KT-451-222

This book should be returned/renewed by the latest date shown above. Overdue items incur charges which prevent self-service renewals. Please contact the library.

**Wandsworth Libraries
24 hour Renewal Hotline
01159 293388
www.wandsworth.gov.uk**

Wandsworth

Gervase
Phinn

The School at the Top of the Dale

HODDER

First published in Great Britain in 2018 by Hodder & Stoughton
An Hachette UK company

This paperback edition published in 2018

1

A CIP catalogue record for this title is available from the British Library

Paperback ISBN 978 1 473 65059 6
eBook ISBN 978 1 473 65058 9

Typeset in Plantin Light by Hewer Text UK Ltd, Edinburgh
Printed and bound in Great Britain by Clays Ltd, Elcograf S.p.A.

Hodder & Stoughton policy is to use papers that are natural, renewable
and recyclable products and made from wood grown in sustainable
forests. The logging and manufacturing processes are expected to
conform to the environmental regulations of the country of origin.

Hodder & Stoughton Ltd
Carmelite House
50 Victoria Embankment
London EC4Y 0DZ

www.hodder.co.uk

For Donna Elsey Phinn

I

'Are you out of your mind?'

The speaker, a striking-looking woman with green eyes and a mass of red unruly hair which tumbled out from under her riding helmet, was astride a large chestnut horse. Her face was flushed with anger.

She was addressing a young man who sat in his sports car which had swerved off the road to avoid her and ended up in a ditch. The driver rested his hands on the wheel, shook his head and sighed. He wound down the window.

'I'm afraid I didn't see you,' he shouted.

'That was patently obvious!' snapped the young woman. 'You came around the bend in that fancy sports car of yours like some mad racing driver.'

The young man got out of the car and approached the woman. 'First,' he replied, nettled by the woman's strident tone, 'I was travelling at a perfectly reasonable speed and secondly, this is hardly a fancy sports car. It's twelve years old as a matter of fact.'

'The age of your car is totally irrelevant,' retorted the woman. 'You could have killed me. Country roads are full of twists and turns. There are signs all along telling drivers to slow down as tractors might be turning.'

'But you are not in a tractor, you are on a horse,' the man told her mischievously. 'I reckon I would have heard a tractor.'

'Is that your feeble attempt at humour?' she asked angrily.

'And I should add,' continued the man, 'that in future I suggest you don't cross a road on a bend where you have no clear view of what might be coming around the corner. It seems to me to be rather foolhardy of you.'

'You can keep your advice to yourself,' she told him sharply. 'I'm not wasting any more of my time arguing with the likes of you.' And with an impatient flick of her riding crop on the horse's flank, she cantered off, stopping a little way down the road to shout back, 'And I hope you stay in the ditch.'

The man rested his hands on his hips and looked down the empty road, screwing up his eyes in the bright sunlight. He leaned forward, craning his neck and peered into the distance in the hope that rescue was at hand. He glanced at his watch. 'Now what do I do?' he asked himself out loud. He examined the vehicle, which seemed undamaged, but there was no way he could drive it out of the ditch. 'Damn and blast!' he cursed. He returned to the car and reached inside for a jacket. Then he sat on the drystone wall which bordered the road to consider his options. He could stay where he was and hopefully be able to stop a car and be driven to the nearest garage, or he could walk in search of a house or a farm from where he could telephone for a breakdown service. Of all things to happen on a day like this, he thought. He glanced again at his watch. The governors of the school, no doubt, would be assembling about now for the interview and wondering where he was. Well, there was nothing he could do. He gazed at the vast panorama which stretched before him. It was indeed a beautiful scene: acres of emerald-green undulating fields studded with grey outcrops of rock and criss-crossed by white limestone walls which rose like veins impossibly high to the lonely hills, largely treeless and austere. Rabbits, their white tails bobbing, cropped the grass at the edge of a nearby field and a fat pheasant strutted along another craggy limestone wall. A swaggering magpie pecked furiously at a piece of roadkill. A few black-faced, lazy-looking sheep peered at him, and above in a vast and dove-grey sky, raucous rooks wheeled in spirals. On the telegraph wires a line of sparrows chattered noisily.

He suddenly became aware of two farmers leaning on a gate on the other side of the road. They had appeared out of nowhere. Both men observed him with a detached kind of indifference. The first was a grizzled individual with a wide-boned, pitted face the colour and texture of an unscrubbed potato, a long beak of a nose with flared nostrils and an impressive shock of white hair. He was dressed in a grubby, long-sleeved, collarless shirt, a waistcoat which had seen better days and ancient wellington boots turned down at the top. His threadbare corduroy trousers were held up by a piece of twine. A cigarette dangled from his lips. His companion was a fair, thick-set young man with an equally weathered face and tight, wiry hair. He was dressed in a loose-fitting grey jumper with holes at the elbows, baggy shorts and large, heavy military-style boots. His legs were wind-burned to the colour of copper.

'Admirin' t'view?' called out the older man. He sucked on the cigarette and then blew out a cloud of smoke.

'I'm afraid I'm stuck,' replied the driver, clambering down from the wall and crossing the road to where the two men stood.

'Aye, I can see that,' said the farmer, rubbing his nose. 'Come off of t'road I see.'

'To avoid a horse,' he was told.

'Tha shun't sit atop o' that wall,' the younger farmer said. 'Thas'll dislodge all t'stones, then t'wall'll collapse an' then t'sheep'll gerrout. You townies are a bloody nuisance leaving gates oppen, not stickin' to t'footpaths an' lettin' yer dogs off of t'leads.'

'I'm sorry,' said the driver. He was minded to remind the speaker that he had not been through a gate or on a footpath and that he didn't have a dog and that the wall was still intact but, needing the men's assistance, he thought better of it. Instead he replied pleasantly, 'I wonder if you could help?'

The older man stared at the car, rubbed the stubble on his chin and gave a world-weary shake of the head. 'Mebbe,' he said. He dropped the cigarette on the grass and ground it with the heel of his boot.

'I should be really grateful if you could lend a hand to get my car out of the ditch for me.'

The old farmer stared for a moment, then, leaving the gate, and, in no great hurry, went to examine the vehicle. He stuffed his hands in his pockets. 'Convertible, is it?'

'That's right,' replied the driver.

'Pity tha couldn't convert it into a tractor.' He chuckled at his own witticism.

The young man smiled weakly. 'Yes, indeed,' he said. 'So could you help?'

'Tha 'as to tek it easy on these rooads,' said the farmer. 'Tha can't drive round 'ere as if it were a racetrack.'

The young man was inclined to tell the farmer that he was not travelling fast and that it was the mad woman on the horse who had caused him to come off the road. However, he thought it best not to prolong the conversation. He was desperate to be away. 'So, could you help me?' he asked for the third time.

''Appen I could,' said the farmer. He turned to his young companion. 'Stop gawpin' and go an' get t'tractor an' we'll give this chap a tow.'

''E shun't 'ave been drivin' so fast,' said the younger man. 'This is a bad bend an'—'

'Never thee mind what 'e should or shouldn't 'ave been doin',' interrupted the other swiftly, 'just thee go an' get t'tractor an' stop thee mitherin'.'

The boy made an irritable puffing noise before ambling off, grumbling to himself.

'And frame thissen,' the old farmer shouted after him. 'We don't want to be 'ere all day.'

'Do this, do that,' the boy mumbled.

'Gerra move on an' stop thee carpin'.'

'Thanks,' said the driver, holding out a hand. 'My name's Tom Dwyer by the way.'

'Well, Mester Dwyer,' said the farmer, 'it were lucky we was in t'area. Tha might have been stranded out 'ere until t'cows come home. Anyroad, we'll soon 'ave thee out o' theer. In an 'urry was tha?'

'I've an interview this morning for a teaching post at Risingdale Primary School. I guess I've missed out on the job now.'

'Naw, they'll 'ang on. Nob'dy's in any gret 'urry, up 'ere in this part o' t'Dale,' remarked the farmer. 'Mester Gaunt, 'e's 'eadmaster, 'e's not t'sort o' bloke to be in any 'urry.'

Tom shook his head. 'I hope you're right. I'm afraid I got lost trying to find the place. There's so many little twisting roads, some of which end up in tracks, and so few signposts, and when I did find a road sign, one arrow pointed one way to Risingdale and another told me to go in the opposite direction. I've been backwards and forwards for nearly an hour.'

'That's because some o' them signposts 'aven't been changed from afore t'War,' explained the farmer. 'They was purrup to confuse t'Germans if they invaded.'

'Well, they certainly baffled me,' said Tom.

'So who did you nearly knock off of t'orse?' asked the farmer.

'A young woman with flaming red hair and a temper to match,' Tom told him.

The farmer chuckled. 'That'll be Janette Fairborn. She's a spirited young woman wi' a reight old temper on her that lass. Teks after 'er father.' He waved a hand in the direction of the surrounding fields. ''E owns most o' t'land around 'ere.'

The chugging of a tractor along the road heralded the arrival of the younger farmer. A few minutes later Tom was back behind the wheel of his car, which had been towed out of the ditch.

'Thank you so much,' said Tom. He reached into his pocket and produced his wallet. 'What do I owe you?'

'Never thee mind that,' replied the farmer. 'My mother used to say that if tha does a good deed for someone, then do it wi'out expectin' any reward but tell 'em to pass it on. 'Appen one day thas'll 'ave t'chance to do a good deed for someb'dy else.'

The farmer's companion gave a hollow laugh.

'Thee do summat for free!' he said. 'That'll be t'day.'

'Thee shurrup an' tek t'tractor back.'

'That's very generous of you,' said Tom to the farmer before starting the car. 'And if I might trouble you again, could I ask you direct me to Risingdale School?'

'Keep goin' along this road for about a mile 'til tha get to t'crossroads,' the farmer told him. 'Ignore t'signpost directin' thee to go left to Risingdale but turn right. Keep goin' for a couple o' miles up a long hill an' you'll get to Lower Bloxton village. Turn left at t'Pig and Pullet pub, signposted Skillington and drive up another steep 'ill an' tha'll end up at Upper Bloxton. Turn right an' you'll get to Risingdale. T'school is at t'top o' t'Dale about a mile out o' t'village. An' mind 'ow tha goes. Tha dun't want any more disagreements wi' 'orses.'

Tom laughed. 'No, I'll go steady. May I know your name?'

'I'm Toby Croft,' said the farmer, 'an' t'lad on t'tractor is my son, Dean.'

'Well, thank you both,' said Tom before driving away.

'Does tha think 'e'll get t'job, Dad?' asked Dean, as they watched the car disappear in the distance.

The old farmer sucked in his bottom lip and scratched his nose. 'Mebbe 'e will,' he remarked, 'but if 'e does, I reckon 'e won't be stoppin' long. I can't see t'likes of 'im settlin' up 'ere.'

After a couple of wrong turnings, Tom found himself in the centre of the picturesque Dales' village of Risingdale. He drove slowly past a row of pretty rose-coloured stone cottages with mullioned windows and blue-slate roofs and the squat grey-stone Primitive Methodist Chapel. He passed by the Norman church with its spire spearing the sky and the adjacent imposing Victorian vicarage built in shiny red brick with its broad gravel drive curving through an overgrown, untended garden. He drove on by the King's Head Inn, the post office-cum-general store, past the village green and duck pond and then up the hill, all the time keeping his eyes peeled for the school.

It was fortunate that Tom was driving slowly and being watchful for as he approached the brow of the hill, a small boy, about ten or eleven years of age, leaped over a wall of greenish-white limestone and darted across the road directly in front of the car. Tom screeched to a halt, missing the child by inches. The boy stood stock-still in the middle of the road like a creature caught in amber. He was a plain-looking, thin little individual with a wide mouth, dark eyes, large ears and tightly curled hair.

His shirt was hanging out from a baggy grey jumper, his socks were concertinaed around his ankles and his shoes were so scuffed it was difficult to tell whether they were originally black or brown. His hands and face were entirely innocent of soap and water.

Tom pulled over to the side of the road and climbed out of the car. 'That was a very silly thing to do,' he said, approaching the little scallywag.

'Sorry, mister,' said the boy. 'I was being chased.'

'Chased,' repeated Tom. 'Who by?'

The boy pointed to a copse a few hundred yards from the road. 'By that lad who is hiding in the trees.'

Tom looked to where the boy was indicating with his finger. Half hidden behind some pine trees was a tall, fat, moon-faced boy with lank black hair. He was scowling.

'Why was he chasing you?' asked Tom.

The boy shrugged. 'He always does,' he replied casually. 'Most times I get away because I'm a good runner and he hardly ever catches me but today he was waiting for me.'

'But why would he want to harm you?'

The boy shrugged again. 'For the fun of it,' he replied. 'He's nothing better to do, I suppose. He doesn't hurt me if he catches me, just clips me around the head and calls me names. Actually, I feel a bit sorry for him. He doesn't have any friends and is bottom of the class at school.'

'Have you told anyone about this bully, to get him to stop picking on you?'

'Like who?' asked the boy.

'Your dad or your teacher.'

'I've not got a dad and the last teacher we had couldn't do much. She had a lot of trouble with him. We'll be getting a new teacher next term.'

'Well, you ought to tell someone to get it stopped,' Tom informed him.

'Maybe I will,' said the boy nonchalantly.

'Well, you get along and don't go running into the middle of the road in future. You might get killed.'

'Yes, I know. I'm sorry about that,' said the boy. 'I'll see you around.'

With that, he set off sprinting down the hill.

Tom saw that the figure in the trees had now disappeared.

After driving for a mile up a twisting, precipitous road, Tom wondered whether he had taken a wrong turning again, but then as the road divided into a track, he saw what he guessed was Risingdale School. It was a solid, square single-storey building with a greasy grey-slate roof and small square windows, enclosed by low, craggy, almost white limestone walls. Beyond rose an expanse of pale and dark greens, cropped close by indolent sheep. It looked like any other sturdy Yorkshire country dwelling. No traffic triangle warned drivers that children might be crossing and there was no board at the front indicating that this was a school. Tom pulled off the road, climbed from the car and approached the gaunt grey building. He could feel the warmth of the late summer sun on his face and catch the tang of leaf and loam and woodsmoke.

'You've arrived then.'

The speaker was a tall man with dark, deep-set eyes, very thick, wild white hair and a large nose which curved savagely like a bent bow. Long eyebrows met above the nose, giving the impression of a permanent scowl. He was leaning back lazily on a bench in the bright sunshine with a lugubrious expression on his long, pale, angular face.

'Oh, good morning,' said Tom brightly. 'I take it this is Risingdale School?'

'It is,' replied the man. There was no trace of a smile.

'And am I speaking to Mr Gaunt, the headmaster?'

'No, you're not. You are speaking to Mr Leadbeater, the caretaker, cleaner, handyman, gardener and general factotum.'

'Well, good morning,' said Tom. 'I'm afraid I was held up.'

'Who are you?'

'One of the candidates for the teaching post. I had a bit of an accident on my way here.'

'Did you?' He didn't sound the slightest bit interested.

'Nearly hit a woman on a horse.'

'Really.'

'And I got lost a few times.'

'A lot of folk do.'

It's like talking to a brick wall, thought Tom. 'I suppose I have missed the interviews.'

'Interviews?' repeated the man.

'For the teaching position at the school. I have been called for interview. Has the headmaster left?'

'He hasn't arrived yet,' the caretaker told him. 'He phoned to say he'd be along later.'

'I see.'

'Two of his sheep got out last night and he's after getting them back. He has a smallholding has Mr Gaunt. Course I don't usually come into the school during the holidays. I've had to make a special effort today to open the place up. It's very inconvenient.' He made no special effort to get to his feet.

'There *are* interviews here today, aren't there?' asked Tom, looking around. He could see only one other car next to his own, an ancient half-timbered Morris Traveller van.

'I don't know anything about any interviews,' the caretaker told him. 'I was just told to open up the school and that there'd be a visitor. Mind you nobody tells me anything around here.'

'I see,' said Tom, wondering what sort of school this was.

'Go in and have a look around if you want,' he said, standing up and stretching.

The previous year Tom had trained at Barton-with-Urebank Primary School and enjoyed every minute of his time there under the guidance of Mrs Stirling, an experienced and dynamic head teacher and the supportive members of staff. He had learnt a great deal, loved the company of young people, knew teaching was the profession for him and had gained his certificate in education with a distinction. That school was an immaculately clean and tidy building with a warm, welcoming and optimistic atmosphere. Paintwork shone, floors had a spotless, polished look, brass door handles sparkled and there was not a sign of graffiti or litter. The display boards, which stretched the full length of the corridor, were covered in line drawings, paintings, photographs and children's writing. Everything looked cheerful and orderly. There was a profusion of bright flowers to the front of the school, and at the rear there was an attractive and informal lawn area with ornamental trees, shrubs, a small pond, garden benches and picnic tables. He could not have trained at any better place. The school inspectors had graded the school as outstanding and Barton-with-Urebank was regarded as the flagship school in the county.

This school was very different. The heavy mud-coloured door, with the tarnished brass knocker in the shape of a ram's head, needed a good lick of paint. It opened with a loud creak into a small vestibule which was dark and unwelcoming with its shiny green wall tiles and off-white paint. From the entrance stretched the corridor, on one side of which were several old pine cupboards and on the other, a line of large, black iron coat hooks. The floor of pitted linoleum was the same colour as the door to the school.

All four classrooms were small and square with hard wooden floors and mean little windows set high up. One classroom, clearly where the infants learnt, had tables and little melamine chairs, some large coloured cushions and a small carpeted area. There was a Wendy house and a modest collection of picture books. Along one wall were pinned children's colourful artwork: round figures with smiling faces, huge eyes and stick-like fingers. On another wall were glossy posters of animals and birds alongside lists of key words and rules of the class-room. On a large table were painting materials, coloured cray-ons, a sand tray and large coloured boxes containing a variety of building blocks and educational toys. The area was tidy and colourful and it was obvious the teacher had made a real effort to provide a stimulating environment for the children.

The other three classrooms, probably for the juniors, varied little. All had ranks of dark wooden desks of the old-fashioned lidded variety, heavy and battle-scarred, with holes for inkwells. They faced a dais on which were a sturdy teacher's desk made of pine, a high-backed chair and a large black-board. Some effort had been made in two of the rooms to make the environment bright and cheerful but the third looked neglected. The room was dark, dingy and airless with a dusty wooden floor. On the walls, devoid of any displays or pictures and painted in a sickly green, were a few dog-eared posters on the rules of English grammar and on famous historical figures. Above, black beams with curved wooden supports stretched across the high ceiling where the paint was flaking. There was a solid cupboard and two old bookcases containing sets of class readers, a stack of dictionaries, some hardback textbooks and a pile of folders. Tom noticed that there were no bright, glossy-backed novels, poetry anthologies or reference books in evidence. Framing the high windows were hung long faded floral drapes; there was a cast-iron Victorian fireplace, its mantle of dark slate and heavy black grate filled with some sad-looking dried flowers and dusty pine cones. Above the teacher's desk were faded samplers in discoloured frames. Tom read them out loud.

'May the children of this school
Earn their teacher's praise,
By being good and working hard,
To walk in Wisdom's ways.

Children to the Lord on high,
Your early honours pay,
While vanity and youthful blood
Would tempt your feet away.

Jesus permit thy gracious heart
To stand as this first effort of Eliza Clark,
And while her fingers on this canvas move,
Encourage her tender heart to seek thy love.
With thy dear children let her play her part
And write thy name dear Jesus on her heart.'

It was like going back in time.

As Tom emerged from the school into the bright sunshine, he cracked his head on the lintel in the porch. He cursed and began furiously rubbing his forehead.

'A lot of people do that,' observed the caretaker unhelpfully. He had resumed his position on the bench. 'It's a tad on the low side. You have to be careful.'

He might have shared this information with me before, thought Tom. He screwed up his eyes to see a lean individual climbing out of a battered pickup truck. The man sported a shabby trilby hat, green corduroy trousers tied at the knee with string, a thick tweed jacket with elbow patches and substantial boots.

'Here's the headmaster now,' the caretaker said, tilting his head in Tom's direction. He made no effort to move from his position on the bench.

'Ah, Mr Dwyer,' said the thin individual, striding towards Tom and holding out a leathery hand. He smiled widely. 'I'm very pleased to meet you. I'm Gerald Gaunt, headmaster of this establishment, for my sins. I'm sorry you have had a long wait but—'

'He hasn't,' interrupted the caretaker. 'He's only just arrived. Had an accident on the way here.'

'Accident?' repeated Mr Gaunt. 'Oh dear.'

'He hit a woman on a horse,' said the caretaker.

'No, I *nearly* hit a woman on a horse,' said Tom. 'I swerved to avoid them and ended up in a ditch.'

'I'm sorry to hear that,' said Mr Gaunt. 'You're not hurt, I hope.'

'No, I'm fine,' Tom told him.

'And the woman and the horse?'

'They are fine too.'

'There's an old Dales' saying,' said the headmaster, 'that one should beware a cow, a horse and a woman, for each of these have time and again proved guilty of the indiscretion of crossing the road on the approach of a tractor.'

Tom managed a weak smile. He smoothed down his hair and straightened his tie.

'I must apologise for my appearance,' he said, looking down at the flecks of dirt on his trousers and his muddy shoes. At college he had been told how important it was to make a real effort with one's appearance and to present oneself for an interview for a teaching position smart and well groomed. First impressions were important and candidates had lost jobs because governors took exception to the way they were dressed.

'No, no, it is I who must apologise for *my* appearance,' said Mr Gaunt, 'I've been trying to find two of my sheep which got out of my field. Some rambler, I guess, had left a gate open. I couldn't go chasing the creatures in a collar and tie. I'm afraid I didn't have time to change.'

'I told him that,' said the caretaker.

'Told him what?' enquired Mr Gaunt.

'That you were after chasing sheep. Did you find them?'

'I'm afraid not.' He turned to Tom. 'Well, let me show you around the school and then we can have a little chat and see if you would like it here.'

'He's had a look round,' said the caretaker.

'I am sure Mr Dwyer would welcome a cup of tea, Bob,' said the headmaster, giving him a look of patient indulgence. 'Would you put the kettle on please?'

There was a pained expression on the caretaker's face. 'I suppose so,' he grumbled, rising from the bench with little enthusiasm. He sighed as if the weight of the world was on his shoulders, scratched his head and headed for the school in no great hurry, pausing only to inform the headmaster, 'There's no milk.'

'Bob is not,' began the headmaster, lowering his voice, 'the most good-humoured, industrious and energetic of men, but he has been caretaker here a long time and I am not one to welcome change. I guess I could employ someone more enthusiastic and capable but better the devil you know, as they say. We are without a cleaner at the moment which has not improved his temper.'

The headmaster's room was small and cluttered and dominated by a huge oak desk with brass-handle drawers. On the top was an old-fashioned blotter, a large glass inkwell, a jam jar holding an assortment of pens and broken pencils, a large mug half full with a pale, cold liquid and a jumble of papers and folders. A battered grey-metal filing cabinet stood by the window next to a heavy bookcase crammed with books and journals, magazines and files. On the floor was a hard, thin carpet and on a pale yellow wall were a few dull prints of various animals and an insipid watercolour of a ruined castle. Propped up in a corner was the strangest-looking contraption: a long wooden trumpet-like instrument over ten feet long with a cup-shaped mouthpiece.

'Come in, come in,' said Mr Gaunt, casually throwing his hat into a corner. He removed a pile of folders from a small spindle-backed chair before sitting behind the desk and leaning back. 'Do sit down,' he said. 'I mean to tidy the place up one day but have never got around to it. Mrs Leadbeater, my secretary, is always nagging me to do it. She's the caretaker's wife by the way.' He smiled genially.

Tom took a seat. The chair wobbled beneath his weight.

'Now,' said the headmaster, 'I've read your application and the references from the school where you trained and from the university where you studied.' He stared thoughtfully at the piles of papers on the desk. 'They are here somewhere. Just can't lay my hands on them at the moment. Never mind, they were very impressive and I think you are just the sort of chap we are looking for.'

'Really?' Tom was quite taken aback. He had expected a formal interview with governors and an education officer firing difficult questions at him. He had taken a deal of time preparing for the event.

'You were a professional footballer, I believe,' said the headmaster.

'That's right,' Tom replied.

'Bit of a change being a schoolmaster.'

'It is,' he agreed, 'but I really enjoy teaching. Since Easter I've been doing supply work in different schools, but just when I get to know the children and the staff, I have to leave. I really would like a permanent post.'

'The head teacher of the school where you did your training says she would have offered you a job had there been a vacancy but she's been prevailed upon to take a redeployed teacher.'

'Yes, that's right,' said Tom.

'As you are no doubt aware, quite a lot of small schools in the county aren't viable any more, with the decline in pupil numbers, and have had to close, with teachers needing to find other positions. Fortunately, touch wood, our numbers have remained pretty static but we shouldn't be complacent, although I think if they tried to close Risingdale, there'd be a riot. It's a very close-knit community as you will find out. They closed one Methodist chapel but when they tried to close the other, they were sent away with a flea in their ears.'

'Yes, I'm aware that a lot of teachers need to be redeployed,' said Tom. 'That's why it's been difficult to find a job. There's been a lot of competition.'

'I've had three teachers who needed redeploying up here to look around, but none of them took to the place and to be frank I and my staff didn't take to them. That Mr Nettles at the Education Department at County Hall, a useless individual who is intoxicated by the sound of his own voice – but that is by-the-by – has given up sending any more, so that's why I went to advert.' There was a meaningful silence. 'Now look, Tom,' he said suddenly. 'I may call you Tom?'

'Yes, of course.'

'To be honest Tom, Risingdale is not one of the county's foremost schools. We never win the sports' cups or the county poetry and art competitions – not that we enter the children for them. It really wouldn't be worth our while. Sadly, I don't have a member of staff confident in teaching these areas. Academically we're quite a bit down the league table but you'll find most of the children are a pleasant enough lot, largely very biddable and well behaved but not top drawer when it comes to ability or intelligence. Of course, we do occasionally get one or two more able children and a couple passed for the grammar school once, but most go on to Clayton Comprehensive where they do reasonably well. The children come largely from the surrounding farms and are not massively keen on school and, to be honest, would prefer to be out and about in the fresh air instead of being stuck behind a desk. In truth I can't blame them. Their parents are not the pushy type and don't have a lot to do with the school, and the governors leave things to me. The Education Office doesn't bother me much and we haven't seen a school inspector for years. Life up here is in the slow lane so if you're looking for excitement, then this is not the place for you.'

'I'm looking for a teaching job, Mr Gaunt,' Tom told him, 'and there are few about at the moment, so I'll take any post which is offered. I'm sorry that sounds ungracious but—'

The headmaster smiled. 'That's an honest enough answer,' he said. 'Well, Tom, I like what I've seen of you. I think you will fit in here so we'll see how it goes. You'll be taking the top juniors. It was Miss Cathcart's class. Sadly, there was an unfortunate incident with regard to that teacher. However, I won't go into that. It's water under the bridge now. I need someone to start immediately which I assume you are able to do.'

'Yes, I can,' replied Tom.

'Well, as I've said, you'd be taking the top juniors, the ten and eleven year olds. The two lower juniors are taught by Captain Cadwallader and Miss Tranter. The captain is a bit of a martinet and does like to spin a yarn, but he is a good sort and a solid enough teacher. Joyce is . . . well, she's a bit unusual, but she runs a tight ship. I am sure you will get on famously with them. The little ones are in the care of Mrs Golightly. She's a tad traditional but none the worse for that. The teachers, you will find, are a decent enough lot and all have been here for a long time. As I said, I am sure you will get on with them.'

'Excuse me for interrupting, Mr Gaunt,' said Tom, 'but do I take it you are offering me the position?'

'Well, yes,' he said, sounding surprised that he had been asked.

'Is there to be no formal interview with governors and an education officer, and are there no other applicants?'

Mr Gaunt laughed. 'Oh no, I don't bother with the governors. As I have said, they leave it all to me. They don't interfere. As regards other applicants, they were few and far between and I could tell they weren't right for this school. I didn't want to waste their time nor mine calling them for interview.'

'So I have the job then?' asked Tom.

'If you want it,' replied Mr Gaunt.

'Well, yes, I do.'

The headmaster rose, smiled widely to show a flash of teeth and proffered his hand. 'Well then,' he said, 'welcome to Risingdale School.'

2

The King's Head had remained unaltered for many years. The country inn, built of honey-coloured stone and with a shiny red pantile roof and brightly painted window frames looked warm and welcoming from the outside. A large wooden board, depicting the portrait of the ill-fated King Charles I in his regal attire hung from a gallows-like structure. To the front of the inn were colourful displays of flowers in tubs and hanging baskets. The pub was a popular hostelry frequented largely by the local farmers and shopkeepers of the village who gathered in the evenings and at Sunday lunchtimes to argue about sport, politics and farming and to put the world to rights.

The outside of the inn belied the interior which was an inhospitable place, dim and stale smelling. The walls, once white, were now the colour of sour cream and were decorated with a few insipid coloured hunting prints, a dark oil painting of a horse, some sepia photographs of farm workers of centuries past, a pair of old bellows, a hunting horn and a couple of antique shotguns. Two shelves displayed a variety of dusty toby jugs, Staffordshire pottery dogs, some tarnished silver sporting cups and a collection of old tankards.

Of course, there were no games' machines, karaoke nights, happy hours or pub quizzes. A few sticky-topped round tables with wrought-iron legs were arranged on the grey flagstone floor with an odd assortment of uncomfortable and unstable spindle-backed chairs and wobbly stools. The one attractive feature of the hostelry was the large and very old inglenook fireplace which took up most of a wall. When one of the Methodist chapels in the village closed, the landlady had bought a job lot of pews which now lined the walls. She had also salvaged a large lectern which stood incongruously in one corner. The departing minister, who had not approved of the 'noisy carryings on and drunken revelries' (as he put it) at the inn was none too pleased to see much of the contents of the chapel ending up in a pub.

When the brewery, which owned the King's Head, sent a representative to suggest the place could do with some refurbishment, the regulars had protested vociferously and threatened to veto the inn if any attempt was made to change things. Like the landlady, the formidable Doris Mossup, they liked it the way it was. The King's Head, they told him, had 'olde-worlde' character and they were opposed to any alterations. In fact there was strong objection to any change of any kind in the village of Risingdale and, as Tom would soon find out, this applied to the school in which he was to teach.

When the new teacher entered the public bar, all conversation stopped and the weathered faces of a few old farmers turned in Tom's direction. The locals were not used to strangers, for the inn was too remote for day-trippers and the steepness of the incline leading to the village and the narrow, twisting roads were unsuitable for caravans and put off many a rambler. Anyway, there was nothing of interest in the village to attract tourists, and as Tom had discovered, the directions to Risingdale were notoriously confusing.

Tom's cheery 'Good afternoon' was received with a few nods of the head and quizzical looks from the locals.

Following the interview at the school, Mr Gaunt had made various suggestions for Tom to consider. His first was for him to get rid of the sports car.

'You'll find the winters up here at the top of the Dale can be especially severe,' he was told, 'and you will never get up the hill to the school in that fancy little car of yours. You'd be skidding off the road and ending up in a ditch again. By December we start to get thick snow and driving winds, then come the blizzards and treacherous black ice. You need a four-wheel drive.' He laughed. 'Or a tractor. Of course sometimes I have to close the school if the snow gets really bad. You might have noticed my alpenhorn in the corner of the room. It comes in very handy when the winters are bad. A few good blows on that echo down the Dale and let the villagers know that the school is closed. Saves the parents trudging up with their children. I bought it in Switzerland and I caused quite a commotion at the airport when I brought it back. I tried to get the education people to pay for it but, as we say up here, they're as tight as a tick's arse.'

The headmaster's second suggestion regarded Tom's accommodation.

'A room at the King's Head is the best place for you to stay, for the time being at least,' he was told. 'Mrs Mossup, the landlady, is a friendly if doughty woman, the rates are reasonable and her food is . . . well, it's just about edible.'

Mr Gaunt failed to mention that the landlady's cuisine was hardly of the gourmet kind and she could only manage the two meals. Her Sunday lunch offering invariably consisted of brown Windsor soup, a slice of roast beef burnt to a crisp, watery overcooked cabbage, charred roast potatoes and lukewarm, lumpy gravy. During the week it was a slab of gristly dry ham or a slice of pork edged in fat, a wilting lettuce leaf, half a rubbery hard-boiled egg covered in glutinous mayonnaise, an overripe tomato and a couple of radishes.

'If you mention my name, she'll give you a good discount,' said Mr Gaunt. 'Of course if you decide to stay with us at the school, you might want to rent or buy a place of your own in the village. We lead an easy-going, peaceful, untroubled sort of life up here but it suits us.' He looked at Tom for a moment with a thoughtful expression on his long face. 'I hope it will suit you too.'

Tom wondered at that moment whether such a quiet life would indeed suit him. Still, he thought, he had a job, the school was in magnificent countryside and he was determined to make a success of his teaching.

So his first visit to the King's Head was to enquire if there was a vacant room that he could rent.

Behind the bar stood a large, healthy-looking girl with curly brown hair, watery grey eyes and prominent front teeth. She wore a tight, low-cut blouse and body-hugging jeans. Her face lit up when she caught sight of Tom and she hurried down the bar to serve him. Most of her customers were elderly farmers so the sight of the very good-looking young man with the tanned face, shiny black curls, long-lashed dark blue eyes and a winning smile was something of a rarity.

'What can I get you?' she asked, smiling coyly. She folded her arms and rested them and her not insubstantial bosom on the counter.

'I'd like to speak to the landlady please,' Tom told her.

'My mam's serving in the other bar,' she said. She tilted her head and smiled coquettishly again. 'Can I be of help?'

'I'm looking for a room.'

The girl couldn't take her eyes off him. 'A room?' she repeated.

'A room to rent.'

'Here?'

'I was told you do have rooms for rent,' said Tom.

'We do but we've only got the two rooms and we're booked up at the moment.'

'Ah well,' said Tom, turning to go. 'Thank you anyway.'

'You're not from round here, are you?' asked the girl, not wishing him to escape so easily. She raised herself from the top of the bar.

'No.' Tom returned to the bar.

'Just passing through, are you?' she asked.

'I'll be moving into Risingdale at the end of the school holidays. I'm the new teacher at the village school. I'll be starting there next week at the beginning of term.'

'The new teacher!' exclaimed the girl. 'You're the new teacher up at the school?'

'Yes, I am,' replied Tom.

'Things *are* looking up,' she said, leaning forward, her corpulence spilling over on the counter again. 'Teachers there are well past their sell-by-date. Mrs Golightly used to teach my mam.'

'I haven't met the other teachers yet,' said Tom tactfully.

'Well, they're all dead old. There's a Miss Tranter who teaches drama but she's no spring chicken either. "Mutton dressed as lamb," as my mam says. Anyway, I reckon you won't stay long,' the girl continued, then she added, 'But I hope you do. Course, there's not much happens up here. Sometimes the Young Farmers have a barn dance at the village hall but that's about the only excitement young people get. Most of the lads don't dance at all but if they do it's only when they're dead drunk and then they look really stupid.' She leaned further over the counter. 'I bet you're a dead good dancer.'

'Sadly not,' admitted Tom. 'Two left feet, I'm afraid.'

'So are tha servin' down 'ere, Leanne, or what?' shouted a grizzled old farmer at the other end of the bar. 'I've nearly tekken root.'

'I'm talking,' she shouted back impatiently, 'so you can hang on.'

A moment later a cheerful-looking middle-aged woman with elaborately coiffured, dyed blonde hair joined them at the bar. Like the girl she displayed a good deal of cleavage.

'Percy wants serving, Leanne,' she told her sharply. 'Frame yourself.'

'I'm going,' replied the girl mulishly, not moving. 'This young man's looking for a room.'

'Mr Dwyer?' asked the woman, turning to Tom.

'Yes,' he replied, surprised she knew his name.

She smiled warmly. 'I'm Doris Mossup, the landlady.' She shook his hand. 'I've been expecting you. Mr Gaunt phoned through to say you would be calling. So you're looking for a room.'

'Yes, that's right.'

'I was telling him that we're all booked up,' said the girl.

'No, we're not,' snapped the landlady. She looked at her with strong reproach.

'We are.'

'Don't argue with me, Leanne,' said the woman, glaring at her, 'and go and serve Percy. I shan't tell you again.'

The girl pouted and stomped off mumbling, to serve the customer who was rapping on the counter at the end of the bar. 'I'll get you a little hammer if you want, Percy,' she told the man crossly, 'then you can knock a bit louder.'

The landlady sighed and shook her head. 'She can be a right madam at times, can that young lady,' she said.

'So, you *do* have a room then, Mrs Mossup?' asked Tom.

'One's suddenly become vacant,' she told him. She failed to reveal that when she had received the call from Mr Gaunt, she had asked the present occupant to vacate the smaller room at the back of the pub, saying it had been booked. She intended to tell the salesman in the better room to move into it when he appeared later that day. She was keen to have the new teacher on her premises.

'So, Mr Dwyer,' she said, with a fixed smile on her round face, 'when will you be wanting to move in?'

'Tomorrow afternoon if that's convenient,' he told her.

'I'll have your room all ready for you.'

'Thank you,' said Tom, turning to go.

'You'll be starting at the school then?' said Mrs Mossup.

'Yes, that's right,' he said, turning back to face her. There was little enthusiasm in his voice. 'I have to admit I am a bit nervous.'

'Oh, the kiddies are mostly no trouble,' he was told, 'and the teachers are nice enough, but not getting any younger. They could do with some fresh blood. Mrs Golightly taught me, would you believe.'

'Yes, your daughter was telling me.'

Leanne reappeared, having served the customer in record time.

'Were my ears burning?' she asked.

'Anyway,' said the landlady, ignoring her, 'I'll put you in the front bedroom overlooking the main street. It's the bigger one and the best I've got. It's nice and comfy and you'll have a lovely view up the Dale.'

'Mr Butt's in that room, Mam,' said Leanne.

'Well, he'll have to shift,' said her mother.

'He'll not be best pleased about that,' said the girl.

'Well, he'll have to lump it, won't he?' the landlady replied. 'I'm putting Mr Dwyer in there now.'

'I wouldn't want to put anyone out,' said Tom. 'I'm sure the other room will be fine.'

'Not at all,' said Mrs Mossup. 'It's only the fertiliser salesman. I'll put him at the back.'

'Shall I show him the room, Mam?' asked the girl.

'No, Leanne, it's not ready yet. Anyway, I'll do that later,' said Mrs Mossup. 'You just attend to what you have to do behind the bar.'

'I don't mind,' said the girl.

Her mother gave her another stern look. 'No, Leanne,' she told her sharply, 'I said I will do it and don't go bothering Mr Dwyer.'

'I'm sure the other room will be satisfactory, Mrs Mossup,'

said Tom. 'There's really no need to ask someone to move out on my account.'

'Do call me Doris,' said the landlady, patting his hand.

'As I said I'm sure the other room will be fine . . . Doris. I do feel rather bad about having someone move out.'

'Oh, don't you bother your head about that, Mr Dwyer,' she told him. 'The room will be ready tomorrow.'

The following day, on a bright Saturday lunchtime, Tom arrived at the King's Head with his belongings. The place was crowded and noisy. He edged his way through a throng of farmers, arguing about the merits of Charolais as opposed to Limousins and the quality of cattle feed and the price of sheep, and placed his cases down at the bar. One of the men, catching sight of him, approached.

'Naah then, lad,' he said.

'Mr Croft.' Tom recognised the man who had come to his aid on his way to Risingdale School the previous day.

'Are tha all reet?' asked the farmer.

'I'm fine,' replied Tom, 'and how are you?'

'Oh, fair to middlin', tha knaas.' The farmer turned to one of his large, raw-boned companions. 'This is t'young fella mi lad I told thee abaat what come off o' t'road in that sports car an' nearly knocked John Fairborn's lass off of 'er 'orse. I pulled 'im out o' t'ditch.'

'It were me what pulled 'im out,' came a voice from the back of the group. The speaker was the farmer's son who had indeed been the one to come to Tom's rescue with the tractor. Mr Croft had done nothing. Leaning on the gate, he had watched Dean do all the work, observing, inspecting, tutting, commenting and criticising as the lad laboured away to get the vehicle back onto the road.

'Who asked thee to stick yer oar in?' snapped the farmer. 'Too much to say for thissen thee.'

'Well, it *were* me what pulled 'im out,' said his son peevishly.

'So this is yon chap what nearly knocked young Jan off of 'er 'orse?' asked one of the farmers. He was dressed in a clean, long-sleeved, collarless shirt, shapeless cardigan, baggy corduroy trousers and heavy boots.

'That's 'im,' answered Mr Croft.

'Well, I 'ope t'lass doesn't gu tellin'. 'er father,' said another farmer. 'John Fairborn's not a man to tangle wi'.'

'Thankfully, no harm was done,' Tom told them.

'Just as well,' said the farmer baldly.

'Anyway, it was very good of you – and your son of course – to help me out,' said Tom, wishing to change the subject. 'I think I owe you both a drink.'

'Oh, well, that's very decent of you,' said Mr Croft before draining his glass in one great gulp and wiping the froth from his upper lip with the back of his hand. 'I'll 'ave a pint o' Benson's Best. Dean's got work to do this afternoon so 'e won't be wantin' one.'

Tom saw the farmer's son stomp off, banging the inn door on his way out.

'Tha's too 'ard on that son o' yourn, Toby,' said one of the farmers.

'Lad's daft as a brush, Percy,' replied Mr Croft. ''E'd lose 'is 'ead if it weren't screwed on.' He turned to Tom. 'Tha got t'job then?'

'I did. It was thanks to you and Dean that I managed to get to the interview on time. How did you know?'

The farmer tapped his long nose. 'It's a small community up 'ere. Mester Gaunt told me. I was 'elpin' 'im round up some sheep what 'e'd lost.' He chuckled. ''E said tha were t'best of a rum bunch but don't thee gu tellin' 'im I told thee. 'E reckon thas'll do. 'E said t'others what come for t'job were barely warm an' breathin'.'

'Well, that makes me feel a whole lot better,' said Tom. The sarcasm was lost on the farmer.

I've barely been in the village for a day, he thought, and people seem to know everything about me.

'Course thas'll find it a bit on t'slow side up 'ere,' continued Mr Croft. He banged on the bar making the glasses rattle and dance. ''As tha tekken root down theer, Leanne?' he shouted. 'We wants servin' when tha's stopped tha gassin'.'

'I've only got the one pair of hands,' she shouted back with a sudden flare of temper, 'so you can hold your horses.'

'Like young Janette Fairborn,' chuckled a farmer. 'I reckon she must 'ave 'eld on tightly when tha nearly knocked 'er off of 'er 'orse.'

Tom gave a weak smile, shook his head and sighed. He decided not to respond. When would he hear the last of the skirmish with Miss Fairborn?

A moment later, grumbling and grimacing, Leanne set off down the bar. Her glowering countenance and strident tone changed suddenly when she saw Tom. She gave him her sweetest smile and put on her sweetest voice. 'Oh, Mr Dwyer,' she cooed. 'I didn't see you standing there. If you give me a minute, I'll show you to your room.'

'When tha's finished chattin' up t'customers, Leanne,' said Mr Croft impatiently. 'Can we get some drinks in?'

The girl coloured up.

'A pint for Mr Croft please,' said Tom, 'and whatever his friends are having.'

Each farmer downed his drink in one swift flick of the wrist and placed his empty glass with a thump on the bar.

Leanne showed Tom to his bedroom, chattering all the way up the stairs.

'Mam wanted to know if you've eaten because if you haven't, I can get you a sarnie.'

'Thank you,' replied Tom, 'but I've had something to eat.'

'Mam says can you have your dinner a bit early as the pub gets really busy on Saturday nights and we're rushed off of us feet.'

'That will be fine.'

'You're to come into the back parlour at six if that's OK. Best not eat in the bar with everyone gawping at you.'

The bedroom was large and comfortable with a huge black-painted iron bedstead covered in a colourful patchwork quilt. There was a deep-cushioned sofa, a small desk and a ladder-back chair, and a thick pink carpet with green and yellow flowers, which had seen better days. In one corner was a washbasin and against a wall was a heavy dark-wood ward-robe. On a small table by the bed was a vase containing some bright flowers.

Leanne sat on the bed and bounced up and down. 'It's got a double bolster,' she said, cocking her head to one side and smiling. 'Dead comfy.' She made no attempt to move. 'You could come down for a drink later if you want,' she said. 'It gets quite lively on a Saturday night.'

'I think I'll just unpack and settle in,' Tom told her. He stood by the door. 'Thank you, Leanne, you've been very helpful.'

She jumped up. 'Well, if there's anythink else, you only have to ask.'

Tom put his cases on the bed and then went and stood at the window. He looked down the main street. Beyond was a panorama which stretched out before him: soft emerald fields dotted with grazing sheep and heavy, square-bodied cattle; an enormous hazy-blue sky streaked with creamy clouds; nest-ling, sunlit farmsteads; the country lane which twisted and turned up the hill to the school and beyond to the swelling hills. The landscape, no doubt, had remained the same for centuries. There was a great sense of tranquillity and timeless-ness about it, as if the noises and concerns of the modern

world had been swallowed up by those rolling pastures, thick
bracken slopes, dark, mysterious forests and misty fells.

There was one other person in the parlour of the King's
Head when Tom entered at six o'clock. A large, flabby individual with an exceptionally thick neck, vast, florid face and
small, darting eyes, he hardly looked like a person whom
Fortune had so singularly favoured. He sat at the table, leaning back expansively on his chair, stretching his fat legs underneath and sucking in his teeth. His stomach, as solid and
round as a football, pushed forcefully against his waistcoat,
revealing a show of white shirt and the top of his trousers.

'Good evening,' said Tom cheerfully, rubbing his hands
together.

The man looked up grim-faced. 'Evenin',' he replied with
cold civility.

'It's been a lovely day.'

''As it?' The man was as stony-faced as a cemetery statue.

'Are you the other guest?'

'I am,' he replied with a bitter twist of the mouth.

'I'm Tom Dwyer.'

'I know who you are.' He gave him a look as sharp as a cut-
throat razor. 'I 'ad to move out o' my room to make way for
thee.' His face was flushed in anger. 'An' I'm no 'appy abaat it
either.'

'I'm sorry about that,' Tom answered, 'I did say to Mrs
Mossup that I would have been perfectly happy in the other
room but she did insist.'

The fat resident treated this information with an unfriendly
grunt.

Tom decided to make no more of an effort with the man so
they sat in chilly silence, occasionally exchanging glances.

Leanne bustled in with two plates, which she placed on the
table before the two men. In giving Tom his dinner, she leaned
over him so he got a full view of the abundant bust displayed

before him. He quickly looked down at the meal. Then his
heart sank into his shoes. Before him were two large slabs of
gristly dry ham edged in fat, a wilting lettuce leaf beginning to
turn brown at the edges, a rubbery hard-boiled egg covered in
glutinous mayonnaise, two overripe tomatoes and several
large radishes. This was accompanied by two heavily buttered
wedges of bread. His dining companion stared first at his plate
and then at Tom's.

'Could tha tell me why t'other guest 'as two slices of 'am
and I 'ave just t'one?' he asked Leanne resentfully.

'There wasn't enough to give you another slice,' she
explained flatly.

'But why should 'e 'ave two slices an' I 'ave just t'one?'
complained the man, in the voice of an injured victim. 'I've been
'ere longer than 'im. An' I notice that 'e 'as a full 'ard-boiled
hegg and I 'ave only 'alf an' what's more 'e's got more radishes.'

'Look, Mr Butt,' she told him, placing her hands on her
hips, 'if you don't like it, then you can take it up with my mam.
Anyway, Mr Dwyer looks as if he could do with putting on a
few pounds.' Then, as an afterthought, she added, 'And you
look as if you could do with losing a few.'

'Now look 'ere—' began the man.

'Enjoy your dinner,' she said, before sweeping out of the
room.

'Cheeky cow,' the man mumbled.

'Do please have one of these slices of ham,' Tom told the
man, sliding a knife under the meat and raising it from the
plate. 'One is quite enough for me and you are welcome to the
radishes.'

'I don't want none,' replied the man like a petulant child.
He forked the half egg and posted it to his mouth and began
chomping noisily.

Tom quickly finished the meal, not wishing to spend any
more time in the company of the disgruntled resident who

was now making a variety of unpleasant munching noises as he devoured his dinner. He placed the thick lumps of bread and the slices of ham surreptitiously in his napkin, deciding to dispose of them when he got the chance.

Later that evening, thinking he might get a breath of fresh air, he decided to walk into the village. It was still light outside as Tom edged through the crowded pub, intending to take a walk around the place which would now be his new home. Saturday and Sunday nights were always the busiest evenings of the week at the King's Head. The locals would congregate and spend all night disputing the qualities of various breeds of sheep and cattle and complaining about the faming subsidies and the price of animal feed. Tom caught sight of a glowering Mr Butt at a corner table with a group of farmers, no doubt complaining about being evicted from his room. At the door his way was blocked by a stocky man in a loud checked tweed suit and with a rugged face the colour of an overripe russet apple, a complexion no doubt derived from his working all day in the outdoors in all weathers.

'Excuse me,' said Tom, trying to push past.

'Hang on a minute,' barked the man, resting a hand as big as a spade on Tom's shoulder. 'I'm wanting a word with you, young man.'

'About what?'

'I think you know what about.'

'No, I'm afraid I don't,' Tom replied. He was inclined to add 'I'm not a mind-reader,' but seeing the man's angry face and the impressive size of the individual, he thought better of it.

'About nearly killing my daughter that's what,' the man told him. The bar went suddenly quiet and all eyes turned in his direction.

'I imagine you are referring to the incident with the horse,' said Tom wearily. 'You must be Mr Fairborn.'

'I am,' said the man. There was a moment's tense silence.

Customers stopped drinking to stare, anticipating the inevitable confrontation.

Tom sighed and shook his head. Would he never hear the end of it? 'Look, it was an accident,' he explained. 'I was in a hurry and maybe I was travelling a little too fast and your daughter should perhaps not have been crossing the road at a bend but no one was hurt and—'

'Don't go blaming my Jan,' said the man furiously, stabbing Tom in the shoulder. 'It was you who was in the wrong. You young speed merchants careering along country roads like bats out of hell in your fancy sports cars like there's no tomorrows are a menace.'

Tom was about to respond but some instinct warned him against it. People around here just didn't seem to listen. He kept a straight face despite his amusement at being described as a 'speed merchant' in a fancy sports car. 'I promise I'll drive very carefully in future,' he assured the man.

Tom's conciliatory manner took the wind out of the big man's sails and he nodded. 'Well, just make sure that you do that or you'll have me to answer to,' he said in a much quieter voice. The man made no effort to move. 'You're the new teacher up at the school I hear.'

'Yes, I am.'

'Well, I hope that you manage teaching the kids better than you do driving a car.' He moved out of the doorway and joined the group of interested onlookers.

Tom walked into the village past the terrace of stone cottages and the Primitive Methodist Chapel until he came to the solid Norman church. An elderly man in a clerical collar was fiddling with a catch on the gate. He was a plump, rosy-faced individual.

'I don't suppose you know anything about locks,' he said, as he saw the approaching figure. He had a strong, well-modulated voice alive with ecclesiastical intonation.

'I'll have a look,' said Tom, 'but I can't say I have any experience in that direction.' He examined the rusty catch and shook his head. 'I think you need a new one.'

'I thought as much,' said the man. 'The gate has to be closed you see, otherwise all sorts of creatures come into the churchyard and leave such a mess.' He smiled. 'All creatures great and small, as the hymn would have it. I've had foxes and cats and dogs and pheasants and rabbits, not to mention the little gentlemen in black.'

'I'm sorry?'

'Moles,' explained the man.

'I shouldn't think that the gate will stop moles,' remarked Tom, 'or most of the other creatures for that matter.'

The clergyman laughed. 'No, I don't imagine so. Oh, I'm sorry, here I am rambling on.' He extended a hand. 'I'm Michael Pendlebury, the vicar here and you, I guess, must be the new teacher. Mr Dwyer, isn't it?' Like the few clergymen Tom had met, the vicar had an exuberantly friendly manner and a tendency to speak with some authority.

Tom shook the cleric's hand. News travels fast, he thought and not for the first time. 'That's right. I'm pleased to meet you,' he said.

'I shall no doubt be seeing something of you,' said the vicar. 'I visit the school occasionally to speak to the children and take the assembly. I am sure you will be very happy there. I can tell from your accent that you are not from around these parts.'

'No, I was born in Ireland.'

'Lovely country,' said the vicar. 'Well, Mr Dwyer, this is a small but friendly community here. You will find the Dales' people are not quite as talkative as the Irish and a bit standoffish at first but they are equally as warm and friendly once you get to know them. They might be economical with words but, when the occasion arises, they are not afraid of voicing their opinions and they do so bluntly. Salt of the earth sort of folk are the people of the Dales.' He breathed in deeply. 'It's such a beautiful spot up here, don't you think? It's so far away from all the noise and bustle of the busy towns and all the troubles of the world.' He gestured to the scene stretched before them: the endless green and grey landscape wrinkled with rocks and further off the cold grey fells, thick bracken slopes and long belts of dark woodland which stretched to distant heights. 'The colouring of the scene is unforgettable on such a evening as this, is it not?' asked the vicar. 'The views up here never cease to fill me with awe. It's not called "God's own country" for nothing. Well, I must not delay your evening stroll any longer, Mr Dwyer. Do call in for a cup of tea when you find the time.' He returned to rattling the lock.

Tom soon arrived at the village green and settled himself on a bench to feed the ducks. He had just begun throwing lumps of the bread he had secreted in the napkin into the water and attracting an armada of hungry waterfowl, when there came a voice from behind him.

'It's not a very good idea to feed the ducks bread you know.'

Tom turned to discover the young woman with the flaming red hair and green eyes whom he had encountered on the road the previous day.

'Oh, it's you,' he said.

'Feeding ducks bread is harmful,' she told him. 'It stops them from eating a natural, balanced diet and it also pollutes waterways, allows bacteria to breed and attracts rats and other vermin.'

'Well, thank you for that fascinating lecture,' replied Tom sardonically. 'Not only are you the spokesperson for the road safety campaign, but you are also the resident expert on ducks.'

The young woman gave a slight smile.

'And you will no doubt be pleased to know that your father has just given me a good ear-bashing in front of all the regulars at the King's Head.'

'My father!' she exclaimed.

'I guess you lost no time in telling him what happened on the road, no doubt embellishing it with exaggerated details of how I nearly killed you and your horse.'

'I never told my father,' she said.

'Oh, really?' He gave a small mocking laugh.

'I don't need my father – or anyone else for that matter – to fight my battles for me,' she told him indignantly. Her face coloured up. 'I am quite capable of doing that myself. You might have already gathered that this is a small community and that news travels fast.'

'Well, we can agree on that,' replied Tom sharply.

'And if I might give you another piece of advice, Mr Dwyer,' she said, not struggling to keep the irritation out of her voice, 'if you wish to be accepted in Risingdale, I suggest you change your attitude. People around here do not like know-it-alls and those who put on airs and graces.'

'That's rich coming from the resident duck expert,' Tom replied, tempted to throw another chunk of bread into the pond. 'If anyone here is a know-it-all, it's you and as for airs and graces . . .'

'I shall not waste any more of my time talking to you,' she said and strode off.

Tom looked out over the still water. The ducks, having realised that no more bread was forthcoming, swam off. The discordant cawing of the crows in a distant wood was the only sound. He closed his eyes and rested his head on the back of the bench and thought for moment. This job was a mistake, he told himself. He had imagined starting his career at a thriving and innovative school with enthusiastic teachers, high standards, good resources and keen and well-behaved children

– like the one at which he had trained. Risingdale School was the very opposite. The headmaster, though pleasant enough, was so laid back he was horizontal, the staff sounded well past their prime and old-fashioned, and the building itself was run down and ill-equipped. But it wasn't just the school. The village was in the back of beyond, the people so insular. Anyone would think that news of a driver avoiding a horse on a country road was the highlight of the year. He thought of the vicar's words: 'People are very friendly and welcoming. Salt of the earth sort of folk.' Well, he had not found them so. He had only been in the place for two days and he had already upset the local land-owner and his precious hoity-toity daughter, and he had clearly made an enemy of the other resident at the King's Head through no fault of his own. He wondered whether or not he wanted the job at Risingdale School. Perhaps he should call early at the school on the Monday morning and speak to Mr Gaunt and tell him that he was withdrawing his application. After all he had not signed anything. 'No,' he said out loud, 'maybe this job's not right for me.'

'Talking to yourself?'

Tom opened his eyes. He hadn't noticed that a small boy had joined him on the bench. He was moving his thin legs backward and forward as if on a swing and holding a thick hardback book to his chest. There was a chill in the air but the child wore the same baggy grey jumper with his shirt hanging out. It was the boy he had met running away from the bully, the plain-looking, bony little individual with skinny legs and tightly curled hair.

'I didn't see you there,' said Tom.

'First sign of madness is that,' said the boy, smiling.

'Pardon?'

'Talking to yourself.'

'Haven't you been told not to talk to strangers?' asked Tom.

'You're not a stranger though, are you?' answered the boy. 'You're my new teacher.'

'And how would you know that?'

'I heard Mrs Bannister talking about you in the village shop.'

Tom decided not to probe as to what had been said about him. He guessed it would not be entirely favourable and there would, of course, be mention of the wretched affair with the horse and its snooty red-headed rider.

'Aren't you cold?' asked Tom.

'No,' replied the boy. 'I spend a lot of time outdoors. I don't feel the cold.' He thought for a moment. 'It's you who nearly knocked Miss Fairborn off her horse.'

'Oh dear,' sighed Tom. 'Yes, I'm the one,' he said.

'She's nice is Miss Fairborn.'

'Is she really? You should be at home,' he told the boy. 'Your mother will be worrying about you.'

'No, she won't,' he answered. 'She plays bingo in Clayton on most Saturday nights. She'll not be back 'til late on. She gets the last bus.'

'I still think you should be getting on home.'

'I come down here a lot,' said the boy. 'I bring a book and I like to sit and read.'

'And what is it you're reading at the moment?'

'It's a novel by Charles Dickens. It's called *Oliver Twist*. It's really good.'

'You must be a good reader to tackle Dickens,' said Tom.

'I am,' replied the boy. 'I say, are you eating this bread?'

'No, I was going to feed it to the ducks but I've been told it's not a very good idea.'

'Could I have it?'

'Help yourself,' said Tom.

The boy began to bite into a piece of bread, remaining where he was on the bench, still swinging his legs. 'My name's Charlie, by the way.'

'I'm Mr Dwyer,' Tom told him.

'I know,' said the boy. 'I'm really looking forward to having you as my teacher. We had Miss Cathcart last year and she was as old as the hills and we learnt nothing. We could do what we wanted so long as we were quiet. She used to sit at her desk, sucking mints and knitting and listening to the radio all day. You'll be different.'

Tom warmed to the bright-eyed chatterbox. 'Will I?' he asked. 'And what makes you think that I will be different?'

The boy wiped some crumbs from his lips and thought for moment. 'I just know, that's all.'

3

On Monday morning and the first day of term at Risingdale School, Tom was up bright and early. He had not slept well for the bed was uncomfortably soft and lumpy, the room stuffy and the noise from the public bar downstairs continued into the early hours. Presumably the landlady was not one to keep to the legal opening hours. Of course, being so far up the Dale, it was unlikely that the hostelry would be visited by the local police who probably knew that the licensing laws were being flouted but wanted a quiet life and were happy to turn a blind eye.

Tom's mind was troubled. He had spent yesterday at his aunt's house in Barton-in-the-Dale. He wanted to be away from the village and the residents (and Mrs Mossup's Sunday lunch) to think about whether or not he wanted the job at Risingdale School.

Mrs O'Connor, Tom's mother's sister, could give Mrs Sloughthwaite, the proprietor of the village store and post office in Barton-in-the-Dale, notorious for her verbosity, a run for her money when it came to talking. Like many of her race, she embroidered the English language with the most colourful and original axioms and expressions, most of which were throwbacks to her old Irish grandmother who had a caustic comment, a saying or snippet of advice for every occasion.

'And how are you keeping, Auntie Bridget?' asked Tom, giving her a hug.

'Let me see,' she said thoughtfully. 'I'm as well as I was before the way I am now. Does that answer your question?' Tom smiled. Sometimes the things his aunt said baffled him. 'Do you know I've not sat down since I got up,' she continued.

That evening she was uncharacteristically quiet for she could see her nephew was worried about something.

'What's troubling you?' asked Tom's aunt as he stared at his untouched dinner.

'I don't really know whether or not I want this job,' he told her.

'And why would that be?' she asked.

'Well, the school is pretty run down, it's in the middle of nowhere, the headmaster is pleasant enough, but he is set in his ways and appears so laissez-faire and the community is so inward-looking. There's so much to do. I don't know if I want to take it on.'

'It takes time to build a castle,' said his aunt.

Tom laughed. 'Do you have an Irish proverb for every occasion?' he asked.

'Just about,' she replied, chuckling.

'It's just that one voice in my head says I should ring up the school tomorrow and say I have reconsidered the position and feel the teaching post at Risingdale is not for me.'

'And the other voice?'

'That I should give it a go, that things might get better. I met one of the pupils, a nice little lad called Charlie. He seemed so excited at the prospect of a new teacher. If I turned down the post, the school would be short a member of staff at the very beginning of term. It seems wrong to let them down. I just don't know what to do.'

'You'll never plough a field, Thomas, if you keep turning it over in your mind,' she said.

'No, I guess not.'

'Well, it's not for me to tell you what to do,' said his aunt, 'but at the very least I think you owe it to the headmaster to go and see him and explain.'

'Yes, I'll do that.'

'And whatever you decide, Thomas,' said his aunt, 'may you have a bright future, as the chimney sweep said to his son.'

So Tom returned to Risingdale that evening.

He was still undecided that Monday morning as he began to get dressed.

He was halfway through pulling up his trousers when there was a loud rap at the door and without waiting to be told to do so, Leanne entered the room bearing a large mug. Tom's cry of 'One moment,' came too late, for the girl was already in the room, staring at him in his underwear with his trousers at half-mast.

'Ooo, sorry,' said Leanne. 'I heard you getting up and brought you some tea.' She placed the mug on the bedside table. She continued to stare. 'Mam says if you put your dirty washing out, I'll do it later.'

'Actually, Leanne,' said Tom, quickly fastening up his trousers, 'I can manage that.'

'How?'

'Oh, I can cope.'

'It's no trouble.'

'Nevertheless, I would like to do it. Thank you all the same. And I wonder if in future you might just wait a moment after you've knocked before coming into the room.'

'OK,' she answered. 'Mam's put your breakfast on.'

Before he could tell her that he only ate a very simple breakfast, the girl had gone.

In the parlour, Tom was pleased to see that the other resident was not at the table. To sit in simmering silence opposite Mr Butt was not the best way to begin the day. His relief soon disappeared when he caught sight of the plate held by the landlady. His heart sank. There were two pale runny eggs, three rashers of burnt bacon, an enormous sausage, a large shrivelled mushroom, a thick circle of black pudding and a small mountain of baked beans. On top was a doorstep of deeply fried bread.

'There we go,' she said, placing the plate before him.

It had to be said sooner or later he told himself and steeled himself for the response. 'Mrs Mossup . . . Doris,' he began.

'Yes, dear?' She was all smiles.

'This is so good of you to cook such a very substantial and appetising breakfast.'

Her smile widened to such an extent that had she been wearing lipstick he imagined she would leave traces of red on the lobes of her ears. 'It's a pleasure and nice to be appreciated.' She patted his hand.

'It's just that . . .' continued Tom, struggling to think of the right words to use.

'Yes, dear?'

'It's just that I only have a slice of toast and a cup of tea in the morning.'

The smile vanished in a flash. 'A slice of toast and a cup of tea,' she repeated as if he had said something indecent. 'I've never heard the like. A full English breakfast is included. Anyway, a growing lad like you needs a good solid meal inside him to start the day, never mind a slice of toast and a cup of tea. You'll waste away on that. You get it down you and you'll feel the benefit.'

'No, really,' protested Tom. 'I couldn't face such a large breakfast.'

'Well, suit yourself,' said the landlady, clearly irritated by the rejection of her efforts. She picked up the plate. 'I'll put this in the oven. It'll do for Mr Butt when he decides to stir himself. I dare say *he* won't turn his nose up at it.' She removed the plate and departed.

'Oh dear,' sighed Tom. Now he had added another name to the list of people he had managed to offend.

Leanne arrived a moment later with a blackened slice of toast.

'Mam sent this,' she said. 'She's in a right mood.'

'I think I might have upset her,' said Tom. 'I just couldn't face such a large breakfast.'

'It'll be first-day jitters, I reckon.'

'Do say I'm sorry to your mother if I have hurt her feelings.'

'She'll get over it,' replied the girl casually. 'Anyway, she's always in a rotten mood on Mondays. By the way I've packed some lunch for you. They don't do dinners up at the school. There's a packet of crisps, two boiled eggs, a pork pie and a couple of nice pieces of ham, same as what you had for dinner on Saturday.'

'Thank you,' replied Tom, looking at the burnt offering before him.

He arrived at the school at eight o'clock to find the place deserted and the door locked. A few melancholy-looking sheep stared at him from the field and a pair of inquisitive rabbits, disturbed from cropping the grass, bobbed up their heads to see what had unsettled them. Two black and white cows, with elaborate indifference, continued grazing. Above in an empty sky, a hawk rode the air currents, sweeping in wide circles. Surely, this was the start of term, Tom thought, but where was everybody? At getting on for half past eight, the ancient Morris Minor chuddered to a noisy stop at the road outside, belching an evil-smelling smoke. The caretaker, dressed in a shapeless grey nylon overall which crackled when he moved and a cap as flat as a cowpat, climbed out, stretched, yawned and, catching sight of Tom, gave a slight nod of the head. Another figure clambered from the vehicle, grumbling to herself. She was a thin, slightly stooped woman with a pale, indrawn face, narrow dark eyes and thick iron-grey hair, cut in a bob. The caretaker shuffled up the path, ignoring the woman's badgering voice behind him.

'How many times have I asked you to get the car fixed,' she complained. 'I might as well talk to a brick wall for all the notice you take. One of these days we'll be stuck halfway up the hill.'

The caretaker, having produced a set of large keys from his pocket, opened up the school. 'You're early,' he told Tom as he passed him.

'You must be the new teacher,' said the woman, approaching and appraising what she saw through unfashionable horn-rimmed spectacles.

'That's right, I'm Tom Dwyer. Good morning.'

'I'm Mrs Leadbeater, the school secretary,' she told him.

'I'm pleased to meet you,' he said.

'Likewise, I'm sure.'

'I rather thought there would be more people here at this time.'

'Oh no,' she replied, sounding taken aback by the observation. 'I arrive with my husband at eight-thirty, that's if that wretched old banger of his manages to get up the hill. Mr Gaunt and the teachers get here at about a quarter to the hour and the children turn up for nine o'clock or thereabouts – well, most of them. Course it depends on the weather how many we get. Come in and I'll put the kettle on. Your classroom's first on the right.'

'Yes, I thought it might be,' murmured Tom.

'It's not in the best of shape I'm afraid,' she said. 'Miss Cathcart wasn't the tidiest of people and the cleaner left at the end of last term, so you'll find it a bit dim and dusty. I did tell my husband it needed a good once-over, but I might as well talk to a brick wall for all the good it does.'

When he saw where he was expected to teach – the dark and dingy classroom he had seen on the previous Friday

– Tom was more determined than ever to tell Mr Gaunt that this job was not for him. It was clear that nothing had been done in the room since the departure of the previous teacher. One would have thought, Tom told himself, that the caretaker, as the secretary had mentioned, might have made an effort to clean the place. After all, he had had plenty of time during the school's summer holidays.

Tom opened the cupboard. It contained a stack of exercise books, a box of blunt pencils and old pens, several bottles of ink, two jars containing some felt tips, and a pile of plain paper. There was a box of chalk, a board duster, two mouse-traps and a packet containing ant repellent. Tom smiled when he saw a couple of knitting needles and a bag of mints. At the back, hidden behind a large and ancient-looking Bible, were a small glass and half a bottle of gin. It appeared that the previous occupant of this Victorian schoolroom had left in something of a hurry.

Ten minutes later the door opened and an extraordinary-looking character entered, holding a large mug of tea. She was a tall, slim woman of indeterminate age with unnaturally shiny raven-black hair, startling glossy-red lips, perfectly plucked arched eyebrows and large, pale eyes. She wore an amazingly tight-fitting crimson turtleneck jumper, a thick black leather belt with a substantial shiny metal buckle and a black calf-length pencil skirt. She sported a pair of impressively pointed black patent-leather shoes with high heels. Silver earrings the size of onion rings dangled from her ears. There was the fragrance of expensive perfume in the air.

'Beryl's sent this,' she said.

'Beryl?' asked Tom.

'Mrs Leadbeater.'

The woman placed the mug down, sat on the corner of a desk and fingered a thin rope of pearls at her neck. She stared at Tom for a moment like someone at an auction wondering if they might make a bid. 'I'm Joyce Tranter, teacher of one of the lower junior classes,' she said. She extended a hand with long scarlet nails which Tom shook. 'You, I am assuming, are the new teacher?'

'Yes, that's right. Tom Dwyer.'

'I hope you don't mind me asking, but what made you apply for a job up here? I should have thought that a young man like you could have had his pick of schools in the county. In my experience primary schools are desperate for young men.' She smiled, showing a set of perfectly even white teeth. 'Up here it's miles from anywhere, the residents live in the Dark Ages, there's more life in a cemetery than there is in the village and the school is not exactly at the cutting edge of education.'

Tom smiled. 'Are you trying to put me off?' he asked.

'Just inquisitive,' she replied.

'It was one of the very few jobs available,' he told her honestly. 'Since some of the small schools are closing, there's a lot of redeployed teachers looking for jobs. Those posts which *are* advertised say the schools are looking for experienced teachers or specialists. I'm neither I'm afraid.' He was minded to tell her that he would not be staying and that as soon as the headmaster arrived, he would explain to him that he couldn't accept the position and would be on his way.

'Well, it's good to have some fresh blood in the place,' said the woman, reiterating what Mrs Mossup had said to Tom earlier. She slid off the desk, exuding a cloud of perfume, and smoothed her skirt as if she were brushing away crumbs. 'It was a quite horrendous time last term what with Miss Cathcart's ... problem. She taught in this mausoleum of a room.'

'It is rather bleak, isn't it?' said Tom.

'But I'm sure you'll brighten it up,' she told him, smiling archly. 'You'll certainly brighten up the staffroom.' She fingered the pearls again. 'We must have a drink sometime. I believe you're staying at the King's Head.'

'For the moment I am,' replied Tom. He wouldn't be there much longer, he thought.

'Well, I'll see you at morning break,' she said, walking to the door and tinkling the air with her long red-nailed fingers. 'Don't forget your tea.'

Through the window Tom could see Mr Gaunt pulling up in his antiquated pickup truck. He went out to meet him.

'Ah, you've arrived,' said the headmaster affably, as he jumped out of the vehicle. He slammed the door and strode towards the school. He was dressed in a light linen suit and a panama hat was crammed rakishly on his head.

'Mr Gaunt—' Tom began.

'Good to see you. Got everything you need, I hope,' he said, not waiting for a reply.

'Might I have a word?' Tom shouted after him. He ran to catch him up.

'Not at the moment, Tom,' replied the headmaster, still striding ahead. 'Not a good time. First day of term and all that. Things to do. Very busy. I'll catch up with you at lunchtime.'

'But I do need to see you,' said Tom. 'I really don't think that I could—'

His words fell on deaf ears, for Mr Gaunt had disappeared into the school.

By now the children had started to arrive.

Tom sighed. What could he do? Certainly not leave these children, walk out of the school, jump in his car and drive off into the distance. He had no option but to stick it out until lunchtime when he could explain things to the headmaster.

At the sound of a handbell a good ten minutes after nine o'clock, the children filed into the building, hung up their coats on the row of pegs in the corridor and entered their classrooms. They sat at their desks, most with arms folded, and waited expectantly.

Tom stood at the front of the room. He had watched keenly as the children took their seats. They stared at him as if he were some rare specimen displayed in a museum case.

He surveyed the faces before him. It was a mixed group of sixteen children: a large, rosy-cheeked boy with a runny nose, a small, gangly boy with a squint and hair like a lavatory brush, a lean, bespectacled boy with a thick mop of tawny blond hair, a sharp-faced boy with untidy hair, two spotty boys, a heavily freckled boy with a head of copper-coloured hair and Charlie, sitting smiling at the front desk. There was a large, ginger-headed girl, a small, pixie-faced girl, owl-like twin girls with tawny hair and large, blinking eyes, a chubby girl with short, rippling sandy-coloured hair, a girl with long black plaits, a pretty girl with mousy-brown hair and pink glasses and an angelic-looking girl with apple-red cheeks and curly blonde hair sticking out at the sides like giant earmuffs.

'Good morning, children,' he said.

'Good morning, Mr Dwyer,' chorused the pupils in subdued tones.

'Ah, I see I don't have to introduce myself.'

'Charlie told us your name, sir,' said the large girl with the ginger hair.

Tom glanced at the boy on the front desk, smiling at him. Charlie made a thumbs-up sign.

'Well, it's good to see such a bright-eyed and keen class of children,' he said, 'and I was impressed by the way you came into the classroom, quietly and quickly.'

The door suddenly burst open and a tall, fat moon-faced boy with lank black hair stamped into the room. Tom remembered him as the boy who had been chasing Charlie. Without a word the boy headed for a desk at the back of the room and slumped in his seat.

The children waited to see the teacher's reaction.

'Just a moment, young man,' said Tom sharply.

'What?'

'Don't just come charging into the room like a wild animal. Who are you?'

'Colin Greenwood,' answered the boy boldly, with the dull glare of a defiant child, 'and who are you?'

'Don't speak to me like that!' exclaimed Tom. 'I'm your new teacher.' But not for long, he thought.

'He's always late, sir,' said one of the twins.

'Well, in future, Colin Greenwood, do not come into the room in that way again. Why are you late?'

'I had jobs to do,' the boy answered crossly.

'Well, get here on time tomorrow,' Tom told him. 'Now then, children, as I was saying, it's good to see you all. I hope you had a pleasant summer holiday and are now ready for some hard work this term.' Not with me though, he thought. There was a grunt from the back of the room. 'I hope we haven't got a pig in the class,' he said, which made the children laugh.

'Ha, ha, very funny,' mouthed Colin.

'This morning,' continued Tom, 'I would like you to write a paragraph telling me something about you and what you have done over the summer holidays, where you have been and—'

'I haven't been anywhere,' Colin shouted out, 'and I don't like writing.'

'Well, you had better get to like it,' said Tom, having heard enough from this particular pupil, 'because that is what you are going to do this morning.'

'Send him out, sir,' said the small blonde-haired girl. 'That's what Miss Cathcart used to do when he was cheeky.'

'No, I am not going to send anyone out,' said Tom. 'Children don't learn anything standing in the corridor. Colin will do as he is told or he will remain in the classroom at breaks and lunchtimes until he does.'

The boy scowled and made an irritable puffing noise.

'And we can do without the sound effects,' said the teacher.

A piece of paper and a pencil were placed on each desk, and the children were asked to begin writing.

The class settled down to work quietly. Tom noticed with some satisfaction that Colin had started to put pencil to paper.

At morning break the children swarmed out of the classroom door before Tom could stop them and rushed madly into the playground where they hooted and shouted and ran about. Had he decided to stay, he would have made it a priority to put a stop to this behaviour. Tom went to the staffroom to meet the other teachers. He was greeted at the door of the small room by an elderly man of military bearing. He was a tall, straight-backed individual, his hair, still untouched by greyness, cropped short and neatly parted, and his moustache a thin white line on his upper lip. He wore a dark blue barathea blazer with shiny crested gold buttons, pressed grey trousers, crisp white shirt and striped regimental tie, knotted tightly under his chin.

'And here is the new addition to our merry band,' said the man jovially. 'Come in, come in, my dear boy, and meet your new colleagues.' He ushered Tom into the room, patting him warmly on the back. Tom made his grand entrance by cracking his head on the top of the door frame. He rubbed his brow crossly and muttered something under his breath.

'I should have warned you to watch your head,' said the man. 'I say, are you all right?'

'Yes, I'm fine.'

'I'm Owen Cadwallader but most people call me the captain, a handle of my former life in the services.'

'Royal Navy?' asked Tom, still rubbing his head.

'No, no. British army. Welch Regiment. Now let me introduce you to the incomparable Mrs Golightly who is busy
pouring you a cup of tea, which I am sure will be most
welcome.' The woman at the sink gave Tom a small smile. She
had the gentle look of a domesticated cat. Dressed in a bright
blue cashmere twinset, she was a plump, cheerful-looking
woman with a round face and tiny darting eyes. Grey hair
tumbled untidily from a bun. She looked like a kindly old
granny. 'You know Joycey, of course.' Miss Tranter, who was
resting back in her chair, nursing a china mug, had a playful
look on her face. She smiled.

'Would you like me to take a look at your head?' she asked.

'No, it's fine,' replied Tom.

'Now you take a seat, dear boy,' continued the captain.

'It's very nice to meet you, Mr Dwyer,' said Mrs Golightly.
'I'm sure you will be very happy here. Milk and sugar?'

'Just milk, thank you,' answered Tom.

She chuckled. 'Sweet enough, eh?' she said.

'Mrs Golightly has been in the school for as long as anyone
can recall,' said the captain. 'Isn't that so, Bertha? She's had a
good few children through her hands in her time.'

The woman passed Tom a large mug of tea. She picked up
an octagonal tin box with a portrait of the young queen on the
front. 'What about a biscuit?'

'No, thank you,' replied Tom, rather overwhelmed by the
hospitality.

'We can't tell you how pleased we are to see you,' she said.

Tom was now feeling guilty. These friendly people would
soon learn that he was not intending to stay.

'Yes, indeed,' agreed the captain. 'As the new term
approached we were getting pretty desperate.'

'We were,' agreed Mrs Golightly.

'We didn't think we'd get anyone at all,' he said, 'and would
have had to double up classes again.'

'Which we had to do following Miss Cathcart's sudden unfortunate departure,' added Miss Tranter pointedly.

'Least said,' remarked the captain, giving her a cautioning look which conveyed some sort of message.

Tom resisted the urge to enquire what had actually happened to the former teacher.

'We had a number of people looking around the school, thinking they might apply for Miss Cathcart's position,' said Mrs Golightly, 'but for some reason it didn't suit any of them.'

And I am going to add to the list, thought Tom.

'And they didn't suit any of us,' added Miss Tranter.

'We were worried that the education people at County Hall might use this as an excuse to close the school,' said her colleague. 'So many of the small rural schools in the county are disappearing. It's so depressing. We are just about hanging on by the skin of our teeth. It used to be such a thriving area up here, but now sadly it is in decline.'

'And whose fault is that?' chipped in Miss Tranter angrily. 'We all know why all these small farms are disappearing.'

'Well, there are a lot of factors, Joycey,' said the captain.

'Nonsense!' she exclaimed. 'It's Sir Hedley and his cronies. They are responsible.'

'Sir Hedley Maladroit is the local landowner,' explained the captain to Tom. 'He has a large estate around these parts and is the biggest farmer in terms of acreage for miles around. You will have passed the iron gates to his house, Marston Towers, just before you entered the village.'

'It's a mock Gothic monstrosity,' added Miss Tranter. 'Sir Hedley thinks he owns everything and everybody. Having driven half the farmers out of their homes, he has acquired their land. He prefers grouse to sheep farming and that is why the population is declining. People are moving out. It's bloody disgraceful. He should know that feudalism and the manorial system have died out. They are a walking mass of out-dated values, the Maladroits. Anyone would think we're living in the nineteenth century. Country squires ruling the roost are a dying breed and the sooner they are extinct the better. As I mentioned to you, Tom, we live in the Dark Ages up here.'

'So we are delighted to see you, Tom,' said the captain, wishing to calm down the atmosphere which was becoming heated. 'Let us raise our mugs and welcome our new colleague.'

Mrs Golightly nodded approvingly. 'And you tell me what biscuits you like,' she told Tom, 'I'll get your favourites in. We tend to go for the Garibaldis.'

Tom felt even worse now. It was like the return of the Prodigal Son. He could not have received a warmer welcome. As he sat there looking at the smiling faces before him and having met the children, he realised he just could not up and leave. He would stay – at least for the time being – and put off seeing the headmaster.

'Now have you everything you need?' asked Mrs Golightly.

'I'm afraid your room is a little spartan,' added the captain.

'That's putting it mildly,' added Miss Tranter. 'It's like a funeral parlour.'

'But I am sure you will have it shipshape and Bristol fashion in no time at all,' said the captain. 'Anything you need, dear boy, just ask.'

'Well, I could do with a few more resources,' said Tom. 'For example, is there any sports equipment?'

'Oh, you're going do some sports,' cried the captain, rubbing his hands. 'Just the ticket. That will go down very well.'

'Splendid,' agreed Mrs Golightly, clapping her hands.

'I thought I'd take the children out some time next week,' said Tom, 'and blow away a few cobwebs.'

'Well, that is an excellent idea, dear boy,' said Captain Cadwallader. 'I'm afraid at my age I'm a bit past it when it comes to sporting activities. Of course I was something of an athlete in the dim and distant past when I was in the army. I won a few cups for running.'

Miss Tranter rolled her eyes. Mrs Golightly gave a small indulgent smile and shook her head.

'I'm afraid none of us here have done much in the way of physical exercise,' admitted the captain.

'That's an understatement,' said Miss Tranter, laughing. 'Not much in the way of – we've done nothing.'

'But that will change now Tom is here,' observed her colleague.

'And I am certainly not for rushing up and down a muddy field in all weathers,' said Miss Tranter, examining a long red nail.

'I think you may find some apparatus in the cupboards on the corridor,' Mrs Golightly told Tom. 'Goodness knows when it was last used.'

'So how have you got on with your class this morning?' asked Miss Tranter.

'Oh, pretty well,' replied Tom. 'It's early days but the children appear friendly and amenable.'

'All of them?' she asked, sounding surprised.

'Well, there is one young man—' began Tom.

'Colin Greenwood,' the teachers said in unison.

'He's a difficult child,' sighed Captain Cadwallader, 'and can be a real handful at times. He caused poor Miss Cathcart a deal of trouble but, of course, the boy has a lot to put up with at home. There's no mother and his father, I gather, is a difficult man by all accounts. Got a reputation hereabouts. Something of a shady character. Been banned from the King's Head a number of times for being drunk and disorderly and got into a spot of bother with the police for speeding in that old tractor of his. Although nothing could be proved, some of the other farmers suspect he was behind a spate of sheep rustling, something which is unforgiveable in these parts. And, of course, I guess, he's not averse to doing the odd bit of poaching. Anyway, don't bother your head about young Colin. You won't see a lot of the boy because he's often kept off school to help on the farm or truanting.'

'If he is a nuisance, send him to Mr Gaunt,' said Joyce. 'When Miss Cathcart taught him, or tried to more like, the boy spent more time outside the headmaster's study than he did in his classroom.'

'As for the other youngsters,' said Captain Cadwallader, 'on the whole they're not the sharpest shears in the shepherd's tackle, but they're nice enough and won't give you any trouble. Most of them when they leave secondary school end up working on the farms, which suits them fine.'

'Provided there are any farms left for them to work on,' interjected Miss Tranter.

'If you ask them anything about tractors and sheep rearing, silage and sheepdogs,' the captain carried on, 'you'll find they are experts. Sadly they don't seem greatly interested in much else. We did have a couple who went on to the grammar, but they were children of "off-comed-uns", as they are known around these parts. They had private tutors to cram them for the eleven-plus exam.'

'I'm sorry,' said Tom. 'What's an off-comed-un?'

'I should explain,' said the captain. 'The off-comed-uns, as the locals term them, are those people who were not born in the Dale, those who move here from the outside. Not generally accepted to be honest.'

'Miss Cathcart used to make him stand in the corridor,' remarked Mrs Golightly who had not been listening, 'or outside Mr Gaunt's room.'

'Who?' asked the captain.

'Colin Greenwood,' she replied.

'I've just told him that, Bertha,' said Miss Tranter.

'Speaking of Mr Gaunt,' said Tom. 'Is he not about?'

'He always spends the first morning of the new term closeted in his room with Mrs Leadbeater,' replied Mrs Golightly. 'He has to deal with all the paperwork which has mounted up over the holiday. He doesn't like to be disturbed. He'll emerge after lunch.'

'Does Mr Gaunt not teach?' asked Tom. He thought of the head teacher of the school where he trained who had a full-time teaching commitment.

'Of course he does, dear boy,' said the captain. 'Except for Mondays, when he takes the remedial children for extra individual help, he teaches a class each morning: infants on Tuesday, Joycey's juniors on Wednesday, my class on Thursday and upper juniors, that's your lot, on Friday.'

'So what do we do while the head teacher is taking our classes?' asked Tom.

'My dear boy, we prepare our lessons and catch up with the marking.'

'I see,' said Tom.

'You will find our headmaster is not the most – how shall I put this – the most energetic of men,' said the captain, 'but he likes the children and they are very fond of him, he is very supportive of his staff and is a thoroughly decent sort who thankfully does not interfere with what we are doing. Well, I hear the bell. Once more into the breach, as the bard would have it.'

After morning break Tom spent the first five minutes telling the children that in future at playtimes they should stay in their seats and, when told to do so, line up quietly at the door before leaving the room.

Colin observed him from under lowered brows and scowled.

Tom set the children to complete the written work he had asked them to start earlier and after a time walked around the classroom to see what they had done. The standard of work varied greatly. A few of the pupils could barely string two sentences together, another used the most bizarre spellings and the writing of David, the small, gangly boy with the squint, was very nearly indecipherable. However, Tom was cheered to see that most children had made a real effort and had produced very creditable work. Carol, the pretty girl with the mousy-brown hair and pink glasses, had written a lively and candid account of how she accompanied her father to the sheep auction to buy a Texel breeding ram; Simon, the heavily freckled boy with a head of shiny copper-coloured hair, described how he went ferreting; Marjorie, the little, pixie-faced girl, had written a charming account of helping her grandmother sew a patchwork quilt; and Charlie had produced a lengthy and thoughtful piece of some quality about his walking on the fells. All Colin had managed to write was one line. 'I live on a farm. I hate it.' Tom decided this was not the time nor the place to tackle the boy. That would wait until later when he could see him alone. He collected the work to mark that evening and spent the rest of the morning teaching some aspects of number work.

At lunchtime the school secretary poked her head around the classroom door. 'I gather you wanted to see the headmaster, Mr Dwyer,' she said. 'He's free now.'

Mr Gaunt sat behind his desk. He stretched out his long legs before him and put both hands behind his head.

'I do so hate the beginning of term,' he groaned. He gestured towards the pile of documents on his desk. 'All this wretched paperwork accumulates over the holiday. It comes over the Dale like the Plagues of Egypt. Why don't those at the Education Department leave us to get on with teaching children instead of bombarding us with this little lot? Anyhow, Tom, how are you settling in?'

'The staff have been very helpful and welcoming,' he said, 'and the children friendly and well-behaved.'

'Colin Greenwood can be quite a difficult boy,' said the headmaster. 'Watch out for him.'

'I think I've got the measure of Colin,' said Tom. 'I've dealt with boys like that before.'

'It's a pity that poor Miss Cathcart never managed to deal with him but that is by-the-by. I think the problem for Colin is women. He responds better to men. Anyhow, if he does misbehave, just send him along to me.' Mr Gaunt looked towards the corner of his room where several canes were leaning against the wall. 'I don't like using the stick but there are occasions when it's necessary. Anyway, enough about Colin, the children here, as I've mentioned, are good-natured and amenable and will give you no trouble. They're not your high fliers so don't go expecting too much of them.'

Tom thought of the words of the head teacher of the school where he trained. Mrs Stirling believed that high expectations and self-esteem were the keys to success in education.

'So what was it you wished to see me about?' asked Mr Gaunt.

'Well, I was wondering if there is a curriculum policy,' answered Tom.

'Curriculum policy,' repeated the headmaster. 'Let me see.' He stared at the mountain of paper on his desk. 'I think something like that was sent by the Education Department. I can't lay my hand on it at the moment. I'll ask Mrs Leadbeater to see if she can locate it. The thing is, Tom, education, in my view, is more about teaching than about paperwork. We tend to devise our own curriculum here. We know what is best for our children. Now, is that all?'

'There are not an awful lot of resources. I wonder if I might have some new textbooks, poetry anthologies and novels, some pens and art materials. The sports equipment is outdated and there is no science apparatus. I realise it seems a lot to ask but—'

'Of course,' interrupted Mr Gaunt, 'you may have whatever you need. Just have a word with Mrs Leadbeater who deals with all the finances. Anything else?'

'The classroom is not in a very good state,' said Tom. 'I wonder if I might—'

'Yes, I meant to ask Mr Leadbeater to give it a good clean. The cleaner left at the end of last term. It was the journey up here that finished her off. I must get on to the Education Office for a replacement again. It's been the devil's own job getting through to that Nettles man.'

'If possible I'd like to give the classroom a lick of paint and put up some display boards and new drapes at the windows.'

'Let me stop you there for a moment, Tom,' said the headmaster. 'Of course it's important that the children work in a pleasant environment, but it's the teaching and learning that are important. If you can get the children to read and write, be able to spell and add up by the time they leave for secondary school, then you will have done a good job.' Mr Gaunt could see from the expression on the new teacher's face that he looked disheartened by his words. He stood, leaned over the desk and patted Tom's shoulder. 'Having said that, of course you may have what resources you need. As I said, Mrs Leadbeater deals with all the finances in the school. I imagine that we have enough to purchase the things you want, and go ahead and decorate your classroom if you wish.'

Tom found Colin sitting alone on a wall in the playground eating his sandwiches. He looked uneasy when Tom came and sat next to him.

'What?' he asked.

'I think you and I need to talk,' said Tom.

'What about?'

'Your behaviour for one thing, and then the work which you didn't do.'

'I told you nothing happened over the holidays and I don't like writing.' He took a bite of his sandwich.

'I'm going to be your teacher from now on,' said Tom, 'so we are going to have to come to some understanding.'

'I don't know what you mean,' he replied with his mouth full.

'I'm sure you do. I won't accept your poor behaviour and attitude and the fact you make no effort with your work. You also disrupt the class with your comments.'

'I don't like school,' the boy told him, spitting out bits of bread. 'I never have.'

'The thing is, Colin,' said Tom, 'that if you carry on as you have been doing, I have certain options open to me.'

'I don't know what you're on about.' There was a wary, resentful look in his eyes.

'As I see it, I have three options. The first is to make you stand outside the classroom in the corridor which I believe is what happened before I came. The next option is for me to send you to Mr Gaunt, and I have been told that is also what happened in the past when you didn't behave yourself. And then there's the third option.'

The boy was interested but his face remained impassive. He stopped eating.

'The third option,' Tom told the boy, 'is for me to come and see your father.'

Colin shot up as if he had been poked with a cattle prod.

'What!' he exclaimed. 'See my dad!'

'I could call out to the farm and tell him that you are not behaving yourself and not working, and see if he can have a word with you.' Of course this was a bluff. Tom had no intention of going to see the boy's father. That would make the boy's life intolerable – for his father, from what he had been told in the staffroom, was a difficult man and likely to take the belt to his son and that was the last thing Tom wanted. His words had the desired effect for the boy was clearly alarmed.

'I don't want you to see my dad,' said Colin. He had a pained look on his face. 'He doesn't like people coming out to the farm.'

'Well then, we need to come to an understanding, don't we?'

The boy looked at him curiously. 'An understanding?' he asked.

'Provided you behave yourself and start to make an effort with your work, I don't see any need to speak to your father. Do you understand?'

'Yea,' he answered brusquely. Tom heard the tremor in his voice and knew that the boy was close to tears. The mention of his father seemed to put the very fear of God in him.

'Oh and, Colin, you can stop the bullying, and before you tell me you don't know anything about it, I saw you chasing Charlie. And one more thing.'

'What?'

'You can start by calling me "sir".'

4

By the end of the week, Tom knew he was going to stay at the school. Mr Gaunt, although not the most go-ahead and well-organised of head teachers, clearly had a good deal of affection for the children. He didn't interfere with what the teachers were doing and remained his easy-going and avuncular self. Tom liked his new colleagues. Although he found them somewhat eccentric, they were cheerful and supportive and he could tell that they had a genuine interest in their pupils, although they made few demands upon them academically. But it was the children who finally convinced him that he should remain at the school. They were eager and good-natured and applied themselves to their work without complaint. It was clear that there was much to do in terms of raising standards but Tom felt optimistic that they would improve. Then there was Colin. Although his work was skimpy and he contributed nothing in the lessons and sat stony-faced at the back of the classroom, Tom's talk with him had clearly made an impression for the boy had been no trouble.

When the bell rang for the end of school, several of the pupils hung back.

'Haven't you children got homes to go to?' asked Tom good-humouredly.

Judith, the girl with the long black plaits and rosy cheeks, spoke first.

'Mr Dwyer,' she said hesitantly, 'we like having you as our teacher.'

Tom laughed. 'Well, I'm very pleased to hear it.'

'We didn't learn much last year,' said Simon, the heavily freckled boy.

'Since you've come,' said Vicky, the large ginger-headed child, 'Colin's started behaving.'

'Yes, he has,' Tom told her.

'We really like your lessons,' said Carol.

The children remained clustered around the teacher's desk as if expecting Tom to say something.

'So was there something else?' he asked.

Matthew, the sharp-faced pupil with the untidy hair, nudged the boy next to him. 'Go on, David,' he whispered. 'Ask 'im.'

'Sir, are you going to stay?' asked the small, gangly boy with the squint.

'Yes, I am,' replied Tom, smiling, 'I'm going to stay.'

'That's champion, is that,' said George, beaming.

Tom had been to see Mrs Leadbeater about the resources and rather expected a raise of the eyebrow, a sharp in-drawing of breath and the usual Yorkshire person's war-cry of 'How much!' To his surprise the school secretary peered over her unfashionable horn-rimmed spectacles and never blinked an eyelid when he listed off all the things he would need.

'Just keep the receipts,' she told him casually. 'And Mr Gaunt tells me you're going to decorate your classroom.'

'Yes, that is my intention,' replied Tom.

'I've been on at my husband to give it a good going-over umpteen times,' said Mrs Leadbeater, 'but, true to form, he's not got around to it. It takes a while for Bob to bestir himself, I'm afraid. He tells me it's the cleaner's job anyway and, as I told you, we are without one at the moment.'

'I don't mind smartening up the classroom,' Tom told her. 'I thought I might make a start this weekend.'

'Well, it certainly wants doing. I don't know how poor Miss Cathcart could bear it teaching in there but that was the way she liked it.'

'Mrs Leadbeater,' began Tom.

'Do call me Beryl.'

'Beryl,' said Tom, 'what exactly happened with Miss Cathcart?'

'You would have to ask Mr Gaunt,' the school secretary told him. 'It's not my place to go into all that. Suffice it to say it was an upsetting time. Now, about doing up your classroom, I'll get my husband to come and give you a hand this weekend if I can drag him away from the football on the television.'

'I wouldn't want to put him to any trouble,' said Tom.

'It's no trouble. It will be good to get him out from under my feet.' She pulled a face. 'I see quite enough of him in school every day.'

So on Saturday, with the help of the caretaker, Tom set about refurbishing the classroom, painting the walls, polishing the floor, removing the samplers and putting up display boards.

Mr Leadbeater had arrived that morning none too pleased to be dragooned into giving up part of his precious weekend, but when he saw the transformation of the room after they had finished, he looked pleased with himself.

'Well, I think we've done a good morning's work, Bob,' Tom said when they stood admiring their handiwork. 'I think you deserve a drink. Would you like to join me at the King's Head for a pint?'

'Thank you very much,' replied the caretaker, allowing himself a rare smile, 'I don't mind if I do.'

The King's Head was unusually quiet for a Saturday lunchtime. Three old men were occupied playing dominoes at a corner table and a couple of hikers sat by the fireplace. Leanne, dressed in a yellow and black jumper and resembling a giant wasp, buzzed down the bar all smiles when she caught sight of Tom.

'Two pints of Benson's Best please, Leanne,' said Tom. He looked round the room. 'Where is everyone?'

'There's a big auction at Durdeyfield Farm,' the girl told him, pulling a pint. 'That's where everybody is. My mam's hoping to get some bargains so she's gone as well. They're selling everything, even the contents of the house. It's dead sad. The Durdeyfields have lived in the Dale for years.'

'That's another farm disappearing,' said the caretaker gloomily.

'Yes, Miss Tranter was telling me about it,' said Tom, paying for the drinks.

'It's the local squire what's behind it,' said the caretaker, before taking a gulp of beer and wiping the froth from his lips with the back of his hand. 'Sir Hedley's buying up the small farms when they go to the wall. He just wants the land for his shooting and so his fancy friends from London can come up and pay for the privilege for blasting hell out of the grouse. He's selling the houses and barns to off-comed-uns as holiday homes and disposing of all the farming vehicles and equipment. It's a real shame. Families who have lived here for generations are moving out of the Dale and that's why the numbers of kids at the school are falling.'

A young man, who had been listening unobserved by the speaker, strode down from the end of the bar.

'Why don't you keep your stupid bloody ideas to yourself, Leadbeater,' he said in a high, querulous voice. His mouth was tight and angry.

The man had a long, bony face like a horse, papery skin as white as milk and the small, down-turned mouth of a peevish child. He brushed back a strand of blond hair like a male model being photographed. He was joined by a companion, another young man, tall and rather better looking, with dark brown eyes and a sharply chiselled face.

The caretaker shifted uneasily on the bar stool. 'Oh, I didn't see you there, Mr Maladroit.'

'That is patently obvious, otherwise you wouldn't go spouting such bloody rubbish.'

The men playing dominoes looked up and listened. The hikers stopped talking to watch.

The caretaker lowered his head and cleared his throat with a small cough. 'I was only saying—' he began.

'Well, don't,' interrupted the young man, 'otherwise if you start slandering my family again, my father will make your life very uncomfortable, very uncomfortable indeed. You know who he is and you know he calls the shots around here. Do I make myself clear?'

Mr Leadbeater licked his lower lip nervously. 'Yes, yes, of course, Mr Maladroit. I'm sorry if I caused offence.'

'Idiot,' mouthed the young man, turning to go back down the bar.

Tom, who had remained silent during this unpleasant exchange, placed his beer carefully on the bar. Although he was generally a quiet and good-humoured man by nature, when he became annoyed or was provoked he had quite a temper. He had been sent off the pitch a good few times when he played professional football. He was now incensed by the man's offensive behaviour. 'You are one of the most witless, ill-mannered persons I have ever met,' he said loud enough for all in the room to hear.

The young man spun around. 'What?'

'I said you are a witless and ill-mannered person,' Tom repeated.

'Leave it, Mr Dwyer,' said the caretaker under his breath, placing a hand on the teacher's arm.

'What did you say?' asked the young man, returning to face Tom whom he regarded with considerable distaste. His small eyes widened, his shoulders stiffened and he breathed out sharply through his teeth.

'I think you heard what I said perfectly well,' answered Tom.

'And who asked you to stick your bloody oar in?' asked the young man.

'I came here for a quiet drink and not to listen to some odious ignoramus shouting the odds.'

'Did you just call me an ignoramus?' demanded the young man. His face was now puce.

'Is there something wrong with your hearing?'

The man came closer and fixed Tom with a malevolent stare. He had never been spoken to in such terms. 'How dare you speak to me like that,' he said. A muscle in his jaw twitched and his small eyes narrowed to slits. 'Do you know who I am?' he demanded. His fists were tightly clenched.

'No, I don't. Perhaps somebody in the bar can enlighten you since you appear to have forgotten.'

'How dare you speak to me like that?'

'You need to learn some manners,' said Tom. 'Go and finish your drink and stop eavesdropping on private conversations.'

'Don't you dare tell me what I should do!' exclaimed the young man.

'Will you please stop this? I don't want any trouble,' said Leanne, looking distinctly uneasy.

'Mind your own bloody business, Leanne,' said the young man, 'and bugger off.' He gripped Tom's arm and stabbed him in the chest with a finger. 'I want an apology,' he said.

'Don't do that,' said Tom without raising his voice.

'Apologise,' shouted the young man, prodding again.

Tom pushed him away with such force that the young man lost his balance and fell with a thump on the floor. The two hikers laughed. Jumping to his feet, the man came forward, swinging his fist. Tom nimbly dodged the first clumsy blow and the second and punched his assailant with a short, sharp jab to the stomach. His would-be attacker bent over like a broken puppet and fell to the floor again, this time coughing and gasping for air.

His companion balled his fist and moved forward towards Tom.

'I wouldn't do that if I were you,' Tom told him coolly. 'You might end up on the floor alongside your pal.'

The man thought for a moment. Something in Tom's expression made him back off. He helped his wheezing companion to his feet and supported him as they made for the door.

The young man, holding his stomach, turned and regarded Tom with a cold, contemptuous look. 'You've not heard the last of this,' he threatened. Then he was gone.

The colour had drained from the caretaker's face. 'That was Jamie Maladroit,' he told Tom. 'He's Sir Hedley's son. I'm sorry I opened my big mouth. I didn't see him at the end of the bar.' He shook his head portentously. 'He's right though, I don't think you've heard the last of it.'

'Oh, I think I have,' said Tom. In this he was to be proved wrong.

That afternoon he drove into Clayton, visiting the White Rose Bookshop first where he bought a selection of bright, glossy paperback novels, poetry anthologies, reference books and modern dictionaries. Then he called at the stationers for some good-quality fountain pens and a selection of pencils, and finally to the art suppliers for paints, brushes and paper. Coming out of the shop carrying an armful of boxes and bags, he collided with a young woman who was hurrying past. His purchases were scattered around him on the pavement.

'I'm sorry,' he said, stooping to pick up the bags and boxes. 'I wasn't looking where I was going.' He looked up to see the young woman with the flaming red hair. She stared down at him. 'You, again,' he sighed.

'Tell me, Mr Dwyer,' she said, giving him a wry smile, 'do you make a habit of not looking where you are going?'

'Do forgive my clumsiness, Miss Fairborn,' he replied in a mock apologetic voice. 'My fault entirely. I do hope you will not tell your father. I really would like to avoid another ear-bashing.'

Her face flushed with anger. 'I have already told you,' she retorted irritably. 'I never said a word to my father. I can fight my own battles. You can believe that or not, just as you choose.' She stopped for a moment, thinking of what next to say and drew a deep breath. 'Do you know, you are one of the most . . . Oh, I don't know why I am wasting my time talking to you.' She strode off.

He smiled. 'Feisty woman,' he said.

Tom's next call was to drop his washing off at his aunt's in Barton-in-the Dale. Before visiting her, however, he called in at the village store and post office. The proprietor and post-mistress, Mrs Sloughthwaite, a round, red-faced woman with a large, fleshy nose, pouchy cheeks and a great bay window of a bust, was the eyes and ears of the village. She knew every-thing that there was to know in Barton-in-the-Dale and was a most efficient conduit of gossip and information. Villagers wishing to know the news only had to call into the shop to receive a detailed and colourful account of the latest happen-ing or hear a fascinating fact about someone's personal life. As was her custom, she was leaning over and resting her substan-tial bosom and her chubby arms on the counter when Tom entered the shop. He found her in earnest conversation with a customer, which she broke off suddenly when he walked through door. She raised her heavy frame from the counter and gave a broad smile.

'Well, well, well,' she said good-humouredly, 'look who the cat's blown in.'

'Good afternoon,' said Tom.

Mrs Sloughthwaite turned to her customer, a tall, frail-looking woman with a pale face and tragic expression. 'This is Mr Dwyer,' she said at full volume, as if talking to a person hard of hearing. 'He used to teach at the village school. He's Mrs O'Connor's nephew. You've met Bridget O'Connor, haven't you? She cleans for Dr and Mrs Stirling at Clumber Lodge and does for Father Daly at St Bede's once a week. She works at the suppository in Clayton next to the church most Saturdays.'

Mrs Sloughthwaite was a mistress of the malapropism and amazingly inventive non sequiturs. She managed to mangle the English language, often to the amusement of her customers.

Tom smiled and said 'repository' under his breath. He was minded to put her right on her misuse of the word but thought better of it. Were anyone inclined to correct her on her many mishandlings of the English language, it would take them an age. He recalled the time she spoke about her cousin's grand-daughter who was something of a child progeny with a photo-genic memory, how she was taking electrocution lessons to sort out her vowels, a girl so bright she could be a member of Mencap, 'that group of clever people with the high IQs'. Once when a customer, worse for drink, had staggered into the store, she had refused to sell him anything, announcing that, as the proprietor, it was her provocative to serve who she liked.

Mrs Sloughthwaite's interest in other people's ailments was legendary.

'Mrs Farringdon is up at the hospital for one of these mono-grams,' she once told a customer. 'They think the tumour might be belligerent.' She informed another patron of her shop that when Mr Pocock was rushed to hospital with a heart attack, 'they tried artificial reincarnation', and she suggested to Mrs Osbaldiston that she might purchase a pair of elastic stockings for her 'very close veins'.

'Mr Dwyer used to be a professional footballer, didn't you?' she asked Tom now. She did not receive nor expect an answer. 'He had to give it up after all the injuries. Damaged a cartridge. His Auntie Bridget was telling me there wasn't a football match when he didn't come off of the pitch covered in bruises and contortions.' She carried on as if the subject of her account was not present.

'He trained as a teacher at the village school under Mrs Stirling and then, when he was fully matriculated, moved to that little school at the top of the Dale. This is Mrs Fish by the way,' Mrs Sloughthwaite told him. 'She's one of my regulars. You might have come across her when you taught at the school. She plays the organ at the church.' She turned to her customer. 'You played at the church, didn't you, Mrs Fish?'

'Yes, I did,' replied the woman.

'She deserted the Anglicans for the Primitive Methodists when you had that falling-out with the last vicar, didn't you?'

'I did,' agreed the customer, a pained expression on her face. 'It was because—'

'He criticised her playing,' said the shopkeeper, finishing the sentence. 'Said she was too slow and kept hitting too many bum notes. I mean anyone can make a few mistakes when they're playing the organ, particularly if they've got bad eyesight like Mrs Fish.'

'I didn't make all that many mistakes,' announced the customer, sounding peeved.

'Anyway, she's gone back to St Christopher's now there's a new vicar,' said the shopkeeper ignoring the interruption. 'You remember Dr Underwood. She's in charge there at the church.'

'I am in a bit of a hurry,' Tom told her. 'I have quite a bit to do this afternoon and—'

Over many years Mrs Sloughthwaite had managed, and was determined, to acquire the most intimate information about everyone and everything in the village. She had become adept at gleaning tittle-tattle from those who patronised her shop and drew them out, at first with a little tactful questioning. Should their answers not prove satisfactory, she employed a more direct approach. The information thus disclosed was then circulated throughout the village. She was not going to let Tom off the hook so easily.

'Do you like it at your new school then?' she asked, fishing for information.

'Yes, very much,' he replied. 'The head teacher is very supportive, the other teachers are friendly and helpful and the children well-behaved. I'm really enjoying it. Anyway, I should like to buy—'

The shopkeeper rested a dimpled elbow on the counter and placed her fleshy chin on a hand. She wasn't going to let him go until she had extracted a deal more information. 'It's a bit remote is Risingdale, isn't it?' she remarked. 'They need oxygen masks up there so I'm told. It's away from anywhere and I bet it's bitter cold come winter. I recall the village was snowed in a few years ago. They had to get the air–sea ambulance out. Fortuitively, we don't get weather like that down here.' She sniffed. 'Course, we don't have much truck with the folks up there.'

It was true there was little communication between the residents of Risingdale and Barton-in-the-Dale. The two villages might have been in different hemispheres. Though there was little more than ten miles between them as the crow flies, the two communities had little contact. It was said that this mutual antipathy dated back to well before the last century over a dispute about sheep rustling. People in these parts had long, long memories.

'So, are you living in the village?' asked the shopkeeper.

'I'm renting a room at the King's Head,' Tom told her, 'but I shall be looking to rent or buy a flat or a small cottage.'

'Then you'll be able to wash your own clothes,' said the shopkeeper. She turned back to Mrs Fish. 'He takes his shirts and underwear to his Auntie Bridget's. She does his laundry.'

Was there anything this woman was not privy to, thought Tom.

'I really must make tracks,' he said, desperate to get away and, taking out his wallet, he placed a ten-pound note on the counter. Before Mrs Sloughthwaite could continue with her interrogation, he picked up a large box of chocolates from a display stand. 'May I have these please?'

'For someone special?' asked Mrs Sloughthwaite, winking.

'Yes, for someone special,' Tom repeated.

'Who's the lucky young lady then?' she quizzed.

'My Auntie Bridget.'

'You're not courting yet then?'

'No, not yet,' replied Tom.

'A good-looking young man like you not courting? I've never heard the like. I reckon you have young women queuing up to be taken out.'

'Chance would be a fine thing,' laughed Tom. 'I think the ten pounds will just about cover it for the chocolates. If there is any change, put it in the charity box please.' And before the grilling could resume, he headed quickly for the door, wishing the two women a hasty 'Goodbye.'

'Give my best wishes to your Auntie Bridget,' Mrs Sloughthwaite shouted after him.

As the door closed behind Tom, Mrs Sloughthwaite returned to her position leaning on the counter and faced her customer. 'His auntie is a good sort but my goodness she could talk for Britain and for as Ireland as well. I can never get a word in when she's in the shop.'

Mrs Fish, who stood glassy-eyed and with mouth open, at that moment lived up fully to her name for she resembled a haddock on a fishmonger's slab.

*   *   *

Mrs O'Connor lived in a small, shiny red-brick terraced house in the village. She was a dumpy, round-faced little woman with the huge, liquid brown eyes of a cow and a permanent smile on her small lips. Her hair was set in a tight perm.

'I expected you earlier,' she told her nephew. 'Where have you been?'

'I got held up,' he told her. He pulled a face. 'In the village store.'

'Oh dear,' said Mrs O'Connor. 'Sure, she's a good-hearted woman is Mrs Sloughthwaite, so she is, but she can talk the legs off a lame donkey, so she can. As my grandmother might have said, God rest her soul, "a silent mouth is melodious to the ears".'

A case of the kettle calling the pan black, thought Tom. 'These are for you,' he said, handing her the chocolates.

'Oh, you shouldn't have bothered,' replied his aunt. No, she said to herself, he really shouldn't have bothered. The chocolates in question had been on the display stand in the village store for more weeks than she could recall. Mrs Sloughthwaite had been trying to shift them since well before last Easter.

'So have you decided to stay at the school then?' she asked.

'I have, yes.'

'Well, for what it's worth,' she said, 'I think you've done the right thing. You wouldn't want to let the kiddies down, now would you?'

'No, I wouldn't want to let them down,' he answered.

'You're a decent young man, Thomas,' his aunt told him, 'with a kind heart. You'll make a fine husband when you find the right girl.'

'Don't you start, Auntie,' laughed Tom. 'I've already had Mrs Sloughthwaite quizzing me about the state of my love life.'

'So, how are you getting along at your new school?' she asked.

'Oh, pretty well,' replied her nephew. 'It's early days yet though.'

'It's a pity that they couldn't give you a job at the village school here in Barton, so it is,' his aunt remarked.

'Yes, I should have really loved to have stayed on but it wasn't to be.'

'Mrs Stirling was after asking about you last week,' said Mrs O'Connor. 'She was wondering how you were getting on at your new school. She said you are greatly missed, so she did.'

'Yes, I miss the school too,' Tom told her wistfully.

Barton-in-the-Dale Primary School had been transformed by the head teacher, Mrs Elisabeth Stirling, in the space of just a few months. With her appointment the school underwent a dramatic change. What had been a moribund place under the management of Miss Sowerbutts, the previous head teacher, soon began to flourish. With Elisabeth's firm and decisive leadership, the once dark and neglected premises were transformed into a bright, cheerful and welcoming place. The introduction of many extra-curricular activities, the improvements in the quality of the teaching, the standards of achievement and the children's behaviour were greatly commended by the school inspector when he made a visit. Parents now, rather than taking their children away, were opting to send them to Barton-in-the-Dale. Within a year it became one of the most successful and popular schools in the area. Tom had trained under Elisabeth's direction and would have dearly liked to have been offered a permanent position at the school, but his hopes were scuppered when the Education Authority insisted that the vacant post was offered to a redeployed teacher. Passing the small, solid, stone-built Victorian structure on his way to his aunt's and seeing the large tubs of bright geraniums by the door, the vivid flowers in window boxes and a bird table on the small lawn to the front, Tom thought of the school at which he now taught and he determined to improve things at Risingdale – and not just the environment.

'You'll stay for some tea,' said Mrs O'Connor now.

'No thanks, Auntie Bridget. I need to get back to the school. I've things to do.'

'On a Saturday!' she exclaimed. 'Sure you should be putting your feet up so you should. Don't you go overdoing it and taking too much on. Everyone lays a burden on a willing horse.'

'Speaking of burdens,' said Tom. 'I've brought my washing. It's good of you to do it for me.'

'Sure it's no trouble at all. My Grandmother Mullarkey, God rest her sainted soul, was wont to say, "May you always have a clean shirt, a clear conscience, and enough coins in your pocket to buy a loaf of bread."'

On the way back to his car, Tom saw his former head teacher making her way slowly down the high street. He caught up with her just as she was about to enter the village store.

'Elisabeth,' he said, coming up behind her.

She turned and smiled when she saw him. 'Hello, Tom,' she said. 'How nice to see you. What are you doing in Barton?'

'I've been visiting my Auntie Bridget's,' he told her. 'I've already called into the village store and been subjected to a thorough cross-examination by Mrs Sloughthwaite, so I won't come in with you. She misses nothing and has this incredible skill of squeezing every bit of information and gossip from her customers. She should be employed by MI5.'

'No, she's not changed,' agreed Elisabeth, 'but she has a heart of gold, so we can forgive her the nosiness. You just have to be a little circumspect what you say when calling into the store.'

'How are you keeping?' asked Tom.

Elisabeth patted her heavily pregnant stomach. 'Not long now, thank goodness,' she said, managing a smile.

'Well, pregnancy seems to suit you. You look blooming.'

'You've not lost the blarney, Tom,' she said. 'And as to pregnancy suiting me, it couldn't be further from the truth. Morning sickness, swollen ankles, cravings for food, nightly visits to the toilet. You men have it easy.'

'You sound like my Auntie Bridget,' he told her, laughing.

'Anyway,' said Elisabeth, 'enough about me. What about you? How are you getting on at your new school?'

'Pretty well, touch wood,' he replied, tapping his head.

'Actually, I was going to give you a call,' said Elisabeth. 'I shall be going on maternity leave soon and the school will need a supply teacher. You're not interested, are you?'

'I'd love to come back to Barton,' replied Tom, 'but not on supply. I've got a full-time position now. I really don't want to go back to supply teaching: I just get settled in a school and get to know the children and staff and then I have to move on when their teacher returns.'

'Of course, I understand that,' she said, 'but if you were offered a permanent position at Barton-with-Urebank, might you consider coming back?'

'I don't know,' he said.

'It's just that numbers in the school are increasing. With the closure of some neighbouring small schools, we have had an influx of children. We will be looking for a permanent member of staff, probably next term.'

'But won't you have to take another redeployed teacher?' asked Tom.

'I already have appointed three redeployed teachers. You will remember Mr Jolly who came from Urebank School and Miss Kennedy who joined us from Sunnydale Infants. I have a Miss Pickersgill with me now. I think this time I can persuade the Director of Education to let me advertise for a new position.'

'I see,' said Tom thoughtfully.

'You would be in with a good chance – more than a good chance,' Elisabeth told him. 'I know that you probably feel honour bound to stay where you are, particularly since you have just started at the school, but – and you must keep this under your hat – I heard when I was at County Hall last week that Risingdale may be among the next tranche of schools for closure. You need to think about your position, Tom. It might be that you will be out of a job again and have to return to supply teaching.'

'If this had come earlier, Elisabeth,' he answered, 'I would have jumped at the chance of coming back to Barton, but as you said, I do feel honour bound to stay at Risingdale. I can't just jump ship after a term.'

'Well, think about it,' she said. 'I am sure you won't mention to the teachers there what I have told you. It is just a rumour and might never happen.' The door to the village store opened and Mrs Sloughthwaite popped her round and jolly face around it.

'Now what are you two talking about?' she asked. 'You've been stood out here chattering on for the best part of a quarter of an hour. I could see you through the window. So what's so interesting?'

Tom sat in the car before he set off back for Risingdale and rested his hands on the steering wheel. Just my luck that a job I had really wanted was now about to come up, he thought. He imagined Barton-with-Urebank Primary School where he had been so happy: wonderful resources, high standards, lively, enthusiastic colleagues, well-behaved and hard-working children, supportive parents, school trips, successful sports teams and a head teacher who set the standard by which others should be judged. No teacher could wish for a better school in which to teach. And it was in the centre of a thriving village of friendly people, not two miles away from Clayton. Then there was Risingdale School, way up the Dale, in the middle of nowhere with its paucity of resources, low stand-ards, eccentric teachers, indifferent parents and a headmaster so happy-go-lucky and undemanding. Perhaps I should give serious thought, Tom told himself, to what Mrs Stirling had said.

In the newly decorated classroom back at the school, Tom cleared the bookcases of the ancient class readers, the stack of old dictionaries, the hardbacks and the pile of folders and consigned them to several bin bags. He put the framed samplers away at the back of the cupboard and would decide what to do with them later. The books he had bought were arranged and then he set about marking the work the children had produced. He couldn't concentrate. The incident in the King's Head had been unsettling but he convinced himself that it would blow over. Then there was Miss Fairborn. Perhaps I was a bit hard on her, he thought, recalling the recent altercation in Clayton. It was clear that the high-spirited Miss Janette Fairborn didn't need anyone to fight her battles. He wished, however, that she would get down from that high horse of hers. But the main thing on his mind was what Elisabeth Stirling had told him, 'Risingdale may be among the next tranche of schools for closure. You need to think about your position, Tom. It might be that you will be out of a job again and have to return to supply teaching.'

5

It was getting on for seven o'clock when Tom arrived back at the King's Head. Being Saturday night the inn was packed and noisy. When he entered the bar there was a sudden hush and faces turned to look at him. There were several nods of the head, a good number of smiles, a few waves, and some of the farmers wished Tom a 'Good evening'.

Mr Croft left his companions and hurried over.

'Naah then, lad,' he said, patting Tom on the back.

'Mr Croft.'

'Are tha all reet?' asked the farmer.

'I'm fine,' replied Tom.

'Let me get thee a drink.' The farmer reached for his wallet which was a rare occurrence.

'That's very good of you,' replied Tom, 'but I've not eaten. Maybe I'll join you later.'

'I'd 'ave given mi back teeth to 'ave been 'ere,' chuckled Mr Croft.

'Been here?' asked Tom, puzzled.

'Earlier today when tha fettled young Maladroit,' the farmer told him. 'That ne'er-do-well's been needin' a good thump for years. I 'eard that tha floored 'im.' He put up his fists like a prizefighter and boxed the air.

'Ah that,' said Tom. It hadn't taken long for that bit of juicy gossip to circulate.

'Well, tha's med a few new friends an' I reckon tha's made an enemy of the Maladroits. I tell thee this, Mester Dwyer, tha're certainly mekkin' tha mark in Risingdale.'

Tom received another warm welcome when he entered the parlour.

Leanne blushed when she saw him. 'Oh hello, Tom,' she said. She was wearing a tight-fitting pair of denim jeans and a bright pink and yellow striped jumper, which clung to her as if she had been poured into it. She looked like a huge chunk of Battenberg cake.

'Hello, Leanne.'

'Mam's cooking you something special,' said the girl.

'Please tell her not too much,' Tom told her. 'I'm not a great eater.'

The girl remained where she was, staring at him. 'I can see that you like to keep in shape.'

'Pardon?'

'I suppose that's why you look so fit,' she said, 'watching your weight. I thought you were wonderful today, the way you sorted Jamie Maladroit out. It was like something on a film. Everyone's talking about it.'

'Yes, I gather so,' said Tom wearily.

'I hope you don't get into any trouble over what happened.'

'I doubt if anything will come of it,' replied Tom, more to reassure himself than anything.

On the Monday morning, the pupils gathered outside the classroom whispering to each other.

'Come along in,' said Tom.

Tentatively, the children entered and looked around, wide-eyed.

'Gosh!' exclaimed David. 'Look at our room.'

'It's all different,' said Judith.

'It's great,' said Simon.

The children began chattering excitedly.

'It stinks of paint,' mumbled Colin, slouching as he went to sit at his desk.

When the children were seated, Tom looked at the eager, smiling faces.

'This is our new classroom,' he told them, 'and I want you all to look after it. There're some new books which you may borrow and everyone has a dictionary which I want you to use. Later this week your work will be displayed on the new boards, neatly written with the fountain pens you will find on your desks. From now on we are going to write in ink.'

The children worked quietly that morning. Thoughts were still going round in Tom's head as he stared out of the window on the expanse of countryside.

His thoughts were interrupted by David.

'Sir, are we going to do some games?'

'Yes, we are,' replied Tom, turning to face the pupil. 'In fact we can have your first lesson tomorrow morning. Put your pens down a moment, children, and listen. I want you to come tomorrow with your games kits. I think we'll start with a game of football.'

'Great!' chorused the children.

Games had not been on the curriculum until Tom arrived at the school. Miss Tranter, as she explained to him as she buffed one of her long nails, had certainly no inclination to run about a muddy field full of sheep droppings and cowpats in the cold and wet; Captain Cadwallader, who, of course, in his youth was something of an athlete, or so he told Tom, now felt he was too long in the tooth for such physical exertions. Mrs Golightly said plainly that the little ones didn't need such things since they got all they needed in terms of exercise on the climbing frame at the rear of the school and by running around the playground.

Tom's first games lesson with his class the following morning was a revelation. He had asked the children to bring into school some suitable clothing meaning, of course, shorts and

T-shirts. The children did not possess any games kits and had no idea what to wear for the lesson, and the motley group, which gathered around the teacher on the tussocky field adjacent to the school, were dressed in the most incongruous outfits. Some turned out in old anoraks and trainers, others in baggy jumpers and jeans, and only one or two wore clothes which vaguely resembled some sort of football kit. Simon turned up in an old pair of wellington boots and a flat cap. Few had boots. Looking at the knot of children, Tom determined that he would have a word with Mr Gaunt about getting some proper kit for them.

There being no playing field at the school, the first games lesson took place on the adjacent field. Two boys had been given the task of erecting four long metal scaffolding poles which had been rusting at the back of the building. These would act as makeshift goalposts and Carol, the little sheep expert, shepherded a small flock of docile-looking sheep and two miserable-looking cows into the adjoining field.

It was a cold and windy morning and Tom did not wish to keep the children standing around listening to him, so he split up the class into two teams and refereed the first game of football played in the school for over a decade. Of course it could not be described as a game of football for as soon as Tom blew his whistle to start the match, the children, with the exception of Charlie and Colin, who watched by the limestone wall, set off running like nests of frantic rabbits. They raced around the field after the ball, moving at a frightening speed. Any pupil who got the ball gave no thought of passing it and some players, if they got in the way of another, were felled like trees. The girls were as ferocious as the boys and the largest in the class, Vicky, thundered down the field like a frenzied carthorse, blowing great clouds of steam and shouldering any opposition foolhardy enough to get in her way. Those she flattened did not stay down long and jumped up to their feet again, racing and dodging, leaping and weaving in pursuit of the ball. Tom had never seen anything like it.

Back in the classroom after the game, he gathered the children around him. He didn't wish to discourage the children but knew things had to be said. Before he could open his mouth, Vicky jumped up and down excitedly. 'That were great!' she exclaimed.

There was a chorus of agreement even from those who had been on the end of her butting.

'It was,' agreed Simon, 'but I don't think we should have lasses playing footie, sir. Can't they do hockey or rounders? Football's for lads.'

'No, it isn't,' countered the girl. 'There are women footballers, you know.'

'I do know,' said the boy, 'but—'

'Just listen a moment,' Tom interrupted. 'All our games lessons will involve everyone in the class. Sometimes we might play rounders and the boys, as well as the girls, will play that game too. There's no discussion about it. Do you understand what I'm saying, Simon?'

'Yes, sir,' replied the boy.

'That's telling him, sir,' said Vicky smugly.

Matthew, the sharp-faced pupil with the untidy hair, nudged the boy next to him. 'Go on, David,' he whispered. 'Ask him.'

'Sir, are we going to have a school football team like in other schools?' asked the small, gangly boy, squinting.

'Yes, we are,' replied Tom, smiling, 'but we need to play a whole lot better than we did today before we enter the school junior league and we need to get some proper kit.'

'My mam won't be able to afford it, sir,' said Judith sadly.

'Don't you worry your head about that,' Tom told the girl. 'I'll sort that out. But we really need to improve the way we play.'

The children looked downhearted.

'Don't look so unhappy,' he told the children. 'It would be wrong of me to tell you that you played a good game. I'm being honest. I was really pleased to see so many of you being so enthusiastic.' He caught sight of a scowling Colin but continued. 'You put a lot of effort into the game but it is not the way to play football. All of you madly rushing about the field after the ball and not passing it to others in the team is no way to play the game. Teamwork wins goals. If we are going to have a team and compete with other schools, then we all have to learn to play as a team. You will need to try and anticipate what the opponents are going to do and be aware of where your teammates are positioned on the field. More importantly, you have to pass the ball. Now I can promise you things will get better. On Monday after school, for those of you who wish to be in the team, we will have a practice and you will start to learn about tactics.'

Tom had noticed that neither Charlie nor Colin had taken any part in the games lesson. He decided to have a word with both of them.

'I'm afraid football is not for me, Mr Dwyer,' Charlie told him during the following morning break. He was sitting at his desk reading one of the new books Tom had bought.

'But you are very fast,' said Tom. 'I've seen how fast you can run.'

'It's true, I am pretty fast,' agreed the boy, 'but I've got two left feet. I'd be a liability on the team.'

Tom found Colin at the edge of the playground at lunchtime, hands stuffed in his pockets, staring over the fields. Tom broached the question of his attending the football practice.

'I'd be crap,' he told the teacher, not looking at him. 'I'm rubbish at sports.'

'I don't believe that,' said Tom, 'and in any case you don't have to be good at something to enjoy it.'

'Well, I wouldn't enjoy it.' He thought for a moment before adding, 'sir'.

'You can't tell unless you try. Why not come to the practice?'

''Cos I don't want to,' he said vehemently. The boy glared at Tom. There was a fierce look in his eye. 'Look at me. I'm fat. I can't run fast like the others. I'm like a knackered donkey and anyway, none of them would want to play with me. None of them like me.'

A sad, withdrawn, mixed-up boy, thought Tom. 'Look, Colin, you probably won't believe this but when I was eleven, I was big for my age and a bit overweight as well, but then I started to play football. I got pretty good at it. It's really all I ever wanted to do after that. Why not give it a try?'

'Is that supposed to make me feel any better?' demanded the boy with a belligerent look on his face. 'Oh, I used to be fat and useless like you,' the boy mimicked, 'and just look at me now.'

'But it's true,' Tom told him calmly.

'Do you think that will change my mind because if you do, then you're wrong! I don't want to play your stupid football. I don't want to be in any team and I don't want to be at this rotten school . . . sir. Can I go now?'

When Tom related this conversation to his colleagues in the staffroom later that day, he was rather hoping for some advice on how to handle the boy. When he was training to be a teacher at Barton, Mrs Stirling had been very supportive when he had encountered a difficult pupil and had suggested strategies and approaches. He had seen how she had dealt with a particularly disruptive and difficult boy. Over the weeks Tom had witnessed how the pupil's behaviour had improved. Disappointingly, his new colleagues were neither helpful nor particularly sympathetic.

'I think you have to accept that Colin Greenwood is a lost cause, dear boy,' said the captain. 'There are some children that the teacher will never get through to and that boy is one. Poor Miss Cathcart, she had a dreadful time with him.'

'It is a fact,' added Miss Tranter, examining her face in a small mirror and applying some blood-red lipstick, 'that those pupils who do not wish to learn cannot be taught. It's a fact that one has to accept.'

'I blame the parents,' said Mrs Golightly. 'They don't exercise enough discipline in the home these days and let their children get away with murder.'

'From what I've been told,' said Tom, 'Colin's father exercises more than enough discipline and that might be the boy's problem.'

'There is always one rotten apple in the barrel, dear boy,' stated the captain.

'I don't consider Colin to be a rotten apple, Owen,' Tom told him sharply. 'He is just a rather angry, mixed-up boy. There must be some reason for his behaviour. Actually, I feel sorry for the lad.'

'Don't start getting sentimental about children,' advised Miss Tranter, who had now started on her eyebrows with a small pair of tweezers.

Tom was reminded of the similar opinion shared by Mrs Robertshaw, a teacher at the school where he had trained.

'Look, Tom,' she had told him, 'you're new to the profession. I've been in it for more years than I'd like to recall. If I may give you some advice: don't get sentimental about children. They need a strong hand and to be kept firmly under control, otherwise they will run rings around you.'

At the football practice there was no sign of either Charlie or Colin. Disappointingly for Tom, the children seemed not to have listened at all to his pep talk given after their first games lesson. Again they raced madly down the field with wild abandon, running and pushing each other with no thought of passing the ball. This was going to be an uphill battle, he thought. As he headed back to the school, he caught sight of a lone figure half hidden behind the large chestnut tree to the front of the building. It was Colin, who had clearly been there all the time, watching. When he looked again the boy had gone.

Tom was getting in his car when he was startled by a strident voice behind him.

'Hello?' It was more of a question than a greeting.

He turned to see a rather threatening figure approaching him. The speaker was a stout, lantern-jawed individual with a red-roughened complexion, heavy grey stubble and a long, bony face like a horse. He wore the attire of the typical Dales' farmer: flat cap, oily and frayed, peaty brown jacket, checked shirt, corduroy trousers and heavy boots. This man also had on a pair of leather gaiters and he carried a hawthorn stick. He was accompanied by two bearded collie dogs.

'Naah then,' he said. 'I wants a word wi' thee.'

'Good afternoon,' replied Tom. 'May I help you?'

'Aye, tha can. Are thy t'bloke what's been usin' my field an' erecting them big bloody metal poles and shiftin' my beeasts?'

'It's your field?' asked Tom.

'Aye, it is,' retorted the farmer, 'an' thee 'ad no business goin' in there.'

'I thought it belonged to the school.'

'Well, it dun't an' tha knaas what thowt did – followed a muck cart an' thowt it were a weddin'. That's my field an' I don't want folk trespassin'. What were tha doin' on theer anyroad, purring metal poles in t'ground?'

'We were playing football.'

'Tha what?'

'We were playing football,' Tom repeated.

'Football!' exclaimed the farmer.

'The poles we were using as goalposts.'

'You were doin' what?'

'I was taking a games lesson with the children,' Tom explained.

'What, in my field?'

'Yes, in your field but, as I said, I assumed it was part of the school. Had I known it wasn't, then I wouldn't have used it. I'm sorry. It won't happen again.'

The farmer rubbed the stubble on his chin. 'Playin' football wi' t'kids,' he mumbled. 'I reckon thy must be t'new school-master then,' said the man.

'I am, yes. Tom Dwyer.'

'Tom Dwyer,' repeated the farmer. 'You're Tom Dwyer?'

'Yes, that is my name.'

'Tom Dwyer. I've 'eard o' thee,' said the farmer.

'Yes, I thought you might have,' answered Tom, 'and before you say it, yes, I am the one who nearly knocked Janette Fairborn off her horse and punched Jamie Maladroit in the King's Head.'

'Did you, by God.'

'You've not heard?' asked Tom.

'Not a word,' replied the farmer, 'but if anyone needed a good 'idin', it's that good-fer-nothin'.'

'Well, I think you must be the only person in the village who hasn't heard. Anyhow, I will not use your field again and will remove the metal poles first thing tomorrow morning.'

'Tom Dwyer,' murmured the farmer, rubbing his chin again. 'Tha's not t'Tom Dywer what used to play for Clayton United, are tha?'

'That's me.'

'Gerraway!' cried the man, coming closer and staring into Tom's face. 'Well, I never did. Tom Dwyer. Tha used to be t'captain.'

'I was.'

'Blood and sand!' cried the farmer. 'Tom Dwyer. Tha was a bloody good player. I reckoned tha'd be playin' for one of t'premier teams by now.'

'Sadly not,' said Tom. 'Too many accidents on the pitch. I had to give up playing.'

'Tom Dwyer,' said the man again, sounding like an echo. 'I can't believe it. An' tha's given up t'football to teach kids?'

'I have, yes,' Tom replied.

'Blood and sand,' said the man again. 'Tom Dwyer, a teacher. Who'd 'ave thowt it?'

'Well, I must be making tracks, Mr . . . er?'

'Sheepshanks,' the man informed him. 'Ernie Sheepshanks.'

'I'll see to removing the metal poles tomorrow, Mr Sheepshanks,' said Tom, 'and not be using your field again.'

'Nay, nay, Tom lad!' exclaimed the farmer. 'Don't thee bother thissen abaat that. I'll shift 'em. Tom Dwyer, fancy meeting thee. I used to come wi' mi lad an' watch thee play every Sat'dy. T'team's gone down pan since thee left. So yer teachin' kids to play football, are tha?'

'Trying to,' answered Tom, 'but not with a great deal of success at the moment.'

'Well, yon field's no good for playin' football on. It's full o' mole 'ills an' rabbit 'oles, sheep droppings and cow shit. I've a much more suitable field up yonder what tha can use and I'll find thee some proper goalposts, an' all.'

'That's very kind of you, Mr Sheepshanks,' said Tom.

'Call me Ernie,' said the man, beaming. He shook his head. 'Well, I'll gu to t'bottom o' our stairs! Tom Dwyer.'

It was on the Wednesday lunchtime when the police car pulled up outside the school. Mr Gaunt stopped Tom as he was heading for the staffroom at lunchtime.

'Sergeant Pollock wishes to see you,' he said. 'I've put him in my study.' To Tom's surprise the headmaster did not enquire why the police had called to see him. It appeared that Mr Gaunt thought it to be an everyday occurrence, either that or he had heard on the grapevine what the visit might concern.

'Mr Dwyer?' asked the police officer, rising from the head-master's chair when Tom entered the room. He was a small, tubby man with a round pinkish face, large blue protuberant eyes and a thatch of black hair. He reminded Tom of one of the brightly painted toby jugs which were displayed in the King's Head.

'That's right,' answered Tom.

'Do take a seat,' said the sergeant, sitting down himself. After twenty years on the force, the officer had developed a detached way of looking at the world and perfected a deadpan expression and a voice devoid of intonation.

'Thank you,' said Tom. He had an idea why the officer had called.

'You're new to these parts,' observed the police officer.

'Yes.'

'Well, you have certainly made your presence felt, Mr Dwyer.'

'Is this about what happened in the King's Head last Saturday?' asked Tom.

'It is. We have had an allegation that you assaulted Mr James Maladroit. He claims he was having a quiet drink with a colleague when you became very aggressive and hit him.'

'Is that what he said?' answered Tom.

'His mother's been on to the superintendent playing merry hell about it.'

'Has she?'

'Not an easy person is Lady Maladroit,' remarked the police officer. He had clearly had dealings with the woman before.

'I guess you would like me to give my version of what happened,' said Tom.

'That is why I'm here, Mr Dwyer, to hear your account of the events,' said the police officer, producing a small black notebook from his pocket and picking up a pencil from the desk. 'You will understand I'm sure that I am obliged to follow these things up.'

'Yes, of course,' said Tom.

He then gave a clear account of the incident, adding that there were several witnesses in the inn at the time, including the school caretaker, who would be able to vouch for what he had said. The officer licked the end of the pencil and wrote down the statement, which amounted to barely a page in his notebook.

'Thank you for your time, Mr Dwyer,' said the sergeant, snapping his notebook shut and popping the pencil into his breast pocket.

'Is that it?' asked Tom.

'That's it,' replied the police officer, getting up from his chair and stretching. 'We might need to speak to you again. If we do, we will be touch,' he said.

Tom went in search of Mr Gaunt and found the headmaster sitting on the small wall which skirted the school. He was surrounded by a group of children and was laughing at something a small child was telling him.

'Could I have a word?' asked Tom.

'Off you go, children,' said the headmaster. When they were alone, Mr Gaunt stood and looked Tom in the face. 'Now then, what is it?'

'About the visit of the police.'

'Oh that,' said the headmaster nonchalantly. 'Don't worry your head about that. Bob filled me in with all the details.'

'And you never mentioned it?'

'Why should I? It happened out of school and is no business of mine.'

'I thought I ought to explain,' said Tom, surprised by Mr Gaunt's reaction.

'No need. Clearly young Maladroit deserved what he got.' He looked up at the sky. 'I think we're in for a bit of windy weather. "If rooks fly high, the weather will be dry. If rooks fly low, we're sure to have a blow." An old Dalesman saying, Tom. Sometimes these time-worn saws are better predictors of the weather than the forecasts on the television. By the way I was meaning to have a word with you. Your classroom looks a picture and you have made a very good impression with your colleagues and with the pupils.'

'Oh,' was all Tom managed to say.

'I thought you'd turn out all right,' Mr Gaunt told him. 'Teachers have to like children and you clearly do. It sounds pretty self-evident that, doesn't it, but there are some in the profession who actually do not like the company of young people. For them teaching is just a job, not a vocation. Schools should be vehicles for building a trusting and nurturing environment, providing children with the grounds for developing their characters.' He laughed. 'I sound like a textbook, don't I? Anyway, keep up the good work.'

With that the headmaster strolled off to talk to the children.

There is more to Mr Gaunt than I first realised, thought Tom.

'In a spot of bother with the constabulary, dear boy?' asked Captain Cadwallader, when Tom joined the teachers in the staffroom.

He explained what had happened.

'You hit him?' asked Mrs Golightly, looking anxious.

'Yes, I did,' Tom told her.

'Oh dear. How very unfortunate.'

'Well, good for you,' said Miss Tranter. 'That arrogant, feckless son of Sir High-and-Mighty needs to be taken down a peg or two.' She fingered the amber beads at her neck and smiled. 'You can obviously handle yourself,' she said.

'I did a bit of boxing in my youth,' replied Tom.

'Really?' Miss Tranter sounded fascinated. 'I do so like a man who can handle himself,' she said.

'I did a spot of boxing in the army,' said Captain Cadwallader. 'Won a few cups.'

'Your mantelpiece must be groaning under the weight of all those trophies you won in the army, Owen,' Miss Tranter remarked sardonically.

The sarcasm was lost on the captain. 'Yes, I was quite a force to be reckoned with when I was in the ring,' he said.

'Do be careful,' said Mrs Golightly.

'Oh, I don't box any more, Bertha,' he told her.

'I didn't mean you,' she said. 'I meant Tom. As you well know, Sir Hedley's a very prominent person around these parts. He's a very influential man. Tom doesn't want to go antagonising the squire.'

'I think he's already done that,' said the captain unhelpfully. 'I suggest you keep your head down for the present, dear boy. Assume a low profile.'

'You are certainly making your mark in Risingdale,' observed Miss Tranter, echoing the words of Toby Croft. 'It was pretty dull around here before you arrived.'

That night Tom found himself unable to sleep. The events of the last week were turning over and over in his head. Of course, in the dead of the night, things always seem worse than they really are but he could not help thinking about what people had said. He never wanted to create an impression but events seemed to have conspired that it should be so. He had only just started the job and already, as had been pointed out a few times, he had certainly made his mark – mostly for the wrong reasons. When he did finally drift off into a fitful sleep, he was awakened by the barking of a fox and the hooting of an owl. The bedroom was oppressively hot for Mrs Mossup had decided that now September had arrived, the heating should be turned on. The huge metal-ribbed radiator beneath the window produced such heat that Tom felt like a side of beef on a spit. He looked at his watch. It was two in the morning. He climbed out of bed, pulled back the curtains and opened wide the window for some fresh air. He was about to close the curtains when he saw an old van with ladders fastened to the roof rack making its way slowly down the main street. One voice told him to go back to bed and not get involved in anything else, but the van looked suspicious. The other voice told him that this needed investigating. Tom changed into a tracksuit and pulled on his trainers and, tiptoeing down the stairs, he let himself out of the inn and jogged down the high street in the direction of the van. It was a mild night. Stars glittered fiercely in a black sky and, save for the distant hooting of the owl, all was still. Tom reached the church and saw by the cold light of the moon the rows of tilted gravestones and the dark outline of St Mary's Church. In the shadows he spotted the vehicle parked by the side of the vicarage with its rear doors open. He knew what those who had driven the van had in mind. Unobserved, Tom crept closer and saw two men on the roof of the church, attempting to lift the lead. He edged around the side of the van, leaned in the open window and removed the keys. Still unnoticed by the thieves, he crept to below where they were busy at work and pushed the ladders which were leaning against the side of the church. They crashed to the ground with a resounding clatter. The thieves shot up as if someone had thrown icy water over them.

'Oi, put them bloody ladders back!' shouted one of the men.

Tom jangled the car keys. 'Now don't go anywhere,' he shouted back. He then ran to the inn to telephone the police.

'My goodness,' remarked Mrs Mossup the next morning at breakfast when she brought in Tom's toast, 'since you've arrived we've never had such excitement since Mr Oswald set fire to his chip pan and nearly burnt his place down. You're certainly—'

'I know, Doris,' he interjected, 'I'm certainly making my mark.'

'You took the words right out of my mouth,' she said. 'By the way, there was a message this morning. Could you call into the police station after school? They need to have a word with you. I hope it's not about the fight you had with Jamie Maladroit.'

That day Tom couldn't concentrate on his teaching. He kept thinking of the forthcoming interview with the police. The words of Toby Croft – 'I reckon tha's made an enemy of the Maladroits – and Mrs Golightly – 'Tom doesn't want to go antagonising the squire' – rang in his head. Clearly, this Sir Hedley had a great deal of influence in the county, was the sort who could pull a great many strings, someone who, as his son had said, 'calls the shots around here'. Leanne's hope that he wouldn't 'get into any trouble over what happened' appeared naïve. Tom stared miserably out of the window at the looming black clouds and a rain-soaked landscape which reflected his sombre mood.

'It may never happen, sir.'

Tom looked round to find young Charlie next to his desk, with a great smile on his face.

'What was that, Charlie?' he asked.

'That's what my mother says when I look sad. It may never happen.'

Well, I hope you're right, he thought.

After school Tom drove into Clayton for his meeting with the police. He was shown into a small interview room with a grill at the window and bare white walls. There was a plain table in the centre with three hard-backed chairs. He waited nervously for the arrival of the police officers, drumming his fingers on the tabletop. There would be two of them of course, probably an inspector and another officer. He'd seen it on the television when lawbreakers were interviewed. They would caution him and then charge him with assault. He felt hot under his collar and his heart began to beat like the hammer on an anvil. Well, this was it, he thought. His career would come to a premature end and he would have a criminal record, all because he had not been able to control his temper. Why had he not, as Mr Leadbeater had said about himself, 'opened his big mouth'? But then again, why should he have kept quiet? The man was rude and aggressive and, as Miss Tranter had commented, he 'wanted taking down a peg or two'.

The door opened and two serious-faced men entered. The first, dressed in a shiny black suit, was a tall, angular individual with a long nose, flared nostrils and a drooping Stalin-like moustache. He was accompanied by Sergeant Pollock.

Tom rose from his chair, his heart still thudding.

'Do sit down, Mr Dwyer,' said the first man. 'Thank you for coming in to see us.' He sat down himself opposite Tom, and rested his hands on the table. His colleague remained standing. 'My name is Inspector Hollis and you know Sergeant Pollock of course.'

Tom placed his hands on his knees and leaned forward, expecting the worst. He took a deep breath.

'I imagine you know why we have asked to see you,' said the inspector. He took out a large blue handkerchief from his pocket and blew his nose noisily.

'I guess it's concerning what happened in the King's Head on Saturday,' answered Tom.

'Indeed,' agreed the inspector. 'Well, Sergeant Pollock here has looked into the complaint and spoken to a number of people, including two hikers and some locals, in addition to the barmaid at the King's Head and Mr Leadbeater, and—' He broke off, sneezed loudly and reached for his handkerchief again. 'Excuse me,' he said, 'I'm think I'm coming down with a cold. I always seem to get one when the weather turns.'

'You were saying,' said Tom.

'Ah, yes. Sergeant Pollock here has looked into the complaint and spoken to a number of witnesses and no further action will be taken in this case.'

Tom gave a great heaving sigh of relief.

'I am satisfied that you were clearly provoked and were assaulted first so we will not be pursuing the matter. Of course, you may wish to make a complaint about the man who attacked you.'

'No, no,' said Tom quickly. (He thought at that moment of his Irish Aunt Bridget, who had a proverb or a word of wisdom for every occasion. 'He who goes to law,' she had once pronounced, 'takes the wolf by its ears.') 'No, I don't wish to pursue the matter.' He wished to lay the unfortunate incident to rest.

'I think that's wise, Mr Dwyer,' said the sergeant. 'Personally, in my opinion if it did come to court, I reckon it's doubtful if anything would come of it.'

'Sergeant Pollock!' snapped the inspector, irritated by his colleague's intervention. After all he was in charge of the interview. 'I don't think there's any more to say.'

Tom stood. 'Thank you,' he said. 'That's a great weight off my mind.'

'There is another matter,' said the inspector, wiping his long nose.

'Another matter,' repeated Tom, sitting back down.

'Yes,' said the officer. 'I should like to thank you for your public-spirited action in assisting us in apprehending the two thieves who tried to strip the lead from St Mary's. They have been systematically stripping church roofs for some time now and we have not been able to catch them. Thanks to your actions we now have them in custody.'

'So you will not be required to give evidence,' said Sergeant Pollock, 'since they were caught red-handed and admitted to the crime.'

'Thank you, Sergeant,' said the inspector and then sneezed loudly. He blew his nose again. 'We do, however, require the keys.'

'Keys?' asked Tom.

'To the thieves' van.'

'Yes, of course. I'll drop them in tomorrow.'

'It's been quite a week for you,' remarked Sergeant Pollock as he showed Tom out.

'It has,' he agreed, 'quite a week and not one I wish to repeat.'

'I have to say, said the officer, 'that since you've come to Risingdale—'

'Don't finish,' said Tom. 'I think I know what you are going to say.'

6

The following lunchtime Mr Leadbeater called in at the staffroom.

'Mr Gaunt would like to see you, Mr Dwyer,' he said.

'Oh dear,' said the captain. 'Summoned to see the big chief. This sounds ominous. I hope it's nothing to do with the punch-up you had in the King's Head, dear boy.'

'It wasn't a punch-up, Owen,' Tom told him, sounding miffed.

'Well, you did land a pretty deadly blow,' said the caretaker. 'Knocked him clean off his feet.'

'And floored the blighter,' added the captain.

'Leave the lad alone,' admonished Mrs Golightly, coming to her colleague's defence.

'I wonder if the assailed is going to press charges,' said the captain tactlessly.

'Assailed!' repeated Tom.

'The chappie you punched.'

'I hit him in self-defence,' Tom told him. 'He made to hit me first and there were plenty of witnesses. You were there, Bob. You saw what happened.'

'I did,' said Mr Leadbeater, 'and he deserved to get punched. That's what I told the police. Anyway, Mr Gaunt wants to see you, Mr Dwyer.' With that he left the staffroom.

'As a matter of fact, I've been interviewed,' Tom told them, 'and as far as the police inspector is concerned, he told me I have nothing to worry about, or words to that effect.' He said this more to reassure himself than to enlighten his colleagues.

'I don't reckon the Maladroits will let things lie,' said the captain. He crunched noisily on a Garibaldi.

'You're right, Owen,' agreed Joyce. 'The likes of the Maladroits have a nasty way of getting what they want, twisting things to get their own way. They can pull strings and know people in high places. I shouldn't wonder if they dine with the Chief Constable and have a high court judge in their pocket.'

'They do indeed hold a lot of sway in these parts,' agreed Mrs Golightly.

'And they have enough money to induce witnesses to change their stories,' added the captain.

'Let's hope Mr Leadbeater doesn't decide to change *his* story,' said Miss Tranter.

'And Sir Hedley has more than sufficient funds to employ a top QC,' said the captain. He was aggravating the wound and Tom began to feel apprehensive. Perhaps something would come of this after all, he thought. 'Have you briefed a solicitor, by the way?' asked the captain.

'No, I haven't!' snapped Tom.

'Might be a good thing to do, dear boy.'

'I could give you the number of my solicitor if you like,' said Mrs Golightly.

'I had better go,' said Tom, not wishing to hear any more gloomy predictions from the prophets of doom.

'Well, sad to say, I don't think you have heard the last of it,' said Captain Cadwallader gloomily.

Mr Gaunt sat in the ladder-back chair at his desk behind a mound of papers when Tom entered his room. There was a copy of *Practical Poultry* on the top of the pile. The headmaster had a pained expression on his face.

'More wretched bumf!' exclaimed the headmaster. He slid the magazine into the top drawer of the desk. 'You know these people in the Education Department at County Hall seem to have nothing better to do with their time than send all this paper out to schools.' He held up a particularly hefty document. 'Look at this. It's about conservation and protecting the environment and recycling, for goodness' sake. Don't they have any conception that every time they bombard schools with this mountain of paper, a rain forest falls somewhere in the Amazon. One would laugh if it wasn't so pathetic.' He smacked the pile of papers. 'They've sent me policies and directives on sex education, libraries, reading, underachievement, health and safety, anti-bullying, healthy eating, the role of governors, head lice, parental involvement and road safety – and another on dog excrement on school playing fields. Can you credit that? Dog excrement! It's endless.' He pushed the papers aside. 'Excuse my grumbling but it does make me so mad. We are here to teach, not spend all day reading all this.'

'You wished to see me,' said Tom.

'Yes, yes, I did. Do take a seat. I won't keep you long.'

The teacher sat down awkwardly on a hard wooden chair and wondered what was in store.

Mr Gaunt steepled his fingers and rested his elbows on the desk.

'Is it about what happened in the King's Head and the visit of the police?' asked Tom.

'No, no. As I said that is your business and what happens out of school is no concern of mine. From what Bob tells me you acted quite correctly and the young man in question whom you hit fully deserved it. It was good of you to come to Mr Leadbeater's defence. That is all water under the bridge now.'

'Well, I hope so,' replied Tom. 'I did call in at the police station yesterday and was told there was no case to answer.' Then he added, 'Which is a great relief.'

'I should mention, however, that I did receive a telephone call from Lady Maladroit asking me to sack you,' Mr Gaunt told him.

'Oh dear,' sighed Tom.

The headmaster laughed. 'Silly woman. Who does she think she is, telling me what I should or shouldn't do? She is a disagreeable and argumentative woman with an inflated idea of her own importance and an out-and-out snob. When she met Sir Hedley, I gather she worked as an assistant in an art gallery in London. After she was married, she reinvented herself as the grande dame. You know, Tom, I have found that those people who could be snobbish are rarely so. It's jumped-up people like Lady Maladroit who think they are a cut above the rest of us.'

'So, she was complaining about me?' asked Tom.

'She was,' replied the headmaster, 'but, of course, I took no notice. Many of us in Risingdale have been on the receiving end of her waspish tongue. I have had a few spats with the woman in the past. She's a very unpleasant piece of work. Don't worry your head about her.'

'Was it Lady Maladroit that you wish to see me about?' asked Tom.

'Yes and no,' Mr Gaunt told him. 'I thought you ought to be aware of the complaint in case you have the unfortunate experience of meeting the virago. Someone, and I guess it is her, has been in touch with the Education Department over the matter, so you might be hearing from them. See me immediately if you do and I shall deal with it.' He leaned back in his chair. 'I don't think Sir Hedley is the sort to complain. He's a decent enough sort of chap. It's that wretched wife of his. How he puts up with her, I'll never know.'

When her son had given her his embellished version of what had happened in the public bar of the King's Head, Lady

Maladroit had gone directly to see her husband to acquaint him with the facts as described to her.

Sir Hedley, baronet, squire, landowner, lord of the manor, owner of half the properties in Risingdale and the land surrounding, controller of many of the villagers' destinies, had peered over the top of the newspaper he had been reading. A portly, red-cheeked individual with a bombastic walrus moustache above a wide mouth, dark hooded eyes, prominent ears and tightly curled hair on a square head, he looked as if he had walked straight out of the pages of an historical novel.

'Well?' Lady Maladroit had asked in a clipped, high-pitched voice. She was standing by the door in the drawing room at Marston Towers, a hawkish-looking woman with a hooked nose and bright eyes, the kind of face that makes you think that at any moment you are about to be pounced upon.

'Well, what?' he had asked, irritated at having his reading interrupted. He knew, from experience, that the shrill tone of his wife's voice signified she was in one of her ill-tempered moods.

'What do you intend to do about it?' she had demanded.

'What do I intend to do about what?' He had continued to peruse his newspaper.

'Don't be deliberately obtuse, Hedley,' his wife had snapped. 'You know perfectly well.'

'I am not a mind-reader, Marcia,' he had told her, disappearing behind the paper.

'Would you please put down your paper,' she had said. 'I am attempting to speak to you.'

Sir Hedley had stifled a sigh and lowered his newspaper.

'I am talking about the unprovoked assault on our son which I have just described to you. What do you intend to do about this thug who attacked James?'

'I don't intend to do anything about it,' her husband had replied. 'He's not hurt, is he? He's not in hospital?'

'No, he isn't,' the baronet's wife had replied, 'but he is traumatised.'

'Traumatised, is he?' Sir Hedley had said in a matter-of-fact tone of voice, giving a dry little smile.

'Yes, he is!' she had replied.

'He wasn't so traumatised when I last saw him playing billiards in the library with a glass of my malt whiskey in his hand.'

Lady Maladroit's face had become suffused with a deep-red flush which made her look ferocious.

'So is that all you have got to say?' she had demanded.

'Very much. If James decides to get himself into a scrap in a public house, that's up to him but he shouldn't expect me to get him out of the scrapes he gets into. I've done that enough times in the past. Anyway, what was he doing in the King's Head at that time? He wants to stop leading the life of the playboy and get a job and do something useful. Now, if I might return to my paper.'

'That's not good enough,' she had huffed. 'You need to contact the police and the County Director of Education first thing on Monday morning and get her to remove this man from the school. It is unconscionable that someone like that should be in charge of children. You need to get in touch with the Education Department and have this man debarred or whatever they do with defective teachers.'

'I shall do no such thing,' her husband had told her.

'Did you hear what James has told me?' Lady Maladroit had asked.

'Every word,' Sir Hedley had replied, 'and most of it, I take with a pinch of salt. As you are well aware, our son and the truth have never had a great deal in common. I do not, I think, need to remind you about his expulsion from his public school when his version of events was rather different from the headmaster's, or when he was stopped for driving over the limit and his account varied not inconsiderably from that of the police. Then of course there was the time—'

Lady Maladroit had held up a bony hand as if stopping traffic. 'Please do not go into all that again, Hedley,' she had interrupted. 'I insist that at the very least you speak to the headmaster about this teacher.'

Sir Hedley had risen from his chair, carefully folded his newspaper and placed it on a small occasional table. He had then approached his wife.

'Let me make this perfectly clear, Marcia,' he had said. 'I shall not contact the police, the Education Department or indeed the headmaster at the school. I do not intend to stir up muddy waters. Now, I do not wish to discuss this subject any further. As far as I am concerned, it is the end of the matter.'

For his wife, however, it was not and she had telephoned Mr Gaunt amongst others.

'The main reason for wishing to have this chat with you,' said Mr Gaunt, 'is to have a word about your colleagues. You seem to be getting on very well with them.'

'Very well indeed,' replied Tom. 'They have been really friendly and helpful.'

'I guess they appear a pretty odd bunch to you?'

'Well, I've not really thought about it,' said Tom. He wondered why Mr Gaunt should be asking his views about the other teachers.

'When I say odd, I don't mean that unkindly,' he said. 'Perhaps a better word might be "idiosyncratic". They do what is asked of them without complaint and the children like them. I have a genuine affection for them.' The headmaster thought for a moment, wondering about the best way of saying what he wanted to say. 'All three of your colleagues are not as they might seem.'

'I'm sorry,' said Tom. 'I don't know what you mean.'

Mr Gaunt leaned back in his chair. 'Take Joyce for example. Don't be fooled by Miss Tranter's air of confidence and self-assurance. She seems to the outside world so cool and confident and very much in control of herself but it is a bit of an act. Joyce is an actress and plays the part very convincingly. She trained at a London drama college, made a career on the stage, and when that didn't quite work out for her, she took up a number of jobs before settling on teaching. She's a good teacher, Tom, and you can learn a lot from her but she is quite a fragile woman, very sensitive and unsure of herself under all that poise. You may have wondered why someone so outwardly self-possessed and artistic should teach in a school like this.'

It had occurred to Tom of course. He recalled what Joyce had told him that, 'Up here it's miles from anywhere, the residents live in the Dark Ages, there's more life in a cemetery than there is in the village and the school is not exactly at the cutting edge of education.' He had wondered at the time why she would want to stay at the school if she disliked Risingdale so much.

'Joyce had a very acrimonious marriage,' Mr Gaunt carried on. 'She met her former husband at drama college. He was, by all accounts, a very controlling and sometimes abusive individual who treated her very badly and undermined her confidence. Eventually she summoned up the courage to leave him but he hounded her, turning up wherever she went. On one occasion he interrupted a performance she was giving at a theatre and he had to be thrown out. You can imagine how that affected her. I think that after that she gave up the stage. Risingdale School has become a sort of refuge for her, somewhere he will not find her. I know she complains about life up here, but I think she feels safe and secure and does enjoy teaching.'

'I had no idea,' said Tom. 'She does seem so self-possessed and sure of herself.'

'She's a very good actress, Tom,' said Mr Gaunt. 'Then there's Captain Cadwallader. He's a character is Owen. He too is perhaps not all that he appears to be either. He is a good-hearted man but as you no doubt have gathered he's a romancer. I am sure you will have been subjected to some of his army anecdotes. They don't do any harm but should not be taken too seriously. He tends to blow his own trumpet, maybe to convince himself that he was once a person of some note. Underneath, like Joyce, he is under-confident. I have often wondered how he managed to become an army officer. He may not appear so, but he is quite an insecure man.

'And then there's Mrs Golightly. Again I think she puts on a show. She appears to the world always cheerful and outgoing but deep down she's a rather sad and, I would guess, a lonely woman. Her husband was killed in a road accident not long after they were married. She has no children to fill the gap he left in her life. She perhaps should have retired by now but would be lost without the job.'

The headmaster became thoughtful. 'So that's a potted history of the lives of the teachers here at Risingdale. I hope you don't feel it is unprofessional of me to talk about the personal circumstances of your colleagues. I just felt you needed to know something of their backgrounds and be aware that all three of them are fragile people. I wouldn't want you to go saying or asking things inadvertently which may touch a few raw nerves.'

'Well, I appreciate you telling me,' said Tom, rather stunned by the revelations.

'In confidence,' said Mr Gaunt.

'Yes, of course.'

'Now I see you have taken my advice about getting rid of that little car of yours.'

'Yes,' he replied. 'I took your advice and bought something more suitable.'

*   *   *

Tom had called in to Classic Motors of Clayton one Saturday.

'So you're up for selling this car, are you?' the owner of the garage had asked. He was a small, snub-nosed man with large ears and was wearing a loud suit and bow tie. A bald patch showed through his stringy hair.

'That is why I am here,' Tom had replied.

The man had walked around the car, stroked the bonnet, kicked a tyre and peered through the windscreen. He opened the driver's door and looked at the dashboard, noting the mileage. 'Well, I can't say that there's much call for sports cars around here,' he had told Tom, sucking in his bottom lip. 'It's all them twisty roads and bends. They don't suit this sort of vehicle.'

'Yes, I am aware of that,' Tom had answered, recalling the incident which had so interested the community at Risingdale. 'That is why I wish to sell it and get something more suitable.'

'Well, I can't offer you much, I'm afraid. These sort of cars don't keep their price and it'll be difficult to shift.'

'Thank you for your time,' Tom had said. 'I'll try elsewhere.'

'Hang on, hang on,' the man had said, reaching for Tom's arm. 'Don't be so hasty. I might be interested at the right price.'

'Why not make me an offer,' Tom had suggested.

'Would you be interested in trading it in?'

'Possibly.'

'What sort of car are you looking for?'

'A small jeep like that one,' Tom had told him, pointing to a vehicle on the forecourt.

'Well, I think this is your lucky day, young man,' the garage owner had said, smiling for the first time. That lovely little four-wheel-drive jeep in immaculate condition, with only a few miles on the clock, one careful owner and a full service history has just this minute come in.'

'It sounds ideal,' Tom had said. 'Of course it depends on the price and what you are prepared to give me for my sports car.'

'Oh, we can come to some arrangement,' the man had said. 'Come along into my office and we'll talk money.'

'Oh and I've been in Yorkshire long enough,' Tom had told him, 'to expect a good deal, a very good deal.'

Tom had felt rather sad some weeks later when he saw the sports car being driven at high speed through Risingdale village. So these sort of cars don't keep their price, do they? he had thought. Well, the man was a car salesman after all. 'I just hope the driver doesn't come across Miss Janette Fairborn and her horse on one of the bends,' he had said out loud.

'So, are you settled at the King's Head?' asked Mr Gaunt.

'For the moment,' answered Tom. 'I would ideally like a place of my own. There's not a lot of privacy living above a pub and Mrs Mossup's food is . . . well, it's—'

'Yes, I did mention Mrs Mossup's food,' said the headmaster, smiling.

'So, I guess I had better start looking for somewhere else. Ideally, I'd like to rent or buy a flat or a small house.'

'I might have the answer,' said Mr Gaunt. 'I gather that Mrs Golightly is minded to sell her cottage and move into the block of apartments where Miss Tranter lives, just along from Rattan Row. It seems a very sensible idea to me. She has found driving up to the school rather burdensome and the last winter rather decided her to move near Joyce. Quite apart from the company, she can travel up with Miss Tranter and share the cost of the petrol. Why don't you have a word with her?'

'Her cottage is probably out of my price range,' said Tom.

'Oh, I don't know. It's a small cottage and I gather needs quite a bit doing to it. You could have a word with your bank manager. I'm sure you could get a mortgage. You have a full-time job, a regular income, good prospects, and you are reliable.'

'Well, it will do no harm to look into it,' said Tom.

'Have a word with Bertha and see what she thinks,' said Mr Gaunt. 'Now, if you'll excuse me, I'm going to pop out for a while. Two of my sheep have taken to wandering off again.'

In the staffroom Tom's colleagues were waiting for a blow-by-blow account of the interview he had just had with the headmaster.

'Well, how did it go, dear boy?' asked the captain.

Tom adopted a suitably disconsolate face. 'I've been sacked,' he said sadly.

'Sacked!' cried Miss Tranter, jumping up and spilling her coffee.

'Sacked,' repeated Tom, shaking his head.

'Oh, goodness me,' said Mrs Golightly, putting a hand to her throat. 'This is terrible.' She looked as if she were going to faint.

'Good God!' exclaimed Captain Cadwallader. 'He can't do that.'

'Come along,' said Joyce, 'we shall all go and see him. This is ridiculous.'

Tom laughed. 'I'm joking,' he told them.

'What!' his colleagues shouted in unison.

'Of course I haven't been sacked. I was joking,' said Tom. 'I was getting my own back after all your gloomy predictions. When I left the staffroom to see the headmaster, I felt like a condemned man approaching the gallows. Everything is fine. Mr Gaunt just wanted to know how I was getting on.'

Miss Tranter strode towards him. She was clearly not amused. She pointed with a red-nailed finger. 'Tom Dwyer, don't you ever do that again,' she said. There was a tremble in her voice.

'No,' said Mrs Golightly. 'It was very naughty of you. We wouldn't want to lose you. You've been like a breath of fresh air.'

'You certainly have,' agreed the captain. He was white-faced and had clearly been shocked by the hoax.

'And if you have any ideas of leaving us,' added Miss Tranter, 'then think again.' For once her mask of sangfroid had slipped. She looked upset.

'No, you won't be getting rid of me,' said Tom, touched by their concern. 'I'm here to stay.' He looked at his colleagues, for whom he had developed a great fondness, and smiled.

Tom wasted no time in having a word with Mrs Golightly about her cottage.

'I gather from Mr Gaunt that you are thinking of selling up, Bertha,' he said.

'Yes, I am,' she answered. 'The place needs a bit doing to it and the garden's got too much for me and after the dreadful snow last winter, it was like driving up an ice rink to get to the school. I've decided to downsize as they say. A nice little apartment will be coming up in the block where Joyce lives and I intend putting in an offer. Of course, I have to sell my place first.'

'I might be interested,' Tom told her.

'In buying my cottage?'

'I'm looking to move out of the King's Head and find a place of my own.'

'And you are thinking of buying somewhere in Risingdale?'

'Yes, I am.'

'So you're intending staying at the school then?' she asked.

'Of course. What gave you the idea that I wouldn't be staying?'

'We all thought it wouldn't be long before you moved on,' said Mrs Golightly. 'I mean, let's face it, you are a very talented

teacher. We're not in your league. As the captain said, you're
of a different calibre.'

'Come on, Bertha,' said Tom, colouring slightly at the
compliment. 'That's silly.'

'I mean look at what you've achieved in the short time you
have been at the school. You've transformed your classroom,
got on really well with the children and sorted young Colin
Greenwood out; you've raised standards and started a football team. We would be very sorry to lose you but we all think
you will move on to a bigger and better school.'

'Well, I'm staying,' said Tom firmly.

'Of course, if the school does close you'll be all right. They
might redeploy you to the school in Barton which you liked so
much.' She sighed. 'The very idea of being redeployed fright-
ens me to death. I'd be like a fish out of water at another
school. I guess Owen and Joyce would too.'

'I really wouldn't worry, Bertha,' Tom reassured her. 'There
are no plans, as far as I know, to close Risingdale School.' As
he said this he recalled Elisabeth's words.

'Let's hope not,' she said. 'Anyway, would you like to come
and have a look around my cottage? You could come up next
Sunday and stay for lunch.'

'That would be great,' said Tom.

On the Sunday, Tom left the King's Head before Mrs Mossup
could present him with the roast beef and Yorkshire pudding.
He told her he had been invited out for lunch. Noticing the
bunch of flowers he was holding, the landlady enquired who
might be the lucky lass but Tom, evading her question, merely
smiled and winked. As he wound through the crowded public
bar, his way was barred by Mr Fairborn.

'Not again,' murmured Tom.

'Goes in one ear and out the other,' said the man angrily and
loud enough for other customers to hear. The bar went quiet.

'I'm sorry, Mr Fairborn,' replied Tom, 'what does?'

'What I said to you about taking more care on the roads.'

'I can assure you I have followed your advice to the very letter and been particularly cautious at the sight of any horses.'

'Don't get clever with me, young man,' said the farmer crossly.

'Perhaps you might explain,' said Tom.

'I saw you last week careering through the village in that fancy sports car of yours, driving like a madman.' He poked Tom's shoulder. 'You, young man, show a reckless disregard for other people. You nearly flattened two ducks and knocked Mrs Partington off her bike. What is it about you people?'

'It wasn't me,' Tom told him.

'What?'

'It wasn't me driving the car.'

'Don't give me that! Of course it was you,' retorted Mr Fairborn. 'I recognised the car. Who else would be driving it?'

'I've no idea.'

'Eh?'

'It wasn't my car.'

'What are you on about, of course it was your car. There isn't another car like yours in the village. Do you think my brains are made of porridge?'

'I sold it.'

'What?'

'I sold the sports car. I now drive a small jeep.'

'Oh,' said the farmer, suddenly lost for words.

'So you see, Mr Fairborn, I couldn't have been the driver,' said Tom.

'I see,' said the farmer in a subdued voice. 'Well, I thought it was you.'

'Well, it wasn't.' He was tempted to repeat Mr Sheepshanks's words about the muck cart and the wedding but resisted.

Toby Croft, who had been listening to the exchange with great interest, came to join them. He rested a hand on Mr Fairborn's shoulder. 'I reckon thee owes this lad an hapology, John,' he said.

'Aye, well, I thought it was him who was driving,' said the farmer.

'We all on us know what thowt did,' said Mr Croft. 'Stuck a feather in t'ground and thowt it'd grow into an 'en.'

'Happen I was bit hasty,' said Mr Fairborn. He looked at Tom shamefaced. 'I'm ... er ... sorry about the misunderstanding.'

'So could I get past?' asked Tom.

The farmer moved out of his way.

As he walked through the village, there was a spring in Tom's step. He chuckled to himself. That certainly put Mr Fairborn firmly in his place, he thought. No doubt the exchange will be the talk of the village by tomorrow. He walked past the duck pond where the coots and moorhens paddled at the water's edge, past the church where he caught sight of the smiling vicar standing at the entrance, shaking the hands of the members of his congregation after Morning Service, on to the post office and general store, past the Methodist chapel, which resounded with loud and joyous singing, and the terraced cottages at Rattan Row until he came to the track leading to Roselea Cottage.

Tom had imagined Roselea to be a small country cottage in honey-coloured stone with a yellow thatched roof, roses around the door, the sort one sees on picture postcards or on the front of tins of biscuits. He was soon disabused when he saw where Mrs Golightly lived. Roselea Cottage stood at the end of a cracked crazy-paved stone path. There was an ancient, broken stone birdbath, an overgrown rockery and a circular flower bed choked with dying flowers and weeds. A track of beaten mud ran down the side. It was a square red-brick building with a sagging slate roof, peeling paint and a neglected garden. Faded green-painted shutters framed the windows. There was clearly much to do to get it into some sort of shape. However, as he stared at the building, he saw the potential. He turned to look at the view, gazing through the trees at a vista of green undulating fields criss-crossed with silvered limestone walls which rose to the craggy fell side, and he marvelled at the scene before him. In a sky as delicate and clear as an eggshell, a red kite soared in circles. Somewhere in a distant field a tractor chugged. Tom knew he had to have the cottage.

'Ah, here you are,' said Mrs Golightly, opening the door. 'I saw you from the window. Come along in.'

Tom was shown into the sitting room, which smelled of furniture polish and cats. The room was furnished with a settee and two matching armchairs covered in a bright, heavy linen fabric, a gateleg table and four balloon-backed chairs, a glass-fronted cabinet crammed with cut glass and china, a bookcase and a small footstool. It was dominated by a heavy oak dresser. Above the fireplace was a large framed print of sunflowers by Van Gogh. The place was a clutter. Every surface seemed to be covered with something: table lamps, a bowl of fruit, porcelain figures, china plates, brass ornaments, photographs in silver frames, glass paperweights, a whole collection of knick-knacks. Fixed to the wall was a large polished brass barometer. The Sunday papers were strewn across the sofa. Mrs Golightly moved them onto a chair, already piled with magazines, for Tom to sit down. He made his way carefully to get to his seat. Before doing so, he looked at a photograph on the mantelpiece. It was of a tall, not unat-tractive young man posing on a sea wall.

'That was my husband Norman,' she told him, her voice full of wistful sadness. 'Taken on our honeymoon in Whitby.

He was killed in a road accident on his way home from work a month later.'

'I'm sorry,' said Tom.

'He loved it here,' she said forlornly, 'the roses round the door, the view up to the hills, the smell of the country. They do say that time is a great healer. Well, not for me. I've never got over losing him. When you are fortunate to find someone to love, to truly love, you imagine that you will be expecting to spend the whole of your life with that person. For me it wasn't the case.' Her eyes were blurred with tears. She sniffed. 'Ah well. Do sit down, Tom, and I'll put the kettle on.'

After a substantial lunch, Tom helped with the washing up. The kitchen was small and painted a sickly yellow. It contained a square Formica-topped table and two chairs, a line of white wooden shelves crammed with crockery, an old-fashioned sink and an ancient gas cooker.

This will need a complete overhaul, thought Tom. He had the same thought when he viewed the bathroom with its avocado-coloured suite and linoleum floor.

After lukewarm coffee they got down to business.

'The cottage is a bit old-fashioned,' admitted Mrs Golightly, 'and not to everyone's taste and it does need a bit doing to it. So, having had a look around, are you still interested?'

'Definitely,' replied Tom.

As Mrs Golightly had said, Roselea did 'need a bit doing to it' but he felt he could manage that. It was the view – that vast panorama which stretched into the distance – which swung it for him. Mrs Golightly agreed to have the cottage valued and he said he would make an appointment to see the bank manger to arrange a mortgage. Then, if all was in order, they could decide on the best time for her to move.

The following Saturday Tom arrived at the bank in Clayton for his appointment to see the manager about borrowing money. He was shown into a small office with a desk and two chairs and told that the assistant manager would be with him shortly. A moment later the door opened and in walked Janette Fairborn. She was dressed in a well-cut black suit and white silk blouse and her abundant red hair was gathered up and tied in a knot behind her head. She carried a folder.

'Oh,' said Tom, jumping up from his chair. 'It's you.'

'Good morning, Mr Dwyer,' she said, a serious expression on her face. 'Do please sit down.' She sat herself behind the desk and placed the folder before her.

'You are the assistant manager?' asked Tom.

'I am,' she replied.

'And you are dealing with my application?'

'That's right,' she told him. 'Do you have a problem with that?'

'Not at all.'

Miss Fairborn placed a small pair of spectacles on her nose, opened the folder and examined the papers it contained.

'So you are looking to borrow from the bank to purchase a property in Risingdale?' she asked, looking over the top of her spectacles.

'Yes, I am,' replied Tom.

She looked down at the papers. 'Roselea Cottage,' she said. 'A two bedroom, detached, Grade 2-listed cottage built around 1815, which I gather is in need of some renovation.'

'That's right,' said Tom.

'And what deposit are you able to put down?' he was asked.

'Deposit?' he repeated.

'I assume you are not applying for a hundred per cent mortgage?' she asked.

'Well, yes,' said Tom. 'I was hoping to borrow the full amount.'

'I see.' She straightened the papers and closed the folder. 'I don't think the bank is in a position to lend you the full purchase price,' she said.

'Does that mean no?' asked Tom.

'Yes, I'm afraid it does,' she replied.

'I do have a permanent job, a regular salary and good prospects,' Tom told her, repeating what Mr Gaunt had said. Then he added, 'And I am reliable.'

'I am sure you are, Mr Dwyer,' she replied, removing her spectacles, 'but the bank is not in a position to lend you the amount you wish to borrow without a deposit. I'm sorry.'

'I see,' said Tom, getting to his feet. 'Well, I don't think there's more to say.'

'Were you to consider something a little more modest, say a flat or a small terraced cottage we could perhaps look again at a mortgage application.'

'Thank you, Miss Fairborn,' said Tom, not wishing to prolong the interview. 'It was good of you to see me. Good morning.'

7

Over the next couple of weeks, there developed in Tom a realisation that his romantic view of those who lived and worked in the Yorkshire Dales was misguided. Having spoken to his pupils and overheard the conversations of Toby Croft and his colleagues in the King's Head, he began to understand that it could be a hard, demanding and unpredictable existence for the farmers in this part of the world. The picture-postcard landscapes of the area depicted some of the most stunning scenery in the country: undulating emerald-green pastures, tall pinewoods and distant sombre peaks, twisting, empty roads bordered by craggy grey limestone walls, clusters of barns and honey-coloured farmhouses. It looked idyllic – a part of the world in which many people dreamed of living, away from the noise, crowds and stresses of the towns and cities. He had imagined that the way of life of the farmers of the Dales was relatively easy and certainly enviable, but he soon came to realise that his notion was an idealised one. In reality the Dales' farmer made a hard and precarious living, constantly fighting the ferocious winds and bitterly cold snowstorms in winter and braving the sweltering heat of mid-summer. Farmers like Toby Croft had to deal with diseases in their animals, vet's bills and the increasing bureaucracy. They rarely had a holiday from their farms, they were up early and to bed late. Sometimes they were forced to pack it all in. The Durdeyfields were not alone in selling up.

In those first few weeks Tom had been at the school, he also developed a genuine affection for and admiration of the children he taught. They were good-humoured, easy-going and interested, and in addition he found them to be shrewd, observant and hard-working. The children of the Dales were expected to play their part at the farm, helping to feed the animals, mend fences and walls, groom the horses, gather the eggs and lend a hand with many other jobs. In consequence their knowledge of farming and the country was extensive.

For example Carol, the pretty girl with the mousy-brown hair and pink glasses, had a comprehensive knowledge of sheep rearing. One lunchtime when Tom sat with her on the school wall in the unseasonable late September sunshine, he was given a lesson about tups and gimmers, hoggits and shearlings, stots and stirks, wethers and tegs. The girl became animated as she realised the extent of her teacher's ignorance, surprised that there were people in the world who couldn't tell a Blue-faced Leicester sheep from a Texel or a Masham from a Swaledale.

She pointed to a field where a small flock of sheep were cropping the grass.

'They're just getting ready for tupping time in the autumn,' she said. Carol looked up at Tom, her eyes magnified behind the large pink glasses. 'Do you know what tupping time is, Mr Dwyer?' she asked.

'I have an idea,' said Tom.

'Them sheep are hoggs.'

'Hoggs,' he repeated. 'I thought those were pigs.'

'Last year's lambs are called hoggs,' the child explained, giving him a somewhat pitying look as an expert might give an ignoramus. 'They spend their first winter down here where the weather's mild and grazing's good, then they go up high on the fells to join the breeding stock. You see you put the tups – those are the rams – with the yows – those are the ewes – to get cracking about the same time every year. Do you know why?'

'I don't,' admitted Tom.

'It's to make sure of an early start for lambing after a bad winter.'

'But aren't the sheep brought down here in the cold weather?' he asked.

'Only if it's really bad,' the child told him. 'They stop up there for most of their lives. The only sheep that stay down here are lowland breeds like Suffolks and Leicesters and cross-breeds. Nesh creatures, as my granddad says.'

'Nesh?'

'Can't stand a bit of cold,' the girl enlightened him. 'They wouldn't last long up there. Too cold and wet and not much to eat.'

'I see,' said Tom.

'You have to check that the tups and yows are ready for breeding,' said the girl. 'Make sure that they are in tip-top condition with no diseases or viruses. Good breeding yows are fit and healthy with a solid body, straight legs, a good set of teeth and two working teats.'

Tom laughed. 'My goodness, you are quite the expert, aren't you, Carol?'

'Well, Mr Dwyer,' said the girl, 'there's not much I don't know about sheep.'

'I can tell that,' replied the teacher.

'Do you want me to tell you how my granddad castrates lambs, Mr Dwyer?' asked the girl.

'No, I think we'll leave that for another time,' said Tom, getting up from the wall.

Marjorie, the pixie-faced girl, Tom discovered, was a little entrepreneur. She explained that she was good at mental arithmetic because she manned the Saturday craft stall at Clayton Market and helped her grandmother sell the patchwork cushion covers and hangings and knitted scarves and gloves they had made.

'Gran's not that good at adding up,' explained the girl, 'and she's a bit forgetful. It comes with age, so I manage the money.'

On another occasion, Tom got to talk to Simon about his interest – ferreting. The boy was one of the quietest in the class but when he was on his own ground, talking about a subject he knew a deal about, he became a lively speaker. Tom was fascinated and educated by the boy.

'Male ferrets are called hobs,' the boy told him, 'and females are jills. Ferrets under one year old are called kits. Did you know that, sir?'

'No, Simon, I didn't,' answered Tom.

'When they get excited, ferrets do a kind of war-dance hopping and leaping about. It's really funny to watch. When they get scared they make a hissing noise and when they are upset it's a soft squeaking sound. I can always tell what mood they are in.'

Tom was genuinely interested. 'Aren't ferrets vicious?' he asked.

'No, not at all.' Simon shook his head. 'Course, they can bite if they get frightened or threatened and are a bit grumpy when they come into the breeding season, but if you get bitten by a ferret it's your own fault.' The boy nodded and smiled. 'They have really sharp teeth though and can bite right through a pencil if they've a mind.'

'But they smell,' said Tom.

'Yer hob gives off a smell to attract the jill when he's ready for mating,' the boy told him, 'but normally they don't smell.'

Listening to this boy, Tom appreciated just how knowledge-able the Dales child could be and how ignorant he was in country matters.

'And you catch rabbits with your ferrets, do you?' asked Tom.

'I do,' said Simon. 'I peg a string net over the rabbit-warren holes and let one of my jill ferrets down. I keep her half fed to make sure she's keen.' The boy sucked in his bottom lip and drew a breath. 'You see, if you underfeed her, she eats the rabbit and won't come up out of the hole. If I overfeed her, she won't go down at all.'

'And she chases the rabbits into the net,' said Tom.

'That's the way to do it. Poachers used to put the ferrets down their pants to hide them from the gamekeeper if they saw him coming. Mind you, I wouldn't go that far. I wouldn't like a ferret down my pants, would you, sir?'

'I most certainly would not!' exclaimed Tom, thinking of what the boy had said about the pencil. 'And when you've caught the rabbit, Simon, what then?'

'Well, I don't keep it as a pet,' said the boy. 'I break its neck and it ends up in the pot.'

'I see,' said Tom.

'I can get you a ferret if you want, Mr Dwyer. They make champion pets. They don't bark, they keep themselves clean and they're mischievous.'

'That's kind of you, Simon,' replied Tom, 'but I think I'll pass on that one.'

'And do you know, Mr Dwyer,' added the boy, 'that jills die if they go too long without sex.'

'No,' said Tom, colouring a little, 'I wasn't aware of that.'

'It's a fact of life,' said the boy philosophically.

Tom discovered that each child in the class (with the exception of Colin who remained uncommunicative and sullen) had his or her own special knowledge about something. For example, Christopher, the large, rosy-cheeked boy with a runny nose could tell a champion sheep from an also ran.

'A champion sheep has a good strong head on him, solid legs and sturdy haunches,' he told Tom. 'We won a blue ribbon at the Clayton Show last year. My dad was well chuffed.'

Tom learnt that George could drive a tractor and chain harrow a field as well as any adult; that Andrew, the lean, bespectacled boy with a thick mop of tawny hair, knew how to build a drystone wall and dig a dyke; that Vicky was expected to lend her father a hand to calf a cow and took charge of feeding the hens, collecting the eggs, rearing the chicks, and tending to the lambs which had been deserted by their mothers. Tom showed a genuine interest in what the children had to say and encouraged them to speak about their lives and their interests. Each child was a little personality but for Tom, it was Charlie who intrigued him more than any of his other pupils. The boy was quick-witted and insightful and had an amazingly retentive memory. His command of mathematics was remarkable and his writing highly imaginative and accurate. Tom had never come across a gifted child before but it was clear to him that this boy had an extraordinary talent.

One afternoon break he asked him to stay behind.

'Well, Charlie,' he said, looking at the boy's work which lay on the desk before him. 'This poem here. Did you write it yourself?'

'Of course, Mr Dwyer,' replied the boy.

'You've not copied it from a book or had any help in writing it?'

'No. I write a lot of poems. They look nicer on the page and you can really say what you feel.'

'It's excellent,' Tom told him. 'It's worthy of being published. I certainly couldn't write poetry of this quality.'

'That's kind of you to say so, Mr Dwyer,' said the boy, smiling.

'May I see some of your other poems?'

'I have them in a portfolio,' said Charlie. 'I keep it at home. I'll bring it in tomorrow.'

'Tell me about Charlie Lister,' Tom asked Mrs Golightly one day after school as she was getting ready to go home.

'He's a nice little lad,' she said. 'I've always had a soft spot for young Charlie. He was the first to read in my class and I've never taught a pupil who is so interested and polite or one who was better at arithmetic. He was good at art as well and at writing and was always well-behaved.'

'He is very bright,' said Tom.

'Oh, he is that. Strange boy in many ways. Rather old-fashioned. I suppose some would say he's precocious, an old head on young shoulders but I always found him a pleasure to teach.'

'What about his parents?' asked Tom.

'Well, Charlie lives with his mother,' replied his colleague. 'I don't think he knows who his father is and has never met him. I remember when he was in the infants he told me that. Mrs Lister, as far as I know, never mentions him.' Mrs Golightly considered what she should say next. 'She doesn't work, so there's a bit of speculation in the village where she gets her money from to pay the rent and deal with all the bills. Some say that she's a bit too friendly with the men but I think that's just idle gossip. She's not a bad mother and clearly loves the boy, but Charlie is left very much to his own devices. He's a bit of a loner, a free spirit, and spends a deal of his time walking in the countryside or down at the public library at Clayton or just sitting by the duck pond reading. He's an avid reader as you've probably discovered.'

'He doesn't live on a farm then?' asked Tom.

'No, no, he lives in one of the tied cottages on Rattan Row owned by Sir Hedley.'

'I think he's a really talented young man,' said Tom, 'and he will have no trouble passing his eleven-plus and getting into the grammar school.'

'Ah well, you need to talk to Mr Gaunt if you're considering entering him for the eleven-plus,' Mrs Golightly told him. 'Children at this school rarely go up to the grammar. We did have a couple of pupils a few years' back who sat the exam and went up there, but their parents were in-comers, "off-comed-uns" as the locals call them. Very pushy they were and got private tutors to cram their children.'

'I think Charlie would really benefit from a grammar school education,' said Tom.

'Maybe he would,' replied Mrs Golightly, 'but you will need to have a word with Mr Gaunt. He's not gone home yet. You might just catch him.'

'Could I have a word?' asked Tom, popping his head around the door of headmaster's study door later that afternoon.

'Yes, of course,' replied Mr Gaunt. 'Do come in.'

'I'd like to read you something.'

The headmaster smiled and sat back in his chair. 'Go ahead,' he said.

Tom read:

> 'The forest is still and silent at dusk.
> No breeze, no movement, no birdcall.
> It's a shadowy, eerie, mysterious world,
> Dark and hushed and lifeless,
> Like a ghostly image in a dismal dream.
> Smell of pine, of earth, of berry,
> But no crack of twigs beneath the feet
> Or rustle of leaves or creaking branches,
> But only the silent stillness of the wood at night.'

'You are quite the poet, Tom,' said Mr Gaunt.

'Oh, it's not mine. It was written by Charlie.'

'Ah, young Charlie Lister,' said the headmaster, not looking in the least surprised. 'I might have guessed. Clever boy with a great imagination.'

'I have his exercise books here, if you would care to see them,' said Tom. 'His work is excellent in all subjects. I think the boy is gifted.'

'I have no doubt that you are right,' agreed Mr Gaunt.

'I was saying to Mrs Golightly that I think Charlie would really flourish at the grammar school and—'

'Let me stop you there, Tom,' said Mr Gaunt, sitting up in his chair, leaning forward and resting his hands on the desktop. 'I have no doubt that Charlie Lister would do very well at the grammar school, but he will do equally well at the comprehensive in Clayton which I think is better suited for that sort of pupil.'

'I'm sorry, Mr Gaunt, but I don't follow. What do you mean by "that sort of pupil"?'

The headmaster gave a tolerant smile. 'I have taught for many years, Tom, and I think you will allow that I know rather more than you who has just started in the profession, what is the most appropriate education for my pupils. I feel it would be more fitting if young Charlie and indeed all the Risingdale pupils went to the comprehensive. The school offers a good all-round education and the students achieve very commendable results.'

'When I first came here, Mr Gaunt,' said Tom, disheartened by the headmaster's response, 'you told me that the children come mostly from the surrounding farms and are not very keen on school.'

'Yes, I did say that,' agreed Mr Gaunt.

'Well, I have to say that I have found the children to be different,' said Tom. 'They seem to like school and are keen to learn and some, like Charlie, are not from a farming background. I have some clever and conscientious pupils in my class who I feel should have the chance of going to the grammar school.'

'I see,' said Mr Gaunt. 'You feel very strongly about this, don't you?'

'Well, yes, I do,' replied Tom.

'Look, I have no problem with grammar schools per se,' the headmaster continued. 'I went to one myself and it was a good, solid education, although coming from a pretty humble background, I did feel a bit of a fish out of water mixing with all these boys from the more affluent homes.'

'But you did well there,' said Tom.

'Yes. I did pretty well but I can't say I was happy, and I don't think young Charlie would be happy at the grammar either. He will do equally well at the comprehensive. Bright students do very well there. I don't believe that the grammar school will suit the boy and, more importantly, his mother couldn't afford to send him there. Quite apart from the uniform and sports' kits, the school trips and all the additional costs she would have to find, there's the bus fares. His mother's a single parent and probably hasn't two pennies to rub together.'

'Mrs Golightly thinks she manages very well financially,' said Tom.

'Not enough, I guess, to cover all the expenses for Charlie to go to the grammar.'

'But there are scholarships and bursaries to help with the expenses,' said Tom.

'Yes, there are.'

'And I am certain a boy with Charlie's talents would get one.'

'Possibly,' said Mr Gaunt, 'but the competition will be fierce.'

'So you don't think I should enter any of the children for the eleven-plus?'

'Look, Tom,' said the headmaster, leaning back again in his chair, 'I guess you might have gathered that I am not a head teacher who interferes with what my staff are doing. Provided the children get a good sound education and the teachers treat them with respect and relate well to them, I don't see any need to get involved. I'm not a dictator. If you wish to look into the question of a scholarship for Charlie and enter him and some of the children for the eleven-plus, then go ahead but before you do, I suggest you have a word with the children themselves and explain what it involves and write to their parents and see what they think.'

'Perhaps the letter might be better coming from you,' suggested Tom.

'No, I think I can leave that in your hands,' said Mr Gaunt, leaning back in his chair again. 'You know, Tom, you are a very dedicated young man and are doing well here but don't overdo the enthusiasm. As I mentioned to you when you started, life up here tends to be in the slow lane. Don't try and change the world. By the way did you have a word with Mrs Golightly about her cottage?'

'I did, and went up to look around. It would have been ideal.'

'And?'

'I was really keen to buy it but have been refused a mortgage by the bank. The assistant manager said I wanted to borrow too much and that I needed a deposit. I had an idea the cottage would be out of my price range.'

'You sound as if you had your heart set on it?' said the headmaster.

'Yes, I did. It was just the thing. I have an aunt who has a word of wisdom for every eventuality, and she would say it's no use complaining, you have to accept what life throws at you and make the best of it. One of her favourite proverbs is, "If the wind fails, take to the oars."'

'Well, you might not have to take to the oars,' said Mr Gaunt.

'I don't know what you mean,' said Tom.

'What if I lent you the deposit?'

'You couldn't do that.'

'I can do whatever I like with my own money. Look, Tom, it's sitting in the bank doing nothing. I could manage a few hundred or so. Of course it would be done properly with a contract setting out payments and such. The interest would be reasonable and you're a safe bet.'

'Are you serious?'

'Never more so.'

'I don't know what to say,' said Tom.

'Wouldn't that aunt of yours say one should never look a gift horse in the mouth? So, are we agreed?'

'Well, yes, that would be fantastic,' said Tom. 'It's very generous of you.'

Perhaps Mr Gaunt's offer of lending the money was not quite as magnanimous as it appeared to Tom. It was a clever move. The headmaster thought that perhaps by offering the young teacher a loan, he would ensure that Tom stayed at Risingdale. He certainly did not wish to lose such a talented teacher. Mr Gaunt had seen how things in the school had changed for the better with the arrival of young Mr Dwyer and like the other members of staff, he had a nagging worry that it wouldn't be long before Tom moved on to bigger and better things.

'So, that's settled,' said Mr Gaunt. 'I shall get in touch with my solicitor to draw something up. Now about Charlie, make some enquiries about this scholarship, but as I said, you need to speak to the boy and find out how his mother feels before you go ahead with anything.'

Later that evening Tom found Charlie as usual sitting on the bench by the duck pond with a large book open on his lap. The light was beginning to fade and the boy was straining to read.

'Hello, Mr Dwyer,' he said when he saw his teacher approaching.

'What's the book this time?' asked Tom, sitting next to him.

'It's called *Nicholas Nickleby*, another of Charles Dickens's novels. Have you read it?'

'No, I'm afraid I haven't. Is it good?'

The boy shook his head and smiled indulgently. 'Mr Dwyer,' he said. 'It's Charles Dickens we're talking about. He's the greatest novelist that ever lived. All his novels are brilliant.'

'What's it about?' asked Tom.

'A teacher, a very good teacher like yourself. You remind me a lot of Nicholas. He likes the children and he sticks up for them. I knew you would be different from Miss Cathcart. She was a nice lady but not a very good teacher.'

Tom was about to ask him about the mysterious Miss Cathcart who his colleagues avoided speaking about but the boy continued.

'I think I might like to be a teacher when I grow up,' said Charlie. 'I suppose that one of the good things about learning and being a teacher is that you can share what you learn with others. Of course, I know I will have to work really hard at school and pass lots of exams.'

'That, in a way, is something I wanted to talk to you about,' Tom told him. 'Charlie, have you thought about what secondary school you might like to go to when you leave Risingdale?'

'I reckon I'll go up to Clayton Comprehensive like everybody else.'

'Have you thought about the grammar school?'

'Not really. I see some of the grammar school boys at the library on Saturday morning when I go to change my reading book. They go there to do their homework. I hear them talking. It sounds a really good school. They do subjects like Latin and Spanish and have a chess club and sing in a choir and perform plays.'

'Do you think you might like to go there?'

'Yes, I suppose I would but I need to think it over and talk to my mother.'

'Of course to go to the grammar school you would have to pass an eleven-plus examination,' Tom told him. 'How would you feel about that?'

'I'd quite like to give it a go,' said the boy. 'It would be a challenge, wouldn't it?'

'And possibly you would be asked to take the scholarship examination as well and attend an interview with the headmaster. Getting a scholarship means everything would be paid for. I will need to write to your mother if you are interested or perhaps I could give her a ring.'

'We don't have a telephone, Mr Dwyer,' Charlie told him.

'Then maybe she could come into the school.'

The boy laughed. 'No, you won't get my mother to come into the school,' he told Tom. 'I think she's a bit afraid of teachers. She didn't like school at all when she was a girl.'

'Well, I'll drop her a line then, explaining what it involves.'

'I'm going home now,' Charlie responded. 'You could come with me and see my mother if you want.'

'I don't think your mother would like me to visit out of the blue, particularly at this time of day,' said Tom.

'Oh, she won't mind,' said Charlie.

Having heard what Mrs Golightly had remarked about the boy's mother, Tom expected a tired middle-aged person so was taken aback when this tall, pale-complexioned woman with violet eyes and an abundant explosion of curly black hair appeared at the door of the terraced cottage.

'This is Mr Dwyer,' her son told her. 'He's my teacher.'

'I hope it's not inconvenient, Mrs Lister, for me to have a word with you about Charlie,' said Tom.

A worried expression clouded the woman's face. 'He's not in any trouble, is he?' she asked.

'Not at all,' Tom told her. 'In fact, quite the reverse. He's a model pupil.'

She smiled, displaying a set of even white teeth. 'He's a good boy,' she said, resting a hand on her son's shoulders. 'Well, you had better come in Mr Dwyer.' She glanced at her watch. 'I do have a visitor later on this evening so—'

'Oh, I won't keep you long.'

The small cottage was warm and homely. A cheery fire burned in the hearth and on the mantelpiece were photographs of Charlie in different stages of growing up. Tom could tell that the boy was loved and wanted. There was a bright, patterned three-piece suite and a bookcase full of paperbacks and old tomes.

'Do sit down,' said Mrs Lister.

Tom explained about his idea of entering Charlie for the eleven-plus and applying for a scholarship to cover the cost of his grammar school education.

'Of course it all depends on whether or not he passes the examinations,' said Tom, 'but I think he will. He's a very bright young man.'

Mrs Lister looked at her son and smiled. 'Yes, I don't know where he gets his brains from. Certainly not me. Would you like to go to the grammar, Charlie?' she asked.

'I think I would,' he replied.

'Well then,' she said. 'That seems to be settled.'

When Tom arrived back at the King's Head and edged his way through the bar receiving a number of friendly acknowledgements from a number of the locals, Leanne called him over.

'There's a woman been asking after you,' she said sulkily. 'I told her you were out but she said she'd wait.' The girl tilted her head in the direction of a corner table and pouted. 'That's her over there.'

Joyce Tranter waved. She was dressed in an exceptionally tight red blouse, which matched exactly the colour of her lipstick and nail varnish, a very short skirt and absurdly high-heeled red shoes. She dripped with an assortment of expensive-looking gold jewellery.

'Hello, Joyce,' said Tom, going over. 'What are you doing here?'

'I thought I would take you up on that drink you suggested,' she said.

Tom recalled the occasion when he had first met her and the fact that it was she who had suggested the drink. He was not in the mood for spending the evening with her but felt it would be ill-mannered for him to refuse, so he managed a smile and asked her what she would like to drink.

'Gin and tonic, please,' she replied.

Tom ordered the drinks.

'I'll bring them over,' Leanne told him, eyeing his companion with a sour expression on her round face.

Tom joined his colleague at the table.

'You appear to have settled into life at Risingdale,' remarked Joyce. 'You seem quite a hit with the locals, judging by the reception you just received, which is no mean feat. They tend to be very aloof with new people.'

'Yes,' he replied. 'I've been made to feel very welcome.'

'I can't say the barmaid looks very sociable,' said Joyce. 'She's been glaring at me since I came in.'

Leanne, as if on cue, came over with the drinks. She placed Tom's pint of beer carefully before him but thumped the gin and tonic on the table, spilling some of the drink.

Joyce gave her a sharp look before turning to Tom. 'Mr Gaunt was telling me—' she began.

'I'll put this on your tab,' Leanne interrupted rudely and in a loud voice, before returning to the bar where she stood, arms folded over her chest, and still with the hostile expression on her face.

'Mr Gaunt was telling me,' Joyce started again, 'that you used to be a professional footballer. You kept that pretty quiet.'

'I did play football,' replied Tom, 'but after a few nasty accidents on the pitch and with age creeping up, I couldn't really continue.'

'Don't you miss it? All those cheering fans, all those starry-eyed girls chasing after you?'

'Not really. It wasn't quite as exciting as people make out,' Tom told her. 'I prefer teaching. What about you? I gather you were an actress.'

'I was,' she told him. 'I did have moderate success on the stage. I was Dandini in the pantomime at the Academy Theatre in Barnsley and got some good reviews, and I understudied Maria in *The Sound of Music* at Rotherham Civic Theatre but things then dried up. I did a course in massage therapy and did that for a while and then I took up teaching.' She failed to mention the abusive husband and the real reason why she quit the stage. 'There wasn't much else I could do. I do miss acting, the buzz, the excitement and all the people.' She took a sip of her drink. 'There's really no one to talk to in Risingdale, well, that is, until you arrived. I find the conversations in the staffroom rather tiresome at times. I mean Bertha is nice enough and you couldn't meet a kinder person, but she can be fussy and you can't shut her up when she gets started. I guess she's quite a lonely person. She lost her husband you know.'

'Yes, Mr Gaunt was telling me.'

'Terrible road accident. She's never got over it and it happened all those years ago. She was devoted to him. As for Owen, well, he is one of life's great storytellers. He can be quite amusing but you have to take most of what he says with a pinch of salt.'

'Yes,' said Tom, recalling Mr Gaunt's words when describing the captain.

'I do like Mr Gaunt,' continued Joyce. 'He's easy-going and undemanding but he's not one of the world's most dynamic head teachers and he rarely gets involved in what we do. Of course, had he intervened with Miss Cathcart it might never have happened.'

'What exactly *did* happen with Miss Cathcart?' asked Tom. 'Everyone seems so tight-lipped about it.'

Joyce sipped her drink again before replying. 'Some people say she took her own life,' she said.

'What!' exclaimed Tom.

'She was found in the river. Of course, it was put down as an accident – that she was walking down the towpath on a particularly windy day, lost her balance and fell in, but I think differently. It was clear to me it was suicide. She was always a nervous, troubled woman and she had been acting strangely. I suppose it just got too much for her. I also have an idea she had a drink problem as well. Sometimes I used to find her asleep in her classroom. She certainly looked as if she was under the influence. She should have stopped teaching years ago but she struggled on and you know Mr Gaunt. He's so laissez-faire and avoids problems and confrontations. He should have encouraged her to resign or got the Education Authority to get her to leave. There was a lot of gossip in the village. Some said it was Colin Greenwood's father who finally pushed her over the edge. I don't mean literally, I mean that he drove her to it. He came into school one day after school to complain. Miss Cathcart evidently had got to the end of her tether with his son and lost it. She hit Colin across the face with a ruler and said some pretty hurtful things to the boy. He ran off home. Mr Gaunt was out of school when Greenwood arrived and Owen made himself pretty scarce. It was left to me to try and calm Colin's father down. I can't say that he was aggressive or loud or anything like that. In fact he was quite calm and spoke quietly which I found rather intimidating. I managed to placate him. Anyhow, it greatly affected Miss Cathcart. She was hiding behind the staffroom door and was in a real state when he'd gone.' She sipped her drink. 'So, there it is.'

'It's tragic that someone should be driven to suicide,' said Tom sadly. 'The act of taking one's own life is beyond my comprehension. Some would say it is the easy way out but I imagine it would take an awful lot of courage. Poor Miss Cathcart.'

'Let's change the subject,' said Joyce. 'This is getting morbid. I was just thinking when we were talking about acting that you might like to join our amateur theatre group.'

'I can't see myself on a stage,' said Tom, shaking his head and laughing.

'I think you would be really good and we are always on the lookout for young men. We will be auditioning for the pantomime soon. You should come along. It's a good way of meeting people and the members are a lively lot,' persisted Joyce. 'I'm sure you must get lonely.'

'Oh no, not at all,' he replied quickly. 'I have all the schoolwork to prepare and the books to mark, and most weekends I go and see my aunt in Clayton.' He took a gulp of his beer. 'I'm also moving into the cottage next week so will have a lot to do there.' The last thing he wanted was to prance about a stage with Joyce.

'You know what they say,' she said, leaning over and patting his hand, '"all work and no play".'

At that moment Janette Fairborn came into the bar accompanied by the tall young man, with the dark brown eyes and high cheekbones, the friend of James Maladroit. She caught sight of Tom and gave the smallest of smiles. Her companion glowered.

'Do you know her?' asked Joyce.

'Not really,' Tom replied.

8

Tom was driving into Clayton on Saturday night to see his aunt when he came across a large black car at the side of the narrow road just beyond the bend where he had had the skirmish with the superior Miss Janette Fairborn and her horse. An urbane-looking middle-aged man with a wide, tanned, Roman-nosed face and carefully combed short white hair and neat moustache, was staring at the bonnet, his hands on his hips. Tom pulled over onto the grassy verge behind and opened the side window of his car and stuck his head out.

'Having a spot of bother?' he called.

'I'm afraid so,' replied the man. He had a cut-glass accent.

'May I help?'

'If you have a spare can of petrol with you, I should be enormously grateful. I appear to have run out.' He shook his head. 'My own fault. Silly thing to do.'

'I'm afraid I haven't any petrol,' said Tom, turning off the engine before getting out of the car, 'but if you like I can drive you to a garage.'

'That's very decent of you,' replied the man. 'I wonder if I might prevail on your generosity a little further. It's just that I am booked to address a meeting at the Town Hall in Clayton in an hour. If I could drop off my keys at the garage and ask them to collect the car, and then if you would be so kind, you might get me to the meeting.'

'Of course,' said Tom.

'Iain Balfour-Smith,' the man introduced himself, as he clambered into the jeep. 'This is very good of you, young man. The meeting promises to be a somewhat lively affair this evening and I really need to be there. It's about the proposed building of a supermarket just outside Clayton. It would have looked an awfully bad show if I had failed to turn up. I'm speaking you see. There's likely to be a deal of opposition. People in these parts are averse to any change.'

Tom laughed. 'I'm aware of that,' he told the passenger, starting the car and pulling onto the road.

'Of course, without change,' continued the man, 'there is no progress. We have to move with the times.'

'So I imagine you will be speaking in favour of the supermarket,' Tom remarked.

The man laughed. 'I am the local Member of Parliament and like most politicians, I have to steer a careful course. I nail my colours firmly to the fence. You must not quote me on that, by the way.'

'I'm Tom Dwyer,' the politician was told.

'And what do you do for a living, Mr Dwyer?'

'I teach at Risingdale Primary School. I started there a few weeks ago. It is my first permanent post.'

'Really,' said Mr Balfour-Smith, 'how very interesting. And are you enjoying teaching?'

'Very much so.'

'I am told it is pretty hard going these days.'

'It is demanding,' said Tom, 'but I do believe it is the best profession to be in. I don't think there is any other job which is so varied and so satisfying – with the possible exception of being the Member of Parliament that is.'

Mr Balfour-Smith gave a hearty laugh. 'Oh, it's varied all right but not always so satisfying. I guess this evening there will be a few raised voices and I'll come in for some criticism. It's all par for the course.'

Gervase Phinn

They drove on.

'I can't say that the teachers I had at the public school which I attended were up to much,' said the politician after a while.

'It depends a lot on background as well as good teaching,' said Tom. 'Family, not the education system, is the main force in children succeeding at school. I'm sorry, I sound as if I'm preaching.'

'No, no, it's most interesting,' said the politician, 'and it is good to hear you being so positive. I've just been appointed to sit on the Select Committee for Education. Perhaps you might like to share your views on how you – as someone new to the profession – feel things are going in schools. I gather quite a lot of teachers leave in the first five years. It would be good to hear the opinion of someone new at the chalkface, so to speak.'

By the time they arrived at the Town Hall, Tom had continued to give his views on the present state of education and in a somewhat forthright manner. The MP had listened with interest. Had Tom been aware that the sharing of his opinions would have consequences for all at Risingdale School, he would have, no doubt, been rather more circumspect.

It was the following Friday morning that the letter arrived. Mr Gaunt, who rarely interrupted any lessons in the school, called into Tom's classroom and asked if he could have a word with him in the corridor.

'I gather you are responsible for this,' said the headmaster with a grave expression. He passed Tom an official-looking letter with the coat-of-arms of the rampant lion and unicorn. It was from the Department of Education and Science. The letter stated that, on the suggestion of the Right Honourable Iain Balfour-Smith, Member of Parliament for Clayton and Urebank, one of Her Majesty's Inspectors, a Miss Tudor-Williams, would be visiting the school a week on Monday to look at the education in a typical small rural primary school. In the letter it explained that Mr Balfour-Smith had discussed a number of issues facing the small rural schools with Mr

Thomas Dwyer, newly qualified teacher, and found he had a lot to say that was of great interest. He had asked the Chief Inspector of Schools to arrange for an HMI visit.

'Oh dear,' sighed Tom. 'I didn't think that . . .' The sentence petered out.

'When did you meet this MP?' asked Mr Gaunt. He did not sound at all pleased.

'His car ran out of petrol,' explained Tom. 'I gave him a lift.'

'And from what it says here you discussed what we do here at the school.'

'No, I spoke generally about education and the direction I thought it was going.'

'You know, Tom, I should think that someone who has been in the profession for such a short time would not have a great deal to say of consequence about the direction of education.'

Tom was stung by the criticism. 'The MP asked for my opinion and I gave it. I was speaking from the viewpoint of someone who has just started teaching. I am sure that the school inspector will be very interested in your opinion.'

Mr Gaunt looked less than convinced. 'Yes, I am sure she will.' He shook his head wearily. 'As I have mentioned to you on a number of occasions, life up here tends to be in the slow lane. We like things to stay as they are without outside inter-ference. You are sometimes a little too impetuous, Tom. You have made a very good start in the school and I have been pleased with how you have settled in but, as I have told you before, don't try and change the world. We have been getting along up here quite happily for many years without the unwel-come attentions of meddling educationalists and the advice contained in the snowstorm of guidelines and policies and directives. It's not paperwork which makes a good school.'

'I did say this to the MP,' said Tom.

'Following what you said to him, it looks now as if we are in for some unwelcome changes with the appearance of a government inspector who will, without doubt, want to alter a lot of what we do. I have only met a school inspector once in my career when I taught in Urebank, and it was not an experience I care to repeat. He was a small, sour-faced individual who found fault with most everything and put the fear of God into the teachers. I really don't know how your colleagues will react when they hear we are to have a visit from an HMI.'

'I'm sorry if you feel I have been at fault,' said Tom. 'I didn't mean—'

'This visit may result,' interrupted Mr Gaunt, 'in the closure of the school if this inspector's report is unfavourable. As you are aware, several small schools have closed recently. Miss Tudor-Williams may sound the death knell for our school.' With that he departed, leaving Tom feeling wretched.

'I can't recall when we last had a meeting after school,' said the captain as the teachers gathered in the staffroom later that day. 'It must be pretty important. I wonder what it's about.'

Tom knew full well what it was about but kept a discreet silence. His colleagues would know soon enough about – and who was responsible for – the visit of the HMI.

'Well, I hope it doesn't go on too long,' said Miss Tranter. 'I have a meeting of our amateur dramatic group committee this evening. We're deciding on our next production.'

'You don't think they are going to close the school,' said Mrs Golightly, 'and redeploy us to the other side of the county. I must say that Mr Gaunt certainly looked down-in-the-mouth when I saw him earlier, and when Mrs Leadbeater came out of his study just now, she looked as white as a sheet.'

Mr Gaunt, accompanied by the caretaker and school secretary, arrived and placed himself on a chair in the centre of the room.

'I've asked Mr and Mrs Leadbeater to join us,' he said, 'because what I have to say concerns them as well as the teachers.' He held up the offending letter. 'This is from the Department of Education and Science.'

'I knew it!' cried Mrs Golightly. 'They are going to close the school.'

'Nobody is going to close the school, Bertha,' the headmaster told her. 'It's not come to that. Just bear with me. This correspondence, which I have received this morning, informs me that next Monday week we are to have a visitation from one of Her Majesty's Inspectors of Schools, a Miss Tudor-Williams.'

'Good God!' exclaimed Captain Cadwallader, shooting up in his chair. 'Did you say the name was Tudor-Williams?'

'Do you know her?' asked the headmaster.

'No, no,' answered the captain quickly. The colour had drained from his face. 'I did know someone of the same name. Probably no relation.' There was a dull empty ache in the pit of his stomach. He recalled his former commanding officer, Colonel Carey Tudor-Williams, and prayed the HMI was no relation. Otherwise, he thought, things could get very difficult for him.

'This visit,' continued Mr Gaunt, 'is not something I welcome.'

'Nor me,' added Miss Tranter.

'But we will have to put up with it,' said Mr Gaunt.

'Why is she coming here?' asked Miss Tranter.

The headmaster glanced for a moment at Tom before replying. 'She's interested in the education of children in small rural primary schools. It is probably just a routine visit. I don't think there is a great deal to worry about but things in the school need to be in the very best order. We must show ourselves at our best. Mrs Leadbeater will give my room a good tidy for start, and Mr Leadbeater will make sure the school has a thorough clean and he will tidy up outside. A coat of paint wouldn't go amiss. I shall get a decorator in. I want all classrooms looking attractive and tidy with the children's work well-displayed.'

'Do we need to do all this?' asked Miss Tranter with a sigh.

'It will do no harm to do a bit of window dressing,' said Mr Gaunt. 'You all might like to come into school at the weekend to get things sorted. Also all exercise books need to be marked up-to-date, and I suggest you jot down some lesson plans for the week in case the inspector wishes to see them. Inform the children that we will be having an important visitor and that they should be on their very best behaviour.'

'It might be an idea to tell Colin Greenwood to stay at home on Monday,' suggested Mrs Golightly. 'Don't you think so, Owen?'

'What?' exclaimed the captain. 'I'm sorry, I wasn't listening.'

'I said perhaps we should tell Colin Greenwood not to come into school on the Monday of the visit,' said Mrs Golightly. 'We don't want any misbehaviour when the school inspector is here.'

'I don't think that will be necessary,' Tom told her. 'Colin's not been any trouble lately.'

Mr Gaunt looked at Captain Cadwallader who sat ashen-faced and staring vacantly ahead of him.

'Are you all right, Owen?' he asked. He had noticed that there was something different in the teacher, a strange sense of distance so uncharacteristic of the usually cheerful and garrulous colleague.

'Oh yes, I'm fine,' replied the captain unconvincingly, before sinking again into self-absorption.

'I am sure you have no need to worry about this school inspector,' said the headmaster, rather more to reassure himself than his colleague. He was as nervous as any and felt his stomach beginning to churn. He was unaware that it wasn't the visit of the school inspector which worried the captain; it was something much more alarming.

On a wet and windy Monday morning, the teachers, who had arrived remarkably early for once, sat apprehensively in the staffroom, awaiting the arrival of the dreaded school inspector. They discussed what they imagined she would look like and settled upon a large woman in thick brown tweeds, heavy brogues, bullet-proof stockings and a hat in the shape of a flowerpot. She would carry a large umbrella with a spike in the end which she would brandish like a weapon.

At ten minutes past eight, the visitor arrived. She was a small woman with a pale, angular face, dark, deep-set eyes, very thick, wild white hair and a large nose which curved savagely like a bird's beak. She stood at the gate staring at the school, observed by Mrs Golightly who had been keeping a lookout at the window of the staffroom.

'She's here!' exclaimed the teacher.

Her colleagues joined her at the window and peered furtively at the figure at the gate.

'Good God!' cried Captain Cadwallader. 'It's worse than I thought.'

'She looks dreadful,' groaned Mrs Golightly.

'Looks can be deceptive, Bertha,' said Tom, trying to sound positive. 'Her bark's probably far worse than her bite.'

'First impressions are very important in my book,' said Miss Tranter. 'I'm always right about people when I first meet them, and this person, who looks as if she could curdle milk with a stare, is very bad news.'

Mr Leadbeater, attired in a new and sparkling nylon overall worn for the occasion, scurried to the gate to greet the important visitor.

'Good morning,' he said brightly, giving her one of his rare smiles and jingling the keys in his overall pocket. 'Welcome to Risingdale School. It is a pleasure to meet you. I am the caretaker Mr Leadbeater and should there be anything you need, you need only to ask.'

'Good morning,' replied the woman without a trace of a smile.

'I trust you have had a good journey,' he continued, still maintaining the obsequious tone of voice and the contrived smile.

'No, I can't say that I have,' she grumbled. 'I waited over an hour for the bus and then it started to rain and the wind up here nearly knocked me off my feet. I didn't realise the school was so far up. It's miles from anywhere.'

'Would you care to follow me,' said the caretaker, imagining the dire things she would have to say about the school. He opened the gate and gave a small bow. 'I am sure you would like a cup of tea before you start.'

'No, I'm not stopping,' said the woman.

'Not stopping,' repeated the caretaker.

'I can't work up here. I've been offered another job at Ruston.'

'You've been offered a job at Ruston?'

'It'll suit me better.'

'Better than being a school inspector?'

'What are you talking about?' snapped the woman. 'I'm not a school inspector. I'm a cleaner. Whatever gave you the idea I was a school inspector? I've been sent by Mr Nettles of the Education Office about a cleaning job, but this school is way too far out for me. I couldn't manage the journey nor the weather.'

The caretaker grimaced and closed the gate with a bang. 'Well, mind how you go,' he said, turning his back on her and returning to the school.

'I don't know what Mr Leadbeater said to her,' remarked Mrs Golightly, still staring through the staffroom window, 'but he's got rid of her.'

Ten minutes later a car pulled up outside the school and the school inspector made her appearance. Everyone was more than surprised when this tall, extremely elegant woman, probably in her late forties, with a streamlined figure, and dressed in a smart grey suit walked into the school. There was the smell of fresh paint in the air.

'It's very good of you to see me,' she told Mr Gaunt as he ushered her into his remarkably tidy study.

'It's a pleasure,' he dissembled. 'I'm delighted to see you.'

Mrs Leadbeater had certainly gone to town in the room. She had tidied the books, changed the dull prints and insipid watercolours for a set of attractive landscapes, replaced the hard, thin carpet with a brightly coloured rug and consigned the alpenhorn to a cupboard. The old-fashioned blotter, inkwell and jam jar containing the pens and broken pencils had been removed from the desk, and on the top she had arranged strategically a neat pile of folders and a selection of official-looking documents – guidelines, curriculum policies and directives from the Education Authority – which had never seen the light of day before.

Mr Gaunt, like the room, had undergone a transformation. His usual attire of old, shapeless sports jacket, baggy flannel trousers and shirt frayed around the collar had been discarded in favour of a smart pinstripe suit, crisp white shirt and college tie. He had also had his hair cut.

'I am sure you would enjoy a cup of tea, Miss Tudor-Williams,' said the headmaster.

'Do you know that would be splendid,' she said, smiling and sitting down in one of the comfortable chairs Mrs Leadbeater had brought from home. She crossed her long legs.

'I have asked my secretary to bring us a cup,' said Mr Gaunt. 'Did you have a good journey?'

The inspector drew a deep breath. 'A very pleasant one,' she replied. 'It's quite spectacular up here, isn't it? I don't think I have seen such beautiful scenery in a long while. The air is so fresh and clean and the sunlight has a purity not to be found in the built-up and busy urban areas where I spend most of my time. I so much wished to live in the country when I was a girl.' She brought her faraway look back to Mr Gaunt. 'It's quite a treat for me to visit a school like this.'

I wish I could say the visit was a treat for me, thought the headmaster.

'Driving up here, there was scarcely a house to be seen,' she said. 'It's so tranquil.'

'At the moment you see the Dale at its best,' Mr Gaunt told her, 'but in winter the wind has the power to penetrate the heaviest of coats, the driving rain is merciless and when the snow comes, it settles in earnest and makes the roads impassable. It's a hard life for the farmers up here.' He looked out of the window. 'But it still has an extraordinary beauty.'

'The children are very lucky to live in such a picturesque part of the country,' observed the school inspector.

'Lucky?' said Mr Gaunt, smiling. 'I am sure most of them would not agree with you. There's not a great deal for young people to do up here apart from help on the farms. I think they would gladly exchange the picturesque scenery for a cinema, bowling alley or leisure centre. It's very isolated and the buses are unpredictable in summer and non-existent in a bad winter.'

The inspector smiled herself. 'I stand corrected,' she said.

Mrs Leadbeater entered with a tray on which was a large teapot, two matching delicate china cups, a milk jug, a sugar bowl and a plate of biscuits. She, like Mr Gaunt, had dressed for the occasion and wore a smart pale-grey suit, a pearl-coloured silk blouse and black patent-leather shoes. She wore her horn-rimmed spectacles on a cord around her neck. It was her idea of what a personal assistant should look like. She placed the tray down on the desk, curtsied and left the room.

When she had finished her tea and further pleasantries had been exchanged with the headmaster, the school inspector was taken to the staffroom to meet the teachers.

'I would like to introduce Miss Tudor-Williams,' announced Mr Gaunt. He turned to the HMI. 'This is Mrs Golightly, the teacher of the infants,' he told her, 'Miss Tranter teaches the seven and eight year olds, Captain Cadwallader takes the class above and Mr Dwyer is in charge of the upper juniors.'

'Good morning,' said the inspector. Her eyes rested on Captain Cadwallader.

'You're a Royal Navy man?' she enquired.

'British Army, ma'am,' he replied.

'My brother Carey was in the British Army. What regiment were you in?'

The captain could not evade the question he had been dreading. He swallowed and gave a small cough. 'The Welch Regiment,' he replied.

'What a coincidence,' said the inspector. 'That was my brother's regiment. You must have been fellow officers. You will recall my brother, of course.'

'Indeed,' said the teacher, looking decidedly uncomfortable. 'A very fine commanding officer.'

'I must remember you to him. I'm sure he would like to meet up with you and talk about old times.'

'I'm sure the colonel is far too busy,' replied the captain with little enthusiasm in his voice.

'Not at all,' said the inspector. 'He likes nothing better than talking about his army days.' She turned to Tom. 'Ah, and this is Mr Dwyer, I assume,' she said, 'the reason for my visit.'

'He is?' asked Joyce.

'Mr Dwyer was speaking to Mr Balfour-Smith, the local Member of Parliament, about the education of children in the small rural school,' explained Miss Tudor-Williams. 'I have been asked by the department to provide Mr Balfour-Smith with more information. He was very interested in what Mr Dwyer had to say.'

'Was he indeed,' commented Joyce, giving Tom an icy look.

The first part of the morning Miss Tudor-Williams spent closeted in the headmaster's study with Mr Gaunt, grilling him about teaching and learning, progress and attainment in the school, then, after morning break, she joined Tom with his class. The lesson could not have gone better. The children were polite, well-behaved and very forthcoming. They stood when the inspector entered the room and wished her an enthusiastic 'Good morning, miss.' Even Colin managed to get to his feet.

'May I ask the children a few questions?' said Miss Tudor-Williams.

'Of course,' said Tom.

'What is your name?' she asked the pixie-faced girl who sat at the front desk.

'Marjorie, miss,' replied the pupil.

'And what subject is your favourite?' she was asked.

'I like them all, miss,' she replied, 'but I suppose I'm best at arithmetic.' Helping her grandmother take the money and give the change at the Saturday market stall had given the child ample practice in adding up and taking away.

'Could you tell me what seventeen taken away from eighty-three would be?' asked the inspector.

'Yes, I could,' answered the girl.

The inspector smiled. 'Well, what is the answer?'

'Sixty-six,' replied Marjorie without a second's thought.

'My goodness that was quick,' said Miss Tudor-Williams. 'Could you tell me what number must be added to the sum of fourteen and fifteen to make forty?'

Marjorie thought for moment. 'Eleven,' she replied.

'Well done,' said the inspector, clearly impressed. 'Let me see if anyone in the class can answer a really difficult poser. Listen carefully, children. If a shepherd had a field of sheep a quarter of which were black, a half of them were white and forty-two were black and white. How many sheep did the shepherd own?'

'It'd be a funny old flock of sheep,' said Carol, 'what with all them different breeds.'

'Breeds,' repeated the inspector.

'Yes, miss,' said the girl. 'What breeds are these sheep?'

'Well, I'm not sure,' replied the inspector.

'Don't you know your sheep, miss?'

The inspector smiled again and glanced at Tom, as if looking for help but he remained silent and bemused. 'No, I'm afraid I'm not that well up on breeds of sheep,' she told Carol.

'You see,' said the little sheep expert, standing up, 'your Texels can be all white and your Swaledales are mostly black and white – white bodies and black faces. Your nearest breed that is all black I reckon is the Herdwick, a Cumbrian breed and very hardy. I don't think any shepherd would have all them different breeds in one field. You see when it comes to tupping—'

'Thank you, Carol,' interjected Tom quickly. 'Let's see if anyone can answer the problem.'

'The answer is a hundred and sixty-eight sheep,' said Charlie.

When Tom had set the children to write an account of what they had done over the weekend, Miss Tudor-Williams went from desk to desk, looking at the pupils' exercise books and talking to them. It became evident to her that Mr Gaunt was speaking the truth when he had told her that the children did little away from the farms on which they lived. Most had spent the weekend helping their parents: feeding the animals, grooming the horses, mending fences and walls, sweeping and washing and cleaning.

David was happy to show the inspector his book, of which he was very proud. 'I used to be really untidy before Mr Dwyer became my teacher and before I got my new glasses,' he said, 'but now I'm a lot neater. I've been practising my writing at home. Mr Dwyer gave me some exercises to do.' He held up his ink-stained fingers. 'I'm still getting used to using the fountain pen though. This one seems to have a life of its own.'

'So I see,' said the inspector.

'He's a good teacher, you know,' said the boy in a confiden-tial tone of voice, 'a very good teacher. You might want to make a note of that, miss.'

Of course Simon, whose account was predictably about going ferreting over the weekend, was keen to tell Miss Tudor-Williams about his pets.

'Now when it comes to mating ...' Tom heard the boy inform the inspector.

When asked what she was writing about, Marjorie regaled the inspector with a detailed account of how she helped her grandmother making a patchwork-quilt wall hanging.

'It's a good way of making use of scraps of old material, isn't it?' commented Miss Tudor-Williams, 'an excellent example of recycling?'

'No, it's not, miss,' replied the girl. 'We use new material like in the quilts that were made years back. The early American quilters always made a deliberate mistake in their work because they believed that only God is perfect. Did you know that, miss?'

'No,' admitted Miss Tudor-Williams, 'I didn't.'

'My grandmother told me that,' said the girl.

When the inspector asked Carol about her weekend, it was as if the child had been wound up for she talked non-stop, unsurprisingly, about sheep.

'The breeds up this part of the Dale,' said the girl, 'are mostly hill sheep and they are tough enough to stay alive on the poor grass on the tops and stay there over winter. My dad cross breeds the Dales' yow, that's a ewe, with a Blue-faced Leicester tup, that's the ram, and the lambs are called mules. I help with lambing because if a lamb gets stuck, I've got a small hand you see and can get it inside the yow and get the lamb in the right position to be born.'

'Fascinating,' said the school inspector.

Miss Tudor-Williams managed at last to move on before Carol could enlighten her any more about the breeding habits of her grandfather's flock. She arrived at Colin's desk. The boy eyed her suspiciously when she sat down next to him.

'And what is your name?' she asked.

'Colin.'

'May I look at your book?'

'It's rubbish,' replied the boy, placing a grubby hand over the cover. 'I don't want you to look.'

'I would like to see it.'

He looked at her with a direct but wary gaze. 'Well, I don't want you to,' he said.

The inspector decided not to pursue the matter. 'And what are you good at Colin?' she asked.

'Nothing.'

'We are all good at something,' she said.

'Well, I'm not.'

'Have you a favourite subject?'

'No.'

'What did you do over the weekend?'

'Same as I always do, working on the farm.'

'That must be very interesting,' said the inspector.

'What!' exclaimed Colin. 'Interesting? I hate it. Look, why don't you go and talk to somebody else?'

What a truculent and angry child, thought Miss Tudor-Williams. She considered moving on but was not one to give up so easily. 'And what have you there?' she asked, seeing a small notebook sticking out of the boy's pocket.

'It's my drawings,' he told her. 'They're no good.'

'May I see?'

'I told you, they're no good.'

He thought for a moment and then gave her the notebook. Inside were delicate line drawings of animals and landscapes, faces and figures, one was a ruined castle.

'These are excellent,' said the school inspector. 'You have a fine eye for detail and perspective.' The boy didn't answer. 'I can see that you like drawing and are very good at it. Has Mr Dwyer seen these?'

'No,' said the boy.

'You should show him. I'm sure he would be very interested.'

Tom noticed that the school inspector had spent more time with Colin than any other pupil so far. He hoped she would have a chance to speak to his star pupil before she left.

Charlie, of course, charmed her. He chatted about the books he had read, his interest in history and astronomy, how he liked to cook, play the ukulele, take long walks and visit the library.

'Have you written this?' asked Miss Tudor-Williams, looking at a page in the boy's exercise book.

'Yes, of course, miss,' replied Charlie. 'I like writing poetry. It looks nice on the page and you can say what you really feel.'

'Would you like to read it to me?' asked the inspector.

Charlie cleared his throat and read:

> 'The day after they cut back the hedgerow
> At the back of our cottage,
> A dormouse found its way
> Into our kitchen.
> It appeared, bright golden brown,
> Its small round ears twitching.
> It cowered in a corner
> And stared at me with large and shiny eyes
> As black as jet,
> Then flicked its furry tail,
> And in a flash was gone.
> My mother said that we should set a trap
> But I said, 'No!'
> How could we kill such a lovely little creature?'

'This is excellent,' said Miss Tudor-Williams. 'You have a real talent for poetry and you're a very considerate young man. I have to say, however, that I tend to agree with your mother. I wouldn't be too keen on having a mouse in my kitchen.'

'But dormice are very rare and we shouldn't kill them, miss,' replied Charlie. 'I got a humane trap and caught him and then let him go, putting him back in the hedgerow.'

'A happy ending then,' said the inspector.

'Well, not really, miss, he found his way back in the cottage. By the way did you know that dormice were first recorded by a Victorian naturalist in Wensleydale?'

'I didn't,' replied Miss Tudor-Williams who, on her travels around schools, was more used to asking the questions and not to answering them. 'I must say,' she said, 'I am learning a great deal from you children today.'

'Tell me, miss,' asked Charlie, 'are you related to royalty by any chance?'

The inspector laughed. 'No, it's just that I am one of Her Majesty's Inspectors. I'm no relation to the Queen.'

'But you see her.'

'No, I don't see her.'

'But you might be a relation,' said Charlie. 'The Tudors were once kings and queens.'

'Mine is not an unusual name in Wales which is where I come from.'

'You never know,' said the boy. 'Maybe you are descended from Henry the Eighth.' He thought for a moment. 'Mind you the Tudors were mostly a bad lot, so it might be better not to look into your ancestry too deeply.'

'I shall make sure I don't,' said Miss Tudor-Williams, shaking her head and laughing.

'Tell me about the boy at the back desk,' said the school inspector when she sat with Tom in his classroom at lunchtime.

'Colin?' replied the teacher. 'He's a mixed-up, unhappy young man and can be sullen and uncooperative. He's the one pupil in the class I don't seem to have got through to. He lives at one of the outlying farms with a father who apparently has little time for his son. I'm told he's a bit of a bully. I have tried hard to encourage the boy, but he is determined to make as little effort as possible with his schoolwork and he's reluctant to take a part in any of the activities. I don't think I've ever seen him smile. Any advice in handling him would be really helpful.'

'Well, Mr Dwyer,' the inspector said, 'it takes a very special sort of teacher to get the child who does not wish to be taught to work hard at school and have the ambition to succeed. I am afraid it is a sad fact that the pupil who is resolute in not wishing to learn presents a real challenge. The good teacher perseveres with patience and understanding and, from what I have seen of your approach this morning, I feel you are on the right lines. I gather you have not seen his drawings?'

'Drawings?' repeated Tom.

'He's a very good artist. Take a look at that little notebook of his. He was showing me his sketches. The boy has a real talent for drawing.'

'I never knew,' said Tom.

'I think that might be the way to get through to Colin,' said Miss Tudor-Williams, 'by means of his art.'

'I'll certainly try.'

'Colin is rather a different kettle of fish from the young man at the front desk,' said Miss Tudor-Williams. 'Quite a contrast.'

'Oh, you mean Charlie.'

'He has such a bright, sunny nature, he is most articulate and his work is excellent. I don't think I have seen such quality in the work of a child of his age for some time.'

'Would you say that he is gifted?' asked Tom.

'Undoubtedly,' replied the inspector. 'Well, I think that's all I have to say, Mr Dwyer, unless you have anything you would like to ask me.'

'Might I ask you if you have gained a favourable impression of the small rural primary school?'

'Yes, I have,' replied the inspector. 'The one salient feature of small schools like this is the family atmosphere, the way that children get along and look after each other. I observed an older child at morning break helping a young one who had fallen over, comforting her and taking her to have a grazed knee seen to. Big schools can sometimes be rather impersonal.'

At the end of the day, Miss Tudor-Williams reported back to Mr Gaunt. She was largely satisfied with what she had seen but singled Tom out for special mention.

'Mr Dwyer is a very talented teacher,' she told the headmaster, 'and the children in his class thrive with his encouragement and instruction.'

'I could see when I appointed him that he would make a first-rate teacher,' Mr Gaunt answered, wishing to share somewhat in the praise. 'Of course, being new to the profession, I have given him a great deal of support and offered advice which he has readily taken aboard.'

'I must say,' said Miss Tudor-Williams, 'that it has been a real education for me this morning. I have learnt about the breeds of sheep, the mating habits of ferrets, the various makes of tractors, how a drystone wall is built, the discovery of dormice and the way a patchwork quilt is made.'

The headmaster sat back in his chair and beamed. 'It's been a pleasure having you in the school,' he told her. 'I have always had the greatest respect for Her Majesty's Inspectors.'

Mr Gaunt gathered all the staff together at the end of the day to report on what the HMI had said. He looked very pleased with himself.

'Well,' he told his staff, 'Miss Tudor-Williams was, on the whole, impressed with what she saw. She thought the children in particular were very well-behaved, attentive and hard-working. The standard of work she found satisfactory and sometimes better and the teaching she felt was generally good although there might be more variety and challenge. Of course she explained that this was not a formal inspection as such but more of a fact-finding visit.'

'Instigated by our very own Mr Dwyer,' added Miss Tranter, pulling a face.

'I didn't actually instigate it,' protested Tom. 'I merely mentioned one or two things to this MP and it was he who got her to visit.'

'Be careful what you say in future,' warned the captain. He still looked ill at ease.

'Because we don't want a repetition,' said Mrs Golightly.

'I must say that it has turned out well,' said Mr Gaunt. 'The inspector seemed pleased that we offer here at Risingdale a good, sound education, comments which can only be good news for us at a time when other small schools in the county are being closed. No doubt her report will find its way to the desk of the Director of Education. To be honest I found Miss Tudor-Williams very personable and someone who talked a lot of good sense. She agreed with me, and this is something I have always said on many occasions, that the keys to educational success in children are self-esteem, self-confidence and expectation. I think the pupils here have all three in abundance.'

Miss Tranter and her colleagues ostentatiously avoided catching each other's eye.

9

The teachers, with the exception of Captain Cadwallader, who was not his usual good-humoured and garrulous self, were in a particularly buoyant mood the day after the school inspector's visit. Amidst all the excited chatter about how things had gone, the captain remained sitting in the corner of the staffroom uncharacteristically silent. He stared distractedly at a mug of cold coffee which was before him on the table.

'Are you feeling all right, Owen?' asked Mrs Golightly.

'Yes, thank you, Bertha,' he answered. 'I'm just a little tired.'

'Well, that inspection did take it out of us, I must admit,' she said.

'You look dreadful, Owen,' said Miss Tranter with all the tact of a sledgehammer.

'I didn't sleep at all well last night,' he explained.

'Well, it's all over now so you can relax,' said Mrs Golightly brightly.

'What is all over?' he asked.

'Why, the inspection of course. It wasn't half as bad as we thought it would be.'

The captain was not thinking about the inspection. Something much more troubling was on his mind.

'The night before Miss Tudor-Williams's visit,' Mrs Golightly chatted on happily, 'I was so worried at what she would say. I imagined she would criticise my reading scheme as being dated, the teaching of phonics as old-fashioned and the way I taught the children their tables inappropriate, but she seemed satisfied and said my methods, albeit traditional, were bearing fruit. Everything went so well, didn't it?'

'It might have gone well, Bertha,' agreed Miss Tranter, 'but we can do without a repeat visit. I hope you are listening, Tom Dwyer. Just keep your comments about the state of education to yourself in future, otherwise we'll have all manner of inter-fering educational pundits descending upon us.'

'Bertha has already warned me,' replied Tom. 'I shall be a bit more guarded in what I say in future, I promise.' He laughed. 'Anyway, Joyce, you came out of this pretty well. The inspector was pleased with what she saw in your classroom, wasn't she?'

'Well, yes, I have to admit that she was quite impressed with my lesson,' said Miss Tranter with a small self-satisfied smile on her face. 'I read a story and, of course with my training as an actress, I came into my own. Good teachers do have a sense of the dramatic, I have always thought. She said I lifted the text from the page with great animation and kept the children's attention throughout.'

'What about you, Owen?' asked Tom, looking at the hunched figure in the corner who was still staring into space and who clearly had not been listening.

'What about me?' he asked.

'How did your lesson go?'

'Lesson?'

'The one the inspector observed.'

'Not too bad,' replied the captain without any further elaboration.

'It was quite a coincidence you being in the same regiment as Miss Tudor-Williams's brother, wasn't it?' said Miss Tranter to the captain.

'Yes, quite a coincidence,' he repeated.

'I suppose you'll be catching up on old times when you meet him.'

'I don't envisage meeting the colonel,' said her colleague flatly.

'Oh, I'm sure he will want to meet up with you,' said Joyce, not letting the matter lie.

'Look, I don't wish to talk about it!' snapped the captain. Leaving his coffee untouched, he stood. 'If you will excuse me, I have to prepare my lesson.'

'Well,' said Miss Tranter when he had left, 'what do you make of that?'

'He's in a very peculiar mood this morning and no mistake,' remarked Mrs Golightly. 'I've never seen him like this. He's not touched a Garibaldi all morning.'

'Probably post-inspection stress,' said Tom.

'No, it's not that,' said Miss Tranter. 'There's more here than meets the eye. Something happened when he was in the army, you mark my words, otherwise he would have been very keen to see this old crony of his. Probably didn't get on with the colonel or they had some falling out. Perhaps he was court-martialled.' She examined a long red nail. 'I'd like to know what it is.'

The evening before, Tom had marked the children's work and had been well-pleased with how their writing had improved Not only was it neater and more accurate but there was a vibrancy and detail in their accounts which made him feel that his efforts were really paying off. Christopher, the large, rosy-cheeked boy, had written a fascinating account of how he had accompanied his father and uncle on the Saturday to do 'a spot of fishing'. As Tom read the narrative, he smiled. He had come to appreciate in the short time he had been in the profession, how children, particularly those who lived in the Dales, were open and honest and oftentimes extremely blunt. A more fitting description of the clandestine activity of the boy's father and uncle, Tom thought as he read Christopher's work, would be poaching.

We went along the muddy bank until we came to a quiet place where my uncle said was the best spot for finding the trout. We had to keep a look-out for the keeper because the stretch of river was on the big estate and we really shouldn't have been there but my uncle said Sir Hedley wouldn't miss a couple of fish and in any case lots of people do it. I spotted a big trout not really moving in the current. My dad told me to move really slowly, lay flat on the ground and put my hand slowly in the water and tickle the fish under its belly. They think that it's the weeds. My uncle told me when I'd done that to stick my fingers in its gills and flip it out onto the bank. As soon as I touched the fish it shot off like a bullet from a gun. Then my uncle had a go and straight away there was a fat brown trout flopping and thrashing on the river bank. My dad hit it on the head and we took it home for tea.

Vicky's account was rather different.

We went round to my grandma's house on Sunday for tea like we always do. My grandma was really upset and in a right old state because she said she'd been accused of something she hadn't done. She used to do the cleaning up at the big house but Lady Marcia had lost some jewellery and she said she thought my grandma had took it. She told her not to bother to come back to do the cleaning any more. My grandma would never take anything. Anyway she didn't like cleaning up at the big house and she didn't like Lady Marcia either. She said she was a stuck-up cow.

Tom predicted that Colin's effort would be like all the other pieces of written work the boy had produced: short and pedestrian and showing no interest or effort. He guessed it would be along the lines of: 'Did my chores and took the dog out and watched television.' He was therefore pleasantly surprised to find that Colin had written rather more than usual, and his description had a blunt simplicity and a no-nonsense lack of sentiment about it.

Our sheep dog died on Saturday. Meg was an old dog but my dad reckons she were the best collie he'd ever had. In the bad winters my dad used to have to fight his way through the snowdrifts to search the sheep what were buried. Sometimes it was waist deep the snow and it was a cruel wind. My dad said that Meg had a gift what not many sheepdogs have. She could pick up the scent of a buried sheep and sniff it out. We buried Meg by the field where she used to like to run.

At afternoon break the captain, who was on playground duty, rushed into the staffroom.

'Could you come please, Tom?' he panted. 'There's a fight.'

Tom followed the teacher into the playground to find Colin and Christopher rolling around in the dust with legs kicking and fists flying. They were surrounded by a group of spectators. Tom dived in and separated the two boys, pulling each one up roughly by the collar of his shirt.

'Stop it at once!' he shouted.

'He started it, calling me names!' cried Christopher. The boy's nose was dribbling with blood. 'Then he hit me. He punched me on the nose.'

Colin remained silent, breathing heavily with a fierce expression on his face.

'I think I'll leave things in your capable hands, Mr Dwyer,' said Captain Cadwallader. 'You seem to have the situation well under control.' He retreated back to the school.

Tom wondered why the veteran of the Welch Regiment, which he had heard had seen furious fighting in the jungles of the world, was unable to separate two boys and had left it to him to deal with.

'All right everybody,' Tom told the onlookers, 'there's nothing more to see. Off you go.' When the children were slow in moving, he shouted, 'Now!' They scurried away. He turned to the two combatants. 'Not you two,' he told the boys as they started to go. 'Over here and sit on the wall. I want to have a word with you both.' The boys sat on the small wall bordering the playground, heads down. 'What was this all about?' asked their teacher.

'He hit me!' cried Christopher, stabbing the air with a finger in Colin's direction. 'Then he called me a fat pig.'

'Did you, Colin?' Tom asked.

'Yea, I did.'

'Why?'

The boy shrugged.

'There must have been some reason,' said Tom.

'He said my dad was a crook and owed his dad money and wouldn't pay him back,' said Colin.

'Did you say this, Christopher?'

'I was only saying what my dad told my uncle last night,' replied the boy, wiping a trickle of blood from his nose.

'So you started it?' said Tom.

'I was only saying what my dad said,' sniffed Christopher. 'Then Colin said I was a liar and called me a fat pig and he hit me.'

'I don't think you would like someone to say your father was a crook,' Tom told him. 'Would you?'

'No, sir, but he shouldn't have called me a fat pig and hit me.'

'No, he should not,' agreed the teacher, 'but then you shouldn't have called his father a crook.'

'It's what my dad said,' mumbled the boy.

'Well, I think you probably misheard,' said Tom. 'Now off you go and get cleaned up.'

'Sir, I didn't mishear him. He said—' began the boy.

'Enough!' barked Tom. 'Let this be the end of it.'

'My dad's not a crook,' said Colin when the other boy had departed. There were tears in his eyes. 'People say things about him but they're not true. They don't know him.'

'Of course your father's not a crook,' said the teacher, 'but hitting someone doesn't solve any problem.'

'You did,' said the boy.

'What?'

'You hit someone in the pub. I heard about it from the other kids and my dad told me. They said you punched Sir Hedley's son in the stomach.'

'That was a bit different,' Tom told him.

'My dad said the person who you punched deserved what he got.' Then he added, 'Just like Christopher. He deserved to get thumped too.'

Tom decided not to pursue the matter. 'Off you go, Colin,' he said. 'And no more fighting.'

'I appreciate you coming to my aid,' the captain told Tom in the staffroom at lunchtime. 'Of course I would have called upon Mr Gaunt had he been in school but he was at a meeting. I felt the situation needed someone much fitter than I to deal with the matter. Of course, in my younger days, I would have had no difficulty in sorting out such high spirits, but I am getting a bit long in the tooth to be struggling with two large boys.' He thought for a moment. 'Perhaps I should think about retiring.'

'Nonsense, Owen,' said Mrs Golightly. 'There's a good few years in you yet.'

'You make him sound like a broken-down carthorse,' remarked Miss Tranter. 'Anyway, where was Mr Gaunt?'

'He had a meeting at County Hall,' Mrs Golightly told her. 'It was probably something to do with the inspection but, then again, it might be about closing the school.'

'I wish you wouldn't keep going on about the school clos-ing, Bertha,' said Miss Tranter impatiently. 'It's becoming rather wearisome.'

'Well, Mr Gaunt being summoned to County Hall sounds a bit ominous to me,' replied her colleague. 'Mrs Leadbeater said an education officer had telephoned Mr Gaunt early this morning and said the Director of Education required the headmaster's presence.'

'We'll soon find out when he comes back,' said Miss Tranter. 'What was this fight about?' she asked Tom.

'Christopher told Colin that the boy's father was a crook.'

Miss Tranter gave a snort. 'Well, he is a crook,' she said. 'Everyone around here knows that the boy's father is a villain, isn't that so, Owen?'

'I'm sorry, Joyce,' said the captain, 'I wasn't listening.'

'What is wrong with you today?' she asked. 'Are you ill?'

'No, I'm not ill,' he replied.

'Well, you are certainly not yourself,' she said. 'And what's all this about thinking of retiring?'

'Just leave it, Joyce, will you,' he retorted. He stood and made for the door. 'I have things to do, if you will excuse me.'

'There's certainly something on his mind,' remarked Mrs Golightly when the captain had gone. 'He's in a very strange mood. He's not touched the biscuit tin this morning.'

For the remainder of the day the captain was very distant. Rather than going into the staffroom to endure another grill-ing from Miss Tranter, he remained in his classroom, which is where Tom found him at the end of the day.

'Can I be of any help,' asked Tom.

'In what way?'

'Something's clearly troubling you. Do you want to talk about it?'

'No, no,' replied the captain. 'I'm fine.'

'I've not known you all that long, Owen,' said Tom, 'but I can tell that something is on your mind. Why not tell me about it?'

'It's very decent of you, dear boy, to take an interest in my well-being,' replied the captain, giving a weak smile, 'but there is nothing you can do.'

'Well, you could try me. It won't go any further, I promise. I can't say that I am the best listener in the world but it's good sometimes to get things off your chest and talk it through with somebody else.'

'It is kind of you,' said the captain, 'but it is something I have to deal with myself.'

'Well, you know where I am if you want to come down for a drink and a chat one evening,' said Tom.

The following morning Christopher's father arrived at school. He appeared outside Tom's classroom, a short, thick-necked individual with a nose as heavy as a turnip and great hooded eyes. He peered through the glass in the door.

'Get on with your work quietly,' said Tom to the class before leaving the room. 'May I help you?' he asked the visitor.

'You our Christopher's teacher?' demanded the man.

'I am, yes,' replied Tom.

'I've come in to see you about what happened yesterday. Our Christopher come home with a bloody nose.'

'He was in a fight.'

'Aye, so he said but he wouldn't tell me what it was about, just that that Greenwood lad punched him on the nose and called him names.'

'Christopher told Colin Greenwood that the boy's father was a crook. He said he overheard you telling his uncle that.'

'Oh, did he?'

'Which I told your son I was sure you never said and that he must have misheard.'

'He didn't mishear. Dick Greenwood is a crook.'

'I really should not go repeating that, Mr Pickles,' said Tom. 'It's slander and could get you into a lot of trouble.'

'Don't you start lecturing me, young man,' said the parent angrily. 'I'm not one of your pupils. You're new to this part of the world but if you had lived in the Dale as long as I have, you would know full well that Dick Greenwood is a thief and a villain and wants locking up. I've lost sheep which I reckon is down to him.'

'And you have, I take it, reported this to the police?' asked Tom.

'Course I haven't,' retorted the parent. 'Bobbies up here are about as much use as a chocolate teapot.'

'Mr Pickles, your son told Mr Greenwood's son that you had said that his father was a crook and repeating this slander is unacceptable and the boy retaliated. Just as your son would do if someone slandered you, Colin defended his father and the two boys got into a fight as a result.'

'Now look here,' said the man, raising his voice. 'Don't get clever with me.'

Captain Cadwallader poked his head around his classroom door to see what the noise in the corridor was and, seeing the two men squaring up, he quickly disappeared back into his room.

'I think it might be better for you to see the headmaster,' said Tom.

'It's not Gerry Gaunt I wanted to see. I want to see you and get things sorted out.'

'Which I am endeavouring to do,' Tom told him. 'Look, Mr Pickles, the boy who hit your son should not have done that or call him names, but in his defence he was standing up for his parent. No child wishes another to say unpleasant things about his father. I am sure you would expect Christopher to defend you if, for example, someone said that you poached fish from Sir Hedley's stretch of river, that you went down there to tickle the trout.'

The man was lost for words for a moment and his face coloured up. 'Who's been saying that I've been poaching?' he asked.

Tom's face took on a deliberately innocent look. 'No one, as far as I know,' he said, 'but if someone *did* say it was the case to your son, I am sure Christopher would spring to your defence.'

The man breathed out. 'Well yes, I suppose he would,' he conceded.

'Boys sometimes do get into scraps,' said Tom. 'It's soon forgotten. Shall we leave it at that?'

'Happen my lad shouldn't have repeated what I said in front of the boy,' granted the parent, clearly pacified. He knew, of course, that Tom must have heard that he was not above a bit of illegal activity himself.

'Your son is doing very well at school, by the way,' said Tom.

'Aye, he seems to like it,' mumbled the man. 'Well, I'll say good morning to you, Mr Dwyer.'

Mr Gaunt appeared from his study. 'Did you want to see me, Mr Pickles?' he asked the parent.

'No, thank you,' replied the man, striding for the door. 'It's been sorted.'

When Tom returned to his classroom, he saw that the children had stopped what they had been doing, which was precious little for they had been fascinated listening to the exchange which had taken place in the corridor. They stared expectantly at him.

'Well, I hope you've all finished the work I set,' said their teacher calmly.

After school Christopher stayed behind after the other children had gone. He looked shame-faced.

'I'm sorry about my dad, sir,' he told Tom. 'I didn't mean for him to come into school. I was dead embarrassed. He's got a real temper on him when he gets mad.'

'It's all sorted out now,' said Tom. 'No more name calling though and no more fights. All right?'

The boy nodded. 'Yes, sir.'

'Off you go,' Tom told him.

Christopher remained where he was.

'Was there something else?'

'Thanks for not telling my dad that it was me who told you about him and my uncle fishing for the trout.'

'That was a made-up account, wasn't it, Christopher?' said Tom, smiling and giving him a knowing look. 'I didn't think that it really happened.'

The boy smiled back and nodded. 'Yes, sir,' he said, 'it was made up.'

As was usual at the end of school, Tom tidied the classroom, marked the pupils' exercise books and prepared his lessons for the following day. It was getting on for six o' clock when he packed his briefcase and was ready to set off for home. Before doing so, he sat at his desk, leaned back and thought about the weeks he had been at the school and how his life had changed. It had been an eventful and on occasions exacting time, but Tom knew that he would stay. His initial reservations about taking on the post of teacher at such an isolated and insular school had disappeared. He had never felt quite as content. He genuinely liked his rather oddball colleagues and got on well with the headmaster. More importantly, Tom loved teaching and felt he was really making a difference in the lives of his pupils. The children were amusing, intriguing and conscientious, with the one exception – Colin Greenwood. The boy had remained resolutely distant and uncommunicative and did the minimum amount of work. He had not been rude or truculent since Tom's conversation with him during the first week of term with the threat that his father would hear about it if his behaviour did not improve, but the teacher's efforts to get him to join in the class activities, contribute in lessons and put more effort into his studies had largely fallen on stony ground. Colin was such a sad and solitary child. It was ironic that the subject of Tom's thoughts appeared at the classroom door at that very moment.

'Hello, Colin,' said Tom, as the boy hovered at the door. 'You should be getting on home at this time. Your father will be worried about you.'

'I wanted to see you,' said the boy diffidently.

'Well, come on in,' the teacher told him.

'It was what you said to Christopher Pickles's dad,' said the boy. He approached the teacher's desk charily. 'We all heard you.'

'Yes I thought you might have.'

'You stuck up for my dad.'

'Anyone would have done the same,' replied Tom.

'No, they wouldn't,' replied the boy firmly. 'Nobody around here sticks up for my dad. They don't think much of him and say he's a thief, but they don't know him.' The boy twisted his hands nervously. 'He's not been the same since my mam died. He's changed. He never used to be like this. My mam used to do all the paperwork, look after the house, pay the bills, help on the farm. We were happy before she died.' The boy fought back the tears. 'My dad's got bad-tempered and moody and he doesn't talk much any more, but he's not bad and he's not a crook, he just gets down about things. Of a night he just sits there. Sometimes he gets drunk. He's let the farm go. He doesn't seem bothered any more. It looks like we'll have to sell up like those at Durdeyfield Farm. I hope he does sell up because I hate it up there. It's dark and lonely and we can't keep on top of things. I don't want to be a farmer like my dad.' The boy's eyes were blurred with tears. He blinked them away.

'I don't know what to do,' he said quietly. 'I don't know what to do.'

Tom knew now why the boy had been so alarmed when he had told him that, if his conduct and attitude didn't improve, he would call at the farm to see his father. It wasn't because his father was violent and would have taken a strap to the boy. It was because Colin didn't want his father having to deal with yet another problem. As he looked at the pathetic figure of the tall, fat, moon-faced boy with the lank black hair and face wet with tears, he felt a surge of pity.

'Have you told your father how you feel, Colin?' asked Tom.

'No, I can't talk to him. He's got enough to worry about. He's dead low at the moment. I worry what he'll do.'

'I think you need to tell him how you feel,' said the teacher.

The boy shook his head emphatically. 'No, it won't do any good. There's nobody I can talk to.'

'There's me, Colin. You can talk to me. What you tell me won't go any further.'

'I know that,' he said quietly, 'but there's nothing you can do. It's just that I wanted to tell someone. I have to go.'

'And what about your drawings?' asked Tom.

'My drawings?'

'The school inspector said you have a talent. She said your sketches were excellent. You showed her your sketchbook.' Colin didn't answer. 'Why have you never shown me your drawings?' The boy shrugged. 'May I see them?'

Colin slid his hand into his pocket and produced a small, grubby notebook. He placed it on the teacher's desk. Then he headed for the door.

'Thanks for sticking up for my dad,' he said.

Tom called after him. 'Colin! Talk to your father.'

The caretaker, who had watched the boy run across the playground heading for home, arrived at the classroom door.

'Have you nearly done, Mr Dwyer?' he asked. 'It's just that I've got to lock up.'

'Yes, thank you, Bob. I'm all finished here.'

'I see you were talking to that Greenwood lad. In trouble again, was he?'

'No, he wasn't in any trouble.'

'You need to keep an eye on that one. He's bad news. Miss Cathcart had a right old time trying to get him to behave himself. He spent more time in the corridor or outside Mr Gaunt's room, than he did in the classroom.'

'Colin has a few problems,' Tom answered. 'He's not a happy boy and has a fair bit to put up with at home from what I hear.'

'Aye, I reckon he has. His father's a difficult bloke – bad-tempered, stroppy and a bit of a villain. Keeps himself to himself up at that farm. There's not many around here have a good word to say for Dick Greenwood.'

'So I gather,' said Tom.

'He hasn't always been like that,' the caretaker told him. 'He used to be a sociable sort of chap but after his wife died he changed. Flew off the handle at the slightest thing.'

'And what about Colin?' asked Tom. 'Has he always been difficult?'

'Well, no,' said Mr Leadbeater. 'I don't remember him being much trouble when he was little.'

'So his behaviour changed like his father's, when his mother died.'

'I suppose so but other kids who lose a parent don't carry on like him.'

'You know,' said Tom, 'it's only those who have lost a parent when they are young who really know how it feels. It has a massive impact on their lives.'

'Happen you're right,' said the caretaker. 'Anyway, if you've done in here, I need to lock up. I'm having to stay late to do all the cleaning. I've been going on and on about getting a part-time cleaner for weeks and I'm still without any help.'

'I might be able to help you there, Bob,' Tom told him.

'What, lend a hand with the cleaning?'

'No, find you a cleaner. Vicky Gosling's grandmother might be looking for a cleaning job. The girl told me she's finished working up at the hall. I gather she found putting up with the lady of the manor a bit too arduous.'

'I can believe that,' said the caretaker. 'She's too snooty by half is Lady Marcia. So you think Mrs Gosling might be looking for another cleaning job?'

'It's worth asking,' replied Tom.

'Right,' said the caretaker, the gloomy countenance disappearing. 'I'll have a word with Mr Gaunt first thing tomorrow. He can give her a ring.'

When Tom arrived back that evening, he found Dean Croft waiting for him outside the entrance to the King's Head.

'Could I 'ave a word wi' thee?' asked the boy.

'It's Dean, isn't it?' said Tom.

'Aye, that's reight.'

'Well, shall we go inside?'

'Nay, I don't want 'er to see me talkin' to thee.'

'Who?'

'Leanne. I'd like to talk to thee out 'ere.'

'All right,' said Tom. 'What can I do for you?'

'I wants to ask thee summat.' The boy scratched his head, looked down and considered what to say. 'I'm no good wi' words like thee.' He scratched his head again and then looked up. 'Does tha like Leanne?' he asked suddenly.

'Yes, I like Leanne,' answered Tom, rather taken aback. 'She's a very nice young woman.'

'But does tha really like 'er?'

'I'm not sure what you mean.'

'Are tha keen on 'er?'

'In what way?'

'Does tha fancy 'er, like?' asked the boy.

'Ah, I see,' said Tom. 'Well, no, I don't fancy Leanne. She's a very pleasant girl but—'

'An' there's nowt goin' on between thee an' 'er?'

'No, nothing is going on.' Tom tried to disguise his amusement and stifled a smile. Dean looked desperate, wringing his hands and breathing heavily. Here was a young man in love, he thought, and it was clear that the object of such ardour was the barmaid at the King's Head.

'An' thee 'as no intentions, like?' asked Dean.

'Intentions?'

'I mean tekkin 'er out and that.'

'No, I have no intentions in that direction,' Tom told him.

'An' yer don't fancy 'er?'

'No, Dean as I've already told you. I like Leanne. She's been very helpful and is good-natured and friendly but I don't fancy her.'

'She fancies thee,' said the boy sadly.

'Well, I'm afraid I can't help that,' replied Tom.

'Can yer put 'er reight then an' tell 'er that tha dunt fancy 'er?'

'That would be a bit difficult,' Tom told him.

'Tha sees, I'm dead keen on Leanne,' said the young man. 'Afore tha came, we was gerrin on pretty well, but now she's got no time fer me. All she does is talk abaat thee. She's fair smitten.'

'Look, Dean,' said Tom. 'I'll have a word with her.'

'And tell 'er that tha dunt fancy 'er?'

'I'll see what I can do,' he was told.

Leanne was at the bar when Tom entered the inn. She was wearing a bright yellow T-shirt, on the front of which was emblazoned in black letters: 'DON'T BE SHY! GIVE ME A TRY!'

'Hello,' she said, giving him a great smile. 'You're late back again. I was wondering where you'd got to.'

'Schoolwork,' Tom told her.

'There's more to life than schoolwork,' replied the girl. 'All work and no play and all that.'

'If you've a minute, Leanne,' said Tom, 'I'd like a word with you.'

'I was wanting to speak to you,' she said, leaning over the bar. 'There's a Young Farmers' barn dance on at the village hall on Saturday and I was wondering if you're up for it.'

Several of the locals turned their heads, listening in to the conversation.

'Could we sit over at a corner table?' asked Tom. 'It's more private there.'

'Yea, sure,' said the girl, moving from around the bar.

'Look, Leanne,' Tom began when they had both sat down, 'I wanted to make things clear regarding you and me.'

The girl smiled coyly.

'Now please don't take this the wrong way,' he continued. 'I like you. You're a very nice and attractive young woman and have made me feel very welcome.'

She beamed and her face coloured up. 'I like you too, Tom,' she replied. 'Since you've been here—'

'But that is as far as it goes,' he interrupted her. 'What I mean to say is that there can be nothing more than a friendship.'

'Oh.' The girl looked despondent. 'I see,' she said.

'I hope I haven't hurt your feelings,' said Tom. 'I just thought I needed to clear things up. I'm sorry, Leanne. I can see that you're upset.'

'Naw, I'm not really,' she murmured. 'Well, a bit I suppose. I should have known you wouldn't like me the way I like you.' She sighed. 'I suppose I was punching above my weight. Oh well. So you won't be coming to the Young Farmers' barn dance then?'

'No, I won't be coming to the dance but I know someone who would love to take you.'

'Who?'

'Dean Croft. He's very keen on you, you know.'

'Oh, him,' Leanne huffed. 'He's dead boring. All he talks about is sheep and tractors.'

'He's quite starry-eyed about you,' said Tom.

'How do you know?' she asked.

'Because he told me,' he answered. 'Give the lad a chance, Leanne. You might discover there's more than meets the eye when it comes to Dean.'

Mrs Mossup emerged from the parlour and caught sight of her daughter and the lodger at the corner table, heads close together and in earnest conversation.

'What are you two up to chattering away about?' she asked. 'You're like a couple of lovebirds.'

The Harvest Festival was one of the most popular and joyful occasions in Risingdale. That year the villagers had been particularly generous and brought to the church a great variety of fruit and vegetables which were displayed on the steps before the altar. Mr Pendlebury, surrounded by tubs of polished apples and pears, plums and damsons, by bright carrots, onions, shiny marrows and dusty potatoes, stood amongst the cornucopia beaming widely to see his church so full. He welcomed the congregation warmly and, following an overly long homily, introduced the pupils of the village school performing a small play on the theme of the harvest.

Five children under the direction of Miss Tranter took up their positions at the front of the rood screen. The first child wore a black smock, the second a brown, the third a blue, the fourth a yellow and the last, a mousy-faced girl with long brown plaits, was dressed in bright green.

'I am the little black seed planted in the dark brown earth,' said the first child, putting her hands together as if in prayer.

'I am the dark brown earth in which the little black seed is planted,' said the second, bending down to touch the ground.

'I am the fresh blue rain which falls upon the dark brown earth in which the little black seed is planted,' announced the third, tinkling his hands as if playing an invisible piano.

'I am the bright yellow sun which shines upon the dark brown earth in which the little black seed is planted,' said the fourth, making a great circle with her hands.

'And I am the strong green plant which has grown, oh so slowly, from the little black seed planted in the dark brown earth, watered by the fresh blue rain and warmed by the bright yellow sun,' declared the last child, stretching out her arms.

The children then held hands and recited: 'And in the world that God had made, in all the seeds of all the yesterdays are all the flowers and plants of all the tomorrows.'

On the way out of the church, Simon, who had watched the play with arms folded and a fixed and unimpressed expression on his heavily freckled face, remarked to his friend, 'I'll tell you what, George, some compost on top of that seed would make it grow a lot faster.'

'Aye, tha reight theer,' agreed the other boy, puffing out his cheeks. 'There's nowt like a bit o' 'orse muck to get things movin'.'

10

The Reverend Mr Pendlebury stood in the porch of St Mary's, surveying the churchyard. He shook his head sadly and sighed. It was not a pretty sight upon which he gazed: a row of tilted, cracked and fractured headstones, heavily coated in moss, broken granite crosses and weathered stone plaques. Dwarfing all the memorials was a huge and elaborate marble mausoleum clothed in thick ivy and surrounded by rusting iron railings. The vicar stared for a moment at the dead flowers arranged in jam jars and the faded plastic bouquets in chipped vases. The area around the churchyard was a mass of dark green clumps of saxifrage, waist-high nettles and choking thistles. Near the gate tangled briars and rampant brambles fought with wild buddleia bushes to gain advantage. The small square of exposed grass was full of molehills and scattered with dead leaves. Litter had been blown by the wind and gathered beneath the walls. The scene of neglect distressed him greatly. The churchyard had been untouched for years. He wished he could do something about it but he had not the funds to hire someone and was too old himself to be tackling such a jungle. When younger he had made an effort to keep the churchyard tidy but it had eventually got the better of him. He knew it would be a costly business and require a great deal of effort to keep the graves in good order, and his was a poor parish; despite his entreaty from the pulpit none of his elderly and dwindling congregation volunteered to help.

Mr Pendlebury loved this church. He had been the priest here since his ordination, first as the young curate, then as the vicar when old Canon Dr Bentley retired. He had no ambitions in the Church, to climb up the ecclesiastical ladder with all the trappings and responsibilities of a dean or an archdeacon. He even declined when asked to become a canon at the cathedral. When it was suggested by the bishop that he might move to a larger and more prosperous parish, he had refused. He was a country parson and wished to remain so. His vocation was to serve the small community and to hopefully make some difference to people's lives.

Sometimes, when the church was silent and empty, he would walk around inside, running a hand along the old, polished oak-panelled pews, his heels echoing on the ancient, glazed tiled floor. He would oftentimes stand in the Norman chancel looking up at the pale stone pillars or kneel before the massive altar slab, which was enclosed by an ornate, carved wooden rood screen which somehow had escaped destruction at the time of Cromwell. Some mornings he would stand, with dappled head and shoulders, beneath the fine perpendicular east window, which was filled with glass of subtle colours, singularly beautiful in the amount of light it allowed to flood through to light up the whole church. This too had miraculously escaped the malicious intentions of the iconoclasts. It was fortunate that Risingdale was so off the beaten track that it had escaped the attention of the vandals.

That morning as he stood in the porch, shaking his head and sighing, Mr Pendlebury caught sight of the very person to whom he wished to speak: the young teacher at the village school. Tom usually went for a run on Saturday mornings and at that moment he was sprinting in the direction of the church.

'Mr Dwyer,' called the vicar as Tom approached, 'might I have a word?'

Tom stopped in his tracks, rested his hand on the gate and got his breath.

'Mr Pendlebury,' he shouted back. 'What a wonderful morning.'

'Indeed,' agreed the cleric, coming to meet him. He raised his hands to the heavens. 'On such a glorious day as this, God is in His heaven and everything has such an absorbing interest and a most considerable charm.'

'What can I do for you?' asked Tom.

'It is what you have already done for me,' the vicar said, resting his hand on the gate. 'You have saved my church, Mr Dwyer. Had it not been for your swift and public-spirited action, St Mary Magdalene's would now be roofless. Not only have you saved my church but, without doubt, you have prevented other churches of being stripped of their lead. The police have been trying to catch the perpetrators for some time. I cannot tell you how grateful I am.'

'It is a lovely church,' said Tom, 'and it would be a great shame to see it fall into disrepair.'

'It would, most certainly,' said the vicar. 'St Mary Magdalene has an especial charm and a long history. Countless generations have worshipped here over the centuries.'

'Yes, it looks very old,' said Tom. He wished to be on his way but Mr Pendlebury now had a captive audience with whom he wished to share his enthusiasm.

'The Norman doorway in the nave has a rare ornamentation with chevron mouldings in a most lavish fashion and the chancel is Norman too,' expounded the vicar.

'Really,' replied Tom, glancing at his wristwatch.

'And the transept is Early English,' continued the clergyman, his voice becoming animated. 'The altar tomb of Sir Marmaduke D'Arbour on the north side of the chancel is unique and in a wonderful state of preservation. Its long inscription detailing the chief events in the illustrious life of the great man, who was considered one of the most eminent persons in the County in the reign of Henry VIII, is most impressive. Sir Marmaduke fought at Flodden Field and distinguished himself at the ripe old age of seventy. Would you credit it? Astonishingly his tomb, which must be numbered amongst the most well-preserved in the country, escaped terrible defacement by some of Cromwell's soldiers. They stabled their horses in the cathedral in Clayton you know. But Sir Marmaduke's effigy is most striking. Perhaps you might like to come in and view it.'

'Maybe another time, Mr Pendlebury,' replied Tom.

'Yes, of course,' said the vicar, 'I have delayed you too long.' His cheerful manner changed. 'But you are right, it would be a tragedy to see St Mary's close. You see we are under threat, Mr Dwyer. My congregation is small and declining and the upkeep of the building is so very high. Sadly, like many other small rural churches we are struggling to survive. I have an idea that the Archdeacon has his eye on St Mary Magdalene's for closure. Had the lead been taken from the roof that would have been the straw which would have broken the camel's back. The cost of repair would have been considerable.'

'Well, I am pleased to have been of help,' said Tom. 'Now I must be away.'

The vicar was not listening but looking at the overgrown churchyard. 'The Archdeacon will be visiting the church in the next couple of weeks,' he said. 'I can guess what he will say when he sees the state of this wilderness. It would take a small army to get it in shape.'

'A small army,' repeated Tom, a thought suddenly coming to him. 'Leave it with me, Mr Pendlebury,' he said. 'I have an idea.'

The vicar laughed. 'I imagine you don't have a small army at your disposal, Mr Dwyer,' he said.

'I think I might,' replied Tom, starting to run. 'I just think I might.'

The vicar had been right, thought Tom as he ran up the high street, heading for the open country. It was a glorious day; the air was fresh, the sky cloudless and a bright sun lit up the sweeping landscape. It being such a mild and sunny day, he decided to prolong his morning run and take a diversion. Leaving the village, he ran up a narrow path which snaked steeply uphill to the right of his usual route. He paused for a moment before tackling the hill, breathed in the fresh air and surveyed the swath of green rising to the fell, dotted with browsing sheep. Rabbits, cropping the grass at the edge of a nearby field, scurried away at the sight of the intruder, their white tails bobbing. A fat pheasant strutted along a craggy limestone wall and an inquisitive squirrel ran up the trunk of an ancient tree, then peered at him between the yellowing leaves. High above in a vast and dove-grey sky, the rooks screeched and circled.

When he had breasted the hill, Tom stopped to get his breath and then stood stock-still and stared in amazement. Before him rose the imposing ruin of a grand castle. The great rectangular space, enclosed by huge corner towers and half-destroyed walls, was now a stackyard for a farm. The southwest angle of one tower was in a good state of preservation, the lowest storey now used as a sheltering place for sheep. The floor was deep in straw under the sheltered walls which looked as if they would crumble and fall at any time. All was still and timeless. The silence was suddenly disturbed by the sound of the fluttering wings of pigeons which had been roosting in the top towers. Tom continued to stare at the ruin, imagining how it would have looked in bygone days. In his mind he swept away the hay and the rubble, the great heaps of fallen masonry overgrown with grass and pictured the grandeur of the fortress, its formidable walls towering over the landscape.

A farmer with a sheepdog at his heels observed him for a moment before approaching. He was a tall, handsome man of indeterminate age with a ruddy, weathered face and abundant black hair. He looked as if he had stepped out of a hot bath. His eyes were large and as deeply brown and shining as a calf's. He was dressed in a shapeless grey cardigan beneath an old waxed jacket and threadbare jeans which had been patched at the knees.

'Can I help you?' he asked. The collie gave a low rumble and showed a set of teeth. The farmer patted the dog's head. 'Quiet, Bess,' he said.

'I'm just looking at this amazing sight,' replied Tom, still staring up at the ruin. 'The last thing anyone would expect up here, away from everywhere, is a castle.'

''Appen it were amazin' in its day,' the farmer told him. 'Now it's just a crumblin', roofless shell.' He thought for moment. He pointed to an overgrown track. 'At one time t'main road passed by 'ere. Quite a busy thoroughfare it were, in its day. Now nobody comes up 'ere save for a few 'ikers an' ramblers and joggers such as thee.'

'It's twelfth century, isn't it?'

'Aye, so I've been telled,' said the farmer. 'Marston Castle. It were built by a gret Norman nobleman, Sir Guilbert D'Arbour. Owned all the land as far as t'eye can see. Came over with the Conqueror.'

'It must be his descendant's tomb is in the church,' said Tom. 'Sir Marmaduke D'Arbour.'

'Aye, it is. T'family lasted fer generations, right into t'last century, then t'line died out. T'castle's all what's left of 'is family and, like yon castle an' t'fancy tomb, they've all been forgotten. Such is life. Time is the big destroyer – how t'once gret an' powerful are brought daan an' soon become ancient 'istory.'

Tom, still staring at the remains of the castle, began to recite:

'Nothing beside remains. Round the decay
Of that colossal wreck, boundless and bare
The lone and level sands stretch far away.'

'It was a poem I learnt at school,' he explained, 'about the great pharaoh, Rameses II who had a huge stone statue built of himself and thought his great legacy would survive him, but, like all leaders and their empires, it disappeared into the dust, rather like Sir Marmaduke and his family.'

'By the sound of it, I reckon tha must be t'new teacher at t'school,' said the farmer.

'That's right,' answered Tom, holding out a hand. 'I'm Tom Dwyer.'

'Tha t'chap what gev young James Maladroit a good hiding.'

'You heard?'

'All t'village 'eard. Tha can't keep owt a secret 'round 'ere.' He shook the proffered hand.

'To put the record straight,' said Tom, 'I didn't give him a good hiding. I was defending myself and it was just the one punch.'

The farmer laughed. 'Fettled 'im though, from what I've 'eard. Anyroad, 'e 'ad 'ad it comin'. My name's Dick Greenwood by the way. My lad's Colin. 'E's talked about thee. I 'ope 'e's behavin' 'issen in thy class. 'E can be a bit of an 'andful. Led 'is last teacher a merry old dance.'

'Colin's no trouble,' Tom told the man. 'At first he was pretty uncooperative and moody and could be rude, but he's a lot better behaved now.'

'I'm glad to 'ear it,' said the farmer.

Tom considered what he should say next. Ought he to leave things at that or should he mention his concerns about the man's son. He decided on the latter. 'He's not a happy boy, Mr Greenwood,' he said at last. 'As I have said, Colin's behaviour has improved but he never laughs and rarely smiles. He doesn't mix much with the other children, he only manages to do the minimum amount of work in class and he takes little interest in what we do in lessons. I'm worried about him.'

Tom prepared himself for a sharp response, assuming that the parent would not take kindly to the criticism of his son from some interfering teacher and was therefore surprised by the man's calm reaction.

The father sighed. 'I know t'lad's not 'appy, Mester Dwyer. It's no life for a lad up 'ere. I can see that. It can get cowld an' windy an' bleak an' sometimes in winter we're cut off. I reckon I'm not much company for t'lad. There's nowt for 'im to do apart from 'elp on t'farm an' 'e's none too keen abaat doin' that. Course it were different when 'is mam were alive.' He looked thoughtful. 'Neither of us 'as been t'same since she was took.'

'It must have been very hard for you both,' said Tom.

'Still is, Mester Dwyer, still is,' said the farmer. 'Anyroad, for what it's worth, I'll 'ave a word wi' Colin an' tell 'im to pull 'is socks up.'

'No, I shouldn't do that Mr Greenwood,' said Tom. 'I don't think he would thank me for speaking to you about him.' He recalled the earlier conversation he had had with the man's son and how upset the boy had become when Tom had threatened to speak to the father. 'I guess any child losing his mother would hardly be very happy. Clearly, he's still grieving for the loss.' Tom could tell by the sorrowful expression on the man's face that the boy was not alone in that. 'I think we need to give it time. As I've said, I have seen some improvement in his attitude of late and I am sure, in time, things will get better. In fact his last piece of written work for me was not too bad at all. He wrote about your sheepdog.'

'Did 'e?' replied the farmer. 'What did 'e say?'

'How she had a rare gift of being able to detect sheep buried beneath the snow, how she could sniff them out.'

'She could do that, all right. Does tha know sometimes a ewe can be buried in a snowdrift for a couple o' days and come out none the worse for wear? Meg saved me many a sheep. Aye, she'll be missed.'

'I think with patience things might get better.'

'In what way?'

'I'm speaking of your son.'

'Aye well,' said the farmer, 'mebbe tha's right.'

'He has quite a talent, you know,' said Tom.

'Colin 'as?'

'Ask to see his artwork. It's really good.'

'I never knew 'e were any good at art. 'E's never said nowt to me,' said the farmer.

'Look at his sketchpad and then you'll see what I mean.'

'I'll do that, Mester Dwyer. It's been good talkin' to yer.' He held out a calloused hand, which Tom shook. 'Anyroad, tha should be on yer way.' He looked up at the sky. 'Don't be fooled by this spot o' mild weather. I reckon it'll not be long afore it gets clashy. That's wet and windy to thee, Mester Dwyer. Things 'ave a nasty 'abit of changing pretty quickly up 'ere. I reckon we're in for a drop o' rain.'

Tom set off running again. The man he had just met, he thought, was nothing like the one described to him, the bad-tempered bully and thief. He seemed a decent man and was clearly concerned about his son.

The sky remained clear, the temperature still mild and there was only a slight wind so Tom decided to continue his morning run. He should have heeded the farmer's advice, for unexpectedly the weather suddenly took a turn for the worse and the once friendly countryside began to take on a menacing aspect. Thickening storm clouds curled upwards from the horizon to cover the last frail traces of the blue sky, and a biting wind, which seemed to blow in every direction, suddenly materialised. A few minutes later, what began as a slight drizzle turned into a thin rain, then into a steady downpour which made the grass sodden and filled the paths with muddy puddles. Cold, hard and relentless water teemed down from the now pewter-grey sky full of dark lowering clouds. The storm moved straight in Tom's direction with perfect timing. There was a resounding crack of thunder, lightning forked the sky and the deluge continued to pummel down in earnest. Tom ran a hand through his wet hair and peered ahead as the rain lashed his face like a whip. He strained his eyes to make out the shape of the track ahead. It was a desolate, rain-soaked landscape before him without a rock or a tree for shelter. The hilly, winding path seemed endless. He could make out the netted walls of gleaming white, the bright green grass and long, dark coppices on the skyline, but not a sign of life save for the few sad, bedraggled sheep which observed him with mild interest. The strong smell of earth, peat and vegetation filled the air. Tom ran on, wet and muddy, skirting the puddles and tussocks of wild grass and leaping over the potholes until he came to the brow of the hill with the valley floor stretching below him.

'I reckon we're in for a drop of rain,' he said out loud, repeating Mr Greenwood's warning words. 'I'll give him a drop of bloody rain!'

After what seemed an age, soaking wet, dishevelled and exhausted, Tom staggered down the high street in the village. He sighed with relief at seeing the sign for the King's Head and made to cross the road. Just as he was about to step off the pavement, a large car raced around the corner and sped through a particularly deep puddle at the side of the road, cascading filthy water into the air and drenching him from head to foot. Tom caught sight of the person in the passenger seat. It was Janette Fairborn.

As he tottered through the public bar of the King's Head, leaving puddles on the floor, he found he was the object of some amusement from the regulars.

'Been swimming in t'beck?' asked one old farmer, chuckling and giving rise to a crack of laughter from his companions.

As Tom, grumbling and cursing to himself, headed for his room, he caught sight of Captain Cadwallader sitting at a corner table, nursing a glass and wearing the expression of a man awaiting his execution. He went over.

'Hello, Owen,' Tom said.

'Ah, dear boy,' said his colleague, looking up and smiling wanly. 'I was hoping I might catch you. My goodness, you're soaking wet. Whatever have you been doing in this dreadful weather?'

'Don't go there,' replied Tom. 'Suffice it to say I will take more notice in future of what the locals say about the climate up here.'

The captain looked ill at ease. 'I would appreciate a few words with you if it is not an inconvenient time,' he said.

'Let me get changed into some dry clothing,' Tom told him, 'and then we can sit down and have a chat.'

Ten minutes later the two teachers sat at a corner table, both with glasses of whiskey before them. Tom could see something was clearly distressing his colleague.

The captain took a sip of the drink. 'It's good of you to see me,' he said. 'I don't know who else to speak to about – well, about what has arisen. I can't speak to Bertha or Joyce and I don't feel able to discuss it with Mr Gaunt. He will find out soon enough. You did say that should I wish to talk about things that you would be willing to listen.'

'Something is clearly upsetting you,' said Tom, 'but I'm sure it can't be that bad.'

'Yes, dear boy, it is,' said the captain, shaking his head.

'Is it the inspection? Miss Tudor-Williams wasn't too hard on you. In fact she had some complimentary things to say about the lesson she observed.'

'No, no, it's not the inspection, well, not directly anyway. It has to do with the inspector though.'

'Miss Tudor-Williams? Whatever is it?' asked Tom.

'It won't be long before I'm found out,' said the captain, 'revealed for what I am and you know what this village is like for gossip. People who know me will feel so let down, many of them extremely angry no doubt.'

'Found out?' repeated Tom.

'Discovered, for the charlatan that I am.'

'You had better explain.'

The captain finished his whiskey in one great gulp. 'I feel like a drowning man seeing my whole life unfurl before me. I always had a feeling that things were too good to last, but in my wildest imagination I could not have conjured up the coincidence of meeting the sister of my former CO.'

Tom tried vainly to get a word in but his colleague continued speaking fast and furious.

'I feel like Christopher Columbus facing a wide and empty sea leading only to the very end of the world.'

'Owen,' said Tom firmly and quietly. 'What is wrong?'

'I'm not a bad person,' he said sadly. 'I know I ramble on and am not a very good teacher, perhaps regarded by some as a bit eccentric, but I am not a bad person. But I've done something very stupid, some would say unforgivable.'

'Go on.'

'When I came out of the army, I took a course at St John's College in Clayton. I was the only mature student as they termed it. All the others on the course were young, straight out of school. I suppose I became something of a father figure to some of them. My appearance, my demeanour, the way I dressed in my blazer and flannels, regimental tie and all that, amused the other students and they nicknamed me "the captain". I got to like the handle to be honest and played up to it. Then some of the lecturers began referring to me as Captain too. I got accustomed to it you see. I had seen the way officers gained so much respect and deference when I was in the army, the way they displayed such confidence and poise and when they spoke people listened. I can't say that many had bothered to listen to me before. It's been the story of my life really. My parents took little notice of me, the teachers certainly didn't. Girls I took out soon tired of me. I was undistinguished, inconsequential, boring, I suppose. That is until I went to college and was taken to be a former army officer. Suddenly I gained respect and people did listen. Anyway, I just went along with this charade. I invented all these stories about being in the thick of the fighting. You see it was a charade, Tom. I never was an army officer. I was in the Welch Regiment but I was a mere lance corporal in the pay corps. I never got beyond a desk.'

'I see.'

'I know I should have said something but I got so used to being a captain. I suppose I almost convinced myself after a time that I had been an officer. It was all a bit of an act. When the college sent my reference to Mr Gaunt, they used the title on the testimonial, assuming I had actually been a captain in the British Army.'

'And you didn't say anything.'

'No, I didn't say anything, which I regret, particularly now when it will come out that I am a fraud.'

'Why do you think it will be discovered now?' asked Tom.

'Miss Tudor-Williams will soon find out,' his colleague said. 'It was just my bad luck that her brother happened to be my commanding officer, and he is sure to remember me and then the cat will be out of the bag.'

'Not necessarily. He might not remember you.'

'Cadwallader is not a common name, is it? Anyway, the colonel was the sort of man never to forget a name or a face.'

'Well, I really don't know what to say,' said Tom. 'You have got yourself into a real fix.'

'I know. Everyone will think very badly of me,' said the former lance corporal.

'Probably they will think you a little foolish maybe,' said Tom, 'but it's not as if you have hurt anyone or done any real harm.'

'But my reputation will be in tatters,' he said. 'The duplicity, the disgrace. I will become something of a laughing stock. I also have an idea that impersonating an army officer is an offence. I think that the best course of action is for me to resign as a teacher at the school and move away to somewhere where I am not known.'

'And why do you think your pretence will be discovered now?' asked Tom. 'Miss Tudor-Williams has probably forgotten all about it and anyway, we are not likely to see her again.'

'Sadly, that is not the case,' said his colleague. 'I learnt from Mr Gaunt yesterday that she is to make a return visit next Monday to drop off a copy of her report on small schools. Of course, she will have spoken to her brother about me, and there is little doubt that my dishonesty has come to light. She is sure to raise the matter.'

'Yes, I guess she will,' murmured Tom.

'I could be in very serious trouble,' said the former lance corporal.

'Shall I tell you what I think,' said Tom. 'For what it's worth, I think you should wait and see what happens before doing anything impulsive. If this comes out then, of course, you need to decide what to do and maybe resignation could be considered, although I feel that's a bit drastic. For the present I feel you should leave things as they are but drop the captain bit. Tell everyone that you have decided that because it is a while since you were in the army, you now wish to be called Mr Cadwallader. I think also that you might stop the reminiscences about your time in the army. Now let's have another drink. I think it's your round.'

On the following Monday morning, former Lance Corporal Owen Cadwallader of the Welch Regiment waited in the staffroom in anxious anticipation for the arrival of his nemesis. He stood staring out of the window before the start of school, twisting his hands nervously behind his back. It was a cold, dreary day which reflected his mood.

'What is wrong with the captain this morning?' Mrs Golightly asked Miss Tranter in whispered tones. 'He's very jumpy.'

'It's probably the prospect of the imminent reappearance of Miss Double-Barrelled,' remarked Miss Tranter, examining a long red nail. 'School inspectors tend to have that effect upon some teachers, though in my own case I can't say that it bothers me. I'm afraid these HMI, swanning around the country poking their noses in, have little idea of what it's really like to stand day-after-day in front of children attempting to get them to learn, and they think bombarding us with snowstorms of paperwork is somehow helpful. They're a bunch of backseat drivers, nothing more.'

'I can't see why she is coming back, and so soon,' said Mrs Golightly.

'Because that is what they do, Bertha,' said Joyce. 'They don't leave you alone once you are on their radar. I was once told that school inspectors are like Rottweilers, the only difference being that Rottweilers, when they've attacked you, eventually let go.'

'Miss Tudor-Williams wasn't like that, Joyce,' said Mrs Golightly, coming to the HMI's defence. 'I think you're being very unkind to her. She was very nice and helpful.'

'Yes, but you've only seen her good side,' Joyce responded. 'I bet in that velvet glove of hers is a hand of iron.'

'Do you know what is wrong with the captain?' Mrs Golightly asked Tom, not really wishing to hear more of her other colleague's diatribe.

'No,' he replied disingenuously.

'Well, he's in a very strange mood,' said Mrs Golightly. 'Hardly said above two words since he's arrived and look at him now. He's a bag of nerves.'

'Do you mind not talking about me as if I were not here, Bertha,' said the subject of their interest tetchily, turning from the window.

'Are you not feeling well, Captain?' persisted Mrs Golightly in a motherly tone of voice.

'Yes, I am very well, thank you very much!' he snapped. 'Now could you refrain from talking about me?'

'You see what I mean,' said Mrs Golightly to no one in particular, 'a very strange mood.'

By lunchtime with no sign of the school inspector, Lance Corporal Cadwallader was feeling a little calmer and as it neared the end of the school day, he felt a great sense of relief, convincing himself that Miss Tudor-Williams would not be making an appearance at this time of day. He was soon enlightened when he saw her car pulling up outside.

'Oh, my goodness,' he sighed as he saw her climb out of her car.

'Captain Cadwallader,' said Mr Gaunt as he saw the teacher creeping out the school just then. 'A word please.'

'Ah yes, headmaster,' replied the former lance corporal.

'Would you come into my study please? Miss Tudor-Williams would like word with you.'

'With me?' he asked feebly.

'Yes, she has asked to speak to you in particular,' the headmaster told him.

As he followed Mr Gaunt into his study, the poor man's heart sank into his highly polished black shoes.

'Good afternoon,' said the HMI, giving a small smile when the teacher entered. 'I was hoping to have a word with you.'

'Oh yes?' He gave a watery smile.

'You will recall that I mentioned on my last visit that my brother was in the same regiment as you?'

'Yes, yes, indeed,' replied the former lance corporal, his face becoming flushed and his gullet rising and falling like a frog's.

'And, as I recall, you said you were a fellow officer.'

'Yes, I did.' He saw the void gaping below him. 'The thing is—'

'I mentioned you to my brother,' continued the HMI, cutting him off, 'and he said he had no recollection of a Captain Cadwallader. He did, however, seem to recall a lance corporal of that name.'

'Oh dear,' sighed the teacher.

'It is very sad,' said the HMI, 'and of course extremely upsetting.'

'I'm so sorry,' said the former lance corporal. He took a deep breath ready to face the retribution. 'Really, I am so very sorry.'

'Dementia, you see,' said Miss Tudor-Williams.

'I beg your pardon?'

'My brother suffers from the early stages of dementia, Captain Cadwallader,' said Miss Tudor-Williams. 'Only recently diagnosed. I have noticed that he had been getting confused of late, losing his car keys, not keeping appointments, forgetting names. My brother had such a sharp mind and very retentive memory; now, I am afraid, these seem to be disappearing. As I said, it is very sad. When I met you, I suggested that you might like to visit him and talk about old times, but it would be distressing, I guess, for you as well as for him.'

The teacher supressed a great feeling of relief and nodded sadly. 'And as I said, Miss Tudor-Williams, I am so very sorry.'

'A close shave, dear boy,' confided the former lance corporal the following morning when he caught up with Tom in the staffroom. He was in a particularly buoyant good-humour which expressed itself in a beaming smile and a friendly pat on the shoulder. He had taken Tom aside to relate the conversation he had had with the HMI. 'Of course it could have been very embarrassing,' he said cheerfully. 'Could have changed my life.'

'Indeed it could,' agreed Tom.

'Ah well, "all's well that ends well" as the bard will have it.'

'And when will you tell the others that you are now to be referred to as just Mr Cadwallader?' asked Tom.

'Dear boy,' said his colleague, patting Tom's arm. 'Do you think that is strictly necessary? The crisis, as it were, has passed.'

'Owen,' said Tom, 'you need to drop the "captain" and the sooner the better. That's the only honourable thing to do.'

'Yes, dear boy, I guess you are right,' he said.

'And Owen.'

'Yes?'

'Could you also drop the "dear boy"?'

II

The following day Tom asked the children in his class to put down their pens, sit up smartly and listen.

'Next Monday,' he told them, 'we are going to do a rural studies project.' The class was in fact to tidy up the churchyard for Mr Pendlebury, but Tom thought calling it a rural studies project sounded more educational and might give the activity greater credence with parents.

'I want you to come to school,' he continued, 'in some old clothes and shoes or wellingtons, and if possible bring along any trowels, small forks or spades that you may have at home.'

'I can bring my granddad's scythe,' said Christopher enthusiastically.

'And my dad has a billhook,' said David.

'Could I bring an 'atchet, sir?' asked George.

'I could bring my sheep shears,' said Carol.

'No, no,' said Tom quickly, 'nothing sharp. We don't want accidents.'

'I can use a scythe, sir,' said Christopher, sounding affronted. 'I use it all the time on our farm and I can drive a tractor.'

'An' I chop wood every week wi' an 'atchet,' George told him.

'And my granddad says I'm a dab hand with the sheep shears,' added Carol.

'Nevertheless,' said the teacher, 'trowels, small forks or spades will be quite sufficient. You might also bring along a pair of gardening gloves.'

'What are we going to do, sir?' asked Vicky.

'Wait and see,' replied Tom. 'It will be a bit of a surprise.'

Tom had explained earlier to Mr Gaunt what he had in mind and as he had predicted there had been no objection.

'Quite apart from making the churchyard look a whole lot better,' explained Tom, 'it's good practical education, gets the children out of school, teaches them about the environment, the flowers and plants and trees, and is excellent for community relations.'

The head teacher held up a hand. 'Tom, you really do not need to justify what you are going to do. I think it is an excellent idea. I wish I had thought of it myself. I would say, however, that you will find that the children know a whole lot more than you or I about the flora and fauna of the area.'

Mr Pendlebury could not have looked more surprised when he opened the vicarage door to discover a class of bright-eyed children armed with a range of implements and accompanied by their smiling teacher.

'It's that small army,' Tom told him.

All morning the children set to work collecting the litter, cutting and pruning, digging and planting bulbs, trimming hedges and raking up leaves. When Vicky and Simon, armed with wire brushes, cleaned the moss from the tombstones, they discovered the names of several of the village's forebears carved into the stone. There were Crofts and Olmeroydes, Sheepshankses and Goslings, Bannisters and Frobishers. Some of the lettering etched on the slate and limestone was short and simple: 'Remembered with love', 'Sleeping until eternity', 'Always loving, always loved'. In contrast was the long and elaborate inscription on the great marble tomb which described the distinguished life and outstanding merits of one Sir Marcus Maladroit, the first baronet. It was surmounted by a headless angel.

Tom crouched before the cracked and overgrown edifice, ran a finger along the gouged lettering and read the inscription:

> This memorial preserves for all time
> The image of a true English gentleman,
> Whose benevolence, directed by serene wisdom,
> Animated by the love of justice,
> Endeared by unwearied kindness,
> And graced by the most generous heart,
> Will be held in the county
> In undying remembrance.

Poor Sir Marcus, Tom thought. Few, if any, would remember him. He recalled the words of Mr Greenwood.

'Time is the big destroyer – how t'once gret an' powerful are brought daan an' soon become ancient 'istory.'

At the end of the morning, the vicar clapped his hands in delight on seeing the transformation of his churchyard.

'It's nothing short of miraculous!' he cried. He beamed with benign pleasure.

The following morning Mrs Pringle arrived at the school. She was a big-boned, shapeless woman with dyed blond hair, a set of double chins and immense hips. She stood before the secretary, clearly angry, her body held stiffly upright and her round face showing an aggrieved expression.

'Is he in?' she asked tersely.

'Is who in?' enquired Mrs Leadbeater, looking up from her desk and peering over the top of her unfashionable horn-rimmed spectacles.

'Headmaster.'

'Mr Gaunt is engaged at the moment,' the visitor was told.

'I'd like to see him. I want to complain about the new teacher.'

'You need to make an appointment.'

'I need to see him now!' snapped the woman.

'Please lower your voice,' the secretary told her. 'There is no need to shout.'

'Well, I need to see Mr Gaunt,' said the woman less stridently.

'What is your name?'

'Mrs Pringle. I'm David's mum.'

'Wait here,' the secretary told her like a teacher speaking to a naughty child. 'I shall see if the headmaster is available.'

She rose slowly from her desk, removed her glasses and placed them down carefully, tidied the papers on the top, smoothed the creases on her skirt and departed in no great hurry for Mr Gaunt's study.

Mr Leadbeater found the headmaster at his desk poring over a page in *The Sheep Breeders Monthly*. She explained that there was a very obstreperous parent in her office wanting to see him to complain about Tom. The headmaster buried the magazine under the pile of documents before him.

'Who is it?' he asked.

'A Mrs Pringle.'

'Show her in, Mrs Leadbeater,' said Mr Gaunt.

Over the years the headmaster, when dealing with antagonistic parents, had perfected the technique of greeting them in the most amiable way and appearing most attentive. He had found this a most effective way of overcoming any hostility. A moment later the parent was shown into the headmaster's study. Mr Gaunt rose from his chair and greeted her with a broad smile.

'Ah, Mrs Pringle,' he said, 'do come along in.' He gestured to a chair before sitting down himself behind his desk. The parent remained standing like some great Eastern statue with an indignant expression on her face.

'I've come—' she began.

'Such a mild morning for the time of year, isn't it?' remarked the headmaster. 'Now, I believe you wished to see me. Do sit down.'

The woman plonked herself in the hard wooden chair which creaked ominously under her weight.

'I've come—' she started again.

'Would you care for a cup of tea?' she was asked.

'No, I don't want a cup of tea,' she said. 'Thank you all the same.' The cheerful greeting from the headmaster had taken the wind out of her sails and she now looked mollified.

'What can I do for you, Mrs Pringle?' asked Mr Gaunt, resting his hands on the desk top.

'It's about our David,' she replied. 'He—'

'Ah, young David,' he interrupted. 'One of our star pupils.'

'He is?' She sounded surprised.

'Oh yes, your son is doing very well. I have noticed a real improvement in his work since Mr Dwyer joined the school. We are so lucky to have such a talented teacher.'

'Well, yes, David does seem to be getting on better this year,' the parent conceded.

'And he seems to enjoy school now. I recall you mentioning to Miss Cathcart when she was your son's teacher that he really didn't like school at all, and you were dissatisfied with the work he was set. I remember you came in to complain on that occasion and were minded to send him to another school.'

'Well, yes, David does like school now,' said the parent. 'I have to admit that and he gets on with the new teacher but—'

'So what is the problem?' asked Mr Gaunt, smiling like a hungry vampire about to sink his teeth into the neck of a victim.

'Well, he come home yesterday in a real state.'

'Oh dear,' said Mr Gaunt, sounding most sympathetic.

'His teacher got him and the other kids digging the vicar's garden. David was covered from head to foot in mud and his hands were filthy. He's also got a rash from the ivy and sting-ing nettles. I send him to school, Mr Gaunt, to learn his letters and his tables, not to go digging the vicar's garden.'

'Ah,' said the headmaster, still with the smile on his face. 'I fear you have got the wrong end of the stick, Mrs Pringle. Allow me to explain. It's not simply a question of digging the vicar's garden as you put it.'

'Well, it sounded like it to me,' said the parent.

'David's class was undertaking a rural studies project,' he explained. He recalled Tom's words. 'It's good practical education you see for the children to get out of school occa-sionally. It teaches them about care for the environment, to gain some knowledge about the flowers and plants and trees, quite apart from being excellent exercise in community rela-tions. Indeed on the recent visit of one of Her Majesty's school inspectors, our curriculum was highly commended and the work undertaken by Mr Dwyer's class was noted as most appropriate.'

'Yes, but David come home covered in mud.'

'Well, of course environmental education does involve chil-dren getting their hands dirty. In my experience boys in particular tend to get a bit grubby at times. I am sure you will agree. Of course if you strongly object to David being involved in future environmental projects of this sort, then I can keep him in school with some suitable work while all the other chil-dren get out and about.'

'Oh, I don't think he'd like that,' replied Mrs Pringle.

'No, I guess he wouldn't. He would feel left out, wouldn't he?'

The parent thought for moment. 'Well, if it's as you say, part of what they have to do in school then I suppose he'll have to do it.'

'Well, that seems to have been sorted out,' said the head-master, getting to his feet. 'Thank you for calling in, Mrs

Pringle. It's always a pleasure to meet a concerned parent. My door is always open.'

The woman rose from her chair and shook Mr Gaunt's hand. 'Well, thank you very much,' she said. She smiled. 'A star pupil, eh?' she murmured as she left.

'This morning, children,' said Tom, surveying the sea of expectant faces before him, 'Mr Pendlebury has come to speak to us. I want you all to sit up smartly and listen very carefully to what he has to say. Now I shall be taking Miss Tranter's class for games while the vicar speaks to you, so best behaviour please. He glanced in Colin's direction and was pleased to see that the habitual scowl was absent from the boy's face. Tom turned to the visitor and said sotto voce, 'You will be all right taking the class by yourself?'

'Oh, yes, yes,' replied the vicar. 'I shall be perfectly all right.' Though he felt the teacher's question was rather condescending, he smiled tolerantly and added, 'I do have a little experience talking to people, Mr Dwyer. I do it on Sundays, you know.'

'I'm sorry,' Tom replied, 'I must have sounded patronising. It's just that—'

'Not at all,' the vicar reassured him, holding up a hand as if to bless him. 'You run along. I shall be fine.'

When Tom had gone, Mr Pendlebury smiled and rubbed his hands together vigorously. 'Good morning, children,' he said brightly.

'Good morning, Mr Pendlebury,' chorused the children.

'You all did a wonderful job tidying up the churchyard. I am very, very grateful.'

'We liked doing it,' Vicky shouted out.

'I'm pleased to hear that,' replied the clergyman. 'Now, this morning, I'm going to talk to you today about a very special person.'

'The Queen,' announced Vicky smartly. 'My gran's got a biscuit tin with the Queen's head on the front.'

'No, no, it's not the Queen,' replied the vicar, smiling indulgently.

'Custard creams,' said the girl.

'I'm sorry?'

'They're my gran's favourite biscuits. She keeps them in the tin with the Queen's head on the front.'

'The special person, children, I am going to tell you about is not the Queen,' the vicar informed the class. 'It's St Francis.'

'My baby cousin's called Francis,' said Judith, jumping up and down as if bursting to go to the toilet. 'We call him Frankie. He was a right little tinker before he was born. My Auntie Norma said he was going to be the last baby she was going to have after all the trouble he caused.'

'That's very interesting,' began the vicar, 'but—'

'He was a breech birth,' continued the girl blithely.

'Dear me,' sighed the cleric. 'I was about to say that—'

'A breech birth is when a baby is born bottom first instead of head first,' explained the child. 'They can't get out you see.'

'Yes, I have heard that is the case,' started the vicar again, 'but—'

'Cows an' ewes can 'ave breech births,' George told him.

'You don't say,' said Mr Pendlebury, thinking it might have been better to have the teacher with him.

'Three of our sheep had breech births,' said Carol. 'My dad sent for me granddad. He's a dab hand at turning the lambs into a head-down position. He does it by applying pressure on its belly and sometimes getting his hand inside. It's a safe procedure although it can be a little uncomfortable. Course by the time labour begins,' continued the sheep expert, 'most lambs settle into a position that allows them to be born head first through the birth canal. That doesn't always happen, though.'

'My goodness,' said the vicar, 'you do know a great deal about sheep. Now, as I was saying—'

'We 'ad a breech calf once,' interrupted George. 'Tha sees, if t'vet can't turn t'calf, t'cow 'as a Caesarean Section. Mi dad let me watch when t'calf was pulled out.'

'Now this is all very fascinating, children,' said Mr Pendlebury loudly, and feeling under some pressure, 'but I want you all to listen.'

'It's not a pretty sight,' said the boy.

'What isn't?' asked the vicar.

'A Caesarean,' the boy told him.

The vicar heaved a sigh. 'Oh dear,' he said. 'This is all very interesting, children, but let's get back to St Francis.' He took a deep breath and decided to speed up his normal delivery to thwart any further interruptions about breech births and Caesarean sections. 'This morning I am going to tell you the story of St Francis. A long time ago, children,' he began, 'there was in Italy the village of Gubbio that had a great problem. A ferocious wolf was eating the livestock and attacking the people. Nothing the townsfolk did protected them from the wolf. Never had they seen such a fierce predator. It killed a shepherd, then the shepherd's brother and father when they went out to deal with this menace.

'The mayor decided to see if Francis of Assisi could help them. He had heard that this holy man could talk to animals and that God talked to him.

'Francis said he would help and listened as the mayor told him of the savage attacks of the wolf and how the people were very frightened. Francis went looking for the wolf and found the animal in the woods. When the creature saw Francis, it growled and showed a set of sharp teeth.

'"Come, Brother Wolf," said Francis. "I will not hurt you. Let us talk in peace." The wolf froze in mid-step. He had been about to eat the saint but something stopped him, and he pricked up his long grey ears and listened. "Why did you kill the livestock and the people?" asked Francis.

'The wolf told him all he wanted to do was to eat. He was sorry for the pain he had caused, but he was hungry. What could he do?

'Francis asked the wolf if the townsfolk fed him would he stop killing the people and their livestock. The wolf agreed and, placing his paw in Francis's hand, walked back with him to Gubbio. And from then on the people of the village fed the wolf and it became their friend. And that is the legend of St Francis. Wasn't that a lovely story, children?' asked the vicar.

There was not a sound in the classroom. The children who had been bubbling with comments now sat in silence. None raised a hand or asked a question; the children just stared with puzzled looks on their faces.

'You see, children,' continued Mr Pendlebury, 'there is a lesson for us all in that tale. Could anyone tell me what it is?' He was hoping that his listeners might have grasped the message that we should love our enemies.

His question was met with complete silence.

The vicar turned to a large, round-faced boy.

'What about you, young man?' he asked.

George pushed back the black curls from his face and shook his head like a wise old man. 'I don't know owt abaat any lesson, but I'll tell thee what, vicar,' he said, 'if some wolf started to tek mi granddad's sheep, 'e'd shoot t'bugger, never mind talkin' to it.'

'So how did the lesson go, Mr Pendlebury?' asked Tom at morning break, as he sat with the clergyman in the staffroom.

'Oh pretty well, you know,' replied the vicar, nursing a mug of coffee.

'So what did you talk to them about?' asked Miss Tranter.

'I was telling the children about St Francis the patron saint of animals,' he replied.

Mr Cadwallader, who had recently, much to his colleagues' surprise, shed his title of 'captain', huffed. 'There's nothing you can tell the children in this school about animals, Mr Pendlebury,' he said.

'No,' agreed Mrs Golightly, looking up from her knitting. 'You get them talking about animals and there's no stopping them.'

So I discovered, thought the cleric. 'You see next Sunday is the Feast of St Francis of Assisi. I am holding a special service at St Mary's to celebrate the saint's day. I have asked the children to bring to church animals for me to bless.'

'Oh dear,' said Mr Cadwallader. 'Not a good idea, vicar, if you ask me.'

'You think not?'

'You never know what they'll turn up with. You could have a church full of pigs and sheep and hens clucking all over the place.'

'And horses,' added Mrs Golightly. 'I wouldn't be surprised to see a cow galloping down the aisle.'

'Could be like Old Macdonald's Farm,' said Mr Cadwallader.

'Oh dear,' sighed the vicar. 'Perhaps it was a little imprudent of me to suggest bringing animals into the church. I was thinking more of rabbits and hamsters, a dog and a cat.'

'Don't worry, Mr Pendlebury,' Tom told him, patting the vicar's arm and laughing. 'I'll tell the children only to bring small pets to the church. You will not be overrun by a flock of sheep, a herd of cows or a drove of pigs.'

'A what of pigs?' asked Miss Tranter.

'A drove,' Tom told her. 'It's the collective noun for pigs or so I was told by one of my pupils. You know it's surprising what knowledge the children have when it comes to animals. They never cease to amaze me.'

'Indeed,' agreed the vicar, nodding sagely. 'Indeed.'

*   *   *

Tom arrived at his classroom on Monday morning to find a small, plump woman wearing a pink nylon overall over a red and white gingham frock which reminded him of the table-cloth in his aunt's house. She was singing to herself as she vigorously polished his desk. The room smelled of lavender furniture polish.

'Hello,' he said, approaching her.

'Oo, you made me jump!' cried the woman, turning around sharply.

'I'm sorry,' said Tom. 'I didn't mean to startle you.'

'I was miles away.' She folded her duster. 'You must be Mr Dwyer,' she said.

'That's right.'

'I'm Mrs Gosling, the new assistant caretaker. Vicky's granny. I've been giving your room a good going-over. Mind you, there wasn't much to do in here, unlike the room next door. It'll take me twice as long to fettle that one.'

'I'm pleased to meet you, Mrs Gosling,' said Tom. 'I know that Mr Leadbeater will be delighted that he's got some help. He's been trying to clean the school single-handedly since the last cleaner left.'

'Well, he's not made a very good job of it, that's all I can say,' she stated. 'Dust everywhere, dirty windows and unwiped surfaces. I found mouse droppings in the staffroom.'

Tom wondered what she would have made of the place prior to the school inspector's visit. The school now was a whole lot cleaner and tidier than it had been. Here was a woman with very high standards.

'And I would like to point out, Mr Dwyer,' said Mrs Gosling, 'that I am the assistant caretaker and not just a cleaner.'

The woman clearly did not mince her words. Tom was amused by her undiplomatic comments. For someone who had just started at the school she seemed particularly forthright.

'Well, I'm sure that now you are here, you'll soon have the school shipshape.'

'It's you I have to thank for getting me the job,' declared the assistant caretaker.

'I doubt that,' said Tom.

'Oh, yes. Our Vicky said she mentioned to you what happened up at the big house with Lady M accusing me of pinching some of her jewellery.' Her face took on an expression of scorn. 'As God's my judge I never touched it. I wouldn't be seen dead in some of the things she wore. Looked like a walking Christmas tree she did when she got dolled-up. All fur coat and no knickers, that's Lady M and as hard and proud as a piecrust. Flew off of the handle when she found her necklace missing and threw accusations in my direction, right, left and centre, like there was no tomorrow. She'll have a hard job getting anyone as hard-working as me, I can tell you that. I scoured and scrubbed, dusted and swept that big place of hers and little thanks did I get. Anyway, I gather you mentioned to Mr Gaunt that I might be interested in a job at the school and he got in touch. I'm going to be much happier up here.'

Tom wondered whether Mr Leadbeater might be much happier having to manage Mrs Gosling and how his colleagues would cope with this formidable presence. She appeared a force to be reckoned with.

'I gather Lady Maladroit is not the easiest of people to get along with,' he said.

'Easy!' huffed the assistant caretaker. 'That's putting it mildly. She's about as easy as a bag full of vipers. I was going to finish there anyway. I couldn't put up with her any more and that useless son of hers. You did the village a service I can tell you when you flattened that young pup. He wanted knocking down a peg or two.'

'I didn't actually flatten him,' explained Tom. 'It was just one punch.'

'Someone should have done it a long time ago. It was well overdue. Thinks he's the bee's knees, and of course for Lady M, he can do no wrong. Sun shines out of his proverbial. Sir Hedley is nice enough, a real gentleman, one of the old school, but his wife and son, they're something else.'

'I'll let you finish here,' said Tom, keen to be away.

'Our Vicky loves it in your class,' said Mrs Gosling before Tom could leave.

'She's doing very nicely,' he replied. 'She's a lively and interesting girl and contributes well in class.'

'Oh, I don't doubt it,' agreed the assistant caretaker. 'She's never been backward in coming forward. Vicky's always had a lot to say for herself. She could talk the hind legs off a donkey.'

'Yes, well—' began Tom.

'Vicky didn't get on with her last teacher,' said Mrs Gosling. 'Poor Miss Cathcart. I'm afraid she wasn't up to dealing with children. They played her up something dreadful so my granddaughter said. You heard what happened to her, I suppose?'

'Yes, I did,' replied Tom. 'It was very sad.'

'Chucked herself in the river. Some said it was an accident but I don't believe that myself. I think that things got too much for her.' She lowered her voice conspiratorially. 'Between you, me and the gatepost, I think she had a bit of a drink problem – and her being a strict Methodist as well. Suicide, that's what I think. They found her floating with the current. As grey as a ghost she was when they pulled her out.' She screwed up her face. 'Some creature or other had been at the body, so Mrs Frobisher who works for the undertaker told me. She was in a dreadful state.'

'Oh dear,' sighed Tom.

'She wasn't a happy woman, Miss Cathcart,' the assistant caretaker went on, shaking her head sadly. 'If you saw her in the village, you'd think she had all the weight of the world on her shoulders. She walked about with this tragic expression on her face. Do you know—'

'I really must get on, Mrs Gosling,' Tom told her. 'Thank you for making my room look so neat and tidy.'

'Pleasure, I'm sure,' she said.

As he headed for the staffroom, Tom thought to himself, I can see where Vicky gets the gift of the gab from.

'A shambles,' announced Mrs Golightly later that day. She was telling her colleagues at break about the service to celebrate the feast day of St Francis. 'I could have predicted it would end in chaos.'

'Never work with animals and small children,' added Joyce. 'The combination is like a time bomb.'

Tom laughed. 'Oh, come on you two,' he said, 'it wasn't that bad.'

'It was bad enough,' retorted Mrs Golightly. 'I have never seen the like in a church or anywhere else for that matter. The smell, not to mention the noise. It will be a long time before Mr Pendlebury decides to do anything like that again. A shambles, that's what it was.'

The service at St Mary's had certainly not been without incident. The children, bubbling with excitement, arrived at the church with a veritable menagerie: various breeds of dog and cat, rabbits, gerbils, hamsters, guinea pigs, mice, tortoises and fish. George brought his pet snake along. The building was full of noisy and restless creatures and noisy and restless children. Simon sat on the front pew gently stroking his ferret, a lithe, sandy-coloured, pointed-faced creature with small bright-black eyes. Next to him the twins, Holly and Hazel, held a small tank of goldfish, eyed hungrily by Marjorie's Siamese cat. Judith nursed on her lap a large, flop-eared rabbit which shivered at the sight of the fierce-looking ferret. Carol had come with her grandfather's sheepdog, an alert, eager-eyed collie which sat obediently at her feet.

Prayers were said, hymns sung, blessings given and all was going well. Then Christopher arrived with his goat. Unwisely, the vicar gestured to the boy to bring his pet down to the front. Christopher, pulling the animal on a long piece of rope, headed in the direction of the altar. Goats are known to be very intelligent and curious creatures and can be stubborn and bad-tempered. In particular they like to explore anything unfamiliar which they come across. Another characteristic of the goat is it will eat almost anything. Having poked its nose into corners and under pews and nuzzled some of the children, the goat took a liking to Mrs Golightly's handbag, which it grabbed with its long yellow teeth and began munching furiously. After much tugging, it let go on catching sight of something tastier – the hymn books. Having nibbled a few of these, it clomped noisily down the aisle on its cloven hooves and began chewing the lacy edges of the altar cloth. The vicar attempted to gently urge the animal to desist and was rewarded by a sharp butt to his legs. At this point Tom came to the rescue and with some force pulled on the rope and took the creature outside, where it began happily munching the grass in the churchyard. Thankfully, things then proceeded without any further mishaps. Excited chatter and laughter filled the church and the children sang the hymn 'All things bright and beautiful, all creatures great and small' with lusty voices.

Later in his study, Mr Pendlebury, rubbing his bruised legs, reflected on the service. It had been a good idea at the time, he thought, but he was sure that even the saintly Francis, patron saint of animals, would have found the service something of an ordeal.

'Could you give me a hand please, Tom?'

Mrs Golightly poked her head around the classroom door.

'Yes, of course, Bertha,' he replied, getting up from his desk and going to join her. 'How can I be of help?'

As usual Tom had been the first to arrive at the school that morning. It was his custom to get there just after eight to prepare his lessons for the day and mark the children's exercise books. He was glad to get out of the King's Head early to avoid the breakfast and the glowering face of Mr Butt. Also Mrs Mossup had not been that friendly lately. When Tom had told her that he was to buy Roselea Cottage in the village and move out over the half-term holiday, she was none too pleased, despite his effusive assurances that everything she had provided for him was more than satisfactory. Leanne had also been less sociable and her sulky face and sharp tongue had drawn comments from the regulars.

'I've just a few boxes in the car with one or two things for the church jumble sale next Saturday,' Mrs Golightly informed Tom. 'I'd be really grateful if you could bring them in for me. Mr Pendlebury's calling into school tomorrow to collect them.'

Tom found that Mrs Golightly's small car was loaded down with a number of large cardboard boxes which were full to bursting.

'One or two things,' he exclaimed, laughing. 'There's half your house contents here.'

'There is rather a lot,' agreed Mrs Golightly, 'but there's just no room in the flat I'll be moving into, so I'm getting rid of it. It's amazing what one accumulates over the years. In those boxes are three full tea-services, countless plates and mugs, table lamps and ornaments, cutlery and pans. I've been quite ruthless. Anyway, it will all go to a good cause. Before they leave have a rootle through them. I'm sure there will be some things you want, for when you move into the cottage.'

Tom had paid a visit to another bank in Clayton and, with the deposit loaned to him by Mr Gaunt, he had secured a mortgage and bought Roselea.

Soon after he had hauled in the boxes and put them in a line which stretched the full length of the corridor, Mrs

Gosling appeared, mop in one hand and a bucket in the other.

'What's all this rubbish doing here?' she asked Mrs Golightly.

'It's not rubbish,' she was told sharply. 'It's some bits and bobs for the church jumble sale.'

'Well, I've just swabbed that floor.'

'It can't be helped,' said the teacher. 'The boxes won't be staying here long. They are to be collected.'

'I hope they won't be here long,' said the assistant care-taker. 'Oh, and while you're here, Mrs G, would you tell the kiddies in your class to tidy up after themselves? It looked as if a bomb's hit your classroom this morning. I mean it doesn't take much effort for them to put all the toys away and tidy the books on the shelf. Oh, and will you tell them not to be messy in the sand and water trays and put the tops on the paint tubs. I mean I've only got one pair of hands.'

'I shall endeavour to do so,' replied the teacher, biting her lip. 'Now if you will excuse me, I have things to do.' She made a hasty retreat to the staffroom but Mrs Gosling had the last word.

'Don't we all, Mrs G?' she shouted after her. She then followed Tom into his classroom.

'Have you heard anything unusual coming from up there in the loft?' She pointed with her mop to the ceiling.

'Now you mention it, Mrs Gosling, yes, I have,' replied Tom. 'It's a sort of scraping and scratching. I think maybe a bird or a bat might have got trapped up there. I was going to mention it to Mr Leadbeater.'

'It's not a bird or a bat,' the assistant caretaker told him. 'It's a rat.'

'A rat!' exclaimed Tom.

'Oh yes,' said the cleaner. 'I can tell a rat when I hear it. We had them at Marston Towers. Sometimes I could hear them running over the attic ceilings and scuttling in the outbuildings. It's the devil's own job to get rid of them. They're clever creatures are rats. They get wise to the traps laid down for them and are immune to the poison. I'm not going up there.

'The caretaker will have to sort it out, if he can frame himself. I've told him about the mice in the staffroom. When he manages to get around to it, he's going to put some traps down. Of course, if you teachers didn't leave biscuit crumbs all over the place, we wouldn't have rodents running riot in the school.'

'You think there might be more than one rat up there?' asked Tom.

'Oh, yes. There's likely a whole nest of them. They breed like nobody's business. Well, I can't stand here gassing all day. I've got Mr Gaunt's study to do.'

When Tom entered the staffroom, he heard Mrs Golightly in full flow, complaining about Mrs Gosling.

'Anybody would think she runs the school the way she's carrying on,' said the teacher angrily. 'I'm sick and tired of her telling me what I should or shouldn't do. I'll tell you this, if I find out who recommended her to Mr Gaunt, I'll have a few well-chosen words to say to that person.'

Tom remained in prudent silence.

'Mr Gaunt will have to have a word with her,' said Joyce. 'Last week she told me that in her considered opinion, it was a waste of time doing drama, that the children would be better occupied reading and writing and doing arithmetic. The woman is a cleaner, for goodness' sake, not some educational expert. She's there to polish, scrub floors, dust shelves, clean toilets and not dictate what goes on in my classroom.'

'Actually, she likes to be styled assistant caretaker,' said Tom mischievously.

'What!' cried Joyce.

'For goodness' sake,' said Mrs Golightly. 'Now she's putting on airs and graces.'

'She threw out the children's models of a Norman castle they had spent a great deal of time making,' said Mr Cadwallader. 'She said she thought it was rubbish.' He crunched a biscuit noisily, leaving crumbs on the floor.

Tom was minded to tell his colleague what Mrs Gosling had said to him earlier about the mice and the biscuit crumbs but thought better of it.

'She's just complained about my boxes in the corridor,' said Mrs Golightly.

'What's in them?' asked Owen.

'Cutlery and crockery and one or two other things I've no longer any use for,' she replied. 'I've told Tom to have a look through all the stuff before they're collected and take what he wants. He'll need a few things when he moves.'

'What about the furniture?' asked Owen.

'Oh, I'll be selling most of that,' said Mrs Golightly. 'A nice, good-looking young man from Smith, Skerrit and Sampson, the auction house in Clayton, came out to see me and is dealing with the sale. He was very helpful was Mr Neville. He suggested that I don't put my things into auction.'

'Why?' asked Tom.

'He said I would be better selling the things privately, in which case I would avoid paying the seller's commission to the auction house.'

'Not necessarily,' said Tom. 'I mean you don't know the value of the pieces you wish to sell. You wouldn't know what to ask.'

'Oh, Mr Neville's doing all the valuations for me. He's going to do an inventory and coming out to see me next Saturday week to make me an offer for my things.'

'*He's* going to buy them?' asked Tom.

'Well, yes,' replied Mrs Golightly. 'Is there something wrong with that?'

'I don't think that is strictly ethical,' said Mr Cadwallader.

'Why do you say that?'

'Because the chappie might be a rogue and a fraudster,' he said. 'Might offer you an amount way below the price your articles could fetch at auction.'

'Oh no, Owen, he seemed such a nice young man,' she told him.

'But he works for the auction house,' said Tom. 'I wonder if his employer is aware of this arrangement? I mean he's doing the company for which he works out of its commission.'

'It smacks of sharp practice to me, Bertha,' said Owen.

'Do you think I should cancel his appointment then?' she asked.

'No,' said Tom. 'Why don't I come out to your cottage Saturday week and see what sort of offer he makes?'

12

Later that week Tom was in the school office giving Mrs Leadbeater the receipts for the strips and boots he had purchased for the school football team, when he heard voices coming from the headmaster's study.

The school secretary placed a finger over her lips.

'Shush,' she said, dropping her voice. 'I want to hear this. Mr Gaunt's got that education officer he dislikes in with him. I reckon there'll be fireworks.'

'I'll come back,' said Tom, placing the receipts on the desk.

'You should stay and listen,' she said. 'It should be good.'

'No, I'll not bother,' he replied, feeling uncomfortable about listening in to a private conversation. The secretary had no such qualms and put her head to the door which connected Mr Gaunt's study and the school office.

'I'll call back,' Tom told her before leaving the office.

Had he known the reason for the visit of the education officer and heard his name mentioned, he would have been sorely tempted to stay and eavesdrop with Mrs Leadbeater.

Just after lunch Mr Nettles, the education officer from County Hall, had arrived unannounced. Mr Gaunt was particularly ill-disposed to surprise visitors from the Education Department appearing at the school, and there was one person he did not wish to entertain and this was the man in question.

The headmaster had discovered that Mr Nettles was an elusive and ineffectual man. On the recent occasions when he had telephoned the Education Office at County Hall, to see if a cleaner for the school had been found, Mr Gaunt had been informed by the snappish clerical assistant that 'Mr Nettles is tied up at the moment. He'll get back to you.' Of course, he never did. Such was the ineffectiveness of the man that he had been moved from department to department in the Education service and in each position he had proved to be inept.

Mr Nettles was a tubby man with thick blond hair sticking up from his head like tufts of dry grass. He wore small steel-rimmed spectacles, which were usually perched on the end of his nose. His chinless face was pasty and drawn.

That afternoon he breezed into the headmaster's study with a cheery 'Good morning' and a broad smile.

Mr Gaunt looked up from his desk with a lugubrious expression on his face.

'Was I expecting you?' he asked.

'No,' replied the visitor.

'I thought not. It would have been courteous if you had made an appointment to see me. I could have been tied up this afternoon.' He used the phrase advisedly.

'Ah,' said Mr Nettles. 'Of course, under normal circumstances I would have, but this is a matter of some import. I considered it judicious to expedite it speedily.'

The education officer was not a man to use a simple word when a more arcane one was at his disposal. In attempting to appear erudite, it made him sound rather shallow and silly.

'A matter of some import,' repeated Mr Gaunt, 'which needs expediting. Perhaps the matter concerns finding me a cleaner.'

'I'm sorry?'

'I take it you are responding to the several messages I left at your office regarding my request for a cleaner, messages to which you have not replied.'

'Yes, yes, Mr Gaunt, I do appreciate that you wished to speak to me, but it has been a very busy time and I did have many pressing matters to deal with.'

'Tied up.'

'I'm sorry?'

'You have been tied up, I suppose.'

'Indeed.'

'Well, I am sorry that you have had a wasted journey, but I have found a cleaner so you have no need to trouble yourself further. The matter is expedited.'

'Oh, I can assure you I did endeavour to procure a cleaner for you,' said Mr Nettles defensively. 'However, it is so isolated up here that I was unable to prevail upon anyone willing to make the journey. But I am not here vis-à-vis the cleaner. I am here on a very serious matter.'

'Well, you better sit down and tell me what this very serious matter is,' Mr Gaunt told him, leaning back in his chair. He assumed an air of indifference which concealed his true feelings of annoyance. Of course, he knew very well what had occasioned the visit – namely Lady Maladroit's complaint about Mr Dwyer. He had known it wouldn't take long for someone at the Education Office to get in touch.

Mr Nettles sat down on the hard wooden chair facing Mr Gaunt's desk and placed his briefcase on his lap. He removed his small steel-rimmed spectacles, blew on the glass, slowly wiped them with a handkerchief and placed them back on his nose. He cleared his throat as if he were to begin to deliver a lecture.

'We have received a letter of complaint at the Education Office,' he said. 'It concerns one of the teachers at this school.'

'Oh yes,' said Mr Gaunt coolly.

'A Mr Dwyer. I believe he has been newly appointed.'

'And?'

'Well, I felt that you ought to be acquainted with the nature of this complaint.'

'And you have come all the way out here to tell me that. There is such a thing as a telephone.'

'It is quite a strongly worded letter from a very influential person, and I felt I needed to speak to you and the teacher concerned personally.'

'And tell me,' said Mr Gaunt, 'if this letter of complaint had not come from a very influential person, as you put it, would you have made this visit?'

'Possibly not,' replied Mr Nettles. He was surprised by the headmaster's apparent indifference.

'One law for the rich and powerful,' remarked Mr Gaunt, 'and one for the hoi polloi, eh?'

The education officer decided not to respond to this. 'I felt you should peruse the letter and ask Mr Dwyer to join us to discuss it, and for me to explain to him that teachers need to be very careful to conduct themselves properly in public and not to bring the school where they are employed and indeed the Education Department into disrepute by their actions.'

'And why do you think Mr Dwyer has brought the school and the Education Department into disrepute by his actions and requires this advice?' asked Mr Gaunt.

The education officer opened his briefcase and produced a large sheet of cream-coloured paper, at the top of which was an elaborate coloured crest.

'Perhaps you might like to examine the letter,' he said, sliding the sheet of paper across the desk.

'No thank you,' replied the headmaster, sliding the letter back.

'I beg your pardon?' said Mr Nettles.

'I do not wish to see the letter.'

'It says that Mr Dwyer assaulted the complainant's son in a public house.'

'Does it really?'

'I must say, Mr Gaunt,' said the education officer, 'that I am very surprised by your lack of concern over such a serious matter as this. The letter is from Lady Maladroit, a woman of some standing. Her husband Sir Hedley, is Chairman of Governors at the grammar school, a Deputy Lord Lieutenant and President of—'

'Let me stop you there, Mr Nettles,' interrupted the headmaster. 'I know who the lady is and of her spurious allegation. She wasted no time in telephoning me about the incident.'

'Oh, I wasn't aware of that,' answered Mr Nettles. 'Then you will know of her complaint that her son was assaulted.'

'Yes, I was aware of the incident in the King's Head and of her erroneous accusation.'

'It says in the letter—' began Mr Nettles.

'Was she there?' asked Mr Gaunt.

'Pardon?'

'Was Lady Maladroit present when this supposed assault took place?'

'If I may—' began Mr Nettles.

Mr Gaunt cut him off. 'She was not and was merely repeating her son's bogus version of what took place.'

'I see that, but—' Mr Nettles began again.

'However,' Mr Gaunt carried on, ignoring him, 'there were people who *were* present and who witnessed the incident: the young woman serving behind the bar, two hikers, some farmers and my caretaker, Mr Leadbeater, and they have given their accounts to the police. I take it you have not spoken to the police?'

'Well, no,' replied Mr Nettles lamely. He shifted uncomfortably in his seat.

'Then perhaps you should do so and they will tell you that they have investigated the accusation thoroughly and have exonerated Mr Dwyer of any blame. Indeed they concluded that the aggressor was the Maladroit son and that Mr Dwyer was acting in self-defence and suggested that he might consider pressing charges against his assailant. Now, I suggest you put the letter back in your briefcase, reply to Lady Maladroit appropriately to acquaint her of this and be on your way. Of course, I guess she already knows this since the police will no doubt have been in touch with her since she wrote the letter.'

'Yes,' replied Mr Nettles, looking crestfallen. 'I shall do that.'

'And had you rung me up, you would have saved yourself the journey and not wasted my time and yours,' Mr Gaunt told him.

Mr Nettles stuffed the letter in his briefcase and got up to go.

'Oh and you might to take this with you,' said the headmaster, plucking a piece of paper from the pile on his desk. 'It's your questionnaire on dog dirt.'

'Apropos that,' replied Mr Nettles, 'we in the Education Department feel it is imperative to ascertain the extent of dog excrement on school playing fields because it is a mounting concern. Indeed the World Health Organisation concludes that it is as toxic to the ecosystem as chemicals and oil spills, an environmental pollutant which is a bona fide health hazard.'

'Well, it doesn't apply to us,' stated the headmaster.

'Forgive me, Mr Gaunt, but it applies to all schools.'

'Even those like ours which don't have a playing field?' asked Mr Gaunt.

Mrs Leadbeater smiled as she watched Mr Nettles making his hasty exit from the school and in so doing treading in a large cowpat near the gate.

'I think we have a rat in the loft above my room,' Tom told Mr Leadbeater later that day.

'Aye, I know. Mrs Gosling's been bending my ear.' He sighed. 'That woman spits words out like a Gatling gun fires bullets. She never stops to draw breath. I can never get a word in. I tell you, Mr Dwyer, she's a mixed blessing is that woman. I mean I've no complaints about the way she cleans the place. She's the best cleaner I've had. Goes through the classrooms like a dose of salts, but she's a law unto herself. I just let her get on with it and keep out of her way.'

'So what do we do about it?' asked Tom.

'About Mrs Gosling?'

'About the rat.'

'I've been on to the Education Office to get someone to get in touch with pest control and I've got nowhere. The lass at the end of the phone said the chap who deals with it was tied up and I've been waiting for his call. I reckon I'll have to sort it out myself. Mind you, I'm not going up there. I'll be seeing Toby Croft in the King's Head tomorrow night, and I'll get him to come and put a trap down. Course he can't use poison what with kids about.'

On the Monday, Mr Leadbeater explained that he had not managed to see Mr Croft at the weekend but he had things in hand. He then scurried off at the sight of Mrs Gosling heading in his direction.

That morning Tom heard the scratching again.

'Can you hear that, sir?' asked Simon.

'Yes, I can,' replied Tom. 'Just ignore it and get on with your work.'

'What is it, sir?' asked Carol.

'It's probably a bird,' Tom told her. 'I'm sure it will find its way out.'

He didn't wish to alarm the children by telling them it was a rat.

'It's not a bird, sir,' piped up Vicky. 'It's a rat. My gran told me when she came for Sunday dinner.'

'Thank you, Vicky,' said Tom. 'All right, children, put your pens down and look this way. I think it maybe is a rat. I didn't want to frighten you but it is likely we have a rat in the loft. It's nothing to worry your heads about. Someone is coming to get rid of it.'

As he looked at the faces before him, no child looked in the least bit frightened or worried; in fact, they looked interested. Of course, Tom was dealing with largely farming children who would have some experience of rodents. This soon became evident to the teacher for the class suddenly became animated.

'On a television programme, sir,' announced Angela, 'it said there's seventy million rats in this country and over six billion on the planet and we are never more than fifteen feet away from one.'

The children looked up at the ceiling where the scratching could clearly be heard.

'We 'ave rats on our farm in t'barns,' said George. 'They're very clever. Did tha know rats' teeth are 'arder than aluminium or copper? They can gnaw through cables, climb brickwork, get into cavity walls an' swim up toilet U-bends. We've got three feral cats which live in t'barn an' they're allus bringin' 'em into t'kitchen an' droppin' 'em on t'floor. Once a rat got in t'house an' my mam 'ad to flatten it wi' a frying pan.'

'Our Jack Russell catches rats,' said Hazel. 'He bites their heads off.'

'Rats carry fleas which spread diseases,' Charlie shared with the class. 'They feed off the rat, sucking its blood, and then pass on the rat's disease to people. That's how the Black Death started.'

'Well, thank you for that, children,' said Tom, hoping that that might put an end to the discussion on rats.

'On this television programme,' announced Angela, 'it said that rats have sex twenty times a day and have babies every four weeks.'

'Oh dear,' sighed Tom. What had he started, he thought.

Vicky waved her hand in the air like a daffodil in a strong wind. 'Mr Dwyer,' she shouted out, 'could we do a project on rats? They sound really interesting.'

After the lesson Simon approached the teacher's desk.

'You don't need to bother getting anyone out to get the rat, sir,' he told Tom. 'I'll bring my ferret in tomorrow. He'll get the little bugger.' He slapped his hand over his mouth. 'Sorry, sir, I meant he'll get—'

'All right, Simon, I get the message. I'm not sure though that you should bring your ferret into school.'

'It'll be no bother. I'll pop him up in the loft and he'll get it in no time at all.'

The following day Simon arrived with his ferret. Tom, having been told by the caretaker that he had had no luck in getting Mr Croft to come up to the school to deal with the rat, decided to let Simon have a go with his pet. The boy had arrived that morning with the ferret in his schoolbag.

The children were fascinated as Simon produced the long, sandy-coloured, pointed-faced creature with small bright-black eyes. He held the animal under its chest, his thumb below one leg, and, using the other hand, he gently stroked the creature down the full length of its body.

'You have to know how to handle them,' said the boy. 'If she gets frightened she might sink her teeth into you. Does anyone want to hold her?'

There was a collective shaking of heads.

Tom placed a stepladder beneath the hatch to the loft and told Simon to be very careful as he climbed up. The children gathered around.

'It's right exciting this, isn't it, sir?' said Vicky.

Simon lifted the hatch and put the ferret inside the loft. Then he closed the hatch.

'Best to leave her in the dark for a bit,' he said.

The children tried to get on with their work but kept looking up at the ceiling. All was quiet and then suddenly there was a scraping and scratching, a frantic scurrying and squealing, and all was silent again.

'She's got it,' announced Simon with a great smile spread over his face.

He climbed back up the ladder and retrieved the ferret, which he held gently to his chest. He then descended. In his other hand he held the dead rat by its tail.

The children cheered.

'Crikey, that's a big one,' said Vicky, who like the other children was not at all fased by the sight of the fat black rodent.

'Well done, Simon,' said Tom, pulling a face as he viewed the dead creature.

'What shall I do with the rat, sir?' asked the boy.

'Just put it outside,' Tom told him. 'I'll dispose of it later.'

The vicar, walking into school that morning to take the assembly, passed a boy in the corridor whistling to himself and holding a dead rat by the tail.

'Morning, vicar,' said Simon. 'Lovely day, isn't it?'

The following Saturday morning Mr Jeremy Neville of Smith, Skerrit and Sampson Auction House arrived promptly at ten o'clock at Roselea Cottage. The handsome young man with the dark brown eyes and high cheekbones and dressed in a fashionable grey suit, looked astonished to see Tom sitting on the sofa, his legs crossed and a cup of coffee in his hand. Tom was equally surprised to recognise Mr Neville – the pal of James Maladroit and boyfriend of Janette Fairborn.

'Do come along in, Mr Neville,' said Mrs Golightly cheerfully, ushering her visitor into the sitting room. 'This is Mr Dwyer. He teaches at Risingdale School with me and has recently bought my cottage.'

'Yes, we have met,' said the man coldly. He shook a lock of hair from his face.

'Good morning,' said Tom breezily. He was going to enjoy this.

'Mr Dwyer happened to call in and I've asked him to stay,' explained Mrs Golightly. 'I'm sure you don't mind. As I mentioned to you when you called before, Mr Neville, I don't intend taking a lot of the heavy old furniture with me as my new flat is too small to accommodate very much.'

'Perhaps I should come back at a more convenient time,' said Mr Neville, giving Tom a black look.

'Oh no,' said Mrs Golightly. 'I'm very keen to get things sorted.' She pointed to the folder clutched to the visitor's chest. 'I guess that is your inventory?'

'It is,' he replied, 'but I really think I should call back.'

'Would you care for a cup of coffee, Mr Neville?' asked Mrs Golightly, ignoring his suggestion.

'Thank you, no,' he replied. His face was a picture of annoyance.

'Well, do sit down,' he was told.

Mr Neville perched on the edge of an armchair, opposite Tom, the folder resting on his lap. He looked uncomfortable.

'Do start,' said Mrs Golightly, sitting opposite him. 'I'm keen to know what everything is worth.'

Her visitor opened the folder. He cleared his throat as if to give a lecture. 'Well,' he said, 'as I mentioned when I visited to look at the items you wish to sell, there is not much call for heavy oak furniture, dark wood sideboards and hard-backed chairs these days.'

'These are Windsor chairs, aren't they?' remarked Tom.

'Yes, possibly.' He gave Tom a bland, patronising look.

'An aunt of mine has one very similar. Eighteenth century, I think. Made of yew. I thought they were quite valuable.'

'Yes, they could very well be if, in fact, they are original. These are most likely reproductions. One can usually tell by the shape and by the grain. The small chest of drawers is an attractive piece but—'

'It's called a Davenport, isn't it?' asked Tom, with a cultivated innocence in his voice.

'Some would call it that, yes,' said Mr Neville. An angry red rash appeared on his neck. 'And has your aunt got one of these as well?'

'No,' replied Tom, 'but I believe they too can be valuable.'

'If they are original but this, in my opinion, is a Victorian reproduction,' he argued shrilly.

'I suppose you can tell by the shape and the grain,' said Tom nonchalantly. 'Actually it looks a lot older than Victorian to me.'

'Tell me,' said Mr Neville, a supercilious look in his face, 'are you an expert in antiques?'

'Oh no,' replied Tom.

'Well, I am. Might I ask what exactly is your interest in this? Mrs Golightly has asked *me* to deal with the sale of her possessions.'

'I'm a friend,' said Tom, 'but I do know a little bit about furniture. My father was a carpenter and did restoration work. If the Windsor chairs and the Davenport are original pieces, they would be worth quite a tidy sum, wouldn't they?'

Mr Neville snapped shut his folder and addressed Mrs Golightly. 'I really do not appreciate my judgements on your furniture being questioned in this way,' he told her, 'so I suggest you put your things into auction.'

'I was going to do that in the first place,' she replied, 'until you said you would make me an offer.'

Mr Neville got up. 'I think I should go,' he said.

'I wonder,' said Tom, as the man made for the door, 'is it the usual practice for the employee of an action house to offer to buy things privately?'

'Why don't you mind your own bloody business!' shouted the man and hurriedly left the room.

'Not quite the nice young man I thought he was,' observed Mrs Golightly.

Tom, on his way to the staffroom at afternoon break the following week, was stopped by Mr Gaunt. The headmaster asked him to step into his study.

'Sit down, Tom,' said Mr Gaunt.

The headmaster had received a disturbing letter from the Education Department that morning, stating that there was the likelihood that more of the small rural schools in the county would be closing in the new year. He – Mr Gaunt – had the uncomfortable feeling that Risingdale might be on the hit list. He felt concerned about what would happen to the teachers but more particularly about Tom if the school were to close. The young man had only just been appointed and might very well, like his colleagues, lose his job or be redeployed to the other side of the county – and he had just bought a cottage in the village. Of course, Mrs Golightly and Mr Cadwallader would no doubt be offered early retirement, as he would, if they didn't wish to be redeployed, and Miss Tranter would have little difficulty in finding another post. It was Mr Dwyer he was worried about. Mr Gaunt was unaware that Tom had been sounded out for another job – back at the school where he had trained. Had the head-master known this, he might very well have advised Tom to apply since things at Risingdale were uncertain. Mrs Stirling, head teacher of Barton-with-Urebank School, who was on maternity leave, had rung Tom the week before saying that a permanent post would be coming up the following term and she would welcome an application from him. Tom had told her that it was good of her to consider him, but he was happy and settled at his new school and had no intention of leaving. She had reminded him of the rumours she had heard at County Hall that Risingdale might have been earmarked for closure and that he should think of his career. Tom, however, had remained adamant. He wanted to stay where he was.

'Is there something wrong?' asked Tom now.

'No, no,' the headmaster reassured him. 'I just thought we'd have a chat and see how things are going.'

'Things are going very well,' replied Tom, 'I think.'

'Good, I'm glad to hear it.' The headmaster leaned back in his chair. 'I guess there's not a great deal for a young and ambitious young man to do in Risingdale,' he said. 'You are probably finding life up here rather parochial and a bit dull.'

'No,' replied Tom. 'I like it.'

'It has to be said that Risingdale has not really moved with the times,' explained Mr Gaunt. 'Over the years, of course, some parts of our way of life have changed. Modern communication, for example, has altered things but we still have the squire, the landowners and the labourers, the vicar, the church and the chapel, the country inn, and of course our school much as it had been a century ago. We have very few incomers or visitors because we are so isolated. The road up to Risingdale goes nowhere else. I suppose eventually village life will be a thing of the past, as indeed will people like me who wish to preserve it.' He thought here of the depressing letter from County Hall which he had received that morning. He knew that closing the small rural schools like his was a way of killing off rural values, something of which those at County Hall had no real understanding. 'Of course, if you do decide to move on, if a post arises in a larger and more challenging school, I will give you a very good reference.'

'Mr Gaunt,' said Tom, getting increasingly worried by the tenor of the conversation, 'I thought you were happy with my work?'

'Good gracious, no! I mean yes, I am very happy with your work. You have made a real impact since you have been in the school. You get on with the staff, the children like you and are working hard and I am very satisfied with your teaching and how you have fitted in here. I just wanted to say that if something better comes up, I shall not stand in your way.'

'I really like it here,' Tom told him, 'and I want to stay. I wouldn't have wanted to buy the cottage if I had a mind to move on.'

'That's good to know,' said Mr Gaunt.

'I'm just about getting used to life in Risingdale,' Tom said. 'Mr Pendlebury once told me that the people are friendly when they get to know you, although I have to say they do like to know your business. News travels fast in the village. You can't keep anything a secret.'

'That's very true,' agreed the headmaster. 'People in the Dale are a very close and curious lot and there is not an awful lot of excitement in their lives. They know more about each other than if they lived cheek by jowl in a block of high-rise flats in the city. You see, they have lived and worked here for generations and many, like Toby Croft, Ernie Sheepshanks, John Fairborn and Richard Greenwood, are descended from long-established farming families. It is a fact that everyone and everything is a source of great interest to them. Speaking of Richard Greenwood, by the way, how is that son of his getting on? Still keeping his nose clean, is he?'

'Well, Colin doesn't put a great deal of effort into his work,' replied Tom, 'but there has been some improvement and he's behaving himself. I know he can be rude and troublesome at times but I feel sorry for the boy. He looks so miserable, he has no friends in the school and I've never seen him smile. I think he has a pretty lonely life living way up the Dale.'

'Yes, Colin is a sad case,' said Mr Gaunt. 'His father's not the easiest man to get on with. He's certainly not liked in the village. He can be very argumentative when he's got a drink inside him. I reckon he's pretty hard on the boy.'

'I've met his father,' Tom told him.

'Have you?'

'I was out for a run and passed his farm.'

'He didn't set his dogs on you then?'

'No, he was very friendly actually. I think perhaps he's been misjudged. He seemed to me a pleasant enough sort of man but like Colin he's just very unhappy. I gather that he was different when his wife was alive.'

'Ah yes, her death did affect him greatly,' said the headmaster. 'She was a lovely woman.'

'Do you think that might be at the root of Colin's problems?' asked Tom. 'Losing one's mother at such a young age must have affected him.'

Tom thought for a moment of his own mother who had died when he was fourteen. He had gone through a bad patch then – moody, short-tempered, angry at God for taking her from him.

'Yes, you are probably right,' agreed Mr Gaunt. 'I have to say though, Tom, that the boy was extremely difficult when Miss Cathcart took the class. She was at her wit's end trying to deal with him. He spent more time outside my study than he did in his classroom. I am pleased he seems to be behaving now, but keep a sharp eye on him.'

'They say that Miss Cathcart took her own life,' said Tom.

'Ah yes, that is what people say,' answered Mr Gaunt. He thought for moment. 'I pray it was an accident. With hindsight I think I could have given her more support. Sadly, she was not a good teacher. Perhaps I should have encouraged her to resign, but then again, I think if I had suggested that it would have devastated her. You see she had nothing much else in her life.'

Following the teacher's death, Mr Gaunt realised he could have done more. He felt a real sense of guilt that he had failed to grasp the nettle and tell Miss Cathcart to accept she was not up to the job and to persuade her to resign. She clearly did not enjoy teaching, parents were complaining and the children in her class were receiving a poor standard of education. But at heart he was a kindly man and felt a great deal of sympathy for the woman. He knew how distressed she would be if he told her she needed to go and yet, if he had, she might still be alive.

'Speaking of Colin,' said Tom, wishing to change the subject, 'I've discovered the boy has quite a talent for drawing. He doesn't seem to have much success in anything else he does in school but his sketches are excellent. Miss Tudor-Williams suggested that encouraging his artwork might be the way of getting through to him.'

'Let's hope so,' said Mr Gaunt. 'I gather young Carol has been giving you an education in sheep farming.' He smiled. 'She was telling me she was giving you a few tips on how to recognise champion tups and yows. Do you know that girl knows more about sheep than most of the farmers in the Dale? I have a small flock myself and if I want any advice, I send for her. If you meet her grandfather, you will find that he has only two topics of conversation: the weather and sheep.'

'Carol's a different kettle of fish altogether from Colin,' answered Tom. 'There's always a smile on her face. I couldn't wish for a better pupil. She is such a good-humoured and helpful girl and you are right, I certainly know a lot more about sheep since I met that young lady.'

'Now tell me, how is young Charlie Lister getting along?' asked Mr Gaunt.

'I've decided to put him in for the grammar school scholarship,' said Tom. 'I've spoken to Charlie and he seems keen, and I had a word with his mother and she has no objections.'

'You've spoken to Mrs Lister, have you?' asked the headmaster. He sounded surprised.

'Yes, I called at her cottage. I've also written to the parents of the pupils in my class asking if any are interested in their children sitting the eleven-plus exam and six have replied positively.'

'You've been very busy in the short time you have been with us,' said Mr Gaunt. 'Don't overdo things, Tom. You need to slow down. There is more to life than school, you know. Take a well-deserved rest over half-term.'

'I'm afraid I'll have little chance of that,' replied the teacher. 'I'm helping Mrs Golightly move into her flat and then will be moving into my new home.'

'So soon?'

'Yes. Contracts have been exchanged, the mortgage from the bank has been agreed and the money you loaned me has come through. I am so grateful for your help. I couldn't have bought the cottage if—'

'Please don't mention it,' cut in the headmaster. 'Well, I think I hear the bell and must let you get back to your classroom. I'm glad we have had this little chat. My door is always open if you want to see me about anything.'

Tom's liking for Mr Gaunt had grown into a genuine affection. He wasn't the dynamic and innovative head teacher of Barton-with-Urebank but he was kindly, generous and supportive. His spirited defence of Tom when the education officer had called (related to him in some detail by Mrs Leadbeater) had impressed and cheered Tom greatly. No, he thought to himself as he walked down the corridor with something of a spring in his step, he was here at Risingdale to stay.

13

On the Monday morning of the half-term holiday, Tom helped Mrs Golightly move into her new flat in the village. It was a small, modern apartment in the same block as Miss Tranter's and overlooked the high street.

The removal van arrived in the morning to take the furniture and effects Mrs Golightly wished to keep: the dining table and four balloon-backed chairs, the sideboard and Welsh dresser, but since the flat could not accommodate any more of her things, she made Tom a gift of a wardrobe and a chest of drawers and included in the sale of the cottage the curtains and carpets. She had approached another auction house to sell the remaining furniture, including the Davenport and Windsor chairs, which turned out to be original pieces and realised a very good price.

'You'll miss the cottage,' said Tom, when he had finished carrying various boxes up the stairs and they were sitting having a coffee.

'Yes and no,' replied Mrs Golightly. 'I shall miss the view of course but the place wanted a lot doing to it and I couldn't manage the garden any more. I shall certainly not miss the journey to school in the bad weather. The flat is much more convenient.' She was thoughtful for a moment. 'You know I was born in the cottage, as were my mother and father and my grandparents. I have many happy memories. I'm just pleased that Roselea has gone to someone who will look after it and appreciate it.'

On the Tuesday, Tom went into Clayton and bought a bed, dining table and chairs, a cooker and a washer, all to be delivered the following Saturday when he intended to move into the cottage. While he was there he called in to see his Aunt Bridget who gave him some towels and linen and then he called into the presbytery at St Bede's to collect an old leather armchair Father Daly had no further use for.

On the Wednesday, Tom made a start at tackling the garden, which had been neglected over the years. In the shed, which smelled of dust and damp and was draped in cobwebs, he had found a spade, a sieve, a rake and a trowel amidst the jumble of junk – broken chairs, packets of slug pellets, a green rubber hosepipe, tins of rusty screws, plastic buckets, seed boxes, cracked plant pots and an old hurricane lamp. He stood on the rutted, tussocky lawn with its bare patches and molehills, deciding where to start. The trees with their long, overhanging branches and clumps of wind-bent thorn and hazel needed pruning, the high hedges and towering laurels trimming, the dead flowers cutting down and the borders, which were clogged with tangled grass and matted weeds, digging over. The first job he had to do, he thought, was to cut back the climbing rose bush that had grown rampant around the cottage door. He had just started clipping when he heard the garden gate click and a moment later Toby Croft ambled down the path to join him, a cigarette between his lips. He was accompanied by his sheepdog, a bright-eyed collie.

The farmer was dressed in the same working clothes he had worn when Tom had first met him: long-sleeved, collarless shirt, shabby waistcoat and threadbare corduroy trousers held up by a piece of baler twine. On his head sat a greasy brown flat cap. In place of the ancient wellingtons, he now sported a pair of black leather boots which had seen better days.

'I see that tha bought yon cottage then,' said the farmer,

after sucking on the cigarette. He stretched his throat from his shirt and scratched it.

'News travels fast, Mr Croft,' replied Tom.

'Folk were talkin' abaat it in t'King's 'Ead last neet. Arnold Olmeroyde waint be best pleased when 'e 'ears.'

'And who might Arnold Olmeroyde be?' enquired Tom.

'Bloke what 'as 'ad 'is eye on it fer donkey's years. 'E's been after gerrin Missis Golightly to sell it to 'im an' hoffered 'er a fair amount. 'E 'as a farm'ouse an' t'fields at t'back of yer. 'E wanted that cottage fer 'is son. I tell thee, 'e waint tek it too kindly 'er sellin' it to thee.'

'Well, I'm sorry to disappoint him,' said Tom, mentally adding another person to the list of those he had upset.

'I reckon tha got it at a good price, an' all,' remarked the farmer, fishing for information.

Tom was certainly not going to reveal what he had paid for the cottage, knowing that it would be spread around the village like wildfire. He tapped his nose and winked.

'Course, there's a bit wants doing to it,' said Mr Croft.

'Yes, I appreciate that,' agreed Tom. 'As you can see, I'm making a start on the garden.'

'Tha wants to go steady choppin' back them roses. They want dead 'eadin' at this time o' year not cuttin' back. Back-endish is not best time to do that. Tha wants to wait till spring to prune 'em. I'll send our Dean down to lop off a few of them branches on yon oak tree an' cut yer 'edges back. 'E'll fettle tha moles an' all – put some traps down. I'll drop off a load o' manure when I'm passin'.'

'That's very good of you, Mr Croft,' said Tom. 'How is Dean?'

'Bloody nightmare,' the farmer told him. 'Can't sit still. 'E's as fidgety as a bee in a bottle.'

'Oh dear.'

''E's frettin' ovver that big lass in t'King's 'Ead, moonin' abaat like some love-sick schoolboy. She wants nowt to do wi' 'im. I've telled 'im, lass's not interested. Mind you, I can't see what 'e sees in 'er, missen. She's been in a reight old mood lately. That Leanne could cut tin wi' that tongue of 'ers. Bit mi 'ead off last neet in t'pub.'

Tom had also seen a change in Leanne of late. He had found she was no longer the cheerful, good-humoured girl, always ready to chat or share a joke with the customers. At one moment, she was irritable and offhand and at other times, withdrawn and preoccupied.

'Well, I had better get on,' Tom told the farmer.

'Aye, I've got things to do,' replied Mr Croft. 'It's a busy time o' year fer me is October. Mi beeasts want dippin' to stop 'em gerrin sheep scab an' lice, then they want gatherin' an' sortin' out an' I tek them what I want rid of to t'auction. Aye, it's a busy time all reight.'

'Well, thank you for the offer of help, Mr Croft,' said Tom. 'I'm very grateful.'

'Don't mention it,' replied the farmer. 'I shan't charge thee ovvermuch to lop off them branches and cut yer 'edges an' sooart out yer moles an' mi manure comes at a very reasonable price.'

Tom shook his head and smiled. 'Thank you, Mr Croft,' he replied. He was reminded of the Yorkshire motto told to him when he had first come to live in 'God's Own Country':

'Ear all, see all, say nowt;
Eyt all, sup all, pay nowt;
And if ivver tha does owt fer nowt –
Allus do it fer thissen

It was later that morning that Tom, looking up from his digging, caught sight of a figure standing at the gate, watching him.

'Hello, Colin,' he shouted.

'Hello, Mr Dwyer,' replied the boy. He had his sketchbook under his arm.

'Where are you off to this morning?'

'I'm going to draw the old barn at Bentley Beck.'

'Come through,' Tom told him. 'I was wanting to have a word with you. Let's sit over here on the bench.'

'Am I in trouble?' asked Colin, walking down the path.

'No, you are not in trouble. What made you think that?'

'Dunno.'

'Well, you are not in any trouble. Come along, sit down. I want you to do me a favour.'

The boy sat on the bench and looked at the teacher, a serious expression on his face. One of these days, thought Tom, the lad might actually smile.

'I'm not being in the football team,' he said firmly.

'No, it's not that but I do think you should come along to the practices,' Tom told him.

'I don't want to.'

'Well, you might change your mind. Anyway, this favour involves you doing a painting for me. I've just bought this cottage. It used to belong to Mrs Golightly and has been in her family for a long time. I am sure that she will miss living here, so I want to give her something to remind her of where she grew up and used to live. I should like to give her a present because she has been very kind to me, and I can't think of anything better than a painting of the cottage. I was wondering if you might do a picture of it for me and I could give it to her. Would you do that?'

'Me?' There was an expression of frowning surprise on his face.

'Yes, you. You're the best artist in the class. You have a real talent.'

'I reckon I could,' said the boy.

'It would be a commission for which you would be paid. I wouldn't expect you to do it for nothing.'

'I don't want any money,' Colin told him. 'I'd like to do it. I'll have a go next weekend.'

'That's splendid,' said Tom, getting up. Colin remained seated.

'You met my dad,' said the boy.

'Yes, I did. We had a very interesting conversation. I didn't know you had a castle in your back garden.'

'It's an old ruin,' said Colin. 'Just a pile of old stones.'

Tom sat down again next to the boy. 'It's a ruin now,' he said, 'but just think what it was like in its heyday – knights in shining armour, battles and sieges, banquets and jousting. It excites me just to think about what it used to be like.'

The boy looked uninterested.

'You never told my dad about the fight I was in,' he said suddenly.

'No, I didn't,' answered Tom. 'There was no need to tell him. It's best forgotten.'

'I'm glad you didn't tell him.'

'Would he have been angry with you?'

'No, but he's had a lot on his mind lately. I didn't want to give him anything else to worry about.'

'I see.'

'My dad liked you,' mumbled the boy.

'Did he?'

'He said you were all right.' Colin thought for a moment. 'Did you like my dad?'

'Yes, I did,' Tom replied.

'A lot of people don't. He's not been the same since . . . well, he just hasn't been the same, not like he used to be.'

'I guess it's a hard life for you both so far up the Dale with just the two of you running the farm.'

'We're selling up,' Colin told him.

'Selling the farm?'

'Yea. My dad's had enough. He says he can't manage it any more. He's sold the farm to him at the big house.'

'Sir Hedley?'

'That's him. He's wanted it for a long time because our farm's in the middle of two big parcels of land that he owns. Now he's got our farm, he owns all the land north of the village, most of it for his grouse shooting. He's going to convert the farmhouse into a holiday let and rent out some of the fields. We've sold the animals and farm machinery to Mr Fairborn. He owns most of the land to the south of the village.'

'I guess from what you wrote for me, you won't be that sorry to leave,' said Tom.

'I'll be glad to go,' said Colin vehemently. 'I hate the place now. It's cold and wet and miles from anywhere. My bedroom's damp, the roof leaks in the kitchen and you can't stop the wind coming through the windows and under the door. We got cut off last winter what with all the snow and lost a lot of sheep. I'm glad we're selling up.'

'And where will you live?' asked Tom.

'My dad's got a job on Sir Hedley's estate. It was all part of the deal when he agreed to sell the farm. He's to be the Assistant Gamekeeper.'

Poacher turned gamekeeper, Tom thought to himself.

'A cottage comes with the job and it's near the village.'

'Which means you have no excuse for coming late to school,' said Tom, smiling.

'Aye, I suppose.'

'Well, I'm glad that everything's worked out for you.'

'I used to like it on the farm,' said Colin, 'when my mam was alive. Things were different then. I miss her a lot.'

'I'm sure you do. You know I think there are few things in life that are as upsetting as losing a parent when you are young. My mother died when I was just a bit older than you and I took it very hard – just like you. It was a terrible time. You think when you are growing up that your parents, like the weather, will always be with you. Then they go. And you never feel quite the same.' It was as if he were speaking to himself and not to the boy sitting next to him. 'I sometimes remember my mother at odd moments, like when I see the rain running down the windows or on a sunny day or when I smell newly baked bread or hear a tune she liked.'

Colin was sobbing quietly. He balled his fists and rubbed his eyes. His body shook.

'Hey, hey,' said Tom, putting an arm around the boy's shoulder. 'It's all right. I didn't mean to upset you.'

'I can't talk to my dad about my mam,' said Colin, sniffing. 'He just won't talk about her. It upsets him. That's when he drinks.' He got to his feet. 'I have to go,' he said and then began running down the path.

On the Friday, Tom spent the day inside the cottage getting things ready for the delivery of the furniture the following day, when he would leave the King's Head and spend his first night in his new home. He lit the fire and sat in the creased brown leather armchair given to him by the priest. When I can afford it, he thought, I shall buy a new three-piece suite. So many people had been generous in helping him set up house. Tom had looked though the boxes destined for the church jumble sale and had stocked the kitchen with Mrs Golightly's unwanted crockery and cutlery, Owen had given Tom a kettle and a toaster and Joyce had provided a set of pots and pans.

As he looked around the sitting room, he thought of the changes he would make. The brightly patterned blue and green carpet would have to go along with the chintz curtains. He would strip the rosebud wallpaper from the walls, remove the white paint from the beams and take up the lino in the kitchen to reveal the quarry-tile floor. There was much to do but he was excited by the prospect.

Later that morning Tom sat on the bench in the garden, leaned back, breathed in the fresh air and surveyed the stunning view before him: the rolling green fields, the limestone outcrops gleaming bone-white in the sunlight, the dark and distant fells, the brown belt of dead bracken, the scattering of grey farmhouses and hillside barns and the endlessly crisscrossing drystone walls. In a vast and dove-grey sky a heron flew lazily overhead, its long legs trailing behind it. In the distance could be heard the whooping cry of the lapwing and the evocative call of the curlew. Tom recalled the vicar's words: 'It's not called "God's Own Country" for nothing.'

Down the track by the side of the cottage that morning came Carol leading a magnificent-looking animal held by a thick rope. Behind her was an elderly man, in typical Dalesman attire, holding a crook with a curved horn handle. The sheep had a thick, shaggy off-white fleece, a jet-black face, bright white around the nose and eyes, black and white mottled legs and great curved horns around its face.

Tom went to the gate to meet the two visitors and the sheep.

'Well, now,' he said, 'what have we here?'

'Oh hello, Mr Dwyer,' said the girl with the smile which was invariably etched on her face. She pushed the pink glasses up on her nose. 'This is my granddad. Granddad, this is my teacher.'

'How do,' said the old farmer. He was a short, lively-faced man, his bright eyes resting in a net of wrinkles.

'Good morning,' replied Tom.

'Grand day.'

'It is indeed. Makes you glad to be alive.'

'I heard you bought Roselea Cottage,' said the man.

Tom smiled. Who hasn't? he thought. 'That's right,' he answered.

'Arnold Olmeroyde had his eye on that cottage.'

'Yes, so I've heard.'

'Not be that chuffed that someone else has bought it,' said the old man.

Tom didn't reply.

'This is Starlight, Mr Dwyer,' the girl told Tom proudly, stroking the head of the sheep. 'Isn't he grand? He won Supreme Champion of Champions at the Clayton Show this year, and last year, that's when I won the Best Junior Shepherdess Shield, he got the Enoch Sheepshanks Memorial Trophy.'

'You were judged the Best Junior Shepherdess were you, Carol?' asked Tom.

'I was, yes, but that was last year. I got a silver trophy and fifty pounds.'

'That's quite an achievement.'

'I reckon so,' said the girl. 'You were well-pleased when I won, weren't you, Granddad?'

The old farmer patted the girl's head. 'I was that, love,' he said.

'Like he was this year when Starlight won.'

'He's a very striking creature,' said Tom, looking at the sheep.

'You can stroke him if you want,' said the girl. 'He won't bite. He's very easy-going. Sheep are like people you know, Mr Dwyer. My granddad says that they have their own personalities. Some of them are grouchy and bad-tempered and others are well-behaved and easy to handle, like Starlight here. That's right, isn't it, Granddad?'

'It is love, yes,' said the old man.

'And what breed is he?' asked Tom, stroking the animal.

'A Swaledale, Mr Dwyer,' she told him. 'Don't you remember I told you what a Swaledale looks like. We do have Texels on the farm but we mostly have Swaledales. They're hardier and better suited to the environment up here, aren't they, Granddad?'

'They are, love,' said the old man.

'And what makes this fine specimen a champion?' she was asked.

'Well, look at him, Mr Dwyer,' said Carol. 'Don't he look like a champion?' The sheep raised its elegant head. 'And as if he didn't know.'

'You see your champion tup,' said the girl's grandfather, who given the opportunity, would talk about sheep endlessly and now had an interested audience, 'has got to be of medium build with low-set horns curled around its head, well-rounded ribs, good solid legs, broad level back, firm loins and eyes quick and bright.' Carol was nodding in agreement. Tom could see from where she had gained her considerable knowledge of sheep.

Carol pointed downwards at the sheep and without the least trace of embarrassment added, 'And he's got to be useful in the downstairs department, hasn't he, Granddad?'

The old farmer nodded. His face broke into a broad grin. 'He has that, love,' he said.

'I see,' said Tom, shaking his head and supressing a smile. He recalled again the vicar's words: 'Dales' people are not afraid of voicing their opinions and they do so bluntly.'

'My granddad said we've got to be extra careful with Starlight because he's worth a lot of money.'

'And are you taking him for a walk?' asked Tom.

'No, no, Mr Dwyer, he's not a dog.' She gave a little giggle. 'You don't take sheep for walks. He's going over to Mr Gaunt's. He wants Starlight to serve some of his yows. His tup is thirteen years old and he's got arthritis and no teeth.' She looked up at the farmer. 'Bit like my granddad really,' she said cheekily.

'You're right there, Carol, love,' said the old man, laughing.

'He's knackered,' the girl added. 'Mr Gaunt's tup, not my granddad. He can't manage more than a few of the slower yows. Starlight will fettle the lot of them though, won't he, Granddad?'

'He will, love.'

'And why has it got red paint on its stomach?' asked Tom.

The child's face creased into a smile.

'You don't know much about sheep, Mr Dwyer,' she told her teacher.

'I don't,' admitted Tom, laughing, 'but I'm learning.'

'It's rudding,' explained the farmer. 'You see you mix some powdered colour with oil and it makes a sort of thick paste which you daub on the tup's belly. When he's mating he marks the yows he's been tupping on their rumps and you can see then where he's been. I change the colour every few days.'

'Why is that?' asked Tom.

'So you can tell what time of the month the lambs will be born. Most yows give birth five months after tupping.'

'Well, it's been a real education this morning,' said Tom. 'Thank you for the lesson.'

'You can come up to the farm if you like, Mr Dwyer,' said the farmer, 'and my Carol will show you around. You never know, we might make a shepherd out of you.'

'I might take you up on that,' replied her teacher.

'Come on then, Starlight,' said the girl, patting the sheep's head, 'let's go to Mr Gaunt's and then you can get cracking.'

Back at the King's Head that evening, Tom found Mrs Mossup in not the best of moods.

'I don't know what's up with our Leanne,' she complained. 'She's mooching about the place with a face on her like the back end of a Clayton bus on a wet weekend. And if I mention anything to her, she either bites my head off or bursts into tears.' She slammed the plate down so hard most of the dinner ended up on Tom's lap. 'I really don't know what's wrong with the lass. I don't suppose she's said anything to you?'

'I'm afraid not,' said Tom, looking down at the daunting plate of thick pink meat edged in fat, greasy roast potatoes, Yorkshire pudding, bullet-hard peas and glutinous gravy.

'Well, something or somebody's upsetting her,' said the landlady.

'Maybe she's had a fall-out with a boyfriend,' suggested Tom.

'Boyfriend!' repeated the landlady. 'She hasn't got a boyfriend.'

'I know that Dean Croft is sweet on her.'

'Dean Croft!' exclaimed Mrs Mossup. 'That gawky youth? She can't stand the sight of the lad.'

'Well, I'm sorry, Doris,' said Tom. 'I really don't know what's bothering her.'

'Do you think she's upset about you leaving?' asked the landlady. 'I know she's got a soft spot for you.'

'I very much doubt it,' said Tom. 'There must be something else.'

He didn't have to wait too long to discover what was troubling the landlady's daughter.

On the Saturday morning , Tom was in high spirits. It was the day he was moving into Roselea Cottage. No more would he have to tolerate the landlady's cooking, the lumpy bed, the noise from the public bar, the sweltering room and the surly expression of Mr Butt every morning.

He had not bothered to shave that morning and wore an old pair of jeans, a shirt with a frayed collar and a baggy jumper. As he stood at the gate, waiting for the deliveries of the furniture and appliances, Tom heard the thump of horse hooves on the bridle path which ran down the side of the cottage. A moment later Janette Fairborn, mounted on a chestnut mare, appeared. She was dressed in cream jodhpurs and a close-fitting hacking jacket. Her red hair fell from beneath her riding helmet. She looked stunning.

'Oh hello,' said Miss Fairborn when she saw Tom. She reined in the horse, patted its neck and looked down at him imperiously.

'Good morning,' Tom replied. Get off your high horse, he told himself. How haughty you look, perched up there like a princess regarding a peasant.

'I see you have managed to buy the cottage,' she said.

No thanks to you, he felt like replying.

'Yes,' he answered, 'I managed to buy the cottage.'

He resisted the temptation to tell her that the manager of the bank opposite to the one where she worked, had been only too pleased to arrange a mortgage but he felt it would be rather mean-minded to do so. He knew the loan was only possible because he had been able to put down a sizeable deposit, thanks to Mr Gaunt.

'Well, I'm pleased for you,' she said.

When Tom didn't answer she looked uncomfortable. 'Actually, I'm glad I've met you,' she said. 'I wanted to apologise for my father. I believe he gave you another ear-bashing in the King's Head.'

'He did,' replied Tom.

'I'm afraid he got the wrong end of the stick.'

'No harm done.'

'He does have a bit of a temper.'

'Yes, I know.'

'You got rid of the sports car then?' she said.

'I did. I was told it was not really the most suitable vehicle for up here, particularly in winter.' Then he could not resist adding playfully, 'And, of course, it didn't handle too well on those winding lanes and sharp bends. You never know what might be behind the corner.'

She gave a small smile. 'Yes, we get some pretty bad weather come December.'

'So I've been told.'

'And one must take great care on the roads.'

Now Tom smiled. 'Definitely.'

'And I believe you had a run-in with Jeremy Neville,' she said.

'Yes, I did,' he answered.

'What was that all about?'

'Oh, I think I'll let your boyfriend tell you about that,' Tom replied.

'For your information, Mr Dwyer, Jeremy Neville is not my boyfriend,' she replied quickly. 'He's just a friend and someone I go out with occasionally. Not that that is any of your business.'

'You're right, it is none of my business,' said Tom, 'but having met the man concerned, I suggest you might choose your friends a little more carefully.'

'And I suggest you keep your unwarranted advice to yourself,' she retorted.

Tom smiled. Seeing her high on the horse, her face flushed with annoyance, the bright eyes flashing and the red hair falling about her shoulders, she looked without a doubt a strikingly handsome young woman. He tugged at a forelock and put on the obsequious voice of one deferring to his betters. 'Sorry, ma'am, beg pardon, ma'am, no offence intended, ma'am.'

Janette shook her head but could not contain her smile.

'Goodbye, Mr Dwyer,' she said, digging her heels in the horse's flank.

'Goodbye, Miss Fairborn,' replied Tom.

$\star \qquad \star \qquad \star$

It was getting on for seven o'clock when Tom arrived back at the King's Head to settle the bill, collect his belongings and say goodbye to Mrs Mossup and Leanne. Being Saturday night the public bar was heaving as he edged his way through to the throng made up largely of noisy farmers discussing gimmers and tups, stirks and hoggs. He noticed that Mr Fairborn and Toby Croft numbered amongst the crowd. Tom's way was suddenly blocked by a giant of a man. He had never met any human being as huge as the towering individual who now stood before him. He was mountainous, six foot six at the very least, broad as a barn door and with arms the thickness of tree trunks and heavy shoulders. He had a weathered face like creased cardboard, the glassy protuberant eyes of a large fish, a bullet-shaped bald head and a neck as thick as a bulldog's. His glass looked like a thimble in his gnarled and calloused hand.

Tom's heart hammered in his chest.

'Excuse me,' he managed to say in a tremulous voice.

Goliath didn't move or speak but stared with the large, expressionless eyes.

Finally he spoke.

'I 'ear tha's bought Roselea Cottage,' he growled. It seemed to Tom that there was a sort of wounded aggression in his voice.

'Yes, I did,' Tom replied. He was aware that the conversation in the public bar had quietened abruptly.

'"Tis a champion cottage is that,' said the man.

'It is indeed,' agreed Tom.

'I was after buying that place for missen.'

'You must be Mr Olmeroyde.'

'Aye, that's me.'

'I'm pleased to meet you, Mr Olmeroyde,' said Tom pleasantly, hoping in being so openly friendly that things would not escalate into an aggressive confrontation. 'I gather that we are going to be neighbours.'

'I reckon so,' replied the man. He rubbed a bristly chin but didn't move. 'Tha teaches up at t'schooil?'

'I do, yes,' Tom answered.

'Took ovver from Miss Cathcart.'

'That's right.'

Still the man didn't budge. He stared at Tom for what seemed like an age and then he rested a large clumsy hand on the teacher's shoulder. He nodded reflectively. 'Our Marjorie, she's mi granddaughter, she's in thy class.'

'Marjorie's your granddaughter?' said Tom, picturing the shy, little pixie-faced child who sat at the front desk.

The colossus smiled. 'Aye. She's t'apple o' mi eye is our Marjorie.'

The man held out a spade of a hand which Tom shook charily.

'I'd like to shake yer 'and,' he said. 'Marjorie's come on a treat since she's 'ad thee as 'er teacher. I just thowt I'd tell thee that, Mester Dwyer.'

'Thank you very much,' said Tom, breathing a sigh of relief. 'Will tha join me fer a drink?'

'That's kind of you, Mr Olmeroyde,' replied Tom, 'but I won't, thank you. I'm moving into the cottage tonight and driving back up there later. Perhaps another time.'

'Another time then,' said Tom's new neighbour. 'Let us know if tha wants any 'elp movin' an' if tha does 'ave a mind to sell yon cottage, I'd be grateful to 'ave t'fust refusal.'

Tom noticed that Leanne was not in her usual place behind the bar. Customers were being served by a harassed, spotty-faced youth who, in the short time Tom had been in the bar, had shouted repeatedly at the impatient drinkers, 'Will yer 'old yer 'orses. I've only got t'one pair of 'ands, tha knaas.'

Over the next few weeks, Tom settled into a contented and fulfilling existence in Risingdale. He had tidied the garden, painted the shed, repaired the gate and decorated inside and outside the cottage. Mr Olmeroyde proved an excellent neighbour. He had rebuilt the drystone wall, delivered a load of logs and arranged for the chimney to be swept. His granddaughter had appeared one Sunday morning with a beautiful multi-coloured quilt which her grandmother had made for Tom as a house-warming gift. On another day Simon had arrived with a dead, glassy-eyed rabbit in a plastic bag.

'Little present for you, Mr Dwyer,' he had told Tom. 'I've had a champion morning ferreting. You need to skin it and gut it and cook it with onions, carrots, celery and parsley. My mum always puts some red wine in as well.'

Tom had thanked the boy and later buried the carcass in the field at the back of the cottage.

Dean turned up early one Saturday with a load of manure, his old tractor chuddering noisily up the drive by the side of the cottage and waking Tom up. The young farmer stayed to cut the overhanging branches from the oak tree, trim the hedges and lay traps under the lawn for the moles. When Tom asked him how much he owed, the lad waved a hand, shook his head and told him he'd have to settle up with his father. Tom felt it politic on that occasion not to mention Leanne to Dean.

He now felt he was being accepted by the residents of Risingdale. The vicar had been right when he had told Tom that Dales' people were a bit stand-offish at first and not quite as talkative as the Irish, but they were equally as warm and friendly once you got to know them. Of late Tom found everyone in the village amiable and generous. Whenever he visited the King's Head, he was greeted cordially by the locals. If he met anyone in the high street, they would smile and ask how he was. On these occasions he found he was beginning to speak like a Dalesman. 'Oh, I'm fair to middling,' he would reply or 'I'm feeling champion, ta very much.'

One evening Mr Greenwood appeared at the cottage door. He was carrying a battered canvas holdall. When Tom had first met Colin's father, he had been dressed in a shapeless grey cardigan beneath an old waxed jacket and threadbare jeans which had been patched at the knees. His dark hair had been unkempt and had looked long and messy and he had had a week's stubble. He was now dressed in a smart tweed suit and wore a collar and a tie. He had shaved and his hair was short and neatly parted. Clearly his new occupation as an assistant gamekeeper had led to this transformation in his appearance.

'I'm not disturbin' you, I 'ope,' he said.

'No, not at all,' said Tom. 'Come in.'

The visitor wiped his feet vigorously on the doormat and entered the cottage. He looked around the sitting room, taking everything in. Although the garish carpet and the chintz curtains had not been changed, Tom had decorated the walls in a pale cream, exposed the dark oak of the beams and repainted all the woodwork.

'There's still quite a bit to do,' he explained. 'When I can afford it, I'll get a new carpet and curtains.'

'Aye, they're not my cup o' tea but tha's med a good start.'

'Take a seat, Mr Greenwood,' said Tom. 'May I get you a drink?'

'No, I'm all reet,' said the farmer, as he sat down.

'Well, what can I do for you?' asked Tom.

'Tha mentioned when I fust met yer that tha liked 'istory. Does tha recall we 'ad a chat abaat t'castle?'

'I do,' replied Tom, 'and you mentioned that the weather would likely change and so it did. I got soaked to the skin and arrived back in the village like a drowned rat.'

'Aye, after tha left it started siling daan. Anyroad,' he reached down and unzipped the canvas bag. 'Ovver t'years I've found bits an' bobs lying abaat t'farm, and one or two things what

I've dug up an' I thowt tha'd be hinterested in some o' t'stuff I've found.'

The canvas bag, which he passed over to Tom, contained an assortment of objects: a rusty knife with traces of silver on the hilt, some lead shot, a tarnished belt buckle, an old sword, bent and corroded, and a misshapen helmet.

'These are fascinating,' said Tom, taking out each object and fingering it.

'And there's these,' said Mr Greenwood. He reached into his pocket and produced a leather pouch. He tipped it up and a small cache of coins spilled out on the table. Tom's eyes lit up. There were several silver shillings dating back hundreds of years, heavy copper pennies and twopenny pieces, worn sixpences, farthings and a shiny Victorian crown. The one that caught his attention was a gold coin, on the obverse of which was King George III in profile and the date 1797.

'I think this is called a spade-ace guinea,' said Tom. 'It takes its name from the spade-shaped shield on the reverse.'

'I thowt it were brass.'

'No, no, I think it's gold and worth a few pounds I shouldn't wonder.'

'Aye, well tha's welcome to it an' t'rest.'

'I couldn't possibly accept them,' protested Tom.

The farmer laughed. 'Well they're no use to me. I reckon you'll value 'em more than me. I think my lad telled thee we're movin'?'

'He did. He seems happy at the prospect.'

'Colin's not liked it up at t'farm since 'is mam passed away,' said the boy's father. 'I can't say as 'ow I've been 'appy theer either. Winter last nearly finished me off then. I lost a lot o' beeasts.' He reached down and picked up the holdall. 'Yer know, Mester Dwyer, Colin's really come on since tha's been 'is teacher. 'E's really tekken to 'is paintin', out theer all t'time wi' 'is sketchpad.'

'As I said, I think he has got a real talent for art,' Tom said.

''E were never suited to farmin',' said the man. 'Mebbe he can mek summat out of 'is paintin', does tha reckon?'

'I think he probably could,' replied Tom.

'I'm pleased t'lad's good at summat,' said the farmer. 'Workin' wi' beeasts dun't suit 'im.'

'I shall take the coins into Clayton Museum and see what they make of them,' said Tom.

'Tha can suit thissen, Mester Dwyer. 'As I said tha're welcome to' em.'

At school things were going well. The children were cooperative, worked hard and were making excellent progress, the football team had had a moderate success, the staff continued to be supportive and good-humoured and the headmaster remained his avuncular self. But of all the things that gratified Tom, it was the way Colin Greenwood had improved. He was no longer the rude and truculent boy who did the minimum amount of work and never contributed in class. He still wasn't the most interested and enthusiastic of pupils, but there had been a distinct change in him. The HMI had been right when she had said that art might be the way to get through to the boy. Since his talent had been discovered, Colin had flourished with his painting. Perhaps, thought Tom, when one day he was watching the boy sketching, his brow furrowed in concentration, it was the first time in the boy's school career when he had gained some recognition and received some praise for his efforts.

It was a cold but bright late November Saturday, the day Charlie was to sit the scholarship examination for the grammar school. Tom had spent several lunchtimes giving the boy some last-minute advice on how to tackle the paper.

'I think the most difficult part,' he had told the boy, 'is the General Intelligence section. I reckon some of the questions here will be tricky. This part requires what is called divergent thinking.' Tom had never come across this term before he started to train as a teacher. His tutor at the university had been very keen on divergent thinking. It was one of the indicators, the lecturer argued, for identifying the gifted child – those exceptionally able children who tended to see things in a different way from others.

'What it means,' Tom had continued, 'is that the obvious answer is not always the right one. It requires you to think creatively. Does that make sense?'

'I think so,' the boy had replied.

'Well, good luck,' the teacher had said. 'And it's not the end of the world if you don't get through.'

The boy had smirked. 'You are beginning to sound like my mother, Mr Dwyer,' he had said.

14

Tom was enjoying a drink in the King's Head on Sunday lunchtime with a group of farmers.

'I 'ear that tha're becomin' quite a bit of a sheep hexpert then, Mester Dwyer,' observed Toby Croft.

'What gave you that idea?' asked Tom.

'I were speakin' to Albert Midgley, young Carol's grand-dad. ''E were tellin' me that 'e were givin' thee a few tips on 'ow to recognise a champion tup.'

'He was,' said Tom, 'but I think his granddaughter knows as much as he does. She's quite an authority on sheep.'

'There's nowt Albert Midgley dun't know abaat sheep – accordin' to 'im, that is,' grumbled Mr Croft's companion, scowling.

'His granddaughter was telling me he won Supreme Champion of Champions at this year's Clayton Show,' said Tom mischievously. He could tell by the tone of the speaker that Mr Midgley was not popular. 'He also got the Enoch Sheepshanks Trophy, I was told.'

'Aye, he did,' said the disgruntled farmer. 'Nob'dy gets a look-in at Clayton Show if he puts one of 'is beeasts in. 'E wants to give other fowks a chance.'

'Same wi' hagricultural show,' complained the third farmer. 'T'bugger cleans up t'prizes theer an all.'

'Course Albert Midgley's got t'brass to buy top-quality sheep unlike some of us.' Mr Croft looked down at his nearly empty glass.

'Let me get you gentlemen a drink,' said Tom.

The three farmers drained the remainder of their beer in great gulps and placed the empty glasses on the bar.

'Daan 'ere, Wayne!' shouted Mr Croft at the spotty-faced youth, serving at the other end of the bar. 'Frame thissen. Tha's got customers.'

Mrs Mossup appeared from the parlour.

'Could I have a word with you, Mr Dwyer, when you've a minute?' she asked in a rather cold tone of voice. She returned to the parlour.

'Yes, of course,' Tom called after her, wondering why she had stopped calling him by his first name and why she was being so formal. Surely, she couldn't be angry with him for moving out.

'I don't know what's up wi' 'er,' remarked Toby Croft. 'She's had a face like a bag o' spanners all week an' t'daughter's same.'

'Tell Wayne I'll settle up with him later,' Tom told the farmer.

In the parlour Mr Butt, legs apart, arms comfortably crossed over his chest, his head tilted a little, sat watching the football match on the television. He grimaced when he saw who had come in.

Tom ignored him.

'Would you mind vacating the parlour please, Mr Butt,' said the landlady, with a heave of her impressive bosom. 'I would like to have a quiet word with Mr Dwyer.'

'Vacate t'parlour?' repeated the man. 'You want me to shift?'

'Yes, that is what I've just asked you. I would like you to go out.'

'I'm watching t'match,' he told her bullishly, not making any effort to get up from the chair. 'I'll not disturb you.'

'It's of a personal and private nature,' the landlady told him. 'So if you wouldn't mind.'

'Actually, I do mind. I'm getting sick o' this, Mrs Mossup,' he responded angrily, 'being pushed out again. First mi room, now t'parlour. 'E's like a ruddy cuckoo in t'nest.'

'Will you move,' snapped Mrs Mossup.

Grumbling to himself, Mr Butt departed but left the door slightly ajar, the better to overhear what was this personal and private matter the landlady wished to discuss. He stood in the hall to listen.

'Would you sit down please, Mr Dwyer,' Mrs Mossup said.

'Is there something wrong?' asked Tom, sitting in the chair previously occupied by Mr Butt.

'Well, yes, there is something wrong,' said the landlady, with great agitation in her voice. 'I've discovered what's wrong with Leanne. It took a lot to get it out of her but I've discovered the reason why she's been acting the way she has.'

'So what is the problem?' asked Tom.

'Now I am not a person, Mr Dwyer,' she told him, 'to mince my words. I'm a straight-talking woman. I always have been. Some people don't like it but I think it's always best to come straight out with it and not beat about the bush and go all around the houses. I think it's always the best policy to be up front and forthright and say what you have to say.'

'And what is it you have to say?' asked Tom, keen to hear what it was.

'Have you been playing fast and loose with Leanne?' she asked.

'I beg your pardon?'

'Taking advantage of her.'

'Certainly not!' Tom exclaimed.

'No carryings-on, funny business, no hanky-panky?'

'Mrs Mossup, I can assure you there has been nothing of the sort.'

'You were very lovey-dovey when I saw you both in the corner of the public bar that day.'

'That's nonsense! We were simply having a conversation. I'm amazed that you should think anything was going on between us.'

'She's always had a soft spot for you,' said Mrs Mossup. 'Ever since you walked through that door, she's been starry-eyed.'

'I really do not wish to hear any more,' said Tom, getting to his feet. 'This is ridiculous.'

'She's pregnant,' said the landlady bluntly.

'What?' He sat down again.

'Expecting.'

'And you think I might have had something to do with it?'

'Well, it has crossed my mind,' she told him. 'You've had every opportunity.'

'So has Mr Butt,' said Tom.

'Do you think she would entertain a big tub of lard like him?' she asked.

The eavesdropper let out a gasp of indignation which was clearly audible in the parlour.

'Just a minute,' said the landlady, getting up. She opened the door and revealed Mr Butt.

'Did you want something?' she asked.

'I . . . er . . . er . . . think I might 'ave left mi paper in t'parlour,' he told her feebly. 'Don't worry, I'll get it later.' He scurried up the stairs, with remarkable agility for one so large.

Mrs Mossup closed the door behind her and returned to her seat.

'Has Leanne not told you who the father is?' asked Tom, leaning forward in his chair.

'She won't say. She's been very tight-lipped.'

'Do you think it could be Dean Croft?'

'She won't give that lad the time of day,' she said. 'So, I want you to be honest with me, Mr Dwyer, and—'

'Let me stop you there, Mrs Mossup,' said Tom. 'I can

tell you categorically I am not responsible for your daughter's present situation and I resent the implication that I am.'

'Well, somebody's responsible,' said the landlady. 'She's not pregnant by some immaculate contraption, is she?'

'Well, it's certainly not me!' exclaimed Tom. 'I suggest you get Leanne in here now and we'll get it sorted out.'

Mrs Mossup went to fetch her daughter, returning a moment later with a tearful Leanne in tow. The girl's eyes were red and puffy.

'Sit down here,' ordered her mother.

Leanne slumped in a chair.

'Now then, young lady, what have you got to say for yourself?'

'Nothing,' she replied, sniffing noisily.

'Leanne,' said Tom gently, 'your mother has got it into her head that I may be responsible for your present situation.'

'What!' exclaimed Leanne.

'That I might be the father of your child.'

'Well, you're not,' said the girl. She wiped her eyes on the back of her hand.

Tom sighed. 'I know that. Tell your mother.'

'He's not,' said Leanne to her mother. 'I don't know what put that stupid idea in your head.'

Tom turned to Mrs Mossup. 'I hope that satisfies you,' he said.

'Oh well,' said the landlady, 'I'm sorry I got the wrong end of the stick.'

'There wasn't any stick to get the wrong end of,' said Tom.

'Well, I'm sorry, I'm sure,' she said meekly. 'It's just that Leanne doesn't know any lads.'

'I do,' countered her daughter with some bitterness in her voice.

'Well, it's now clear that you do,' said her mother angrily.

The words she had bitten back came flooding out. 'One of these lads you've been carrying on with, has landed you with an illegitimate child. People in the village will have a field day if they find out.' She looked at Tom.

'I'm sure you won't say anything, will you?'

'No, of course not. So what are you going to do, Leanne?' Tom asked the girl.

'I'll tell you what she's going to do,' cut in Mrs Mossup, before her daughter could reply. 'I'm packing her off to stay with my sister in Scarborough, and when we've given it some more thought, we'll decide what to do.'

Leanne began to sob.

'It's no good turning on the waterworks, young lady,' said Mrs Mossup. 'You've made your bed. Now you will have to lie on it.'

'Well, I'll make tracks,' said Tom, wishing more than anything to be away from the domestic crisis and back to his new home. He stood up.

'I'm sorry, Tom, about thinking it was you,' said the land-lady. 'Anyway, no harm done.'

In this, she was soon to be proved wrong.

Later, after Tom had paid for the drinks and left, Mr Butt went into the public bar for his usual couple of pints before retiring. After buying himself a drink, he joined Mr Croft and two other farmers at a corner table. He tried to keep in with the farmers – after all they were his livelihood – but he wearied of their constant talk of sheep staggers and scabby mouth, rattle belly, bovine diarrhoea and swine pox, and their endless complaints about the price of animal feed and the state of the weather. He didn't like their company and the feeling was mutual – the farmers didn't like his. Mr Croft and his compan-ions tolerated the fertiliser salesman because he was some-times good for a pint.

''As tha done wi' t'dippin' then, Toby?' asked Mr Croft's fellow farmer, a small, wrinkled individual with wisps of white wiry hair combed across his otherwise bald pate and a dimpled, veined nose.

''Ave I hell as like,' retorted Mr Croft. 'I've got 'alf a bloody flock to do. I tell thee this, Percy, if tha wants owt doin' properly, then do it for thissen. I gev job to our Dean an' what did t'daft'apeth do? Only went an' poisoned hissen.'

''E did what!' exclaimed Percy.

'Ended up in Clayton Royal Infirmary, that's what. Does tha know 'e's abaat as much use as a chamber pot wi' an 'ole in t'bottom. I telled 'im afore 'e started dippin' to gu steady wi' OPs. Course 'e took no notice and were swishing dip abaat like there were no tomorra. I sometimes think t'lad's limp under t'cap.'

'Thee 'as to be very careful usin' organophosphates,' volunteered Mr Butt. 'Ovver-hexposure can 'ave nasty side-effects.'

'Tha dunt need to tell me that,' replied Mr Croft snappily. 'I've been dippin' bloody sheep for donkey's years.'

'I were just sayin',' said Mr Butt feebly.

'So tha think your Dean's 'ad a big dose then?' asked Percy.

'Aye, I reckon so,' replied Mr Croft. ''E started wi' these headaches, then got confused and began forgettin' weer 'e'd put stuff, 'e couldn't sleep an' were off of 'is food. I thowt at fust lad were love-sick. 'E's been mooning abaat Leanne but she wants nowt to do wi' 'im, not since that teacher up at t'school started. I think she's sweet on 'im. Anyroad, when 'e started seein' things – giant rabbits an' dancin' foxes, I knew summat were up. Then he keeled ovver, so I took 'im to CRI. They're keepin' 'im in 'til it wears off.'

'Well I 'ope t'lad'll be all reight,' said Percy. 'An' speakin' of Leanne, I 'an't see 'er behind bar for a bit. She's p'raps sickenin fer summat. Mebbe it's that stomach bug what's still goin' round.'

'Well, it's a peculiar stomach bug what meks tha purron weight,' observed Toby. 'She's allus been a big lass but by heck she's purron some pounds lately. I telled 'er mam she were fillin' out and she telled me to mind mi own business, lass 'as a lot on her plate.'

'Oh, she's sickenin' for summat, all right,' said Mr Butt, with a self-satisfied look on his round face, 'an' it's not a stomach bug.'

'What's up wi' 'er then?' asked Mr Croft. 'Does tha know?'

'She's keepin' a low prolife,' he was told.

'What fer?'

Mr Butt leaned forward and confided in a throaty whisper, ''Es only gone an' put 'er in t'club.'

'Tha what?' exclaimed Mr Croft.

'Got 'er pregnant,' answered Mr Butt.

'Who 'as?'

'That teacher.'

'Mester Dwyer?'

'Aye, 'im,' said Mr Butt. 'Missis Mossup confronted 'im earlier. I 'eard 'er in t'parlour.' (He had not, of course, been privy to the end of the conversation.) 'She asked 'im if 'e 'ad been playing fast an' loose wi' 'er daughter an' 'e 'ad no answer to that.'

''E's got t'lass pregnant?' asked Mr Croft.

'That's what I said,' answered Mr Butt.

'Well, I don't know,' said the farmer, shaking his head. 'I would nivver 'ave thowt it of Mester Dwyer.'

'Dark horse,' said Mr Butt. 'I've seen t'other side of 'im. Devious, that's what 'e is. Only been in t'King's 'Ead no more than five minutes an' 'e 'ad me chucked out o' mi room. 'E's a cuckoo in t'nest.'

'I've allus found 'im such a nice young fella,' said Mr Croft. He looked down at his empty glass. 'An' 'e's allus good for a drink.'

'Oh, I'll get these,' said Mr Butt, taking the hint.

When things were quiet in the village store and post office in Barton-in-the-Dale, the proprietor occupied herself by scouring the local newspaper for any juicy items of gossip which she could later share with her customers. Not only had Mrs Sloughthwaite a remarkable talent for drawing out from those who patronised her shop the most intimate information, she had an exceptional memory. Nothing escaped her notice and nobody who walked through her door was spared from an interrogation.

It was the Monday after Tom's unfortunate interview with Mrs Mossup when Mr Butt called into the village store. Rattling the doorbell on its spring, he pushed his way through the door.

Mrs Sloughthwaite raised herself from the counter on which she had been leaning, smiled and wished the first customer of the day a cheery 'Good morning.'

'Mornin',' he grunted. 'Give us a couple of them chocolate bars, a quarter of pear drops, a bag of them salted peanuts and a packet of fags.'

'Please,' murmured Mrs Sloughthwaite, pulling a face at the man's rudeness.

'Eh?'

'Is that all?'

'Aye.'

'Would you like a bag?' He could do with a bag, she thought, over his head.

'No.'

'Thank you,' she murmured.

'Eh?'

'Nothing.'

He paid for the items, scooped them up with the change and stuffed them in his pocket.

Mrs Sloughthwaite was inclined to let this disagreeable customer leave, but it was not in her nature to let anyone who came into her store evade a cross-examination. Rarely did she abandon the attempt to extract more information.

'Just passing through, are you?' she asked before the man could escape.

'No, I'm 'ere on business.'

'And what would that be, if you don't mind me asking?'

'Chemical enrichment constituents for farmers,' he told her.

'Fertilisers?'

'Aye, summat like that.'

'And are you staying in the village?' she asked.

'Thee asks a lot o' questions, missis,' he told her.

'I just like to show an interest in my customers, that's all,' she said.

'Well, for your information, I'm stopping at t'King's 'Ead in Risingdale. Does that answer your question?'

'Oh, a nephew of one of my regular customers is staying there. A very nice young man. You will have come across him – Mr Dwyer.'

'Oh aye, I've come across 'im all reight, an' as for being a nice young man, well that's a matter of hopinion.'

'You don't get on with him then?' she asked, intrigued.

'No, I don't,' answered Mr Butt. 'I was evicted from mi room to mek way for 'im an' 'e got preferential treatment from t'landlady. Anyone'd think 'e were royalty t'way she carried on. Mind you, 'e's got 'is come-uppance.'

'In what way?' asked the shopkeeper.

'Got a barmaid pregnant. She were allus mekkin' eyes at 'im, an' 'e took advantage of 'er. Anyroad, 'e's left t'King's 'Ead pretty sharpish.'

Well, well, Mrs Sloughthwaite thought to herself, that is a turn-up for the book. She wondered if Mrs O'Connor knew.

Before she could resume her grilling, the customer left, banging the door after him.

It was later that afternoon when Mrs O'Connor made her appearance.

'It's cold enough for two pair of shoelaces, so it is,' said the customer.

Mrs Sloughthwaite sometimes found it hard to understand the meaning of the woman's words of wisdom but nodded sympathetically as if she did.

'Have you heard from that nephew of yours lately, Bridget?' asked the shopkeeper.

'Oh yes, Tom called in last week. He's got some very exciting news, so he has.'

'Really?' said Mrs Sloughthwaite.

'He's bought himself a cottage in Risingdale. He's taking me over to see it next Sunday. I'm so pleased for him. He's a lovely lad, so he is. Tom was after being a priest, you know, but he found he was allergic to the incense. Anyway, he loves teaching. His poor mother, God rest her soul, would be so proud of him.'

'I should have thought a good-looking young man like your Tom would have a girlfriend by now,' remarked Mrs Sloughthwaite.

'Oh, he's no time for girls,' replied Mrs O'Connor, 'what with his new job and having to get things done at his cottage.'

'No time for girls,' repeated Mrs Sloughthwaite.

'There's another bit of interesting news you might be interested in,' her customer continued.

'Oh yes,' said Mrs Sloughthwaite.

'I saw the baby. He's the spit-and-image of his father, so he is. Lovely blue eyes and such a smile.'

'You know about the baby then?' asked Mrs Sloughthwaite.

'Of course I do,' replied the customer. 'Mrs Stirling's hardly been keeping it a secret, has she?'

'Oh, *that* baby,' said Mrs Sloughthwaite.

'A baby is such a blessing,' said Mrs O'Connor.

I wonder if she will think her nephew's baby is such a blessing when she finds out about it, thought the shopkeeper.

Tom as usual arrived early that Monday morning and found Mrs Gosling polishing the desks. The woman always welcomed him with a warm smile and then spent a good ten minutes chattering away inconsequentially. That morning she was uncharacteristically quiet.

'Good morning, Mrs Gosling,' said Tom cheerfully.

She remained with her back to him. 'Morning,' she replied tersely, turning her head slightly and giving a laconic nod. Then she carried on polishing the desks.

'I'm hoping that I can persuade Mr Gaunt to replace those old desks with some new tables,' Tom told her. 'They must be the devil's own job to keep clean.'

She didn't reply.

'I thought I'd walk to school this morning,' he told her. 'It's brisk but nice and dry. Makes you glad to be alive on such a day.'

'Does it?' she said, turning to look at him. There was a severe expression on her face.

'Are you all right, Mrs Gosling?' asked Tom, with concern. 'You don't seem your usual self.'

The assistant caretaker gave him a penetrating look. '*I'm* all right, Mr Dwyer,' she said, 'but there are them what are not.'

'Yes, we are very lucky,' he replied. 'There is so much trouble and unhappiness in the world. We should thank God for our good fortune.'

'You think yourself lucky then, do you, Mr Dwyer?' She pursed her lips.

'I do,' he replied.

'Well, there's one young woman who's not so lucky, is she?' answered the assistant caretaker. Disapproval was writ large on her face.

'I'm sorry, I don't follow what you are saying,' said Tom.

'I'll say this, Mr Dwyer,' said Mrs Gosling, stuffing the duster in her pocket and then clasping her hands together under her solid bosom, 'I am very surprised that you, of all people, a teacher who should be setting a good example to the children, should carry on as you have done.' She picked up a tin of furniture polish and marched out of the classroom before Tom, stunned by this outburst, could reply. 'The way you've behaved is shameful,' she said loudly, as she hurried off down the corridor.

When Mr Gaunt arrived at school, he asked Tom to step into his study and told him to sit down.

'This is a tad delicate,' said the headmaster. He leaned back in his chair. 'It is a matter I feel I ought to raise. As I said to you over the unfortunate incident in the King's Head with the Maladroit son, what you do out of school is your business. However, I feel I have to mention this. I am sure you are aware by now how gossip spreads in this part of the world. The thing is, I met Mr Croft yesterday morning and he was telling me about something which concerns you.'

'Oh yes?' said Tom.

'There is a rumour going around the village concerning yourself and a young woman.'

'Oh dear,' sighed Tom. Now he knew why Mrs Gosling had been so reproachful. She had obviously heard the rumour. It now appears that all Risingdale would know about Leanne and assume he was the father of her child. And how did that piece of information get out, he thought. Who, apart from the three people who sat in the parlour at the King's Head on Saturday night, knew about Leanne?

Mr Gaunt carried on. 'The rumour is that the barmaid at the King's Head is . . . well, she is . . .'

'Expecting a baby,' Tom finished the sentence.

'Well, yes.'

'And that I am the father,' said Tom.

'Yes, that is what people are saying. Is there any truth in this?' asked Mr Gaunt.

'None at all,' replied Tom.

He then described the interview with Mrs Mossup.

'Of course,' said Mr Gaunt, 'I dismissed this rumour as nonsense and I said so to Mr Croft. I have known you long enough to know that you are a decent young man who could never behave unkindly or unchivalrously. However, I felt I ought to mention it to you. I don't know what mean-minded individual has been spreading such gossip.'

'I've no idea,' said Tom. 'As far as I know there are only the landlady, her daughter and myself who are aware of the girl's condition. I can't believe that either of them would say anything and they would certainly not tell people that I was the father. I'll have a word with Mrs Mossup after school today.'

'I think that is a very sensible idea,' said the headmaster. 'Now, on another matter, I have a letter here from the grammar school.' He passed it over to Tom. 'It says the scholarship examination will take place at the end of the month on a Saturday morning. I see from what it says here that you have entered young Charlie Lister.'

'That's right,' answered Tom. He could not get the previous conversation out of his head. What was the source of this rumour, he asked himself. Who could have spread such a thing?

'It might be a good idea to give the boy a bit of coaching,' continued Mr Gaunt. 'He won't have had much experience of sitting a timed examination. I believe this one is extremely demanding.'

'Pardon?'

'Give Charlie some coaching for the scholarship exam.'

'I've been doing that,' Tom told him, 'and I think he'll walk it.'

On the way back to his classroom, he took Mrs Gosling aside.

'A word please,' Tom said to the assistant caretaker. 'You have no doubt heard the rumour going around the village concerning myself and Leanne Mossup. I assume that it was this to which you were referring earlier.'

'It's none of my business, Mr Dwyer, but, I will say this—'

'Listen to me for a moment please, Mrs Gosling,' interrupted Tom heatedly. 'It is true that Leanne is having a baby but I am not the father. Let me say that again so you will be in no doubt. I am not the father. And to repeat your words, I am surprised that you, of all people, should believe such a thing of me. There is no foundation in the malicious rumour and the sooner you and all the other villagers understand that the better. If you do not believe what I have told you, then I suggest you ask Leanne or her mother.'

The assistant caretaker, shocked by the virulence of the teacher's angry avowal, opened her mouth to speak but snapped it shut. For once she was lost for words.

'So I hope that is clear enough,' said Tom.

Mrs Gosling managed to find her voice. 'Yes, Mr Dwyer,' she replied, looking shamefaced, 'perfectly clear.'

At lunchtime Colin appeared at the classroom door.

'Can I see you, Mr Dwyer?' he asked.

'Of course,' replied Tom. 'Come along in.'

'I've done the picture of Roselea Cottage for you,' he said. 'It's not all that good. I could do a better job in summer when there are flowers in the garden and roses round the door. It looks a bit dull.'

He placed his sketchpad on the desk and opened it to where he had painted the cottage. It was a boldly executed watercolour, beautifully detailed, which depicted the cottage exactly.

'Colin, this is brilliant,' said Tom.

'Not really,' the boy said diffidently.

'Listen to me,' said Tom. 'I'm telling you this is really, really good.'

'You like it then?'

'Like it? I'm over the moon with it.'

The boy's lips formed the ghost of a shy grin.

'Did I see you smile, Colin Greenwood?' asked Tom. The boy's smile widened. 'Look, this painting is exactly what I hoped. I didn't want the sort of picture like you see on the front of chocolate boxes and birthday cards with all the bright colours. I know Mrs Golightly will be delighted with it. I've told you this before, and I'm not just saying it to make you feel good, I really mean it. You have a real talent for art. May I see the painting you did of the barn at Bentley Beck?'

The boy turned to another page in his sketchbook.

'This was a bit tricky because I'm not used to doing water,' the boy told him. 'There's not much colour. It's more like a black and white photograph.'

There was another perfectly executed drawing. It was a bleak, remote scene that the boy had painted. Lowering storm clouds curled upwards on a slate grey sky. In the foreground was a squat barn with thick walls and small windows picked out in detail and the stream with the narrow stone bridge. Clumps of wild grass and tufts of sedge broke the surface of the beck. A weeping willow bent over from a bank, knotted with nettles and wild flowers, its hanging branches stroking the rippling water. A few rough fell sheep cropped the grass.

'May I hang on to this?' asked Tom. 'I would like to show it to Mr Gaunt.'

Colin nodded and tore the paper carefully from the pad.

'Did you know people are talking about you, Mr Dwyer?' he asked suddenly.

'Yes, I know,' replied Tom.

'My dad heard people talking and saying you'd got a girl into trouble.'

'And do you know what that means?'

'It means that she's having a baby.'

'That's right,' said Tom. 'Well, let me set things straight so all these people will know the truth and stop spreading rumours about me. I have not got any girl in trouble as you say. It's tittle-tattle. Rumours, particularly in a small village like Risingdale, spread like wildfire. Sometimes people find pleasure in gossiping and believe the worst about a person. It is unkind and very hurtful. Does that make any sense to you?'

'Yea, it does,' answered the boy, nodding. 'People say bad things about my dad and they're not true, like when Christopher said my dad was a crook and owed his dad money and wouldn't pay him back.'

'So you know exactly what I mean,' said Tom.

'Yea, I do. I'll tell my dad that what people are saying about you isn't true.'

'You do that,' said Tom.

'Thanks for what you're doing for me, Mr Dwyer,' said the boy. He tore another sheet from his sketchpad. 'This is for you.' Before Tom could say anything the boy picked up his sketchpad and left the classroom.

Tom looked at the picture. It was of the ruins of Marston Castle.

'Did you want to see me, Mr Dwyer?' Charlie had appeared at the door a moment later.

'Yes, I do. Come along in,' said the teacher. 'I have the date for your scholarship exam at the grammar school. It's to take place in a couple of weeks on Saturday.'

'I know, my mother received a letter last Friday,' the boy answered.

'Can you make it?' asked the teacher. 'It will be at the grammar school.'

'I can get the bus,' said Charlie.

'Are you nervous?' asked the teacher.

'Actually I'm quite looking forward to it,' replied the boy. 'Anyway, it's not the end of the world if I don't get the scholarship.'

'It will be a pretty tough exam, you know,' Tom told him, 'but I think you will cope with it. Anyway, sit down and we will have a go at a few more questions similar to the ones that may come up. As you know, there will be questions on arithmetic, general English, comprehension, General Intelligence and an essay.' Tom flicked open a paper. 'What about this one? "Out of a six-thousand-pound donation, one thousand pounds was given to a local school and half of the remainder was given to charity. The rest was divided amongst four children. How much did each child get?" Would you like a piece of paper to work it out?'

'The answer is six hundred and twenty-five pounds,' said Charlie, after some thought.

Tom smiled. 'I can't see you will have a lot of trouble with the arithmetic,' he said. 'I think the General Intelligence questions may prove a bit difficult. I know when I looked at some of them, it took a lot of thought and others I just could not do.'

'Could I have a go at a couple?' asked Charlie.

'All right,' said the teacher, looking at the paper. 'What about this one to which I got the wrong answer: "In an abandoned house, there is a fish tank containing three big fish, four medium-sized fish and five small fish. Five of the fish die. How many fish are in the tank?"'

'That's easy,' said Charlie. 'There's twelve.'

'And how do you come to that conclusion?' asked the teacher.

'Well, if the house was abandoned, there would be nobody to take the dead fish out of the tank, would there, sir,' answered the boy.

'Do you know, Charlie Lister,' said Tom, 'I don't think you need any more coaching. I reckon you could teach me a thing or two.'

At the end of the day Tom was about to leave to see Mrs Mossup at the King's Head when Mrs Gosling put her head around the classroom door.

'I'm ever so sorry what I said, Mr Dwyer, I feel awful. What must you think of me?'

Tom was cool with her for he had been very angry about her outburst.

'Just get the facts right next time, Mrs Gosling,' he said, 'and don't listen to scurrilous rumours.'

After school Tom called in at the King's Head to see Mrs Mossup. The few regulars smiled and nodded and the new barman behind the bar waved when he entered. He found the landlady in the parlour.

'I know why you're here, Tom,' she said. 'I was expecting you. Sit down and I'll put the kettle on.'

'Not for me thank you, Doris,' he said. He smiled. 'You know my Auntie Bridget is of the firm belief that a cup of tea is the remedy for most everything, it cures all ills.'

Mrs Mossup gave an opaque smile. 'Well, it won't cure this one, that's for sure. It's all around the village about Leanne,' she said.

'And me,' he added.

'Yes, and about you, I'm afraid – but you don't need to worry your head about that, I've put people straight. Last night half the public bar was asking me about it. It doesn't take long for things to get around the village. Course, I couldn't deny Leanne's situation but I told them in no uncertain terms that you had nothing to do with it. It was a malicious rumour that you had.'

'But how did anyone find out?' Tom asked. 'There were only the three of us who knew.'

'No, there weren't,' replied Mrs Mossup. 'I know who is responsible and when he gets back here, I shall give him a piece of my mind.'

'Mr Butt,' said Tom. 'Of course.'

'He was listening at the door. I remember I saw it was slightly open and when I got up to shut it, he was outside. He'd been earwigging all the time and this was confirmed by Toby Croft who said *he'd* been the one to spread the rumour. He'd only heard half of what we said and went up to his room before Leanne came down, so he didn't hear her say that you had nothing to do with it.'

'And where is your daughter now?' asked Tom.

'I sent her off on the Scarborough train yesterday. She's to help my sister out at her B & B until the baby arrives. She's minded to keep the child and I shan't stand in her way. She's not a bad girl you know, Tom. When I'd calmed down, we had a long chat and sorted things out. There's worse things that happen in the world than having an illegitimate child. I didn't press her about who was the father but, no doubt, I shall find out eventually. I'm just so sorry I dragged you into this.'

'It's water under the bridge now,' said Tom.

'Thinking about it,' said the landlady, 'in a sense I wish you were the father. I couldn't think of anyone better.'

'And where is Mr Butt?' asked Tom, feeling embarrassed by her words.

'Selling his fertiliser,' said Mrs Mossup, 'but he's due back tonight and I shall be waiting for him with a few well-chosen words.'

Soon after Tom had gone, the villain of the piece arrived at the King's Head to find his cases by the door. He found Mrs Mossup in the hallway, arms folded over her chest, awaiting his appearance. She had seen his car pull up at the back of the pub.

'What are mi cases doin' out 'ere?' he asked her, as he came in through the door.

'I want you out of here now!' she barked. 'Get your cases and take yourself off. I don't want to see you ever again.'

'What 'ave I done?' demanded the man.

'Don't you dare play the innocent with me!' Mrs Mossup cried. 'You're a nasty, evil-minded, big-mouthed scandalmonger, spreading that wicked rumour about Leanne and Mr Dwyer.'

'I were only sayin' what I ovver'eard,' stated Mr Butt weakly, in a futile attempt to defend himself.

'And what were you doing listening-in to other people's private discussions?' she demanded angrily.

'I couldn't help but hear,' he told her, shocked by the virulence of her outburst. 'You were speaking very loudly. I could hear you in my bedroom.'

'Don't you give me that! You're a liar as well as a gossipmonger. You were outside the parlour door and you only heard half of what was said. If you had have heard the full conversation you would know that Mr Dwyer had nothing to do with our Leanne's situation. I've no doubt that he will be in touch with his solicitor to take you to court for defamation of character.'

'If yer must know—' began Mr Butt, in a voice that sounded far from contrite.

'I don't wish to hear any more from you.' She thrust a piece of paper into his hand. 'And you can settle up before you go.'

'Be reasonable, Mrs Mossup,' he pleaded.

The landlady's face remained disobligingly blank. 'I want you gone and if you are still here in five minutes, I shall have you thrown out.'

As he made his way through the public bar several minutes later, Mr Butt's way was barred by the colossal frame of Arnold Olmeroyde.

'Mester Croft wants a word wi' thee,' he told the man.

'I . . . I . . . I'm in a bit of an 'urry,' said Mr Butt, trying to push past.

''E's ovver theer at t'corner table,' said Mr Olmeroyde, grasping an arm. It was like a vice.

'Come along.'

There were three farmers at the table with Mr Croft.

'We don't like liars an' troublemekkers around 'ere,' he told Mr Butt, 'so I wouldn't bother showin' tha face around these parts any more. I shan't be buying owt from thee again, an' I reckon no other farmer around 'ere will either. Now bugger off!'

15

Sir Marcus Maladroit Boys' Grammar School was named after its founder, a wealthy landowner, manufacturer of shoddy goods and philanthropist, and the great-grandfather of the present baronet.

It was an unprepossessing building constructed of shiny red brick with a great central clock tower and small mullioned windows, standing at the end of a sweeping drive.

Charlie walked into the school to sit the scholarship examination. The entrance smelled of old wood and floor polish. All along one wall were large, polished pale-wooden panels on which were written in gold lettering the names of former pupils who had achieved academic excellence. On another wall were the portraits in oils of former headmasters attired in black gowns. They stared down from their frames with suitably serious expressions on their faces. On a heavy oak table was a bronze bust of a man with large ears and hooded eyes.

A sign with an arrow directed the young applicants to where the examination was to take place. Outside the hall was a knot of boys, around ten or eleven in number and the same age as Charlie. They shuffled nervously and whispered to each other. Most were in school uniforms, some in bright blazers. All wore white shirts, grey flannels and polished black shoes. Charlie stood out in the blue jumper his mother had knitted, baggy jeans and scuffed trainers. The boys stared at him as if he were some strange creature that had found its way into the entrance. Charlie did not feel at all embarrassed but looked back at them and smiled. Presently, a poker-faced teacher in a black gown arrived and the group fell into silence.

The teacher didn't introduce himself but told the boys to pay attention. He was not in a good mood for he had been dragooned by the headmaster into giving up his precious Saturday morning to invigilate the examination.

'In a moment you will be shown into the school hall where you will sit the scholarship examination. You will find your name printed on a card on the desk where you are to sit. Do not open the paper until you are told to do so. You will have one hour in which to answer the questions and you must not leave the hall until the time is up. Write neatly and clearly. I do not think I need to remind you that there will be no talking and to keep your eyes on your own paper.' He paused to let his instructions sink in. 'Are there any questions?' he then asked. No one raised a hand. 'Good,' said the teacher, glancing at his watch. A moment later the bell in the clock tower began to sound ten. 'Follow me,' he instructed. The boys trailed behind the teacher down a long, dark corridor and arrived at the school hall. The teacher pulled on a polished brass handle on the door and ushered the boys inside.

Charlie sat at the designated desk and took out his fountain pen. He rattled through the questions, finishing well before the hour was up.

The teacher with the black gown and the unfriendly face approached.

'Have you finished?' he asked testily.

'Yes, sir,' replied Charlie, smiling.

'You have answered all of the questions, have you?' He sounded surprised.

'Yes, sir.'

'Then I suggest you read through them and make sure you haven't made any mistakes,' the teacher told him.

Charlie was minded to tell him that he really didn't feel it necessary to check his answers for he was confident he had got them right. However, he merely smiled again and nodded.

At the end of the hour, the boys were told to put down their pens and the papers were collected.

'When will we know the results?' Charlie asked the teacher.

'All in good time,' was the reply. 'Now run along.'

On the way out one of the boys in a blazer caught up with Charlie. He was small and spotty and wore large glasses.

'Where are you from?' he asked.

'Risingdale School.'

'I'm at Barton-with-Urebank. How do you think you got on?'

'I think I did all right,' Charlie told him.

'There were some real stinkers, weren't there?' said the boy. 'That last question about the aeroplane got me stumped.'

The last question described an aeroplane flying in a straight line at 355 miles per hour. It passed over point 'A' at 2.35 p.m. and then passed over point 'B'. It stated that the distance between 'A' and 'B' was 71 miles and asked at what time did the aeroplane pass over 'B'?

Charlie worked out the answer in his head but didn't wish to appear big-headed so he nodded. 'Yes, it had me stumped too,' he said.

'My name's Rupert,' said the boy.

'I'm Charlie.'

'I hope we both get in, then there will be someone I know,' he said.

While Charlie was answering the final question on the examination paper, Tom sat with his aunt at a corner table in the Ring o' Bells café in Clayton. After morning coffee he was to take her up to see his newly refurbished cottage, but he wanted to tell her about the rumours that had been flying around the village about him and the fact there was no truth in them. He thought that word might have reached her and he wanted to put the record straight.

(Later Mrs O'Connor was to acquaint Mrs Sloughthwaite with this information. The shopkeeper, when she had been told, resisted the temptation to say that she had already heard the gossip, but only said, 'I just can't be doing with people who tittle-tattle. As if anyone would think such a thing about such a well-brought-up young man as your nephew. The very idea.')

That morning Tom had collected Colin's painting of Roselea Cottage from Tonicraft in Clayton where it had been framed. He had decided rather than giving it to Mrs Golightly himself, he would ask Colin to do it the following week.

'So that's where you live?' said Mrs O'Connor, examining the picture. 'It looks charming, so it does, but won't you be a bit lonely there all by yourself?'

'No, I'll be fine,' answered Tom.

'My Grandmother Mullarkey, God rest her soul, had something similar in Ballinaslow – a small cottage just like yours but with a thatched roof and white walls. Do you know she raised eight children in it. She used to say that a home is not a home unless you hear the patter of tiny feet.'

'Well, I can assure you, Auntie Bridget,' said Tom, 'there will be no patter of tiny feet in my cottage – at least for a long time. Unless, of course, it's a dog.'

When Tom went to pay the bill, there at the counter stood Janette Fairborn.

'Hello,' he said.

'Mr Dwyer,' she replied, turning. He was certainly a striking figure, she thought, with his shiny black curls, long-lashed dark blue eyes and engaging smile. She locked eyes with him for a moment, blushed and looked away. 'And how are you?' she asked, glancing down and fumbling in her purse for some change.

'Fair to middling,' he replied.

She looked up and laughed. 'You are beginning to sound like one of the locals. And how is your cottage coming along?'

'Ee, reight, champion,' said Tom, mimicking Toby Croft. 'I tell thee what, it's comin' on a treat.'

They both laughed.

'Something seems to have amused you.' Jeremy Neville, with a scowl on his face, had appeared like the villain in a Victorian melodrama.

'Ah, Jeremy,' said Janette. 'I thought we said we would meet at ten o'clock.' Suddenly there was an edge to her voice. 'I've been waiting here for half an hour.'

'I got held up.' He looked like a petulant child.

'You know Mr Dwyer, of course,' she said.

'Of course,' he replied, not looking at Tom. There was a withering condescension in his voice. 'Shall we go?' He walked to the door.

Janette paid the bill and said goodbye to Tom.

'Who was that attractive young lady?' asked Mrs O'Connor when Tom had returned to the table.

'Oh, just somebody I've met in the village,' he told her. 'Nobody special.'

'You really didn't need to be so rude, you know,' Janette told Jeremy as they walked down the high street.

'I can't stand that man,' he spat out.

'And what has he done to upset you. You never did tell me.'

'Oh, just forget it, will you,' he said tetchily. 'I don't want to talk about it.'

'Well, I would like to know.'

'I've told you,' he snapped. 'Did you not hear me? I do not wish to talk about it, so just let it drop.'

'You don't need to be so bad-tempered. I don't know what Mr Dwyer has done to you, but you were really rude in the café. It was embarrassing.'

'Oh, I'm sorry. I embarrassed you, did I?' he said sarcastically.

'Yes, you did.'

'And why are you so interested in this Dwyer chap all of a sudden?' he asked.

'I'm not interested in him. I just thought you were so ill-mannered. So what did he do to make you behave like that?'

'You know, sometimes, Jan, you can be a bloody pain in the neck.'

'And so can you,' she countered.

They drove in virtual silence back to the village.

Before she got out of his car, she turned to him. 'I don't feel like seeing you for the time being, Jeremy,' she said.

'Suit yourself,' he replied peevishly.

'Oh, I always do,' she replied.

Driving back to Risingdale with his aunt, Tom caught sight of Charlie sitting in the bus shelter in Clayton High Street reading a book. He pulled over.

'Jump in the back, Charlie,' said Tom. 'I'm going your way. I'll drop you off.'

'Oh, thanks, Mr Dwyer,' said the boy, getting in the car.

'This is Mrs O'Connor,' Tom told him. 'I'm taking her to see my cottage.'

'Hi,' said Charlie.

'Hello, love,' she replied.

'He's my star pupil,' Tom told his aunt, 'and has been sitting an examination this morning at the grammar school. So how did it go, Charlie?'

'All right, I think,' the boy replied. 'The questions weren't that hard but you were right that the tricky ones were in the General Intelligence section.'

'Sounds like something out of a spy novel,' observed Mrs O'Connor. 'Isn't that what the Americans have?'

'That's the CIA, Mrs O'Connor,' Charlie told her, 'the Central Intelligence Agency.'

'How did you get on with the essay?' Tom asked his pupil.

'I thought the questions were a bit silly to be honest,' replied the boy. 'We were asked to pretend to be an ant and describe what we saw crossing a garden or write an imaginary conversation between an eagle and a pigeon. I don't think they would have much to say to each other – the eagle would have killed the pigeon and eaten it. I put a note at the bottom of the paper saying I thought they could have set more interesting questions.'

'Did you indeed?' said Tom, wondering how that would go down with the headmaster.

The following week, when the teachers were on their morning break, Miss Tranter tried to recruit Tom to be in the Christmas pantomime she was producing.

'It's always so difficult,' she sighed, 'to get the right people for the parts. I have a young woman in mind for the female lead, but it's the principal man who presents the problem. Most of the men in CRAP are well past their sell-by date. To have one of those playing the prince, he would be a laughing stock.'

'CRAP!' exclaimed Mr Cadwallader. 'What the devil is CRAP?'

'Clayton and Ruston Amateur Players,' explained Miss Tranter.

'A rather unfortunate acronym,' observed her colleague.

'What is the pantomime you are doing this year?' asked Mrs Golightly.

'It's *The Sleeping Beauty*,' replied Joyce. 'I first considered *Snow White* but was told it is politically incorrect to use the term "dwarf" these days. It's regarded by some as offensive. The correct term is "vertically challenged". I mean you can't have "Snow White and the Seven Vertically Challenged Men". Then I thought of *Cinderella* but came up against the same obstacle.'

'What's wrong with *Cinderella*?' asked Mr Cadwallader.

'You can't describe people as ugly any more,' Miss Tranter told him. I mean *Cinderella* wouldn't be the same without the Ugly Sisters.'

'It's political correctness gone mad,' said Mrs Golightly.

'I don't agree,' said Tom. 'Terms such as "dwarf" and "ugly" are derogatory.'

'How moralistic you sound, Tom,' observed Miss Tranter. 'Well, anyway, to avoid any objections I've opted for *The Sleeping Beauty*. As I said, I think I've found the princess, but it's the handsome prince I know I'll have difficulty in finding.'

Tom felt three pairs of eyes upon him.

'Oh no,' he said. 'You needn't look at me. There's no way I'm playing a prince.'

'But you'd be perfect for the part,' said Joyce. 'You have the looks, the bearing and the legs for it.'

'What have my legs got to do with it?' asked Tom.

'The prince has to wear tights,' Joyce told him. 'He needs to have a good pair of legs. I can't have someone on the stage with sparrow legs. He would be the laughing stock. You've got firm, muscular legs, just right for the part.'

'I sound like a prize Swaledale tup,' he said.

'You have got nice legs, Tom,' said Mrs Golightly. 'When you are in your games kit—'

'Stop right there!' exclaimed Tom. 'There is no way that I'm prancing across a stage in tights.'

'Well, you used to cavort around a football pitch in shorts,' observed Mr Cadwallader. 'What's the difference?'

'A great deal,' said Tom.

'I think you would be right for the part,' said Mrs Golightly. 'You would make a lovely prince.'

'Yes, I agree,' said Mr Cadwallader.

'You would certainly make a few girls' hearts flutter,' added Mrs Golightly.

'You see,' said Miss Tranter, 'we are all agreed.'

'No, we are not all agreed!' snapped Tom. 'I am not playing any prince, so get that right out of your head, Joyce.' He got up to go. 'I've got football this afternoon and need to put the nets out,' he told his colleagues. 'So if you will excuse me.'

'He has got nice legs,' remarked Mrs Golightly as she saw him leave.

Outside the staffroom door, Tom found Colin waiting.

'You wanted to see me, sir,' said the boy. 'Am I in trouble?'

'No, of course not,' said Tom. 'Just wait here one moment.' He hurried to his classroom and returned with the framed painting Colin had done of Roselea Cottage. He gave it to the boy. 'I think it might be nice if you gave this to Mrs Golightly yourself. Just wait a moment.' He went into the staffroom. 'I know it's not usual for pupils to come in here,' Tom told his colleagues, 'but I think we might make an exception on this occasion. Come along in, Colin.' The boy entered the room shyly. 'This young man,' said Tom, putting a hand on Colin's shoulder, 'has painted a very special picture and he would like to present it to you, Mrs Golightly. It's a thank you for all you have done for me, and I hope it will remind you of the happy times you have spent in Roselea Cottage.'

Colin gave the picture to the teacher. 'I hope you like it, miss,' he said.

'Oh my,' said Mrs Golightly, looking closely at the watercolour, 'it's lovely. I'm quite overcome. And you did this, Colin?'

'Yes, miss.'

'Well, it's wonderful. I shall treasure it.'

The boy smiled shyly.

'Now, come along,' said Tom to his pupil, 'Mr Gaunt wishes to see you in his study.'

The smile quickly disappeared from the boy's face. The only times he had been in the headmaster's study was when he was in trouble.

'What have I done, sir?' he asked.

'The headmaster will tell you,' Tom replied.

'Ah, young Colin Greenwood,' said Mr Gaunt, when the boy and his teacher entered the room. 'Come along in and stand in front of my desk.'

'What have I done, sir?' asked the boy again. He eyed the cane displayed on the wall.

'I shall tell you what you have done,' replied Mr Gaunt. He held up an envelope. 'I have a letter here which says you have won the County Art Competition with your watercolour painting of the barn at Bentley Beck. What about that then?'

Colin looked incredulous. 'I w . . . won,' he stammered.

'Mr Dwyer entered your picture and it was judged to be the very best,' Mr Gaunt told him. 'It says here that your watercolour painting was a good composition with a nice use of colour and tonal contrast. Well done.'

The glimmer of a smile returned in the boy's face.

'Well, perhaps if you hadn't been so precipitous,' remarked Sir Hedley, peering over the top of his newspaper, 'you would not be without a housekeeper.'

Sir Hedley Maladroit and Lady Marcia were in the drawing room at Marston Towers having another of their frequent disagreements.

'Precipitous!' repeated the baronet's wife angrily. 'And what pray do you mean by precipitous?'

Her husband looked at the hard face, thin, pursed mouth and habitual frown for a moment without replying. How he had come to dislike the woman with her screwed features, strident hectoring voice and constant complaints. Many had been the time when he had considered divorce but then decided that it would be such a bother and, of course, a costly business with half of his estate disappearing with her. Best just to put up with it, keep his head down and see as little of her as possible.

'Are you listening to me, Hedley?' she asked when he didn't reply.

'Every word,' he replied sardonically.

'Well, might you then tell me what you meant by precipitous?'

Her husband folded his newspaper carefully and rested it in his lap. He stroked his moustache. Sir Hedley was a wordsmith, with an extensive vocabulary. He could complete *The Times* crossword in an hour. 'What I mean by precipitous,' he told her, 'is that your action in sacking Mrs Gosling was hasty, impulsive, rash and impetuous – ergo, precipitous. It was by no means certain that she took your jewellery.'

'Then pray tell me who do you think stole it? Apart from Mrs Gosling, the only other person who goes into my bedroom is me. She had ample opportunity to take it. Or do you imagine that there is some thieving fairy that flew in through the window and stole it?'

'Has it occurred to you, Marcia,' said her husband, 'that you might have misplaced the necklace?'

'No, it has not occurred to me,' she retorted. 'I am not in the habit of misplacing things. I always put my jewellery in the tortoiseshell box on my dressing table. That peridot and pearl necklace was one of my favourites. It belonged to my grandmother and has great sentimental associations. I well recall placing it in the box.'

Sir Hedley examined the crossword on the back of his folded paper. 'Well, now you have sacked Mrs Gosling,' he remarked casually, 'you are without a housekeeper and cannot find anyone in the village, which has no doubt rallied to support her, willing to take her place. Furthermore, you have given the residents of Risingdale yet more ammunition to criticise us.'

'Oh, for goodness' sake, Hedley,' she answered, 'they have had ample ammunition already. Let's be honest, they don't like us because we own most of the land, have money and position and live in a big house. It is pure envy. Some people cannot bear to see others with more than they have. I was snubbed in the village shop by two of the customers yesterday, and I am certain that the shopkeeper gave me last week's bread. When I asked if I could have my orders delivered in future, she told me they don't have that facility. It's just too much.'

'So you are doing your own shopping now,' observed Sir Hedley with a slight smile on his lips.

'Well, of course I'm doing the shopping, for the moment anyway. Who else could do it?'

'Now that you have sacked Mrs Gosling,' Sir Hedley told her, 'then I suppose you will have to do it, won't you, and if you don't like the village shop, then you can always use the supermarket.'

'I do not intend to patronise a supermarket,' his wife said.

'Well, that is up to you,' he replied, returning to his crossword and considering a clue: 'Retribution seems in order.'

'And while I was in the shop this morning, I overheard a conversation concerning that new teacher at the village school,' continued Lady Maladroit.

'Nemesis,' said the baronet.

'What?'

'Retribution seems in order. "Nemesis" is the answer to the clue.'

'You have not heard a word I have been saying, have you?' she demanded. 'Will you please listen? I was saying that while I was in the village shop this morning, I overheard a conversation concerning that new teacher at the village school.'

'There's another instance of your being precipitous,' remarked her husband.

She shut her eyes for a moment, as if composing herself before she spoke. 'What?'

'You sent off letters right, left and centre about the incident in the King's Head only to discover it was our own dear son who was at fault.'

'I don't believe James was at fault,' she countered. 'He was attacked.'

'So the police and the witnesses were all wrong, were they?' asked her husband.

'About what?'

'About what happened in the King's Head.'

'Because they do not like us and never miss an opportunity of trying to get the better of us, those witnesses must have fabricated their evidence,' said his wife.

Sir Hedley sighed. 'So the hikers who happened to be in the bar were lying as well as the locals, the barmaid and the school caretaker?'

'I don't wish to discuss this any more,' she said. 'I was talking about the theft of my necklace.'

'By sacking Mrs Gosling, you have yet again been rash,' the baronet told her. 'I don't believe for a minute that she took your jewellery. You should get the facts right before jumping in at the deep end.'

Realising she was losing the argument, Lady Marcia changed tack.

'In the village shop,' she told her husband, 'I heard more disturbing news about that teacher at the village school. Evidently he has seduced the young woman who serves behind the bar at the King's Head. She is expecting his baby. So that will be another illegitimate child brought into the world and a single parent living off the benefits provided by hard-working people.' Sir Hedley was inclined to remind his wife that she did not number amongst the hard-working people as she had not done a day's work since she married him. However, he let her ramble on and returned to his crossword.

'Prevent strife in dungeon – the silence follows,' was the clue. 'Keep the peace,' he muttered.

'What?'

'Answer to the clue: "Keep the peace".'

'Would you please put down your paper,' she said. 'I am attempting to speak to you.'

Sir Hedley stifled a sigh and lowered his newspaper.

'Not only is that teacher a violent thug but he is also some-one without any morals. And he is supposed to set a good example to children. I think not.'

'I have no doubt that you have it in mind to send a few more letters to the headmaster and the Education Authority and anyone else you think will listen to you,' said Sir Hedley.

'Yes, I shall,' she answered. 'I feel very strongly about it. Immoral people should not be in charge of children.'

The baronet threw the newspaper on the floor and stood. He had had enough. 'Have you heard a word I have been saying? I said you should get the facts right before jumping in at the deep end. Well, let me warn you, Marcia, if you see fit to write another of your letters, you will be opening a can of worms, and I should be very careful, very careful indeed, in making accusations based on some rumour you have overheard in the village shop.'

'One of these days, Hedley,' said his wife, 'you will surprise me by actually agreeing with what I say.'

She then flounced out of the room.

It was later that day Sir Hedley found his wife in the drawing room, sitting at a small desk with gold tasselled drawers folding a large piece of paper and placing in an envelope. The baronet had to admit to himself that he was feeling rather smug.

'Written your letters, have you?' he asked.

'Yes, as a matter of fact, I have just finished,' she replied.

'Then I suggest you tear them up.'

'What?'

'I have just been speaking to Mr Greenwood, the new chap I've employed to help the gamekeeper.'

'And what is that to do with my letters?' she asked.

'Quite a bit actually,' replied her husband. 'Mr Greenwood was telling me how well his son is doing at the village school with his new teacher, you know the one you are complaining about.'

'Well, what of it?'

'The subject of the landlady's daughter came up and Mr Greenwood tells me there is no truth to the rumour concerning the teacher. He is not the father, just the object of some malicious rumour. It is just as well you have not posted your letters, isn't it, Marcia, otherwise the young man in question might get it into his head to take legal action for your defamatory comments.'

Lady Marcia felt it prudent, on this rare occasion, not to respond.

'And where is the Prodigal Son this afternoon?' asked the baronet.

'Please!' interrupted his wife, holding up a hand. 'You never have a good word to say for James. You are forever criticising him.'

'With good reason,' said her husband.

'For your information,' Lady Marcia informed him, 'he is helping out Jeremy Neville at the auction rooms this afternoon.'

'Well, when he has finished that,' said Sir Hedley, 'perhaps he might like to help you out cleaning the house and doing the shopping, since you no longer have a housekeeper.'

Before his wife could respond, the baronet departed for the library to finish his crossword.

To say the son and heir was 'helping out' was something of an overstatement. The man in question was sitting on a stool with his friend at the bar in the King's Head. Mrs Mossup had made it clear when he arrived that, should there be any more trouble, he would be barred.

'Might I remind you, dear lady,' he told her with a disdainful look on his face, 'that it was not I who threw the punch. It was your lodger. He should be barred if anyone is.'

'If you persist on arguing with me, Mr Maladroit, I shall ask you to leave,' she told him.

'And where is that lovely daughter of yours this afternoon?' he asked.

'She's not here.'

'Yes, I can actually see that. Where is she?'

'She's in Scarborough. Now I've told you, any more trouble and you're barred.'

'Silly cow,' he mumbled as she walked off down the bar to serve another customer. 'Do you fancy going into town tonight?' he asked his friend. 'See a bit of action.'

''Fraid not, old chap. I have to sort out the lots for next Saturday's auction.'

'I might have a few things to put in,' said his friend. 'If I do, can you waive the seller's commission?'

'I suppose so. It will not go through the books. Old man Sampson is a stickler for details, so if he finds out, I'll be in hot water. What sort of things do you want to put in anyway?'

'Oh, just a bit of stuff, nothing big, which I've no longer any use for. I need the funds. The old man is as tight as ever.'

'I'm sorting out the catalogue tomorrow, so drop them in.'

'Are you getting anywhere with the delectable Miss Fairbody?' asked James.

'Fairborn,' Jeremy corrected. 'Actually no, she's still a bit of an ice maiden. Our relationship has cooled off lately.'

'I hate it here,' said James suddenly, before taking a great gulp of his drink.

'It is a bit dead,' agreed his friend, 'but the beer's good.'

'I didn't mean this dump. I meant the whole place. It's so claustrophobic. I hate the snooping people, the stinking farmers, the gossipy women. I hate everything about it. All I get at home from the old man is, "Why don't you get a job? When are you going to do something useful? Why don't you make something of yourself?" He goes on and on. It drives me mad.' He took another gulp of his drink. 'I'll be glad when he's dead.'

'Come on, Jamie. You don't really mean that,' said his friend.

'Too bloody right I do. When I inherit the estate, the first thing I'll do is put all the rents up. The old man is too soft with the tenants. Then I'll spend a couple of weeks each year in the south of France and get myself a decent car.'

'You've just got a new car.'

'Hardly new. That little sports job was the only one I could afford. The old man's cut my allowance after what happened in here. Ma gave me the cash. I mean a decent car.'

His friend, wearying of the constant complaints, finished his drink and got up. 'Well, I must go. I've got to sort out all the lots. The boss wants it all done by tomorrow. You can come and help me if you like.'

'I'll give that a miss,' replied James, draining his glass. 'I'm getting another drink.'

At the staff meeting after school, Mr Gaunt held up a letter.

'This concerns the fate of the county's small schools,' he said.

'I knew it!' exclaimed Mrs Golightly. 'They are going to close Risingdale School down.'

'Please, Bertha,' said the headmaster, 'do let me finish. The letter does not say that the Education Authority is closing us down, but it does say that it is, at present, considering whether or not it is viable to keep some of the small schools open. We are numbered amongst several others they are thinking about closing. Let me reassure you that nothing has been decided, so let's not start thinking the worst. Before any decisions are made, there will be a period of consultation where all interested parties will be asked to give their views. This letter is inviting me to a meeting with the Director of Education on Friday morning with some of the Education Sub-Committee to present my argument for keeping Risingdale open.'

'Oh well,' scoffed Mr Cadwallader, 'this so-called period of consultation is a mere cosmetic exercise. They have already decided to close the school, that's certain. They are just going through the motions to give the impression that they are prepared to listen when in fact it has all been decided. I have no confidence at all in elected members. Two-faced most of them. I wouldn't trust them as far as I could throw them. I recall once being told that politicians are like bananas.'

'Bananas?' said Miss Tranter.

'Yes,' said her colleague, 'like bananas. They start off green, become bent, turn yellow and end up rotten.'

'Don't tar all politicians with the same brush, Owen,' said Mr Gaunt. 'Some are dedicated and honest.'

'I have yet to meet any,' retorted his colleague.

'I think Mr Balfour-Smith is a decent sort,' said Tom. 'He was really interested in small rural schools.'

'Two-faced the lot of them,' said Mr Cadwallader. 'I wouldn't count on getting help from him. They will close us, you mark my words.'

'Don't be so pessimistic,' said Mr Gaunt. 'I am sure that if I can present a sound enough argument, we will get a reprieve. After all, we did receive a very favourable report from the HMI, and I shall be contacting the parents asking them to write to their elected member and the Education Authority to lobby them to keep Risingdale open. I shall also seek the support of Mr Pendlebury and Sir Hedley Maladroit.'

'I wouldn't bother with Sir Hedley,' said Joyce. 'Nothing would suit him better than for the school to close. He would buy the building for a shooting lodge.'

'No, Joyce,' replied Mr Gaunt. 'I don't believe so. I think you do Sir Hedley an injustice. He is a man of principle and I am sure we can rely on his backing.'

'I feel sorry for you, Tom,' said Mrs Golightly. 'You've only just started your career and they go and close the school. It's not fair at all.'

'Bertha,' said the headmaster firmly, 'they are not closing the school, not yet at any rate. Let us try and be more optimistic. Now to more cheerful news, Mr Pendlebury has asked if we can stage the Nativity play again in the church. He says in his letter, and I quote, that "last year, although not an unmitigated success, it is so much a part of the Christmas celebrations it would be a shame not to have the Nativity play this year."'

'I don't know what he means by not being an "unmitigated success",' said Mrs Golightly, irked by the comment. (She had produced the play.) 'I thought the children did very well.'

'But you have to admit, Bertha,' said Joyce, 'that things didn't go all that well.'

'Well,' replied her colleague, like a sulky child, 'if you think you can do better, then you produce it.'

'I have the pantomime to direct, which will take up a deal of my time,' replied Miss Tranter. 'I couldn't cope with the Nativity play as well.'

'I am sure that this year, Bertha,' said Mr Gaunt, 'things will go well and, as for last time, I thought you did a sterling job, despite the few problems.'

'Thank you, Mr Gaunt,' she said, looking at Joyce. 'It's nice to be appreciated.'

'The other news is that the football team has won the last match against Ruston which makes three successes in a row. We have Tom to thank for that.'

Following a few weekly football practices, the team started to get things together, the pupils spreading out across the pitch, passing the ball and playing tactically. Although getting beaten by the teams from the bigger schools, the Risingdale players were winning matches against the smaller ones. It was particularly pleasing to Mr Gaunt that his school had beaten Ruston, the neighbouring preparatory school.

'Also I heard this morning,' he continued, 'that Charlie Lister has passed the examination he sat at the grammar school and has been called for interview for a scholarship. The headmaster was most impressed with the boy's paper. Another piece of good news is that Colin Greenwood has won the County Art Competition.'

'Good gracious,' said Mr Cadwallader. 'Did you say Colin Greenwood has won?'

'I did,' Mr Gaunt told him. 'Perhaps Tom might tell us more.'

'Well, Colin has quite a talent for art,' the teacher told his colleagues.

'He did that lovely watercolour of the cottage for me,' said Mrs Golightly. 'He's very good.'

'I entered one of his watercolours – the barn at Bentley Beck,' Tom told the staff. 'It really is a most impressive picture which was judged to be the best of the entries. He wins a twenty-five pound book token, some art materials, and his painting will be displayed in Crompton Museum and Art Gallery.'

'I must say that is a turn-up for the books,' said Miss Tranter.

'All credit to you, Tom,' said Mr Cadwallader. 'The lad was unteachable when poor Miss Cathcart had him in her class.'

'You see,' said Mr Gaunt, 'all your active involvement in the life of the village and all these successes we have had in school will add to my ammunition when I appear before the Education Sub-Committee.'

'Let's hope so,' said Mr Cadwallader doubtfully.

On Remembrance Sunday, Mr Gaunt, the teachers and some of the older pupils of the school gathered around the small war memorial in the village with members of the Royal British Legion and a goodly number of the inhabitants of Risingdale. Following an overlong homily by the vicar, a reading from the diary of a soldier who fought in the Battle of the Somme and the recitation of poems by Carol and Simon, wreaths of poppies were laid on the steps beneath the monument and a bugler sounded the Last Post.

At the conclusion of the service, Simon approached an elderly man wearing a maroon beret and a chestful of medals. He had remained staring at the names carved into the stone on the cenotaph. He stood straight-backed, his arms straight at his sides. He sensed he was being watched, turned and smiled at the boy, who was looking up at him.

'Hello, son,' he said.

'You have a lot of medals,' remarked Simon.

'Just a few,' replied the old soldier.

'You must be very brave.'

'There were many much braver than I,' replied the man reflectively, 'and quite a few of them never made the journey back.'

'Could I ask you something?' asked the boy.

'Of course.'

'Why are the men wearing different coloured hats?'

'They are berets, son, not hats,' the old soldier told him, 'and members of the different regiments wear different coloured berets. I was in the Parachute Regiment, so mine is maroon.'

'You jumped out of aeroplanes?'

'I did.'

'Gosh. Can I ask you something else?'

'Of course you can.'

'After the War were you allowed to keep your gun?'

'No, no. Service weapons had to be given up.'

'Could you keep your helmet?'

'Yes, I kept mine,' the old soldier told him. 'It's behind the tank in my attic.'

'Wow!' exclaimed Simon. 'You have a tank in your attic?'

16

Mrs Lister placed the letter into her son's hand.

'What's this?' asked Charlie.

'You had better read it,' she said, smiling broadly.

Her son studied the paper. 'I passed the exam,' he said. 'I got through.'

'That's what it says,' said his mother. She bent and kissed his cheek. 'My clever son. I'm so proud of you.' She affectionately ruffled his hair. 'I don't know where you get your brains from – certainly not me.'

'Maybe from my father,' said the boy.

'Yes, love, maybe from your father,' she replied. Her face clouded over.

Growing up, Charlie had often asked about his father. His mother had always been evasive when he raised the matter before and had told him that when he was older and able to understand she would explain. She knew the time would come and was not looking forward to it. On his ninth birthday, when her son had asked again, she decided it was time to tell him some of the things, but not all, about his father. She had sat him down and told him that his father was a kind and decent man and very clever, but circumstances meant that he couldn't live with them.

'You see he has another family,' she had explained.

'He's married then,' her son had said bluntly.

'Yes, love, he's married,' she had replied. 'Not very happily, but he's married.'

'So you were never married to him,' the boy had stated.

'No.'

'Well, if he is unhappy, why can't he leave his wife and come and live with us?' Charlie had asked. 'People do that. They get divorced.'

'It's complicated, love,' his mother had told him.

'Why is it complicated?'

'It would make his life and ours very difficult if he were to get divorced.'

'Why?'

'He's a very important man and he . . . it's just complicated.'

'Is he called Lister like us?'

'No, Lister is my maiden name,' she had answered. 'I call myself Mrs Lister. It stops a lot of gossip.'

'You mean about having a son and you're not married?'

'Yes, love.'

'Will I ever get to meet him?' Charlie had asked.

His mother had considered at the time telling her son who his father was and that he had met him. After all, her son had a right to know. But then she thought of all the trouble it would cause particularly for her and Charlie should this information become common knowledge so she decided against it. She knew how gossip spread in the village and how people could be judgemental and cruel. 'One day, when you're grown up,' she had told him, 'I promise I will tell you everything.'

'What is he like?' her son had asked.

'He's kind and clever and people who know him like him. He's also very important.'

'Does he know about me?' Charlie had asked.

'Yes, he knows about you.'

'Does he like me?'

His mother had stifled her tears. She had given her son a hug and kissed his cheek. 'Yes, love, he likes you a lot.'

Charlie had nodded and had asked no further questions. He could see that raising the question of his father distressed his mother but he needed to know. She was wrong not to tell him, he thought. He was old enough to understand. Why was it such a mystery? Why was it so complicated? When would he be told who his father is?

Two weeks before, when he had been sitting at that hard wooden desk in the great school hall at the grammar school and had completed the scholarship paper, he had tried to imagine the father he didn't know. His mother had told him he was a clever and an important man. Perhaps he was like the severe-looking teacher in the black gown who now patrolled the aisles or a rich farmer like Mr Fairborn or maybe someone like Mr Gaunt.

When Tom arrived home from school late one afternoon the following week, he found Mrs Lister waiting on his doorstep. She was holding a large plate covered in a muslin cloth.

'Hello,' he said.

'Good afternoon, Mr Dwyer.'

'It's Charlie's mum, isn't it?'

'That's right,' the woman replied. 'I hope I've not come at an inconvenient time.'

'Not at all. I'm pleased to see you,' he told her, unlocking the cottage door. 'Come in, come in.'

'I brought you this,' she told him, as they entered the hall. 'It's an apple pie, a small thank you for all you are doing for Charlie.'

Tom took the plate from her. 'That's very kind of you,' he said. 'I'll pop it in the kitchen and put the kettle on.'

'Oh, I won't stay,' she replied quickly.

'Do go into the sitting room and stay for five minutes. I'd like to have a chat about Charlie.'

Mrs Lister perched on the end of the settee.

'Charlie's passed his grammar school examination and he's got an interview to see if they will give him a scholarship,' she said.

'Yes, Mr Gaunt told me,' answered Tom. 'He said the headmaster at the grammar was very impressed with your son's paper. I am confident he will sail through the interview. He's a very clever young man and a credit to you. You must be very proud of him.'

'Oh, I am,' said Mrs Lister. 'He's never been any trouble. Charlie's always been good-natured and well-behaved.' She looked down at her feet, thinking what she might say next.

'Was there something you wished to see me about?' asked Tom.

'Well, yes, there is,' she replied. 'You probably know that Charlie's father doesn't live with us.'

'Yes, he told me.'

'Did he say anything else?'

'No, nothing else.'

'I thought he might have said something more to you.'

'No.'

'It's just that as he grows up he's raised the matter a few times, asking about his father. I've been very vague and just told him he is a good and kind man.'

'So you still see Charlie's father then?' asked Tom.

'Yes I do.'

'And he knows about Charlie?'

'Oh yes, he knows he has a son. The problem is that he is a married man. People in the village assume I'm a widow. I don't say I'm any different if I'm asked. You are the first person I've told, in confidence.'

'I see,' said Tom, wondering why she felt it necessary to share this information with him.

'Charlie's father has made certain that we are very well provided for. I don't pay any rent for the cottage and I get a monthly allowance to pay the bills. When I told him that Charlie was to enter for a scholarship to cover the costs of the grammar school education, he said he would pay for anything that was needed and there was no need for Charlie to sit the examination, but I was adamant that he should not have to spend any more money on us. I don't want to take advantage of his generosity. I suppose you think that is rather silly.'

'Not at all,' said Tom.

'Anyhow, Charlie's been asking more and more about his father lately, and it's presented me with something of a dilemma. One part of me says he is old enough to know the truth and another that if I tell him there will be all sorts of . . . of consequences. It would be very difficult for his father and for Charlie and me if it becomes common knowledge.'

'I see,' said Tom. 'And what about Charlie's father? What does he think?'

'The same as I do. We really don't know what to do for the best. You are probably wondering why I am telling you this, Mr Dwyer,' she said. 'Well, the reason is that Charlie likes and respects you, and if there is one person who he can trust and be open and honest with, it's you. I know that.'

'As I've said, Mrs Lister,' replied Tom. 'Charlie hasn't mentioned anything to me about his father. He's a happy, well-adjusted and very clever young man. He's also very mature for his age, and I am sure will take anything you choose to tell him in his stride. Of course, it is for you and his father to decide what or what not to tell him.'

'I know that,' she answered. 'I just wanted to make sure that Charlie was still happy in school and not fretting about things. As I said, I thought he might have confided in you.'

'Well, he hasn't,' Tom told her, 'but if he does, I shall let you know.'

'I'd appreciate that,' said Mrs Lister. 'Thank you for listening.'

Tom walked with Mrs Lister down the path. She stopped at the gate to shake his hand. 'I hope you like the apple pie,' she told him.

At that very moment, Miss Janette Fairborn trotted down the bridleway on her chestnut mare. She stared for a moment at the tall, pale-complexioned woman with the abundant explosion of curly black hair who stood by the gate, then gave Tom the characteristic small smile, while nodding her imperious head.

The interview at the grammar school took place the week after Mrs Lister's visit to Tom's cottage. Charlie had to miss school to attend.

'Just be yourself,' Tom had advised his pupil the day before. 'Don't try and tell the panel what you think they want to hear. You've passed the first hurdle and I know you'll get over the next. Good luck.'

Charlie and his mother now waited in a small reception room at the grammar school. They had made their way that morning through a crowd of chattering pupils, all dressed alike in blue blazers with gold beading. They looked so confident. The headmaster's secretary appeared. She was a tall woman with a round red face and tiny, very dark eyes and had a pair of glasses on a cord around her neck.

'Would you like to come this way, Mrs Lister,' she said, smiling, 'the panel is ready to see you and your son now.'

Charlie and his mother were shown into the headmaster's study. It was a plain room containing a large mahogany partner's desk, a set of heavy oak bookcases filled with old-looking tomes and folders, several hard-backed chairs and a row of ugly olive-green metal filing cabinets. There was a square of carpet on the polished wooden floor and a large portrait in oils in a gilt frame of the school's founder on the wall. Sir Marcus stared down with a suitably stern expression on his face.

Three people sat behind the desk: an angular man in tweeds with greying curly hair, close-set, unsmiling grey eyes and heavy black eyebrows, who sat upright and straight-faced like a cemetery statue; the Chairman of Governors, the portly, red-cheeked Sir Hedley Maladroit; and sandwiched between them a fair, good-looking man approaching middle age. This individual smiled widely, rose to his feet, shook hands with Charlie's mother and wished her a 'Good morning.' He then gestured to two chairs which had been placed before the desk and asked her and her son to take a seat.

'I am Kevin Crawford, the headmaster,' he told them. 'I am delighted you have been able to come and see us.'

The mother was clearly very nervous. He noticed how her hands were shaking. She had an anxious look on her face and sat straight-backed in the chair, her legs pressed together and her hands twisting a ring on her finger. The boy, by contrast, appeared to the headmaster to be remarkably composed and looked around inquisitively with his dark eyes taking everything in. Most of the other young candidates who had appeared before the panel had either fidgeted apprehensively or stared frozen like frightened rabbits caught in the headlight's glare. Despite the headmaster's friendly and encouraging manner, they had answered the questions in trembling voices. This young man was intriguing. He had a steady gaze and looked perfectly at ease. There was something about the boy that reminded the headmaster of someone – the wide mouth, dark eyes and large ears.

'May I introduce my colleagues,' said Mr Crawford. He looked to his right. 'This is Councillor Brewster, one of the foundation governors.' The man gave the slightest of nods. There was not a trace of a smile. The headmaster turned to his left. 'And this is the Chairman of Governors, Sir Hedley Maladroit.' The baronet, for some reason lost on the headmaster, shifted rather uneasily in his chair but managed a smile. 'Good morning,' he said.

'Good morning,' replied Charlie's mother, almost inaudibly.

The baronet coloured a little and gave a small cough.

'I do know Mrs Lister,' he said. 'She is one of my tenants. She rents one of my tied cottages on Rattan Row. I visit there occasionally to ensure that everything is satisfactory.' Then he added purposefully, 'I do that with all my tenants.'

The headmaster wondered why his Chairman of Governors felt it necessary to share this information with the panel, but he moved on.

'Well, let's make a start,' he said, tapping a paper on his desk. 'You performed exceptionally well in the scholarship examination,' he told Charlie. 'Mr Evans, who was the invigilator when you took the test, tells me you completed the paper before everyone else.' The teacher in question had been to see the headmaster with the papers on the Monday morning and mentioned the strange little boy who, in his baggy jumper and jeans, looked so different from the other candidates.

'I enjoyed doing it,' said Charlie.

'Your answers were particularly neat and well-written,' remarked the headmaster, 'and in ink.'

'Mr Dwyer, my teacher at Risingdale likes us to use a fountain pen,' Charlie told him.

'I prefer a fountain pen to a biro myself,' admitted Mr Crawford. 'I gather you were not very impressed with the essay questions,' he remarked, glancing down at Charlie's comments on the paper. He had an amused expression on his face.

'Well, I thought we might have been asked to write something rather more interesting than pretending to be an ant crossing a garden or about two birds having a conversation. I'm afraid they didn't leave much to the imagination.'

'And what would you suggest?' asked the headmaster, intrigued by the boy's sureness.

'A favourite time of year maybe or a holiday or a visit to somewhere special,' replied Charlie.

Mr Crawford smiled. 'Well, we will see if we can improve on the essay questions next time,' he said.

'I liked the part on General Intelligence,' said Charlie, 'and the arithmetic.'

'The tricky sections,' said the headmaster, The boy had performed better than any of the other candidates in these parts of the paper. 'Well now, would you tell me something about yourself: what you enjoy doing in your spare time, the things you think you are good at, what subjects you like at school.'

'I like to go for walks,' said Charlie. 'I enjoy fishing and am a keen birdwatcher.'

'And what birds have you seen?' asked Councillor Brewster, thinking his question would catch this young man out. Several of the previous candidates, wishing to impress, had informed the panel they had an interest in politics, current affairs or history, only to be found wanting when asked to elaborate.

'I've seen lots,' replied Charlie.

'Such as?' asked Councillor Brewster.

'Snipe, redshank, black grouse, golden plovers, sandpipers, woodcock, curlew. There are too many to mention. My favourite bird is the red kite. I love to watch him diving down from the sky.'

'On my grouse,' added Sir Hedley, chuckling. 'I can't say that the red kite is my favourite bird.'

'And what else do you like doing in your spare time?' the headmaster asked Charlie.

'I've taught myself the ukulele and one day, when my mum can afford it, I'd like to get a guitar,' said Charlie.

'And you like reading, don't you?' added his mother. 'His nose is never out of a book.' She felt her son was doing himself no favours by talking about birdwatching and playing the ukulele.

'What are you reading at the moment?' the councillor asked Charlie.

'I'm reading *Nicholas Nickleby*. It's by Charles Dickens.'

'Yes, I know who wrote it,' said the councillor with a slight unfriendly smile. 'I assume you are reading the simplified version,' he added condescendingly. 'The original novel, I imagine, would be too long and difficult for a boy of your age.'

'Oh no,' replied Charlie confidently, looking the man in his grey eyes. 'I read the originals. Actually, I've read quite a few of Dickens's novels.'

'And what others have you read?' inquired the governor, raising an eyebrow.

'*David Copperfield, Oliver Twist, Martin Chuzzlewit, The Old Curiosity Shop* and some others.'

'Really,' said the man. He gave another thin smile that conveyed little more than feigned interest.

'And what appeals to you about the novels of Charles Dickens?' asked Mr Crawford.

The boy sat forward in his chair. 'Well, the stories are really good for a start and full of suspense,' he said, 'and the characters are interesting, not just the good ones, but the villains like Fagin and Mr Murdstone, Bill Sikes and the headmaster of Dotheboys Hall, Wackford Squeers. Mr Squeers is stupid but also cruel and uses the cane on the pupils.'

Sir Hedley gave a hearty laugh. 'Well, young Charlie,' he said, 'if you come to this school you will find the headmaster here not at all like your Mr Squeers. He is certainly not stupid.'

'But may on occasions use the cane on those boys who do not behave themselves,' added Councillor Brewster.

'Do you know, Councillor,' Mr Crawford told him, piqued by the irrelevant interventions, 'in the eight years I have been headmaster at the school, I have never had recourse to the cane.'

Mr Brewster, a great believer in corporal punishment, felt this was not the time to argue the efficacy of using the cane. He would leave that until the next governors' meeting.

'And you play the ukulele?' he asked. His tone sounded patronising.

'Yes, I do,' replied Charlie. He wrinkled his brow before adding, 'but not very well.'

'And what about sports? Do you like football and cricket?'

'I'm afraid I'm not very good at football and I've never played cricket. I'm not really a team player.'

'I see.' The councillor turned his attention to Charlie's mother. 'Your husband was unable to make the interview this morning, Mrs Lister?' he asked.

'No.'

'I always think it is important that both parents take an interest in their child's education.'

'I don't have a husband.'

'I see,' said the councillor. A one-parent family, he noted. 'And tell me, Mrs Lister, what do you do for a living?'

Charlie's mother had taken a dislike to the man and answered frankly, 'I don't have a job at the moment.'

'So you are unemployed,' said Mr Brewster.

'Yes, I am.'

'You will appreciate I am sure, Mrs Lister,' continued the governor, 'that competition for a scholarship is fierce and that we have to be certain that the parents, or parent, is fully supportive of the school and will encourage their child to work hard, and will also have sufficient funds to cover certain costs, not contained within the bursary, that may be incurred.'

Before Mrs Lister could answer any further intrusive questions, the headmaster, who had wearied of the grilling, interjected, 'I am sure Mrs Lister is well aware of that, Councillor Brewster,' he said. 'Shall we move on? Sir Hedley, have you any questions?'

'Tell me, Charlie,' asked the baronet, 'why do you want to come to this school?'

'Well, I never really thought about coming here,' the boy answered. 'It was just that my teacher, Mr Dwyer, suggested that I try for a scholarship. He said a school like this would suit me.'

Sir Hedley thought for a moment. He had heard a lot of late about the young teacher who had started at the village school. He had certainly made an impact since he had been in Risingdale. He would be interested to meet him.

'Mr Dwyer is a very good teacher,' continued Charlie. 'He reminds me of Nicholas Nickleby. He's kind and clever.'

'It is good to hear you speaking so highly of your teacher,' said Sir Hedley. He turned to the headmaster. 'I can't say that I have many good things to say about my teachers at the boarding school I attended.' He then added for the benefit of the other governor, 'Too handy with the cane for my liking.'

Following another series of questions, all of which Charlie answered honestly and with self-assurance, the headmaster asked the boy if there was anything he wished to ask.

'I can't think of anything, sir,' he said.

'And if you were offered a place,' said Sir Hedley, 'would you get to school on time, look smart, finish your homework and do what the teachers tell you to do?'

'Yes, sir,' replied Charlie. 'I'll do my best.'

'That is all we ask of any boy who comes to this school,' said Mr Crawford, 'to do his best.'

'That being the last candidate,' said Mr Crawford, when Charlie and his mother had left, 'we can now consider which of the boys should be awarded the bursaries. You will be aware that we have had a record number of applicants this year and, as you have mentioned, Councillor Brewster, the competition is great. Most of those who sat the scholarship examination performed very well. It will be a difficult task to select the final six.'

'I do feel we can discount the last candidate,' said Mr Brewster.

'Why?' asked Sir Hedley.

'I felt the boy was rather too cocky for my liking,' said the governor. 'What was all this about not liking the essay questions on the paper? I thought that to be impudent. He had far too much to say for himself. I question whether he has actually read all those Dickens's novels that he claimed. I think he was probably prompted by his teacher to say what he thinks we wished to hear and to try and impress the panel.'

'Perhaps you should have asked him to read an extract,' said Sir Hedley wryly, 'then you would have discovered if he was telling the truth or not. For my money, I believed the boy.'

'Quite apart from that,' continued the councillor, 'he can't play any instrument except for the ukulele and has no interest in sports. Surely, we are looking for boys who can add something to the school – take part in the orchestra, play sports, act in the school plays. He said himself he is not a team player.'

Mr Crawford thought for a moment as the governor, as was his tendency, rattled on. This boy was clearly talented and would add immeasurably to the school. He was bright, interested and could express his views with enthusiasm. Such youngsters, often described as precocious by those who felt that children should be seen and not heard, were often not liked. He, however, was very taken with the boy.

Councillor Brewster was still in full flow. 'Also I feel that his mother would not be as supportive as we would wish. Furthermore—'

'I am sure you have made your feelings very clear,' interrupted Sir Hedley. 'And I should add that we are not here to interview the mother.'

'But I do feel—' started the councillor.

'Might I be allowed to say something?' said the baronet, turning to Mr Crawford.

'Of course,' said the headmaster, thankful for the intrusion.

Sir Hedley leaned forward towards the desk and turned to his fellow governor. 'I should like to remind Councillor Brewster for whom these awards are intended,' said the baronet. 'My great-grandfather established the bursaries for children from less-well-off homes, whose parents had not the wherewithal to pay for the expenses, children such as young Charlie Lister, whom I found enthusiastic, confident and likeable, and, by his performance on the scholarship paper, he is clearly very clever as well. Some of the boys we have seen are from homes with parents who can well afford to pay for the costs of coming here. I completely disagree with you and I fully support Charlie Lister's application.'

'If I may respond to that, Sir Hedley—' began the other governor, 'I should just like to point out—'

'I don't think we will agree,' the baronet told him, 'so it would prove fruitless to discuss this any further. I suggest we leave it to the headmaster to decide. He has the casting vote.'

Before the other governor could respond, Mr Crawford spoke up. 'I agree with Sir Hedley,' he said. 'I would like to offer Charlie Lister a bursary.'

After Sir Hedley and Councillor Brewster had departed, Mr Crawford became pensive. That last candidate did remind him of someone. His eyes were for some reason drawn to the portrait of the school's founder. Of course, the boy looked like Sir Marcus. He had the same dark eyes, large ears and wide mouth, the features of the founder's great-grandson. Mr

Crawford leaned back in his chair smiled. 'I wonder?' he said out loud. 'I just wonder.'

County Hall was a solid and imposing grey-stone building, like many a Yorkshire town hall, standing in the centre of Clayton. Its sturdy and prominent presence was equalled only by the great pale stone cathedral. Built in the late nineteenth century when the city flourished as an important mill town, County Hall, with impressive pillars and decorative porticos, exuded wealth and self-importance. It stood in stark contrast to the crumbling, concrete post-war civic buildings which disfigured some neighbouring towns. Surrounding County Hall were formal gardens with carefully tended lawns, box hedges, symmetrical herbaceous borders and neat gravelled footpaths.

Mr Gaunt stood and stared up at the building, with a fixed expression on his face. It had been over twenty years since he had been inside, when he had been called for an interview for the headship of Risingdale. He recalled the occasion well and his nervous anticipation as he walked up the long drive to the entrance. He had spoken at that time of the importance of the village school, how it was at the very centre of a community and should be preserved. He now had to argue the case again and felt as nervous, possibly more so, because that morning much depended on the persuasion of his argument. Over the years, people often wondered why he had remained at that small village school for so long. Surely a better-paid position in a bigger, more challenging school should have attracted him. They didn't know, however, how deep was his affection for Risingdale, for the children, the community and the village.

A young man in a blue overall and large boots, pushing a barrow-load of hedge clippings and dead flowers before him, stopped and observed the headmaster.

'Champion day,' he said.

'Yes, indeed,' replied Mr Gaunt. 'Lovely and bright and quite warm for the time of year. The gardens look very neat and tidy by the way.'

'Well, I do try my best and you can't do more than that, can you?' he said, chuckling, and resting his barrow for a moment. 'Course they'll look better in spring and summer. You don't recognise me, do you?'

Mr Gaunt screwed up his eyes and looked into the young man's face. 'I'm afraid not,' he replied.

'I've grown a bit since you last saw me. You used to teach me. I'm Lloyd Cooper.'

'Lloyd Cooper,' repeated the headmaster. He thought for a minute. 'Yes, yes, I do remember you and you are right, you have changed a bit.' The young man, he recalled, had been a shy, nervy, underconfident child who found schoolwork hard. His reading had been poor and he had struggled with his writing but he had a sunny disposition and was helpful and well-behaved.

'I wasn't much of a scholar, was I, sir?' said the young man.

'But you were good-hearted,' replied Mr Gaunt, 'and you tried your best.'

'I loved Risingdale School,' said the young man. 'It was like being in a big family. Everybody knew everybody else and we all got along. Wasn't like that at the big school. It was too big and unfriendly. I was in the bottom group and the teachers didn't bother with us much. Headmaster didn't know my name. I was glad to leave.' He smiled and looked around at the gardens stretching before him. 'I love this job, being in the outdoors, seeing things grow, keeping everything neat and tidy. I've done pretty well considering. I'm the head gardener here.'

'I'm glad for you, Lloyd,' said Mr Gaunt.

'I have two kids and both of them have brains to burn. They get it from their mum.'

The young man held out his hand. 'I want to thank you, sir, for all you did for me. You were good-hearted too and tried your best,' he said, grinning and repeating the headmaster's words.

Mr Gaunt shook the young man's hand. 'It's been a pleasure to see you again, Lloyd,' he said.

'Likewise,' replied the young man.

The interior of the building was like a deserted museum, silent and cool, with long echoing oak-panelled corridors, high, ornate ceilings, marble figures and busts, leather-covered benches and highly polished doors. Huge framed portraits in oils of former councillors, mayors, aldermen, leaders of the Council, high sheriffs, lord lieutenants, members of parliament and other dignitaries lined the walls. The men featured in the paintings (and they were all men) stared down self-importantly from their gilded frames. It was a gloomy and intimidating place.

Mr Gaunt was shown into a large and impressive room smelling of wood and furniture polish. A solid mahogany desk inlaid with an olive-green rectangle of leather dominated the centre. Tall glass-fronted bookcases lined one wall and framed pictures and prints were displayed on the other. Opposite the bookcases a huge window gave an uninterrupted view over Clayton, busy and bustling with morning traffic. He stared out of the window and rehearsed in his head what he would say and thought of the questions he might be asked.

He was soon joined by the Director of Education. Ms Tricklebank was a dumpy, rosy-faced woman with grey appraising eyes. Mr Gaunt had only met her twice and only briefly. She had the reputation of being a strong-minded and formidable woman.

'Good morning, Mr Gaunt,' Ms Tricklebank said in a brisk, business-like manner. 'Thank you for coming.'

'Good morning,' he replied. 'I appreciate the opportunity of sharing my views with you.'

'Let us move to one of the committee rooms,' she said. 'There's a bit more space there. Joining us this morning are several councillors who sit on the Education Sub-Committee. I should say at the outset that no decision on the future of Risingdale School has been taken and it will not be resolved today. This is merely an exploratory meeting for us to share our views. I want to assure you that I am greatly in favour of keeping open schools like yours and have argued the case strongly for their retention. You will appreciate, however, that the decision is in the hands of the elected members, who are looking to make savings in the education budget.'

In the committee room, three people were seated around a large oak table. There was a lean man in tweeds with greying curly hair and close-set, unsmiling grey eyes, a plump woman of indeterminate age with a pale, oval face and black hair drawn back into a loose knot and a thin, youthful-looking individual who sported a shock of ginger hair.

'May I introduce Mr Gaunt, the headmaster of Risingdale School,' said Ms Tricklebank.

There was a chorus of 'Good morning.'

'And at the table,' she continued, 'are Councillor Brewster, Councillor Staniland and Councillor Cooper.'

Mr Gaunt sat opposite the three figures. Ms Tricklebank sat next to him.

'We have asked you to come along this morning, Mr Gaunt,' said the Director of Education, 'as part of our consultation exercise concerning the future of the small schools in the county. The elected members are most interested in your views and to learn something about the school where you are the headmaster and to gain an insight into the work and life in a small rural primary school. So if you would like to start.'

'Good morning,' said Mr Gaunt. He took a breath. 'As I mentioned to the Director of Education, I welcome this opportunity of sharing some of my views on small schools. There are three areas I wish to cover: the safety of the children, the effects on the community should Risingdale School close and the education we provide. I shall try to be as succinct as possible.

First, it is essential that children feel safe and secure. I am sure we can agree on that. The school where I am headmaster is at the very top of the Dale. It is set in the most stunning Yorkshire countryside but is subject to the bleakest winters and the most inclement weather at other times. Sometimes the snow falls in earnest and we are cut off. There is only one road into the village and the school is a mile further north. Were Risingdale to close the children would have to be bussed to neighbouring schools. Sometimes, as a consequence of the extreme weather conditions, the road is impassable and the pupils would not be able to leave the village or surrounding farms. They would therefore miss their education. Of course, for any bus which braved the snow and ice, the journey would be a hazardous one to say the least.

'If I may now turn to the effects on the community should the school close. Much has remained unchanged in the village for over a century. There is still St Mary's Church, the duck pond, the village hall, the country inn, the village shop and the school. To close Risingdale School, which has the unique position at the very centre of the community, would have a disastrous impact upon the lives of the people who live in the area.

'As regards the education which the school provides, I would argue that it is second to none. The classes are small and staffed by dedicated, fully qualified teachers who have chosen to work in this kind of school rather than the big city ones because they are passionate believers in the type of education the small school can provide. The caretaker, cleaner and school secretary are former pupils and feel as committed as the teachers. The classrooms are clean and cheerful and we have ample resources. Our children are drawn from largely farming backgrounds; they are well-behaved and work hard and they achieve a good standard of work. All our children have a deep knowledge of the environment, not only relating to farming but also about the flora and fauna which flourish in the area. They have a sound knowledge of the history and the geography of the region and beyond. We teach them to value this part of the country, to take care in the appearance of the school but also of the village. There is a strong tradition of service in the school. The older pupils look after the smaller children in the playground. Recently, a group of older children transformed the overgrown churchyard, cutting and pruning, digging and planting bulbs. We have an active relationship with the church. The vicar is a regular visitor to the school to take assemblies and speak to the children and a while ago encouraged the pupils to take part in a special service on the Feast of St Francis. Ours is a close-knit community. To my mind, education is about developing healthy, happy, well-behaved children who are caring and truthful, who love to learn and achieve excellent academic standards. Now, should there be any questions, I should be pleased to answer them.'

Councillor Brewster leaned back in his chair and sucked in his bottom lip. 'That is all very well,' he said, 'but I am sure you will appreciate that the Education Authority has to make cuts to balance the budget. The maintenance of small schools is very expensive. We have to find the money from somewhere.'

'Of course I appreciate that,' replied Mr Gaunt, 'but I would hope that the money can be found from some other source.'

'Perhaps we should invite you to look at our finances and advise us from where this other source might be,' said the councillor condescendingly. He glanced at his notes. 'Now you say that Risingdale School provides an education as good as or even better than in the big schools.'

'Yes, I said that.'

'Rather an extravagant claim, isn't it? Can it really offer the broad, balanced and challenging curriculum found in schools of a greater size than yours?'

'Indeed it can. I would like to draw your attention to the recent report from Her Majesty's Senior Inspector of Schools, Miss Tudor-Williams, who visited Risingdale School and judged our curriculum to be very good.'

'I have a copy of the report should you wish to see it,' Ms Tricklebank interjected.

'Does the curriculum include sporting activities?' continued Councillor Brewster.

'Yes, the children play a range of sports and we have become successful in competitive games. Indeed our school football team has won its third successive match against teams from much bigger schools. One of our teachers was a former professional footballer.'

'What about art and drama?' asked Councillor Staniland.

'These subjects are on the curriculum and the children perform well in both. Recently, one of our pupils won the County Art Competition. As regards drama the pupils have a lesson each week. We have a former professional actress on the staff. This year some of our children will be performing in the pantomime at the theatre in Clayton, and, of course, there is the traditional Harvest Festival service and the Nativity play performed in the church.'

'But how do you cater for the wide range of ability within the school?' persisted Councillor Brewster.

'Very effectively,' he was told. 'There is, as you say, a wide range of ability amongst the children, from high flyers such as the boy who recently was offered a full scholarship at the grammar school to those who need extra help in their studies. The latter group I take each week for special support.'

'Perhaps I might come in here,' said Councillor Staniland, irked by her colleague's domination of the proceedings. 'Risingdale sounds to me to be a remarkable school, Mr Gaunt, and you and your teachers should be congratulated for all the work you do.'

'Hear, hear,' agreed Councillor Cooper and before Councillor Brewster could start the interrogation again, he continued. 'I really don't think we need to take up any more of your time. I am sure you are keen to return to Risingdale School.'

Ms Tricklebank walked with Mr Gaunt to the reception area.

'As I have said,' she told him, 'I have been arguing the case with the elected members for maintaining our small schools for some time with little effect, I fear. Your presentation this morning, I think, has had a much greater impact than mine and I thank you.'

17

'I suppose we shall have to show our faces,' said Joyce wearily. 'Mr Gaunt was keen that we should all go, although I could think of better ways of spending my evening.'

The teacher was on yard duty with Tom one Friday morning break.

'Actually,' he replied. 'I am rather looking forward to it.'

'I take it you don't get out much, do you?' said Joyce.

'Pardon?'

'You must lead a pretty tedious life,' she said, 'to describe attending the unveiling of a plaque at the Church Hall as exciting. Watching paint dry would be more thrilling.'

'Least said the better about paint,' replied Tom. 'I've got paint coming out of my ears with all the decorating at the cottage.'

'Well, I'm warning you,' said Joyce, 'the evening promises to be deadly dull.'

'It will give me a chance to meet more of the villagers,' replied Tom, 'particularly the parents of some of the children I teach.'

'I see quite enough of them at parents' evenings without meeting them socially,' replied his colleague. 'They'll be bending your ear all night.'

'When are we going to have a parents' evening?' asked Tom.

'Next term,' she answered. 'Mr Gaunt keeps them down to a minimum.'

Their conversation was interrupted by a small ginger-headed boy of about seven with a face full of freckles and a small green candle emerging from his crusty nostril. He ran up to the teachers, frantically waving his hand in the air.

'Miss! Miss! Miss!' he cried. 'Mark has just used a rude word.'

'Well, ignore him,' said the teacher casually. 'And wipe your nose.'

The boy rubbed his nostrils on his coat sleeve and sniffed. 'He used the "R" word, miss,' said the boy with a shocked expression on his small face.

'The "R" word,' repeated Joyce, racking her brain to think of the offending expletive.

She looked at Tom. He shrugged and shook his head.

'What word was it?' she asked the child.

'It's very rude, miss, and I don't want to say it,' the boy answered.

'Well, whisper it,' said Joyce intrigued. She bent and placed her ear next to the boy's mouth.

'R-sole,' muttered the boy.

'Go and tell Mark I wish to see him,' said the teacher.

The boy ran off with a smug expression on his freckled face and returned a moment later with the reprobate, another small, freckled individual with a runny nose.

'Did you call Nicholas Wilkinson a rude word?' Joyce asked the boy. She put on her stern expression.

'Yes, miss,' replied the child, 'but he called me a name.'

'What did he call you?' asked the teacher.

'A pikelet.'

'A what?'

'A pikelet, miss.'

Joyce turned to Tom and shrugged.

'I think he meant pillock,' he told her sotto voce, and supressing a smile.

Miss Tranter directed her attention back to the two little boys. 'If I hear either of you two calling each other rude names again, you will stay in all lunchtimes this week. If I had used words like that when I was your age, my teacher would have washed my mouth out with carbolic soap and cold water. Do you both understand?'

The two boys nodded and answered, 'Yes, miss,' despite the fact they had never heard of carbolic soap.

'Off you go then,' said the teacher.

The children scurried off.

'As I was saying,' said Miss Tranter, 'tonight will be tiresome and entirely uneventful.'

In this she was proved wrong.

When Tom, dressed in a smart suit, crisp white shirt and college tie, arrived at the church hall that evening, the place was buzzing. It seemed that the entire village had turned out. A knot of farmers, including Toby Croft, Ernie Sheepshanks and Arnold Olmeroyde, were in animated conversation; Mrs Mossup, in a colourful outfit like a converted curtain, was in full flow with a group of women; and John Fairborn and his daughter were chatting to a large man, a sour-faced woman and a distinguished-looking cleric. As he made his way to join his colleagues, Tom was buttonholed by the vicar.

'Ah, Tom,' said Mr Pendlebury, 'I am so pleased to see you. Do come along and meet the bishop. He is very keen to have a word with you.'

The Right Reverend Charles Atticus, suffragan Bishop of Bilsdon, was not a handsome man in any conventional sense, but he had a thoughtful, intelligent face and kindly eyes. His calm, warm and attentive manner endeared him to all those with whom he came into contact. At the approach of the vicar, he stopped talking to his companions: the stout, ruddy-cheeked individual with an impressive walrus moustache and dark hooded eyes and the lean woman with a lined, pinched face.

'May I introduce Mr Thomas Dwyer,' said Mr Pendlebury. 'This is Sir Hedley and Lady Maladroit, the Bishop of Bilsdon and I guess you know Mr Fairborn and his daughter Janette.'

'Good evening,' said Tom.

There was a look of majestic indifference on Lady Maladroit's face. The bishop smiled and extended a long priestly hand. The farmer and his daughter said 'Good evening' and Sir Hedley nodded. Lady Maladroit gave Tom a hostile stare and remained stiffly silent.

'My dear, Mr Dwyer,' enthused the bishop, 'it is indeed a pleasure to meet you. Mr Pendlebury has been singing your praises. Thank you so much for your prompt and public-spirited action.' He turned to the others in the group. 'Mr Dwyer,' he explained, 'foiled the thieves who were attempting to strip the lead from St Mary's roof. Had it not been for him, I have little doubt but that we would have had to close the church.'

'It was lucky that I saw something suspicious,' replied Tom. 'I am sure that anyone would have acted in the same way.'

Lady Maladroit looked distastefully at him. Not a muscle of her face moved.

'Not so,' said Sir Hedley, 'I am afraid that these days people tend to mind their own business. They see a fight and look the other way.'

Tom wondered if this was an oblique reference to the incident in the King's Head, concerning the speaker's son when he had not minded his own business. However, when the baronet continued, he was reassured that this was not the case. 'Most folk don't get involved if they see a wrongdoing,' said the baronet. 'You are to be congratulated, young man.'

Disapproval was writ large on his wife's face.

'Actually,' continued the baronet, 'I have come across your name before, Mr Dwyer.'

Oh dear, thought Tom. His argument with the man's son would, no doubt, now raise its ugly head. He braced himself for the rebuke.

'Yes,' continued Sir Hedley. 'You were mentioned by one of your pupils, who spoke very highly of you. I interviewed quite a remarkable young man for a scholarship at the grammar school. I am the Chairman of the Governors there.'

'That would be Charlie Lister,' replied Tom, relieved that the incident in the King's Head was not mentioned.

'Indeed,' said Sir Hedley. 'He was awarded a full scholarship. Lively little lad he was and bright as a button.'

Lady Maladroit remained in simmering silence and continued to glare at Tom. She was furious with her husband for being so amiable to the man who had attacked their son. Of course it was so typical of him, she thought. Her husband had become so fractious of late. She determined she would have something to say to him later.

The honoured guest, the Right Honourable Iain Balfour-Smith, Member of Parliament for Clayton and Urebank and newly appointed Minister of State for Education arrived. He had been invited to unveil the plaque. Mr Pendlebury hurried off to meet him and returned to the group a moment later with the esteemed visitor.

'I think you know Sir Hedley and Lady Maladroit, Mr Balfour-Smith,' the vicar said to the politician.

'Yes,' he replied. 'How are you, Hedley?'

'Very well, Iain,' the baronet replied.

'And how are you, Marcia?' he asked, looking at the hard, lined face and down-turned mouth.

'I'm well, thank you,' she answered, managing a small smile.

'May I introduce Mr Fairborn and his daughter, Janette,' said the vicar.

'Good evening,' said Mr Balfour-Smith, before turning to Tom.

'And I know this young man. It's good to see you again, Tom.' He shook his hand warmly. Lady Maladroit raised an eyebrow and scowled.

'Tom saved my bacon,' explained the politician. 'I foolishly ran out of petrol on my way to a meeting about the proposed supermarket, and he not only ran me to the venue but arranged for my car to be collected. We had a most interesting conversation about education in small rural schools and I arranged for an HMI to visit Risingdale where he teaches. She was most impressed, I have to say, particularly about Mr Dwyer's teaching.'

'Well, well,' said Sir Hedley, 'you appear to have made quite an impression in the village, Mr Dwyer.'

Lady Maladroit stared angrily at Tom. 'Yes,' she said coldly, 'quite an impression.' She drew her lips together into a tight little line and stared at him with Medusa ferocity. 'We should meet some of the others, Hedley,' she said to her husband, walking away.

The vicar took Mr Balfour-Smith off to explain the proceedings, leaving Tom with Mr Fairborn and his daughter.

'My goodness, Mr Dwyer,' said Janette, 'you do seem to be the flavour of the month, praised by the bishop and lauded by the MP.'

'Perhaps one day I might be in your good books too, Miss Fairborn,' countered Tom. His blue eyes flashed and a broad smile lit up his face.

'I heard you've bought Roselea Cottage,' remarked Mr Fairborn.

'Yes, I did.'

'You're certainly getting your feet under the table,' said the farmer. 'Most folk thought you wouldn't be stopping long. Very few people settle in Risingdale. Too far up the Dale and there's not much going on, particularly for a young man like you. Of course, when the school closes, I suppose you'll be moving to pastures new.'

'I wasn't aware that the school is closing,' said Tom. 'Perhaps you know something that I don't, Mr Fairborn.'

'It's just a rumour but it stands to reason it's not viable to keep the place open, particularly now that numbers of children are declining. I guess after what I've heard this evening you'll not have any trouble finding another job.'

Miss Tranter, thinking Tom was looking uncomfortable, decided to rescue him and breezed up.

'Do forgive me,' she said pleasantly, and slipping her hand through his arm, 'but might I drag Mr Dwyer away. There is someone I wish him to meet.'

Despite her earlier comments to Tom about the tedious evening ahead, Joyce had made a real effort with her appearance. She was dressed for the occasion in a stylish, tight-fitting grey suit, crimson silk blouse and black lacy stockings. She wore absurdly high stiletto heels and was bedecked in an assortment of jewellery. Her make-up was immaculate, her long nails were impeccably manicured and not a hair on her head was out of place.

'I thought I'd rescue you,' she told Tom, as they walked away. 'That was Janette Fairborn who gave you all that grief about driving too fast, wasn't it?'

'Yes, it was,' said Tom, who would have quite liked to have remained in the young woman's company.

'She's terribly snooty,' said Joyce. 'I guess that just because her father owns a lot of land around here, she thinks she's a cut above everyone else. I saw you being dragged along to meet the dreadful Maladroits. That woman could freeze soup in pans with a face like that and as for her husband, I hear he's bought yet more land and driven Colin Greenwood's father off his farm and . . .'

Tom was not listening as Joyce babbled on. He was looking in the direction of Janette Fairborn. Snooty she might appear, he thought, but she looked stunning. She looked back at him and smiled.

'Did you have to be so pleasant?' Lady Maladroit demanded of her husband when they were well away from the others. '"You are to be congratulated",' she mimicked his voice. '"One of your pupils spoke very highly of you." Congratulated for attacking James?'

'Don't be ridiculous, Marcia,' replied Sir Hedley. 'You know as well as I that the man was not at fault. James started it and he got what he deserved.'

His wife was not listening for she had caught sight of what Miss Tranter was wearing around her neck.

'I don't believe it,' she cried.

'What don't you believe?' asked her husband wearily.

'That woman, she's wearing my jewellery.'

She strode off and intercepted Joyce before her husband could stop her.

'May I ask where you acquired the necklace you are wearing?' she asked sharply.

'I beg your pardon?' asked Joyce coolly.

'The necklace! Where did you get it?'

'I bought it,' she replied.

'From where?'

Joyce did not like the strident tone of the woman's voice. She knew, of course, who it was who had addressed her and was not going to be intimidated.

'If you must know,' she replied loftily, 'I purchased it from Smith, Skerrit and Sampson, the auction house in Clayton. Why do you ask?'

'Because that necklace happens to be mine,' said Lady Maladroit. 'It was stolen.'

'Well, I bought it in good faith,' said Joyce, fingering the jewellery and affecting a cool air of indifference. 'Perhaps it is similar to the one you lost.'

'It is the same necklace,' Lady Maladroit insisted, raising her voice. 'It was my grandmother's and I would recognise it anywhere. And for your information I did not lose it. It was stolen and I would like it back.'

Miss Tranter gave a small, sardonic laugh. She was not at all abashed by the woman's hard and penetrating stare. 'Well, you will have to take it up with Smith, Skerrit and Sampson because I am certainly not parting with it.'

'Did you understand what I just said?' asked Lady Maladroit, angered by the cool calm of the woman. 'It is stolen property.'

'I understood you perfectly,' declared Joyce in an unruffled tone of voice. 'Perhaps you didn't understand what *I* said.'

'Now look here—' began Lady Maladroit, with a sudden flare of temper.

People were turning their heads. The farmers stopped talking, the MP stared, the vicar looked decidedly embarrassed and Mrs Mossup and her companions stared with naked curiosity. The angry outburst from the lady of the manor was proving to be the principal excitement of the evening.

Sir Hedley, hearing the exchange, glanced uneasily over his shoulder, then quickly joined his wife, gripped her arm and pulled her a little apart from where she was standing with Miss Tranter. 'Marcia,' he said in a muted voice, 'you are causing a scene. If you think it is your necklace—'

'It is,' she interrupted.

'If it is,' Sir Hedley told her, 'then we will speak to the auction house tomorrow.' He lowered his voice even further and hissed in her ear. 'Now, for goodness' sake, pull yourself together.'

'But that is my necklace,' she persisted, stabbing the air in Joyce's direction, 'and I want it back.'

'Could I have your attention,' shouted Mr Pendlebury, considering this was an appropriate time to start proceedings before the altercation could escalate, 'I think we are ready for the unveiling. I shall ask the Right Honourable Iain Balfour-Smith, our Member of Parliament, to say a few words.'

As Tom was making his way out, Janette Fairborn approached him.

'Look, I hope you don't think I was mocking you,' she told him.

'Mocking me?' he repeated.

'For saying you seem to be the flavour of the month, being praised by the bishop and the MP. I regretted what I said as soon as I said it. It must have sounded like I was poking fun at you.'

'Not at all,' said Tom, with a flash of white teeth. 'Actually I found it quite amusing. You know, I've got to rather like our little exchanges.'

Janette too enjoyed the badinage. Her opinion of Tom was beginning to change. She stared for a moment into long-lashed dark blue eyes.

'I just hope that your father is wrong,' he told her.

'I'm sorry,' she said, not having heard a word.

'I was saying that I hope your father is wrong – about the school closing.'

'Oh yes. It would be a pity, but it is just a rumour. As you know my father sometimes gets things wrong. Anyway, if the school does close, as he said, you won't have any trouble finding another job, probably in some place rather more exciting than Risingdale. I guess there will not be much to keep you in the village if the school closes.'

'Oh, I don't know about that,' replied Tom, smiling.

The following afternoon Mr Julian Sampson of Sampson, Skerrit and Smith Auction House arrived at Marston Towers. Sir Hedley had rung him that morning and explained the situation, asking if the auctioneer might call and see him at his earliest convenience.

Mr Sampson was a distinguished-looking man with a head of carefully combed silver hair and the face of a Roman senator. He wore an expensive-looking woollen overcoat unbuttoned to reveal an equally expensive-looking charcoal-grey suit with narrow chalk stripes and matching waistcoat with gold chain and fob. He sported a blue-and-white silk bow tie.

He stood in the hall at Marston Towers on the black and white marble floor, facing an ornate oak staircase. He removed a pair of half-moon gold spectacles from his pocket, placed them on his nose and cast a professional eye over a particularly fine inlaid Regency mahogany centre table with decorated bronze edging and central arabesques, supported by a concave platform. He ran a gloved hand tenderly over the dusty surface and the auctioneer in him valued the piece at thirty to forty thousand pounds. He was shown into the drawing room by Mrs Moody, the new housekeeper, a stout woman with a hennish bosom, severely permed chestnut hair and an overemphatic voice. She had large, bulging eyes and an anxious, even slightly alarmed expression on her round face. Having been the only applicant for the post advertised in the *Clayton Gazette*, Mrs Moody had been appointed but she had proved less than satisfactory. Mrs Gosling had cleaned and dusted, wiped and polished with a vengeance. Her successor merely flicked a feather duster and occasionally, when she felt inclined, washed a few dishes. Her bad legs meant she could not climb up a ladder, her bad back meant she could not bend and her allergic reaction to furniture and metal polish (and rubber gloves) meant the silverware remained dull and the surfaces dusty. Unlike Mrs Gosling, she didn't 'know her place' and had no conception of status, rank or position in the world and treated everyone exactly the same – usually like naughty children. Sir Hedley and his wife, who rarely agreed on anything, were in accord that Mrs Moody should be given her marching orders as soon as a suitable replacement could be found. Finding a suitable replacement was proving extremely difficult, for people in the village had rallied to support Mrs Gosling who they felt had been shabbily treated by the lady of the manor.

Mrs Moody, dressed in a striped frock and apron and carrying a yellow duster for effect, threw open the library door without as much as a knock.

'There's a Mr Sampson here to see you,' she told Sir Hedley, thrusting her head around the door. 'Do you want to see him?'

'Yes, yes, Mrs Moody,' he replied, 'I am expecting him. Please show him in here to the library.'

'You're to go in,' she told the visitor and made a hasty retreat before her employer could ask her to bring in some coffee.

The visitor, an observant man, removed his kid gloves and looked around. The room was lined with fixed bookcases set between tall sash windows, overlooking a long, walled garden. Everything exuded comfortable opulence, from the heavy plum-coloured velvet curtains to the thick carpet, from the delicately moulded ceiling to the deep armchairs and magazine-laden tables. He noted the shaft of sunlight, solid with motes of dust, which stretched between him and the Sheraton kidney-shaped desk. He studied the piece of furniture. Thirty thousand at least, thought the auctioneer.

'Ah, Mr Sampson,' said Sir Hedley, rising from the settle to greet him. 'It is so good of you to call.'

'Good afternoon,' said the visitor. He looked none-too-pleased to be summoned to Marston Towers on a busy Saturday auction day, but the baronet, who had explained about the necklace, had been quite insistent.

'Do take a seat,' said Sir Hedley.

'I should prefer to stand, thank you,' replied Mr Sampson. 'I am hopeful this will not take long. I have a very busy day.'

Lady Maladroit, sitting ramrod straight by the window on an elegant mahogany armchair with padded back, fixed the visitor with an icy stare, her mouth pulled tight. She gave a slight nod of acknowledgement. Her fierce, beaky face reminded him of an affronted eagle.

'I must say, Sir Hedley,' said Mr Sampson, 'this is a most unfortunate state of affairs.'

'Indeed,' agreed Lady Maladroit before her husband could reply. 'I should have thought that a supposedly reputable auction house would not be peddling stolen goods.'

Mr Sampson bristled. 'My auction house does not peddle stolen goods,' he retorted. His face flushed with anger. 'This is the first instance since the inception of Smith, Skerrit and Sampson that such a situation has occurred. It is most distressing.'

'Shouldn't you establish the provenance of the items you put up for auction?' asked Lady Maladroit petulantly.

The auctioneer made a supreme effort of self-control. 'We cannot possibly ensure that every piece we sell is bona fide,' he answered. 'However, in this case one of my former employees was assured that the seller owned the item.'

'I am the owner,' Lady Maladroit reminded him, with controlled impatience, 'and I certainly did not agree that the necklace should be sold. It is stolen property. I hope you have informed the police so that the thief can be apprehended.'

'I have not,' replied Mr Sampson.

'Why ever not?' she demanded crossly.

'I felt it prudent to talk to Sir Hedley first,' he replied.

'Well, I shall most certainly be contacting them,' Lady Maladroit told him with withering condescension.

'That is up to you,' said Mr Sampson indifferently. He was getting increasingly irritated by the woman's strident voice and argumentative manner.

She stiffened and narrowed her eyes. 'I think it is very remiss of you, Mr Sampson, that you did not see fit to inform the police.'

The auctioneer's annoyance did not diminish. He was minded to respond in kind but restrained the inclination to do so. Then he smiled inwardly at the thought of what he was about tell her. That will take the wind out of the woman's sails, he thought.

'Are you able to tell us who put the necklace into the auction?' asked Sir Hedley. He too was getting increasingly irritated by his wife's strident voice and argumentative manner.

'Indeed I can,' replied Mr Sampson. He paused for effect and then delivered the bombshell. 'It was your son.'

'What!' exclaimed Lady Maladroit. She snapped upright as if she had received an electric shock. A little spasm touched her face.

Mr Sampson, with no great hurry, folded his gloves and put them in his pocket before producing a piece of paper, which he held out before him. 'I have here the catalogue with the details of the lots which were sold at the auction and the necklace is not listed. An employee, Mr Neville, who happens to be a friend of your son's and who has since left the company, put the necklace in as an extra item, to save your son paying the usual auction house commission. It did not appear in the catalogue. In effect, Smith, Skerrit and Sampson did not sell your necklace. Your son colluded with Mr Neville to avoid paying the seller's commission of twenty per cent of the selling price of the item.'

'This is nonsense!' she snapped with a sort of disgusted wince as if she had just tasted something unpleasant.

'No, Lady Maladroit, it is not nonsense,' responded Mr Sampson angrily. 'However, if you choose to dispute what I have told you, then I shall place the matter in the hands of the police.' He turned around abruptly and walked to the door.

'One moment, Mr Sampson,' said Sir Hedley, getting to his feet and approaching the visitor. 'My wife is in no way questioning the truth of what you have said.' He gave her a sharp look. 'She is, as I am, deeply shocked by what we have heard. I should be very grateful if you would leave the matter in my hands. I would not wish the police to be involved. I shall, of course, have words with my son.'

Mr Sampson stopped and swivelled around dramatically. 'The reputation of my auction house has been tarnished by this incident, Sir Hedley,' he said indignantly.

'I apologise for all the upset this has caused,' said the baronet.

'Very well, Sir Hedley,' answered Mr Sampson, feeling somewhat mollified. 'I shall leave things with you.'

'And I would ask you to be discreet and not mention my son's involvement in this affair.'

'And what about my necklace?' asked Lady Maladroit who had regained her composure.

Mr Sampson gave Lady Maladroit a dismissive stare. 'Your son sold it,' he told her, 'Miss Tranter bought it and she is not obliged to sell it back.'

'Then I shall speak to her myself,' announced Lady Maladroit.

'No, you will not,' snapped her husband. 'Perhaps, Mr Sampson, you might be prepared to have a word with Miss Tranter. I will, of course, buy the necklace back and give her an additional financial consideration. If you would accompany me to my study, I will write out a cheque.'

'Very well, Sir Hedley.' Mr Sampson looked again at Lady Maladroit. 'Although this is most inconvenient, I shall appeal to Miss Tranter's generosity but, as I have just pointed out, she is not obliged to sell the item back. The item was placed in the auction in good faith and she bought it in good faith.'

Lady Maladroit opened her mouth to speak but not being disposed to hear any more from her, the visitor wished her a muttered 'Good afternoon,' turned his back on her and walked away without a backward glance. Sir Hedley gave his wife a sharp look and followed him.

Outside the door they bumped into Mrs Moody who had been eavesdropping. She was carrying cups and saucers, a milk jug and coffee pot on an old tray. 'Where do you want this?' she asked.

'In my study please, Mrs Moody,' Sir Hedley told her. 'I'm sure Mr Sampson would welcome a cup before he goes.'

'I do apologise for my wife, Mr Sampson,' said the baronet, as he sat at his desk in his study and began writing out a generous cheque. 'You will understand that she was very distressed at the loss of her necklace and the revelation about our son was . . . well, I won't go into that.'

The auctioneer felt sorry for Sir Hedley. He is a courteous and considerate man, he thought, and is a martyr to put up with that virago of a wife.

Sir Hedley's sanctum, his study, was a large room dominated by a heavy mahogany desk, on which were an impressive brass inkwell in the shape of an eagle with outstretched wings, a stationery holder and a pile of papers. Displayed on the walls were oil paintings showing different animals: grazing cattle, fat black pigs on stumpy legs, bored-looking sheep, leaping horses and packs of hounds.

'You have some very fine pieces of furniture, Sir Hedley,' said Mr Sampson, placing the cheque in his pocket. He never missed the opportunity of promoting his business. 'Should you wish to part with any item, I should be only too pleased to handle the sale. The Regency table in the entrance hall is of a particularly fine quality. I estimate that if it came to auction, it would fetch in excess of thirty thousand pounds.'

The baronet gave an ironic smile. 'Oh, it's not my most valuable piece,' he told him. He pointed to the tray of coffee Mrs Moody had brought in and placed on a marble-topped gilded wood console table. Mr Sampson stared at the tray, on which were two delicate china cups, each containing a tea bag floating in the milky water like a drowned mouse. 'That tray is much more valuable. It's worth at least double the value of the Regency table.'

The item in question was a crudely made object of cheap wood with misshapen handles and clumsy joints.

'I'm sorry,' said Mr Sampson, 'I don't understand.'

'My son James spent three years at a top independent boarding school. I spent over sixty thousand pounds on his education and he left passing just the one exam – woodwork.'

Later that afternoon the reprobate faced his furious father.

'You have done some deceitful things in your time,' said Sir Hedley, 'but stealing from your mother is beyond the pale.'

'It's just a bit of a misunderstanding, Pa,' replied James.

'Please do not insult my intelligence,' growled the baronet. 'There has been no misunderstanding. You have stolen from your mother and proved yourself to be not only a liar, but now a thief as well.'

'I know it was wrong,' replied his son, attempting to look suitably remorseful. 'I'm sorry, I really am, and wish I hadn't done it. It was stupid and very wrong. I see that now.'

'And as a result of your dishonest actions, your mother discharged the housekeeper, blaming her for the theft, and your friend at the auction house has been dismissed for his part in the affair.'

'It's just that my allowance didn't cover some of my outgoings.'

'Outgoings!' erupted Sir Hedley. 'And what the hell do you mean by your outgoings?'

'I've borrowed some money and needed the cash pretty quickly.'

'So you are now a debtor, to boot,' sighed his father.

'I knew you wouldn't let me have any money. You see, if you had only seen your way to increasing my allowance when I asked, then—'

'So it is my fault for not giving you more money?' The baronet gave a hollow laugh.

'Well, no, of course not, but my allowance didn't stretch to—'

'Ah, we keep coming back to the allowance,' interrupted Sir Hedley. 'Well, let me tell you this. As from today there will be no more allowance. I have been too indulgent with you, but no more. You will get a job and support yourself.'

'But Pa—' began James.

His father pinched the bridge of his nose and sighed. 'You have brought disgrace upon this family and I can only hope that there is nothing else you have done or will do to make me more ashamed of you.'

Sir Hedley did not have to wait very long.

Back in his office, Mr Sampson telephoned Miss Tranter and arranged to visit her the following afternoon. He arrived for the appointment just after lunch to find Joyce waiting for him at the door of her flat, dressed for the occasion in a shell-pink, tight-fitting, roll-top sweater and cream slacks. She had observed her visitor's arrival from the window as he parked his shiny black Mercedes in the small parking area to the front of the apartments.

'I am very grateful to you for seeing me, Miss Tranter,' said the auctioneer, as he was shown into the tidy sitting room. Mr Sampson looked around. From experience he could tell something about a person's character by the way they furnished their rooms. Here was a woman of taste, he thought, taking in the pale green walls, long lime curtains and the expensive cream-coloured sofa. A large crystal vase, containing carefully arranged flowers, stood on a low table and on the polished oak floor was a bright Turkish rug. There was the aroma of freshly brewed coffee. 'I would not have disturbed your Sunday but the matter, as I explained on the telephone, is of some importance.' He reached for her hand and held it for a moment longer than was necessary.

'Oh, that's quite all right,' replied Joyce. She exuded a cloud of perfume. 'Do sit down. I am sure you would enjoy a cup of coffee.'

'That would be splendid,' Mr Sampson replied, 'that is, if it is not too much trouble.'

Miss Tranter gave him one of her most charming smiles. 'No trouble,' she said. She noted how well-groomed and polished her visitor was: the carefully combed silver hair, clean nails, the smell of expensive cologne, the gold cufflinks, the silk tie and the expensive-looking charcoal suit.

Having served the coffee, Joyce sat on the sofa, leaned back and crossed her long legs. She watched her visitor as a cat might spy on a tree full of birds – hungrily. 'You mentioned on the telephone your visit concerns the necklace I purchased.'

'Indeed,' nodded Mr Sampson.

'I thought someone from the auction house would be getting in touch. Lady Maladroit accosted me at the village hall, demanding the necklace back. She was quite belligerent. It sounded as if she thought I had stolen it. I found her attitude intolerable and will not be bullied.'

'Yes,' agreed Mr Sampson. 'I too have found her to be a very difficult woman.' He resisted the temptation to add that she was the haughtiest and most ill-tempered woman he had ever met. 'It is most embarrassing, Miss Tranter, for me to be put in the position of asking you to sell back the necklace.'

'I imagined that she would want it back,' said Joyce. 'But you have no need to feel any embarrassment, Mr Sampson. After all you were not to know it was stolen property. You are the innocent party.'

'You are most understanding, Miss Tranter,' he said.

'Do drink your coffee,' said Joyce. 'It's getting cold.'

'I did point out to Lady Maladroit,' he said, after taking a sip of his drink, 'that she has no claim on the piece. There is no obligation for you to part with it.' He considered for a moment revealing that it was the woman's son who had stolen the item and that were it up to him he would tell Joyce not to return the jewellery. However, he had promised Sir Hedley to try his best to persuade Miss Tranter to sell the necklace back.

'Well, I don't feel inclined to part with it,' said Joyce.

Mr Sampson reached into his pocket and produced the cheque given to him by Sir Hedley. He passed it to Miss Tranter. 'Perhaps this might change your mind,' he said.

Joyce glanced at the cheque. It was indeed more than generous.

'Oh my,' she said. 'This is nearly twice the amount I paid for it.'

'So are you willing to sell the necklace?' asked Mr Sampson.

'I'll get it,' said Joyce, jumping up from the couch. 'To be honest I don't really like it. As soon as I got it home, I thought it too flashy. Rather too ostentatious for my liking.'

'Yes, I agree,' said the auctioneer. 'I think you would suit a more delicate piece, perhaps a Belle Époque rose-cut diamond pendant. You know, my late wife could have had the choice of so many different items of jewellery which came into the auction house for sale but she always chose the more delicate and simple pieces.

'So your wife has passed away, Mr Sampson?' asked Joyce, assuming a most sympathetic tone of voice.

'Sadly, yes, she died three years ago after a long illness.'

'Oh, I am sorry,' she said.

'I tend to live a lonely life these days, Miss Tranter.' He sighed.

'I can relate to that, Mr Sampson,' said Joyce. 'I too live a lonely life.'

'You live here alone then?'

'I do,' said Joyce. Then, smiling to herself, she told him, 'I'll fetch the necklace.'

It was getting on for three o'clock when Mr Sampson finally got up to leave.

'My goodness,' he declared, glancing at his expensive gold wristwatch, 'just look at the time. I've taken up far too much of your Sunday. I must leave you in peace.'

'It has been a pleasure,' replied Joyce, rising from the sofa and extending a carefully manicured hand, which her visitor held in his for a moment.

'And it has been a real pleasure for me too,' he replied. 'It is quite some time since I have had such an agreeable afternoon.' He released her hand and stared at her, considering what to say next. He gave a small cough. 'I wonder,' he said, 'if, as a small thank you for your kindness and understanding over the necklace, you might consider joining me for a meal one evening?'

'I should like that very much,' said Joyce.

'Oh, that's splendid,' he said. 'There is a very smart French restaurant in Clayton, Le Bon Viveur,' he told her. 'I go there frequently but would welcome your company. It is not quite as convivial dining there alone. So shall we say next Saturday?' he asked.

'That would be fine,' said Joyce.

'I could pick you up at say seven o'clock and then we will have time for a drink before the meal.'

'I look forward to it.'

'Well, I'll take my leave, Miss Tranter. Until Saturday then.'

'Do please call me Joyce,' she told him.

'Joyce,' he repeated, smiling widely. 'I'm Julian.'

*　　*　　*

While Miss Tranter and Mr Sampson were spending a pleasant afternoon in each other's company, Sir Hedley called upon Mrs Gosling. He had asked his wife to accompany him to apologise to the former housekeeper for the false accusation and offer her old job back, but Lady Maladroit had been obdurate.

'I hope it is not an inconvenient time?' he asked his former cleaner, as he stood on her doorstep.

'No,' she replied. 'You had better come in.'

Sir Hedley stood with his back to the fire and stroked his long moustache. 'I am here to apologise for the way you have been treated,' he told her. 'It was quite unacceptable for my wife to . . .' He struggled to find the right words to use.

'Accuse me of stealing,' said Mrs Gosling, completing the sentence for him.

'Yes, indeed,' he conceded. 'I imagine that you have already heard that we have recovered the jewellery?'

'Mrs Mossup, who was at the "do" in the village hall on Friday told me. I gather Miss Tranter bought it at an auction.'

'That is indeed the case,' the baronet concurred.

'So how did it end up in an auction?' asked Mrs Gosling.

Sir Hedley equivocated. 'We are not entirely sure at the moment,' he said, 'but it is certain that you had nothing to do with its disappearance. I can only express my deepest regret for what was said.'

'I didn't like being accused,' said Mrs Gosling. 'It was very upsetting.'

'Of course,' said Sir Hedley. 'As I have said, I can only apologise on behalf of my wife for her jumping to the wrong conclusion.'

It's a pity Lady Hoity-Toity didn't stir herself to come and apologise, thought Mrs Gosling.

'You are greatly missed at Marston Towers,' continued Sir Hedley. 'Between you and me, the cleaner we have at present is not really up to the job.'

'If you are wanting me to come back,' said Mrs Gosling, 'well, I'm not. I've got fixed up with a job at the village school as the assistant caretaker which suits me much better.'

'I never expected you to return after . . . well, after what was said.'

'I have always found you to be a decent and approachable person, Sir Hedley, who appreciated what I did,' said Mrs Gosling. 'You're a real gentleman, but now I am not in your employment, I feel I can speak my mind. Your wife—'

'Please, let us leave it at that, Mrs Gosling,' interrupted the baronet, knowing full well what she was about to say.

Sir Hedley's former housekeeper watched her visitor walk down the path. She had an expression of smiling satisfaction on her face.

Walking through the village, Sir Hedley came across Charlie. The boy, wearing a thin jacket and without scarf, gloves or woolly hat, was sitting in his favourite spot on the bench by the duck pond, his nose buried in a book. He was reading with a distant, serious expression on his face.

'Hello, young man,' said the baronet, sitting next to him.

'Oh hello,' replied Charlie, looking up and smiling.

'I say, it's a little cold for you to be sitting out here, isn't it?'

'I like the fresh air,' replied the boy, 'I'm a bit of an outdoor person.'

'Yes, you told us as much when you came for the interview. Do you remember me?'

'Oh yes, you're one of the governors at the grammar school.'

'I am and I was very impressed with you. You did very well answering all those questions.'

'I enjoyed it,' Charlie told him. He closed his book. 'You were very nice to me but I didn't like the man at the end.'

'He was a bit stuffy,' admitted Sir Hedley. He winked. 'I didn't like him either.'

'He kept staring at me with a very serious face. I liked the headmaster though.'

'Well, I think you will be happy at the grammar school.' He looked at the thick tome on the boy's lap. 'Reading, I see. Is it another Dickens?'

'You've guessed right,' said Charlie. 'It's called *A Tale of Two Cities* and it's all about the French Revolution. "It was the best of times, it was the worst of times."'

'I'm sorry,' said Sir Hedley.

'That's how it begins,' said Charlie.

'"It was the best of times, it was the worst of times",' the baronet repeated, thinking how true that was of his present state.

'I've got to the part where they are chopping off the heads of all the rich landowners and aristocrats,' Charlie told him almost gleefully.

'I reckon I wouldn't have stood much of a chance if I had been there,' chuckled the baronet. He coughed and looked out over the water. 'It's a lovely day. You know I prefer this time of year to the summer.'

'So do I,' said Charlie.

Sir Hedley sighed. The man and the boy sat there in companionable silence for a while, watching the ducks.

'Has your mother ever mentioned me to you, Charlie?' asked Sir Hedley.

'No . . . well she's told me we rent the cottage from you and that you are kind.'

'Nothing else?'

'No.'

'I see. Well, she must be very proud of you.' He nodded. 'Yes, indeed, very proud. You have a great future ahead of you, Charlie, a great future.'

18

Miss Tranter was in a particularly buoyant mood the following Monday. The auditions on the Saturday for the Christmas
pantomime had gone well with a large turnout of hopeful
amateur thespians wishing to have a part, she had a fat cheque
from Sir Hedley to put in the bank and she looked forward to
an intimate dinner later that week with the well-to-do owner
of the auction house.

'That was a right old carry-on at the church hall, wasn't
it?' remarked Mr Cadwallader, before taking a large bite
out of a Garibaldi biscuit and showering his waistcoat in
crumbs.

Two of her colleagues were in the staffroom at morning
break. Tom had taken his class on a school trip to the museum
in Clayton.

'I thought that Lady Maladroit was most disagreeable,'
remarked Mrs Golightly. 'The way she spoke to you, Joyce,
was inexcusable.'

'Completely out of order,' added Mr Cadwallader.

'Everyone could hear. Poor Mr Pendlebury didn't know
where to look, the MP was aghast and Sir Hedley was red in
the face with embarrassment. It must have been very upsetting for you, Joyce.'

'Not at all, Bertha,' replied Miss Tranter casually. She examined a long nail. 'I wasn't in the least upset. If I am confronted
by some objectionable person who starts shouting the odds, I
tend to go into role. That's my drama training, you see. I don't

rise to their antagonism but I stay perfectly calm and controlled. This annoys them even more.'

'What are you going to do about the necklace?' asked Mrs Golightly.

'I've sold it back,' replied Joyce. 'I can't say that I really liked it when I put it on. It was far too showy.'

Mr Cadwallader raised an eyebrow and exchanged a glance with Mrs Golightly.

'That was very generous of you,' he said.

'Not really,' Joyce told him. 'I got a whole lot more for the necklace than I paid for it. I made a tidy little profit.'

'I wonder how Tom is getting on at the museum,' said Mrs Golightly. 'It's such a risk these days, taking children out of school. All that health and safety palaver.'

'I couldn't agree more, Bertha,' said Mr Cadwallader, dusting the crumbs from his waistcoat. 'Fraught with potential mishaps.'

When he had informed his colleagues of the planned excursion, they had shared with Tom a series of dire warnings.

'Take a bucket,' Mrs Golightly had advised. 'Someone is sure to be sick. I recall when I took the infants to see the animals on Mr Olmeroyde's farm and little Betty Bentley was sick all over her coat, her dress, her shoes, the seat, and then all over me. I stank of vomit all afternoon. Mr Olmeroyde said that something smelled worse than his pigs and all the children pointed at me. I was so embarrassed.'

'And make sure you count them on and off the bus,' Miss Tranter had said. 'Do you remember when we lost Nicholas Wilkinson's older brother, who used to come to this school, when we went to Whitby for the day? He wandered off and was discovered in the amusements, soaking wet with one shoe missing, with candyfloss on a stick and without a care in the world.'

'And we were frantic,' Mr Cadwallader had added.

'And the silly boy was sick on the way home,' Miss Tranter had said.

'Make sure they go to the toilet before they board the bus,' Mr Cadwallader had told Tom. 'You don't want any wet seats.'

Tom had been on a school trip when he taught at Barton-with-Urebank School and was very familiar with what was required and some of the potential dangers, but he had kept quiet and thanked the teachers for their suggestions. When he had mentioned the proposed excursion to Mr Gaunt in the corridor on Friday morning, the headmaster had told him it was a very good idea, but that there would need to be more than one adult to accompany the children and help supervise them. He couldn't spare another member of staff. Mrs Gosling, a seasoned eavesdropper, had then piped up.

'I'll go with you, Mr Dwyer,' she had announced. 'I'd quite like a trip to the museum. I haven't been for ages.'

So it was agreed that the assistant caretaker would go along.

The class congregated at the bus stop in the village at ten o'clock on the Monday morning, chattering excitedly. Tom smiled as he saw Mrs Gosling, striding up and down, marshalling the children like a sergeant major, making them get into an orderly line and keep the noise down.

'Calm down,' she ordered. 'Now Mr Dwyer and me do not want to see any silliness.' She stabbed the air with a gloved finger. 'No smearing the display cabinets with grubby fingers, no wandering off, no touching anything and watch where you're walking. We don't want you knocking over some priceless object.'

The ten o'clock start meant that the party had missed the rush hour and the Clayton bus was not busy. The bus driver, a miserable-looking individual with thin wisps of sandy hair retreating from an otherwise bald pate, warned Mrs Gosling, as she boarded the vehicle, that he wanted no misbehaviour from the children. He knew from experience driving the school run what children were like these days, jumping up and down in their seats, running down the aisles, shouting and swearing and smoking, and making rude signs through the back window at drivers. Any trouble, he warned her, and they would all have to get off. Mrs Gosling was not the sort of person to be hectored. When she had worked at Marston Towers, she had given as good as she got when Lady Maladroit complained about something or other. She told the bus driver sharply to drive the bus and keep his comments to himself. These children were well-behaved she told him. When the class alighted outside the museum, the driver commended Mrs Gosling on the good behaviour of the children, assuming that she was the teacher in charge.

'There ought to be more teachers like you, missus,' he told her. 'You know how to handle kids.'

Mrs Gosling had visited the museum with her granddaughter when the child was small and warned Tom to be wary of the crusty, old, sour-faced curator in the grey suit who watched them like a hungry hawk, who insisted on no talking and who clearly did not approve of children on the premises. It was therefore a pleasant surprise when they were greeted at the entrance to the imposing building by a friendly young woman. Tom stared at her – the pretty face, flawless complexion, long blonde hair and eyes the colour of the large, polished jade vase which stood on the mahogany table. She had a look on her face of a woman quite aware that she was being admired.

'I'm Dr Merryweather, the new curator,' she said, 'and I am delighted to see you all. I should be happy to show you around and describe some of the exhibits.'

Tom had brought with him the samplers he had found in the classroom when he had first arrived at Risingdale School. He told the curator that they had been stuck in a cupboard and asked if she would like them for the museum.

'They belonged to a teacher at the school,' he explained. 'Perhaps if you do want them, you could say they were donated by Miss Cathcart.'

'That's very kind,' said the curator. 'Do thank Miss Cathcart for her generosity.'

'She's dead,' announced Vicky, who had overheard the conversation. 'She fell in the river and drowned and when they found her—'

'Thank you, Vicky,' interjected the teacher. 'Now you go and look at the dinosaur bones.'

When Tom showed Dr Merryweather the cache of coins Mr Greenwood had found, her eyes lit up.

'I'm no expert on coins,' she told him, 'but I think some of these might be quite rare. If they were discovered locally, then they are of great interest. I need to show a colleague at the York Museum who knows about old coins. Are you able to leave them with me?'

'Yes, of course,' said Tom.

'I'll give you a ring when I have found anything out and could pop out to Risingdale and tell you what I have discovered. I have an aunt in the village and often visit her at the weekend.'

'That would be splendid,' said Tom.

'She's a bit of all right, that curator, i'n't she, sir?' George remarked when Tom went to join some of his pupils. The boy winked.

'Yes, George,' the teacher replied. 'I have to agree with you there, she is.'

'I wonder if she's married, sir. Shall I ask 'er if she's married? Tha could be in with a chance.'

'Do nothing of the sort,' Tom managed to splutter out before the curator came to join them.

The visit was a great success. The children were interested, enthusiastic and well-behaved and bombarded the curator with questions, which she answered with pleasure. They were captivated by the giant ammonite fossil, the bandaged remains of an ancient Egyptian mummy, the case upon case of insects and the collection of weapons but what attracted their attention most was the magnificent specimen of a Cape lion which dominated the gallery displaying animals from around the world. Greyish-yellow in colour with a dark mane, a snarling mouth and enormous clawed paws, the impressive creature stretched out in a huge glass case.

'This is Horace,' explained the curator, as the children gathered around her.

'It's a bit of a daft name for a lion, miss,' said Vicky. 'I've got an Uncle Horace.' She turned to Mrs Gosling. 'Uncle Horace's not a bit like a lion, is he, Gran?'

'No, he isn't,' agreed Mrs Gosling, thinking of her daughter's lazy husband. 'More like a sloth,' she said under her breath.

'The lion should be called Nero or Goliath,' suggested David.

'Maybe you're right,' said Dr Merryweather, 'but Horace seems to me to be a friendly sort of name. Perhaps he was a mild-natured animal.'

'He doesn't look it, miss,' said Marjorie.

'My Uncle Horace isn't very friendly and he's certainly not mild-natured,' stated Vicky. 'My dad says he a miserable old git.'

'Victoria Gosling!' exclaimed the girl's grandmother.

'Thank you, Vicky,' said Tom. 'I think we've heard enough about your Uncle Horace.'

'Lions don't have a reputation of being friendly and mild-natured, miss,' remarked Judith. 'I certainly wouldn't like to meet one like Horace.'

'There's no chance of that, I'm afraid,' replied the curator. 'Cape lions were exterminated by European settlers who colonised South Africa and these wonderful creatures are now extinct. Like a lot of species, man has wiped them out. It's very sad, isn't it?'

'How did he get here, miss?' asked David, pressing his nose to the glass and squinting.

'He was brought to England over a hundred years ago and kept at the London Zoo,' he was told. 'People came from miles around to look at him. Even Queen Victoria came to see him. Horace lived to be twenty-five years old, which is a lot longer than most lions in captivity. When he died, he was stuffed and mounted and given to the museum by his owner, the great-grandfather of Sir Hedley Maladroit.'

'He has a collection of stuffed animals and birds up at Marston Towers,' said Mrs Gosling, screwing up her face. 'Nasty dusty creatures they are with staring glass eyes and sharp beaks.' She thought for a moment of Lady Maladroit. 'I can't see the point of being stuffed myself.'

The children queued up outside the museum for the trip back to school, chattering happily and discussing what they had seen. Mrs Gosling walked down the line like a general inspecting the troops.

'Keep the noise down,' she ordered. Tom watched indulgently.

On the bus, going back to school, Carol stared out of the window, looking pensive.

'I can guess what you are thinking,' Tom told the girl. She turned and peered at him through her pink glasses. 'You're thinking how sad it is that such a majestic beast like Horace should be now extinct and end up stuffed in a case.'

'Oh, I'm not, Mr Dwyer,' she answered cheerfully, 'I was thinking that when Starlight dies, I'd like to have him stuffed and mounted.'

*   *   *

Tom, keen to find out how the interview at the grammar
school had gone, sat next to Charlie on the bus back to
Risingdale. Much to his amusement, Mrs Gosling had taken
charge of the class again, lined up the children, warned them
to behave themselves and counted them on the bus. Tom was
happy for her to do this for it gave him a chance to talk uninterrupted to Charlie. He had not had the chance to speak to
the boy since he had heard the news of Charlie's scholarship
award. The boy was uncharacteristically quiet that morning
and had remained silent during the museum visit. He now
stared out of the window, looking preoccupied.

'I'm really proud of you, Charlie,' said the teacher, sitting
down next to him. 'I was so pleased to hear you've been
offered a scholarship for the grammar school. Your interview
must have gone really well.'

'Pretty well, I think,' replied Charlie, turning to face the teacher.

'What were you asked?'

'Just general things.'

'Such as?'

'Oh, what I liked doing in my spare time, what were my
favourite subjects at school. That sort of thing.'

'Well, you clearly impressed them.'

'Maybe,' said the boy, looking out of the window.

'So, you think you will like studying at the grammar school?'
asked the teacher.

'Oh, I guess so, Mr Dwyer,' replied Charlie, turning to face
the teacher again.

'You don't sound all that sure.'

'I liked the headmaster and the Chairman of the Governors
but wasn't keen on the teacher I met. He looked very glum
and wasn't very nice. I hope they are not all like him. I could
tell he didn't like me.'

'I'm sure you're imagining that and anyway, there are plenty
of others who aren't like him.'

'Maybe,' replied Charlie thoughtfully.

'You do want to go to the grammar school?' asked Tom.

'I don't really know if I do, Mr Dwyer. I've mixed feelings.'

'I see,' said Tom. 'Is that what is on your mind? You are not usually this quiet.'

'Well, now you mention it, Mr Dwyer,' replied the boy, 'there is something on my mind. It's been on my mind for quite a while now.'

'Would you like to tell me about it?'

'You know, of course, that I haven't got a father,' said Charlie. 'Well, I have got a father, everyone's got a father, but mine doesn't live with us.'

'Yes, I do know that,' said Tom.

'I've never met him,' said the boy, 'and I don't know very much about him apart from what my mother has told me, that he is kind and clever and an important man – a bit like you I suppose, Mr Dwyer.'

'Oh, I'm not your father, Charlie,' Tom told him, smiling.

'Oh, I know that. You're too young and didn't know my mother ten years ago. I think I would like to have a father like you though. You'd be very good at it.'

'Well, thank you for that vote of confidence,' said Tom, laughing.

'Anyway,' continued the boy, 'the thing is, I would like to know who my father is. I've been thinking about it quite a lot lately. My mother says she will tell me about him when I am older, but I think I'm old enough to know the truth. Don't you agree, sir?'

'I don't think that's for me to say,' answered Tom diplomatically. It was clear the boy's mother had not told him about her visit to see his teacher. 'I'm sure that your mother has a good reason for not telling you.' As he said this, he thought about what Mrs Lister had told him. Although he had not said it to her at the time, he had thought Charlie was certainly mature enough to understand. He should be told the truth. It would be the right thing to tell him about his father. It is always best to be honest with children. Charlie should meet his father, Tom believed, but he felt it wasn't his place to interfere so he kept his thoughts to himself. However, he would have a word with the boy's mother when the opportunity arose.

'My mother told me that if people found out who my father is, it will cause all sorts of problems for him and for us,' Charlie told the teacher. 'I can't understand that, you see.' He sighed, shook his head and looked back out of the window. 'I really would like to meet him,' he said, more to himself than to his teacher.

'There's a woman in the hall wanting to see you,' announced Mrs Moody loudly, as she walked through the door without knocking.

Sir Hedley, sitting at the desk in his study and looking through some papers, raised his head and sighed. The woman would have to go, he thought. Not only was she sluggish when it came to cleaning and dire at cooking, but she was blunt to the point of rudeness.

'It's a Mrs Mossup,' the housekeeper told him.

'Mrs Mossup?' he repeated.

'Landlady at the King's Head,' he was informed. 'Said it was important. Mutton dressed as lamb, if you ask me,' she added, uttering her thoughts as always without the least inhibition. 'Do you want to see her or shall I tell her you're busy?'

'Yes, I'll see her. Will you show her in please?'

Sir Hedley rose from his chair to meet his visitor.

'Good morning, Mrs Mossup,' he said, moving around the desk and extending a hand which was shaken charily.

'Good morning, Sir Hedley,' she replied. She gave a slightly lopsided bow and licked her lips. 'It's good of you to see me. I hope that I'm not inconveniencing you.'

'Not at all, Mrs Mossup,' he replied, gesturing to a chair. 'Do sit down.'

'I wouldn't have troubled you, but there is something I need to say.' She sat straight-backed and rested her hands on her lap. The baronet sat opposite her and smiled.

'Now, what can I do for you?' he asked.

'It's a bit difficult,' the landlady told him. 'It's about a rather delicate matter.' She seemed to be momentarily at a loss for words. It only lasted a short time but it was enough for Sir Hedley to understand that it was a struggle for the woman to say what she had come to tell him. He noticed that her hands trembled on her lap.

'Please continue,' he said.

'Well, it will no doubt have come to your ears that my daughter is expecting a baby.'

'Yes, I did hear something of the sort,' replied the baronet.

'I'm not surprised that you know,' said Mrs Mossup. 'Gossip spreads like wildfire in the village. Anyway, Leanne, that's my daughter, is staying at present with my sister in Scarborough. She may come back to the village when she's had the child but nothing's been decided yet. She intends to keep the baby.'

Sir Hedley glanced at the carriage clock on his desk and wondered why the woman was telling him all this. He had a very busy morning ahead and was keen to get back to the estate accounts. However, being a well-mannered man, he smiled and appeared to look interested.

'You are, no doubt, wondering why I am here to tell you about it,' she continued.

'That has occurred to me, Mrs Mossup,' answered Sir Hedley.

'If you could bear with me,' she said. 'Leanne's been very tight-lipped as to who the father is. At first I thought, quite wrongly as it turned out, that it was the young teacher at the village school.'

'Mr Dwyer,' said the baronet.

'Yes, Mr Dwyer, but it's not him.'

'So, how does this concern me?' asked Sir Hedley, wishing she would get to the point.

'As I've said, Leanne has up to now refused say who the father is but my sister has managed to wheedle it out of her.'

'I'm sorry, Mrs Mossup,' said Sir Hedley, 'but I can't see what this has to do with me.'

'Well, it does,' said the landlady. 'It's your son who is the father.'

'What!' bellowed the baronet.

'Evidently, it happened after the Young Farmers' barn dance. I gather, from what Leanne said, they both had a bit too much to drink and one thing led to another.'

Sir Hedley sat open-mouthed and was completely lost for words. Then he sighed deeply and heavily.

'I just thought you ought to know,' said Mrs Mossup weakly.

When Mrs Mossup had gone, Sir Hedley sent Mrs Moody to ask his son to join him in the study.

James had a hangdog expression as he faced his father across the desk and shifted his feet nervously. He had kept a very low profile following the incident of the necklace. He now braced himself for another scolding. He found, to his surprise, that Sir Hedley was remarkably calm and restrained.

'I have had a visit from the landlady of the King's Head,' Sir Hedley told his son.

'What did she want?'

His father did not speak for some seconds, then continued. 'She had some very interesting news.' He paused again for a moment of reflection and then looked hard at his son. 'It appears that you are the father of her daughter's child.'

James went pale and opened his mouth to speak but his father held up a restraining hand.

'No, no, James, don't say anything,' said Sir Hedley. 'I can easily predict the whole gamut of excuses and vindications which you are about to spout: the baby isn't mine, the girl threw herself at me, her mother is only after money, etc., etc. Your paternity can be easily established by a simple medical test so don't bother denying it.'

His son gnawed his bottom lip and remained white-faced but silent.

'Now, what are we going to do about it?' It was a rhetorical question. 'Let me tell you what I have decided. I have assured Mrs Mossup that I shall support her daughter in every possible way, financially and otherwise, and agreed that your – what shall I call it – your indiscretion, will remain a secret for the time being at any rate. Of course, I am aware that gossip travels fast in the village, so eventually your being the father will become common knowledge and be a further embarrassment for your mother and myself and add to your already tarnished reputation.'

'Look Pa—' began his son.

'Be quiet!' snapped Sir Hedley, banging the flat of his hand on the desktop. 'Just listen! This afternoon I have spoken to the General Manager at Hamish Reid whiskey distillery in Melrose. I have a financial interest in the company. I have arranged for you to work there and accommodation will be provided. Yes, James, you are to actually get a job. You will leave on Monday, which gives you ample time to pack and sort out any business you have here.'

'But Pa, I know nothing about whiskey,' protested the son.

'You surprise me, James,' said his father with a sardonic smile. 'I assumed that since you consume so much of it at the King's Head every week and from the decanter in the library that you would be something of an expert in that field.'

'But Pa,' began James.

Sir Hedley held up his hand.

'There will be no more discussion. You will leave for Scotland next week. I have nothing more to say. Please close the door on your way out.'

Sir Hedley sat at his desk, pondering. The time has come, he thought, to do something I should have done before. The events over the last few weeks had focused his mind. He would now deal with it without delay.

As he was putting on his coat in the hall, Lady Maladroit appeared.

'What's wrong with James?' she asked. 'He's just rushed up the stairs in a real state. What have you been saying to him?'

'I suggest you ask him,' replied her husband.

'Where are you going, Hedley?' she asked.

'Into town,' he told her, 'and I shall eat at my club this evening.'

'Was that the landlady of the King's Head I saw earlier?'

'It was.'

'What did she want?'

'Oh, nothing of any real importance,' her husband told her. 'Just to inform me that James is to be the father of an illegitimate child. We are going to be grandparents, Marcia.'

His wife, for once, was too stunned to speak but stood open-mouthed like a fish on a slab.

Lady Maladroit, devastated by the news that she was to be the grandmother of an illegitimate child and was to become associated with the common barmaid at the King's Head and her odious mother, was in the worst of moods. Adopting her habitual rigid posture and sour expression, she went in search of the housekeeper, who she found sitting at the long, scrubbed white-pine table in the kitchen, her chubby hands encircling a large mug of coffee.

'I have something to say to you, Mrs Moody,' she said, standing stiffly at the door.

'Oh yes?'

'Yes,' Lady Maladroit told her. 'I have to say that I am far from satisfied with your work.' Mrs Moody did not respond but raised the mug to her lips and took a large gulp of coffee.

'The floors are grubby, the furniture dusty and the carpets dirty. Things cannot continue like this. You must bestir yourself.'

'Bestir,' repeated the housekeeper. 'What is that supposed to mean?'

'You must apply yourself more assiduously,' Lady Maladroit informed her. 'I would like to see a vast improvement. Before you leave today, I want the sitting room, the study and the drawing room given a thorough clean.'

'Oh, do you now?' snapped Mrs Moody, colouring up.

'Yes, I do. Furthermore, my husband and I find your manner disrespectful. You are far too familiar for a domestic servant.'

'And who do you think you are talking to?' demanded the housekeeper, banging down the mug so heavily it made Lady Maladroit jump. She rose to her feet. 'I'm not standing for this. Domestic servant indeed! I've never been called such a thing.'

Lady Maladroit was unaccustomed to being confronted with such barefaced insolence and was dumbstruck.

'And if that's how you feel,' Mrs Moody told her, 'you can stuff your job.'

With that she marched out of the kitchen, leaving Lady Maladroit, for the second time that day, standing open-mouthed like a fish on a slab.

When Charlie arrived home from school, he found that his mother had a visitor. Sir Hedley Maladroit, his large frame filling the small armchair, sat in the corner of the front room, nursing a cup of tea on his lap.

'Oh hello,' said the boy brightly.

'Hello, Charlie,' replied the baronet.

'You remember Sir Hedley, don't you, love?' said Mrs Lister to her son. He noticed that his mother looked anxious, like she had at the interview. Her hands were shaking and she had an uneasy look on her face. 'Sir Hedley sometimes calls round to see me and we met him at the grammar school. Do you remember?'

'Oh yes,' said her son, 'and we had a most interesting chat down by the duck pond.'

'We did indeed,' said the baronet. He too looked a little uneasy.

'Is everything all right?' asked Charlie. He noticed how straight-backed his mother sat on the sofa and how she twisted the ring on her finger. He could tell she was nervous about something. He looked at Sir Hedley. 'Are you here to tell me I didn't get a scholarship after all?'

'No, no,' he replied, 'I'm not here to tell you that.'

'Well, what's wrong?' the boy asked his mother.

'Nothing's wrong, love, everything's fine,' she said unconvincingly. There was a slight tremble in her voice. There was an uneasy silence.

By the way the two adults were acting, Charlie knew there was something troubling them.

'And how are you, young man?' asked Sir Hedley, after a moment when no one spoke.

'I'm not a hundred per cent, I'm afraid,' replied the boy. 'I think I'm coming down with a chill.'

'I'm sorry to hear that.'

'Of course, you have to expect it at this time of year,' said Charlie, sniffing. He looked at his mother, who remained strangely quiet.

'If you look behind the sofa,' Sir Hedley told him, 'there's something for you.'

Charlie discovered the guitar, bought earlier that day.

'Wow!' he exclaimed, picking up the instrument and running a hand down the shiny wood. 'Is this for me?'

'It is,' Sir Hedley told him. 'I recall you mentioned that you hoped to get a guitar one day when we interviewed you.'

'But I didn't think you would get me one,' said Charlie. 'Thank you very much. It is really kind of you.' He looked at his mother. 'Isn't it kind of Sir Hedley?'

'It is, love,' she replied.

'Could I go and practise in my bedroom, please?' he asked.

'Not at the moment, Charlie,' she told him. 'Come and sit down next to me. I've . . . we've . . . got something to tell you first.' The boy joined his mother on the sofa. She put her arm around him and then reached for his hand and squeezed it. She took a deep breath. She swallowed hard. 'You remember last week you asked me about your father.'

'Yes,' said Charlie, 'and I mentioned it to my teacher.'

'What did you say?' she asked.

'I said I would like to know who my father is. I said I had been thinking about it quite a lot lately and that you said you would tell me about him when I am older.'

'I see.'

'I said I thought that I was old enough now to know the truth and asked Mr Dwyer if he agreed with me.'

'And what did he say?' asked Mrs Lister.

'That he was sure you had a good reason for not telling me.'

'A good answer,' remarked Sir Hedley.

'Well, I think it's time that you should know,' said the boy's mother. She looked at Sir Hedley who had put his cup down. There was a moment of awkwardness. 'Hedley,' she said, giving him the cue to speak.

'I'm your father, Charlie,' he said, standing up.

'Oh,' said the boy in a small voice. His mother squeezed his hand tightly.

'It must come as something of a shock,' said the baronet.

'More of a surprise really,' replied the boy. 'Have you always known about me?'

'Yes, I have always known about you and been very, very proud of you.'

'So you are my father?'

'I am,' replied Sir Hedley.

'I did hope it would be someone like you.'

'That is very good to hear,' said the baronet. 'Would you shake my hand, Charlie?'

The boy stood and shook his father's hand and then gave him a hug.

'My goodness,' said Sir Hedley, not expecting such a reaction. He was greatly moved by the gesture and rested his hands on the boy's head, his eyes beginning to fill up. Charlie's mother got up and put her arms around them both. They stood there, a motionless tableau, clinging to each other for what seemed an age. Then, drawing away at last, Mrs Lister kissed Charlie gently on the cheek.

And Sir Hedley Maladroit, baronet, thought to himself at that moment that although he had maybe lost one son, he had certainly gained another.

It was two weeks after the visit to the museum when Dr Merryweather telephoned Tom. She apologised for not getting in touch sooner, but told him that the coin expert at the York Museum had wanted a second opinion on a couple of the coins. She suggested meeting him at lunchtime on the Saturday at the King's Head, which she said was a most appropriate venue for what she had to say. When Tom asked why it was an appropriate place to meet, she told him all would be revealed when they met.

On the Saturday, Tom arrived at the pub in good time. It was a cold December day and there was a sting in the air and a light dusting of snow covering the landscape. He was greeted as he entered the inn by Toby Croft who was propping up the bar with a couple of other locals. The three farmers were pleased to see him for he was always good for a drink.

'Nah then Mester Dwyer,' said the farmer. ''Ow are tha gerrin on wi' that cottage of yourn? 'As tha fettled it yet?'

'It's coming along very nicely,' Tom replied. 'Your Dean has done a grand job in the garden. He worked solidly all morning cutting and pruning and wouldn't take a break. He's a really good worker.'

'Aye, well, I'm glad 'e's good for summat,' conceded the farmer grudgingly. 'Thing abaat that lad o' mine is 'e's strong in t'arm an' weak in t' 'ead.'

'Now come on, Toby,' said Tom, 'you are too hard on your son.'

'Too 'ard on 'im!' exclaimed Mr Croft. 'I reckon 'e never telled thee what 'appened when 'e were dippin' t'sheep, did 'e, Mester Dwyer?'

'No, he never mentioned it.'

'Only went an' covered hissen in poison chemicals an' ended up in t' 'ospital wi' side effects.'

'Is he all right now?'

'As reight as 'e'll ever be,' grumbled the farmer. He looked down the bar and held up his glass. 'Are tha servin' down 'ere, or what, Wayne?' he shouted.

The barman, who had been talking to a group of hikers, came to join him.

'What can I get you?' he asked.

The three farmers looked simultaneously in Tom's direction.

'A pint for me,' said Tom, producing his wallet, 'and whatever these gentleman are having.'

'Very decent of you, Mester Dwyer,' said Mr Croft. 'Pints all round.'

The three farmers drained the remainder of their beer in great gulps and placed the empty glasses on the bar.

'I thought I heard your voice, Tom.' Mrs Mossup appeared from the parlour, all smiles. 'I'll serve these, Wayne,' she told the barman. 'Pints, is it? I wondered if you were keeping away after what was said.'

'I wouldn't blame 'im if 'e did,' said Mr Croft. 'Nasty business was that, being accused o' putting your Leanne in t'family way.'

'He was never accused of anything of the sort for your information,' retorted the landlady, pulling the first pint. 'It was all a misunderstanding and you should know better than to listen to malicious rumours started by people who had no business earwigging on other people's conversations.'

'No, I've not been avoiding you, Doris,' Tom reassured her. 'I've been a bit busy lately.'

'It was only what we was told,' remarked Mr Croft, not letting the matter lie.

'Well, you were told wrong!' snapped the landlady.

'That unfortunate episode is all water under the bridge now,' Tom told her, keen to move on from the altercation. 'How is Leanne keeping?'

'Bearing up, you know.' She continued pulling a pint.

'Is she keeping the bairn then?' asked Mr Croft.

The landlady jerked her head around like an angry hen and glared at him. 'Never you mind,' she said tartly, before plonking the glass of beer down before him and spilling some of the contents in the process. 'I'm having a private conversation with Mr Dwyer, so you sup your pint and keep your nose out.'

'I was only saying—' began the farmer.

'Well, don't!' she told him.

Their exchange ceased with the appearance of a slim young woman with an exquisite figure, wonderful hair and fetching eyes who had entered the room. She looked around, saw Tom, smiled and waved and came to the bar to meet him.

'Hello, Dr Merryweather,' he said.

'Hi,' she replied. 'I'm Pat by the way.'

'And I'm Tom. Let's go over to that corner table,' he told her. Then he whispered in her ear, 'Walls have ears in here. I'll get you a drink.'

'Just an orange juice, please.'

'I'll bring it over with your pint,' said Mrs Mossup, who, like the farmers, was scrutinising the young woman.

'You've intrigued me,' Tom said, sitting down next to Dr Merryweather.

'In what way?' she asked.

'How is the King's Head such a fitting venue for us to meet?'

'Do you know what king it is on the board outside?' she asked.

'Charles I who lost his head. How is that significant?'

'I shall tell you,' she said.

Mrs Mossup arrived at the table. 'Here we are,' she said, putting down the drinks. She stood, as if waiting to be introduced.

'Could you put these drinks and what the farmers are having on my tab please, Doris?' asked Tom. 'I'll settle up later.'

'I've not seen you in here before, dear,' said the landlady to the young woman.

Dr Merryweather smiled. 'No,' she said, looking around. 'It's very, er . . . olde-worlde.'

'That's the way we like it,' replied the landlady.

'Thank you, Doris,' Tom told her.

'Now,' said Pat when the landlady had returned to the bar, 'let me tell you about the coins you left with me.' There was a real excitement in her voice. She reached into her handbag and produced the small pouch containing the coins. 'There is not much of interest or value in here.'

'A pity,' said Tom. 'I thought there might be. One of them is gold, isn't it?'

'No, the coin you're thinking of is a brass card counter. Some of them looked very authentic and people tried to pass them off as the real thing. It's worthless, I'm afraid. As I have said, there is nothing of interest and value here. There's a George III twopenny piece known as a cartwheel coin because of its shape and weight. It weighs two ounces, so as you might imagine these coins were very unpopular at the time. Having a few of those in your pocket would prove pretty heavy. There are several silver sixpences, some copper pennies and a few very worn farthings. Two of the coins, however, are of real interest, so much so that an expert from the British Museum travelled all the way to York to look at them. I've left them at the museum. There's a Charles I silver milled shilling minted in York just after the start of the Civil War, dated 1643 or 1644. Although the expert said there's a little wear, this coin is a desirable piece. York was Charles's second capital after he was forced to leave London in early 1642 and he arrived there in March. This coin is rare and would probably raise a few hundred pounds at auction.'

'Good gracious!' exclaimed Tom.

'The other coin is even more interesting,' said Dr Merryweather. 'The small rectangle of misshapen silver is a siege piece minted in Scarborough and formed from a portion of flattened domestic silver. The Scarborough siege issues include various odd denominations, due to their being made from roughly cut-up pieces of metal derived from plates, dishes, jugs, spoons, etc. They were flattened out and bore a value equivalent to the weight of the piece. The one you have has a stamped depiction on its obverse of Scarborough Castle with a gate to the side and the letters V and S for five shillings. According to the expert it is excessively rare and possibly there is only one other example in existence. It is far too valuable for me to carry around in my handbag – that is why I have left it at the museum.'

'How valuable?' asked Tom.

'Oh, about twenty thousand pounds,' she said casually.

'What!' cried Tom, spilling his drink. 'I don't believe it!' Such was the loudness of, and the shock in his voice that all those in the pub stopped talking and looked in his direction.

Dr Merryweather rested a hand on Tom's. 'It's true,' she told him.

At the bar Toby Croft exchanged a look with the landlady. 'Somethin' 'as come as a bit of a surprise to our young Mester Dwyer,' he said, nodding sagely. 'Are you thinkin' what I'm thinkin', Mrs Mossup?'

'And what would that be?' asked the landlady.

'That the young schoolmaster might not 'ave put your Leanne in t'family way but it sounds to me, from what I've just 'eard, that there's one young woman who 'e 'as.'

19

'Do you know,' remarked Mrs Golightly to Mr Cadwallader at lunchtime in the staffroom, 'what's upsetting Joyce this morning? Last week she was on top of the world but today she's down in the dumps. She's sitting in her classroom, slumped over the desk like a puppet which has had its strings cut.'

'Things might not be going too well with her ardent admirer from the auction house,' suggested Mr Cadwallader. 'Perhaps she's had a tiff with the captivating Mr Sampson. As you say, she's been full of the joys of spring recently.'

Joyce had indeed been in a buoyant mood of late. The intimate meal at Le Bon Viveur with Mr Sampson had been a great success. He had been the perfect gentleman and clearly delighted in her company, finding her lively and interesting and, of course, attractive. For her part Joyce had found the auctioneer charming and attentive and, of course, he had the added attraction of being very well-to-do. They had talked and laughed all evening and were the last diners to leave the restaurant. When Mr Sampson – Julian – had suggested they should have a meal together again, Joyce had readily agreed. The following Monday she had regaled her colleagues with a blow-by-blow account of the evening, from being collected in the Mercedes to coffee back at her flat.

Joyce came into the staffroom now. She didn't speak to the two teachers but stood by the window looking despondent. Mrs Golightly asked her what the matter was.

'I don't wish to talk about it, Bertha,' she replied miserably. 'It's too distressing for words.'

'A trouble shared is trouble halved,' said Mr Cadwallader. 'Come along, Joycey. You can tell us.'

'Well, if you must know, it's the wretched pantomime. I wish I had never agreed to do it.'

Mr Walker, manager of the Clayton Civic Theatre, had asked her to produce the play. He had been most persuasive, telling her that with her experience on the stage and with her obvious expertise in theatre production, that she was ideal. Joyce had been swayed by his blandishments and consented to take it on.

'So, what's the problem?' asked Mrs Golightly.

'The principal man is a pain in the proverbial,' she said angrily. 'He's the assistant manager at Cheap and Cheerful, the food outlet in Clayton, but anyone would think he is a West End star the way he carries on. He struts around the stage like some constipated peacock, giving unwanted and unneeded advice to the other actors. I wish I had never offered him the part but I was desperate for a young man and he was the best of a bad lot. At the last rehearsal he had the brass neck to say he could improve on the script. So now he thinks he's a playwright.'

'Who wrote the script?' enquired Mr Cadwallader.

'I did,' replied Joyce. 'What's more this prima donna wishes to go on the programme with a stage name, I ask you.' She snorted and pursed her lips. 'He's an amateur, for goodness' sake, but he thinks he's God's gift to the acting profession.'

'What's his stage name?' asked Mrs Golightly, intrigued.

'Lawrence de la Mare,' Miss Tranter told her. 'His real name is Darren Biggerdyke. He's got up everyone's nose and if I wasn't so reliant upon him, I would tell him to sling his hook. He got into a real argument with the Wicked Fairy at the rehearsal, telling her how she should say her lines. Mrs

Crabb is Maleficent, the Wicked Fairy. She works in Eye-Savers, the opticians in Clayton.'

'I can't see Mrs Crabb standing for any nonsense from anybody,' remarked Mr Cadwallader. 'She scared the life out of me when I went for an eye test. I've never seen the woman smile and she can be very offhand with customers.'

'Yes, she can be difficult,' agreed Joyce, 'and she will wear these huge coloured bifocal spectacles with lenses like the bottoms of milk bottles. They magnify her eyes so much she looks like some myopic frog.'

'It's nice to see some of the pupils from the school taking part in the pantomime,' Mrs Golightly told her, changing the subject.

'The children are fine,' said Joyce, 'although George would not have been my first choice for the part of the prince's page. He's in it because his father only agreed to build the stage sets if his son was in the pantomime. The boy is willing enough but he's clumsy, can't remember his lines, and of course a royal servant would not have such a pronounced Yorkshire accent.' She sighed. 'I was disappointed that Tom wouldn't take a part in the pantomime. As you said, Bertha, he would have made a perfect prince.'

At that moment, the subject of the conversation, who had been taking the football practice that lunchtime, entered the staffroom. He was dressed in his tracksuit top and shorts.

'Brrr, it's cold out there today,' he said. He rubbed his leg vigorously.

'What's wrong with your leg?' asked Mrs Golightly.

'An old football injury,' he told her. 'I still get these muscle spasms and cramps, particularly in the cold weather.'

'What you need is a therapeutic massage,' said Joyce, getting up. 'Sit down and I'll give you one. In between the rest periods actors often have, I did an intensive course in massage therapy. I think I told you. Let me look, Tom.'

'No, no, really, Joyce,' he began.

'Don't be silly. Sit down and stick out your leg.'

'Really, Joyce,' Tom began again, but he was pushed into a chair and his leg was pulled out before him.

Joyce began to knead the leg. 'Muscle strain is a common injury among those who participate in sports,' she told him. 'Lay back,' she ordered.

'Actually, it's bit lower down,' Tom told her, feeling himself colouring up.

'The muscles at the top of the leg need manipulating,' said his colleague, continuing with the massage. 'The problem is with this bulging muscle in the calf. It's a very powerful muscle which runs just above the knee. You see by all that running and jumping and the fast movements, you have damaged it and are therefore prone to spasms and painful involuntary contractions. Now when we get further up the thigh—'

Tom shot to his feet as if someone had cracked a whip behind him. 'Do you know that feels a whole lot better? Thank you, Joyce.'

'But I've hardly started,' she replied.

'Well, it's fine.'

'I can do a full body massage if you are interested,' she said.

'N . . . no, no,' stuttered Tom.

'Well, I'd be interested,' said Mr Cadwallader.

'Now I come to think of it, I'm a bit tied up with the pantomime at the moment, Owen,' she told him. She looked at Tom, 'And speaking of the pantomime . . .'

At the end of the school day, Tom asked if could have a word with Colin.

'I thought I might walk home with you to Castle Farm this afternoon,' he told the boy.

'Why, sir?'

'I need to have a word with your father.'

'About me?' The boy instinctively braced himself to hear bad news.

'No, not about you.'

'What is it about, Mr Dwyer?' asked the boy.

'Wait until I've spoken to your father and then you'll find out,' Tom told him. 'Don't look so worried. It's nothing to be concerned about.'

Colin was quiet and thoughtful as they headed through the village to take the path by the church to Castle Farm. With his hands dug deep in his pockets, he walked a little ahead of Tom.

'So how are things going with the move?' asked the teacher.

'OK,' muttered the boy without further elaboration.

'So, when will you be moving?'

'Next weekend.'

'And are you all packed up and ready to go?'

'Yea, just about.'

'It will be a big change for you and your father.'

'Yea, I suppose it will.'

Tom stopped. 'Colin, would you just wait a moment.' The boy halted and stared ahead of him. 'Look at me.' The boy turned. There was a miserable expression etched on his face. 'What's troubling you?' asked the teacher.

The boy looked down. 'Nothing,' he mumbled.

'Is it the move?'

'No.'

'Well, what is it? Come along, Colin. I can see that there's something wrong.' The boy's bottom lip began to tremble and his eyes were pricked with tears. 'Do you want to tell me about it?'

He nodded and rubbed his eyes. He looked up.

'Mr Dwyer,' he said, after a pause, 'when you were a kid, did you sometimes not like yourself?'

Tom was taken by surprise at the question. He looked at Colin for a moment. 'That's a strange thing to ask,' he replied.

'But did you sometimes not like who you were and what you did and wish you were somebody else?'

'No, I don't remember wishing that I was somebody else,' the teacher told him. 'I was maybe a bit shy and wanted to be more confident like some of the other boys in the school but I never really envied them. Every now and then I was sorry for something I'd done or said, and I didn't feel very good about myself then, but I never felt unhappy about the person I was.'

'I sometimes don't like myself,' said Colin with feeling. 'I sometimes hate myself.'

'Why?' asked the teacher, looking at the boy's piteous face.

'I was angry and mixed up after my mam died,' said Colin. 'I think that's what made me do horrible things. I was mean to people but, it's hard to explain, I sort of couldn't help it. I was like somebody else.' His eyes began to fill up. 'I knew that what I said was wrong and that it hurt people and made them unhappy but I didn't stop doing it. I suppose I wanted them to be unhappy like me. I didn't like the person I had become.' He rubbed his eyes on the back of his hand. 'I still don't.'

'We have all done things which we wish we regret,' Tom told him. 'You're not alone in that.'

'I was a bully,' said the boy.

'I know you were,' said Tom. 'You were chasing Charlie Lister the first time I set eyes on you.'

'I wanted to be like him,' said Colin, 'I wanted to be happy like him. That's why I picked on him. I was jealous.'

'But you're not a bully now, are you?' said the teacher.

'No, I'm not a bully now.'

'Well, that's all that matters, isn't it?'

'No, it's not,' said the boy, shaking his head and rubbing his eyes again.

'Look,' said the teacher, staring at the tortured face with tears running down the cheeks, 'when I first met you, to be honest, I didn't like you very much. You were rude and lazy and answered me back but you're a different boy now. Do you hear what I say, you are a *different* boy. You behave yourself, are working a lot better, you don't bully any more and you are a fine artist. You have a talent that nobody else in the school has. I've changed my mind about you. I like you and am really pleased that you are in my class. Now let's hear no more about you disliking yourself.'

'I can't,' the boy told him. 'I said things to Miss Cathcart which I wish I had never said, cruel things. I sort of bullied her as well. I think that I made her do what she did.'

'And what was that?' asked Tom, knowing full well what the boy meant.

'You know, jumping into the river. I sometimes think that I made her kill herself.'

'No, Colin. You didn't do that.'

'But you don't know that, do you, Mr Dwyer?' He gazed at Tom through his tears. 'I was really nasty to her in one lesson, calling her awful names and shouting at her and the next day they found her in the river.'

'It was an accident,' Tom told him. 'Miss Cathcart must have lost her footing and fallen in.'

'That's what some say, but it's not true,' said the boy. 'She took her own life. Most people know that.'

'And you think you drove her to do it?' asked Tom. 'You blame yourself?'

'Yea, I do.'

Tom considered what words to use. Maybe the boy was right, that his actions did indeed push Miss Cathcart over the edge, maybe it was the last straw for the poor woman. Tom could never know for certain, but he couldn't have Colin reproaching himself for the rest of his life. 'From what I've been told,' he said, 'Miss Cathcart was an unhappy woman and there were lots of things which made her feel unhappy. It wasn't just the way you treated her.'

'Do you really mean that, Mr Dwyer,' asked the boy, 'or are you just saying that to make me feel better?'

'Look, Colin,' said Tom, resting a hand on the boy's shoulder, 'of course you were not to blame for Miss Cathcart's death. It was wrong of you to be unkind to the teacher, you know that now, but you must not feel responsible for what happened, so put it out of your head.'

'I can't,' said the boy, beginning to sob. 'I just can't.'

'Well, you must,' Tom told him. 'You can't keep blaming yourself. As I've said you're a different boy now from the one I first met. Now, come along, I've got something very exciting to say to your father.'

The boy didn't move. 'I've not told anyone else what I've just told you,' he replied. 'You won't tell my dad what I've said, will you?'

'Let's keep it to ourselves, shall we?' said Tom.

At Castle Farm Tom found Mr Greenwood leaning on the gate, staring out over the open fields.

'Naa then, Mester Dwyer,' he said, catching sight of the teacher approaching.

'All set to go?' asked Tom.

'Aye, just abaat. T'sheep an' t'cattle gone, t'farm machinery and tractor sold, most o' t'stuff in t' 'ouse flogged or given away. In some ways I'll be sorry to leave, but in others not.'

'Mixed feelings,' said Tom.

'Summat like that.' He looked at his son, 'Hey up, Colin. Cat got thee tongue, 'as it?'

'Hello, Dad,' muttered his son.

''As this lad o'mine been behavin' hissen then, Mester Dwyer?' asked the farmer. 'I 'ope tha's not up 'ere to bring me bad news abaat 'im.'

'Not at all, Mr Greenwood,' replied Tom. 'Quite the reverse. Colin's doing just fine.'

'It's good to 'ear,' said the farmer, looking at his son and smiling.

'He gave me a present last week,' Tom told the farmer.

'Did 'e now?'

'A really lovely picture of Marston Castle. I shall treasure it. As I've said, your son's got quite a talent. Fancy him winning the County Art Competition.'

'Aye, fancy.' He looked at his son. 'I'm dead chuffed wi' 'im an' I know 'is mam would 'ave been too. Mi wife was quite an artist, thaa knaas.'

Colin stared at his father. This was one of the few occasions when his mother had been mentioned. 'I didn't know that,' he said.

'Aye, she was. 'Din't 'ave much time fer 'er paintin' though, what wi' runnin' t'farm.'

Both father and son looked thoughtful.

'Could I have word with you, Mr Greenwood?' asked Tom.

'Tha'd best come in out on cowld. You go an' gerron wi' your 'omework, Colin, while I 'ave a word wi' yer teacher.'

'I'd like your son to stay, please, Mr Greenwood,' said Tom. 'What I have to say concerns him as well.'

'I thought you said it hadn't anything to do with me,' said the boy, looking worried.

In the farmhouse, sitting at the old pine table opposite the farmer and his son, Tom related the first part of the conversation he had had with the curator at the Clayton Museum and Art Gallery, telling them that most of the coins were well worn, of base metal and of little interest and that the golden guinea turned out to be a worthless brass card counter.

'I thowt they'd not be worth much,' said the farmer. 'I could tell by t'feel of 'em that there were no gold there. Anyroad, yer welcome to 'em.'

'I'm afraid I couldn't accept them, Mr Greenwood,' Tom told him.

'They're no good to me, Mester Dwyer. I gev 'em to yer, an' tha's welcome to 'em.'

'Perhaps when you hear what I have to say,' said Tom, 'you may change your mind.'

He smiled and leaned back in the chair, anticipating the reaction he would receive when the farmer and his son heard the news about the two special coins.

'Two of the items, however,' Tom said, 'were of great interest and value. There was a Charles I silver shilling which the curator estimated would fetch a few hundred pounds at auction—'

'What!' exclaimed the farmer.

'And an exceptionally rare coin called a Scarborough siege piece worth rather more.'

'More than hundreds of pounds?' asked Colin, his eyes wide.

'Just a bit more,' said Tom, relishing the moment. He paused for the maximum effect.

'How much more?' asked the boy, leaning eagerly across the table.

'Oh, possibly in the region of twenty thousand pounds,' replied Tom nonchalantly.

The room echoed then with the Yorkshireman's war cry:

"Ow much?' roared Mr Greenwood and his son in unison.

'Where's Joyce?' asked Tom at afternoon break. 'It's not like her to miss a cup of tea.'

'She's in a terrible state again,' replied Mr Cadwallader, reaching into the biscuit tin. 'She's licking her wounds in her classroom.'

'So, what's the problem now?' asked Tom.

'She called into my flat last night,' said Mrs Golightly. 'She was in floods of tears.'

'Is it the pantomime again?'

'It is,' replied his colleague. 'The principal man has pulled out and he's taken his girlfriend who was playing the Sleeping Beauty with him. She's lost her principal players.'

'Oh dear.'

'Evidently he got into a furious argument with the Wicked Fairy,' said Mrs Golightly. 'From what Joyce has said, they have been at loggerheads since the first rehearsal – him telling Mrs Crabb what to do, how to act, where to stand, how to say her lines, and she telling him to mind his own business and keep his clever comments to himself. And she added that if he didn't stop harassing her, she would tell her husband who would punch his lights out. Poor Joyce was in the middle. Anyway, after a real ding-dong, it came to a head at the rehearsal yesterday when he came on stage and changed his lines.'

'What did he say?' asked Tom.

Mrs Golightly recited:

> 'I am the handsome Prince,
> Of whom you are so fond,
> Now shall I tell the Wicked Fairy
> Where she can stick her wand?'

Tom dropped his head to hide his smile.

'Oh, it's not funny,' scolded Mrs Golightly. 'The Wicked Fairy did stick her wand but not in the place where the prince imagined. Joyce had to pull them apart. Talk about amateur dramatics. Anyway, the principal man told Joyce that he could no longer be on the same stage as Mrs Crabb and it was either him or her, one of them would have to go. Of course, he imagined that him having the leading part, he was indispensable and that Mrs Crabb would be given her marching orders, but Joyce had had enough of his behaviour and reminded him she was the producer, not him and not to be such a drama queen. At this, he flounced out, with his girlfriend following, telling Joyce where she could stick her pantomime.'

'Oh dear,' Tom repeated.

'She's managed to get someone to take on the part of the Sleeping Beauty,' said Mr Cadwallader, 'but without the leading man, it looks likely that the pantomime will have to be cancelled.' He nibbled on a biscuit.

'It's such a shame,' added Mrs Golightly. 'Joyce and the cast have worked so hard and the children were so looking forward to performing.'

'If only there was someone who could help Joycey out,' said Mr Cadwallader meaningfully, 'some good-hearted soul to take on the part of the handsome prince.' He exchanged a glance with Mrs Golightly. They both then looked pointedly at their colleague.

'Oh no!' spluttered Tom, feeling their eyes fixed firmly upon him. 'I couldn't possibly . . .'

'Of course you could,' said Mr Cadwallader. 'You would make the perfect prince. You are made for the part.'

'It's out of the question,' said Tom decisively. 'Quite out of the question.'

'Well, it's a great pity,' sighed Mr Cadwallader, reaching into the tin for another Garibaldi.

'Poor Joyce,' sighed Mrs Golightly. 'All that hard work gone to waste.'

Miss Tranter entered the staffroom, looking as if the whole weight of the world was on her shoulders. She sighed theatrically and slumped into her usual chair, despondency carved on her face.

'Cheer up, Joycey,' said Mr Cadwallader brightly. 'You never know. You might find a replacement.'

'Not at this late stage, I won't,' she told him miserably. 'When I think of all the work I and the cast and the backstage crew have put in, all the time we have devoted to this production, I feel I am at the edge of a precipice.'

'You have to put it behind you,' suggested Mr Cadwallader. 'Life is full of ups and downs. You just have to hang on in there and move forward with confidence.'

'I shall have to break the news at the next rehearsal that the pantomime is off,' groaned Joyce. 'And when I think of the children's faces, wet with tears, when I tell them,' she lamented, 'I want to weep myself.'

'All right, all right!' exclaimed Tom. 'I'll do it.'

'What?' cried Joyce.

'I said I'll take on the part of the prince.'

Miss Tranter leapt up from her chair. 'Oh, will you, Tom?' she said excitedly. 'Will you really?'

'I suppose so,' he answered, not sounding at all enthusiastic.

'You darling man!' Miss Tranter exclaimed and, rushing across the room, she planted a massive kiss on Tom's lips just as the door opened and the headmaster appeared.

'Am I interrupting something?' Mr Gaunt asked with raised eyebrows.

'Tom has agreed to be my handsome prince,' she announced.

'Congratulations,' said the headmaster.

That afternoon everyone at Risingdale School was in particularly high spirits. Joyce, of course, was euphoric on learning that Tom had agreed to take on the part of the prince in the pantomime. A beaming Mr Gaunt arrived at the staffroom with the news that the Education Authority had been in touch to inform him that the school was saved from closure. His joy was infectious and Mr Cadwallader and Mrs Golightly had cheered so loudly that they could be heard by the assistant caretaker who was busy cleaning the sinks in the girls' toilets. Mrs Gosling, for her part, was in an exuberant frame of mind.

She had felt triumphant when she had discovered that Lady Maladroit's necklace had turned up, exonerating her of all blame, and even more so after the visit of the local squire. At lunchtime she regaled Tom with a long and embroidered account of Sir Hedley's visit to her cottage, when she related how he had expressed deep regret and begged her to return as the housekeeper at Marston Towers.

'I told him there was no way I would return,' she said haughtily. 'I told him I was very happy in my new post as assistant caretaker, thank you very much.'

That afternoon, Tom's class was also in a bubbly mood. Colin's revelation about the rare coins caused great excitement amongst the other pupils. Charlie was in a jaunty mood, although unlike Colin he had kept his exciting disclosure a secret, something his mother had asked him to do for the time being. Simon, talking ten to the dozen, described in detail to anyone who would listen how his ferret had given birth, and David, sporting a new pair of glasses with large, colourful frames, announced happily he could now see properly. Marjorie and Vicky could hardly contain their excitement, for both had been cast as fairies in the pantomime. They were loudly discussing what costumes they would wear. George announced that, as Prince Floribund's page, he had a leading part in the pantomime and hoped to take up acting as a career when he left school.

Carol too was also in very good humour.

'You are in a sunny mood today,' Tom told the girl.

'I am, sir,' she replied.

'And why is that?'

'Starlight had a very lucky escape yesterday, sir,' she explained.

'In what way?' asked the teacher.

'He got his head stuck. My granddad said that he might be a handsome beast and God's gift to the ovine world but he's daft as a brush and dead greedy. Ovine, by the way, means to do with sheep, Mr Dwyer,' explained the girl.

Tom smiled. 'Go on, Carol, I'm intrigued as to what happened.'

'When I put Starlight's food in the feeder,' the girl continued, 'he was so eager to get to it, that he ran straight at it and pushed his head through the metal bars and got it stuck.'

'What did you do?' asked Tom.

'I fetched my granddad and my dad. Well, when Starlight tried to pull his head out, his horns wouldn't let him and he started jumping and tugging and twisting. My granddad and my dad tried to push him forward and lift him up, but Starlight kept pulling and started kicking and nipping which made my granddad use a very rude word which I won't repeat. My dad telephoned Mr Olmeroyde, who farms next to us, and he came with the vet. Starlight was in a real state and the vet said he could suffocate if they didn't get him out pretty quick. My granddad said he knew that and used another rude word which I won't repeat. The vet gave him an injection to calm him down – the tup, not my granddad – and then said the best thing to do would be to cut off his horns to get him out. My granddad—'

'Used another rude word which you won't repeat,' interrupted Tom, chuckling.

'He did,' said Carol, nodding, 'and he said there was no way he was going to have the horns removed what with him being a show sheep and all. Mr Olmeroyde went to fetch a metal saw and he cut the bar on the feeder and freed the tup. Starlight's now in my granddad's bad books and sulking and off his food, but maybe it will teach him not to be so greedy in future.'

When Tom arrived at Clayton Comprehensive School for the rehearsal of *The Sleeping Beauty*, he found the main hall noisy with people. He stood at the back and caught sight of Joyce, dressed in tight-fitting denim jeans, black leather boots with ridiculously high heels and a garish multi-coloured jumper. She was wearing scarlet lipstick and heavy black mascara which made her look severe and dramatic, as she argued with a small woman with frizzy hair whose face was dominated by a pair of huge black-framed glasses. This, Tom guessed, was the Wicked Fairy. Joyce stopped speaking when she saw Tom. She waved at him and smiled.

'May I have your attention!' she shouted. 'Will everyone please take a seat?' She clapped her hands. 'Quickly, quickly. We have much to do this evening.' When the actors had seated themselves and she had got all their attention, Joyce continued, 'Now, as you are all aware, Darren Biggerdyke is no longer the prince.'

'Good riddance!' the small woman with the frizzy hair and large glasses called out. This was accompanied by some supportive grunts and murmurs from the others.

'Quiet please!' ordered Joyce. 'Now, I have to admit that I was getting rather desperate about whether we would be able to find suitable replacements for the two principal players in time, but I have managed—'

She stopped talking abruptly when a thin individual with floppy dyed-blond hair, a pale complexion peppered with freckles and a long, prominent nose came through the door at the back of the hall and sauntered towards her. He was dressed in a startlingly bright-pink shirt, crushed strawberry-coloured corduroy trousers and black leather jacket. It was clear the young man thought a great deal of himself. Behind him was a tall, thin-featured young woman with a beaked face.

'Hi, everyone,' he said in a clipped and rather exaggerated accent, and waving a theatrical hand at the group of actors sitting in rows facing the stage. This was greeted by complete silence.

'What are you doing here?' demanded Joyce, as he approached her. He brushed a strand of hair from his face.

'The thing is, Joyce,' he said loftily, 'I've been mulling over the situation after the last rehearsal when matters got a bit overheated.'

'Really,' she replied, not as a question but more a way of making him shut up. She folded her arms.

'And I thought that by backing out, Davina and I would let you all down. We don't want to do that so we have decided to continue to play the part of Prince Florimund and Princess Aurora.'

'Have you indeed?' said Joyce.

'I realise that at this late stage you won't be able to get suitable replacements, and I guess without us you will have to cancel the pantomime.'

'Well, actually, Darren,' Joyce told him with a triumphant intonation to her voice, 'I have found more than suitable replacements.'

'What!' he cried. The man looked dazed as if he had been smacked in the face.

'After you walked out in a huff and told me where to stick my pantomime,' Joyce continued, 'I looked for a couple of people who would be willing to take over the parts. I am pleased to say I have found a new handsome prince and a most suitable Sleeping Beauty.'

'But it's our parts,' protested Darren's companion.

Joyce smiled a tolerant, patient smile, one she often employed in the classroom when explaining things to a child. 'Not any more,' she said. She pointed to the end of the front row. 'Here is our Princess Aurora and at the back of the hall is our new Prince Florimund. Come along down, Tom, and meet the rest of the cast.'

Darren shot around. He gave Tom the glare of a defiant child.

'Now if you two do want to join us again,' Joyce went on, 'you could assist with the scene changes, Darren, and Davina could help look after the properties.'

'Not bloody likely!' he shouted, and marched angrily for the door, followed by his girlfriend, who would later have a few well-chosen words to say to him.

There was loud applause and heads turned in Tom's direction. All had enjoyed the performance and could see their producer was in her element.

Tom had not expected that he would make such a conspicuous entrance and walked self-consciously to join Joyce at the front.

'This is Tom Dwyer, one of the teachers at the school where I work,' said Joyce. 'He has very kindly stepped into the breach. I won't introduce everyone to you, Tom. You will get to know them in due course. However, you do need to meet our new leading lady.' She looked in the direction of a slim young woman with a mass of auburn hair, who was sitting at the end of the row. Unlike the other members of the cast, she had stared ahead when Tom had walked down to the front. 'This is our Princess Aurora, the Sleeping Beauty,' said Joyce. The young woman turned her head, looked at Tom and gave that small familiar smile. 'I think you know Janette Fairborn?'

20

'I have always thought that the innocence of young children is wonderfully illustrated at Christmas when the infant Nativity takes place,' Mr Pendlebury told the staff.

The vicar was sitting in the staffroom two weeks before the school broke up for the Christmas holidays. He was visiting the school to take the assembly and to stay to watch the rehearsal for the play which was to be performed at St Mary's the following Friday afternoon.

'Small children acting out one of the greatest stories of all time capture the very essence of this very special time of year,' he continued speaking as if he was declaiming from his pulpit. He sighed. 'To see Mary cradling a large doll representing Baby Jesus never fails to bring a tear to my eye, and Joseph, wide-eyed and innocent-faced, in a tartan dressing gown and a thick multi-coloured towel over his head always occasions a sympathetic smile.'

'Well, I can't say that the Nativity play has that effect on me, Mr Pendlebury,' said Miss Tranter. 'I'm afraid I have little patience with infants. They are notoriously unpredictable and unmanageable. You can never foresee what might happen once they are in front of an audience. They fidget and shuffle, twiddle their hair, scratch and pick their noses, and as soon as they catch sight of their parents and grandparents they start waving and blowing kisses and forgetting their lines. I just hope that this time we don't have a repetition of last year's fiasco.'

'Excuse me, Joyce, it was not a fiasco,' said Mrs Golightly, feeling peeved by the unfavourable comment. She was the teacher who produced the Nativity each Christmas and it took her a deal of hard work and effort. 'The play was very well received and I think one has to expect a few mishaps where young children are concerned.'

'Oh really, Bertha,' said her colleague, 'it was more than a few mishaps.'

'I must admit,' said the vicar, recalling last year's Nativity play, 'there were a few unforeseen and unfortunate incidents. I am sure that this year there will be no misadventures.'

'I hardly think a few hiccups could be described as "misadventures", Mr Pendlebury,' retorted Mrs Golightly, getting increasingly wounded by the criticisms. 'I thought the children did very well, all things considered.'

At the Nativity play performed in the church the year before, there had indeed been a few unforeseen and unfortunate incidents. The boy playing Joseph, a plump, pale-faced child with a crop of wild ginger hair, had been wearing a long brown poncho, which had been clearly too big for a small child. As he had made his entrance, he had trodden on the bottom of the costume, tripped, fallen and knocked over the manger. He had then used a word that St Joseph would have never uttered. Later, when the play seemed to be going well, an angry little angel, in a silk gown and tinsel halo, who had been masked by another infant, had shouted offstage, 'Can you tell the palm tree to shift, Mrs Golightly, he's blocking my view and I can't see my Nana.'

'You need to make sure they all go to the toilet before the play this time,' Mr Cadwallader instructed his colleague. 'We all remember what happened last year.'

The boy playing the palm tree had opened the performance. He had stood at the front of the church with arms outstretched. The child had been encased in dark brown crêpe paper, draped in papier-mâché coconuts with card-board fronds attached to his hands. He had sported a bright green woollen balaclava helmet through which his little face had peeped. Seeing the packed church and all eyes on him and hearing their titters, he had become frightened and had wet himself. His 'little accident' had seeped through the brown crêpe paper in a dark stain. The child had wriggled uncomfortably, as if suffering from chronic worms, and bits of the wet paper had fallen off revealing his electric blue underpants. At this, the audience had laughed volubly and the little palm tree, sobbing pathetically, had exited stage right clutching his papier-mâché coconuts. Things had not improved. One of the little shepherds, with a tea towel over his head and sporting a cotton-wool beard, had spent most of the play scratching his chin and exploring a nostril with a finger. His little companion had announced during a render-ing of 'Away in a Manger' that he needed a wee and the third shepherd fell asleep. The innkeeper, a sturdily built child with spiky ginger hair and his two front teeth missing, had upstaged everybody by announcing indignantly to the audience, when he opened the inn door, that he wanted to be Joseph. When Mary and Joseph arrived he had told them, 'Clear off! There's no room.'

'And I hope this year we are not having the appearance of the Little Drummer Boy,' said Miss Tranter. 'He wouldn't shut up, banging that wretched tin drum.'

The overenthusiastic little boy, dressed in a soldier outfit and taking on the part of the Little Drummer Boy, had proceeded to bang the metal drum around his neck loudly and with gusto. The infant playing Mary, an angelic-looking child with a rosy prettiness, one could see was getting increas-ingly annoyed. Finally her face had changed to a sort of pent-up fury. She had placed Baby Jesus carefully back in the manger (a large pink doll with frizzy hair) and had shouted at the boy, 'Will you shurrup, Darren! I'm trying to gerrim off to sleep. You're doin' mi 'ead in!'

'And if I were you, Bertha,' suggested Miss Tranter, 'I would tell the parents of the Three Wise Men not to go overboard on their children's costumes this year. I mean it's not a contest to see who the best dressed king is.'

The parents of the children playing the Magi had indeed gone to town on the costumes. The three little boys had entered the stage in regal splendour, holding their precious gifts. The first king had had a huge silver turban perched on his head and a purple cloak (a velvet curtain) embellished with sequins draped around him. The second king had worn a headdress of coloured feathers, white gloves and a scarlet pashmina. King number three had sported a most impressive bejewelled cardboard crown. The jewels in his crown were in fact coloured wine gums which had been glued on to look like rubies and emeralds and they had shone brilliantly under the lights.

As the play had progressed, the third king had begun to get rather bored and had started yawning and scratching and stretching. Then he had proceeded to detach the wine gums one by one from his crown, pop them in his mouth and chew them vigorously. The other two kings had watched him with interest. Finally the second king had leaned over and said in a loud stage whisper, 'Give us one, Jason.' The third king had obliged. The drama had concluded with the children singing, 'O Little Town of Bethlehem' accompanied by the loud chomping of the Magi.

Mrs Golightly, hearing this surfeit of comment and criticism, stiffened and narrowed her eyes. 'Well, thank you very much for all those helpful suggestions,' she remarked sarcastically. 'It is always good to be told how things could be improved.'

'Don't take it the wrong way, Bertha,' said Miss Tranter. 'I was only offering some constructive criticism. After all, I do know something about acting.'

'You were not very receptive to constructive criticism, were you,' countered her colleague acerbically, 'when Darren Biggerdyke gave you the benefit of his advice at the pantomime rehearsal.' It was out of character for the teacher to be so cutting.

'That was different,' replied Joyce sharply. 'He was—'

'Well, I am sure things will be fine this year, Mrs Golightly,' interjected the vicar reassuringly, and observing the fixed expression on the infant teacher's face, 'I am so grateful for all the time and effort you have put in and I know that the children will be splendid.' Mr Pendlebury was not a man who liked any sort of confrontation and he could see that this exchange between the two teachers could escalate unless he intervened. Having said that, after the previous year's performance, he felt decidedly apprehensive and could not resist one final comment. 'Oh and could the children get the words right for the carol. We don't want a repetition of last year when they sang "The First O Hell"!'

Mrs Golightly pulled a face. 'I shall bear that in mind, vicar,' she said tetchily, and wondering why she had let herself in for this.

Mr Pendlebury's observation of the rehearsal later that day did nothing to allay the fears he had regarding the performance the following week.

The vicar, having taken the assembly, joined Mrs Golightly in her classroom. The tables and chairs, sand and water trays, book boxes and teacher's desk had been pushed up against the wall to make a space for the children to perform.

'Now settle down, children,' said the teacher, raising her voice and clapping her hands to stem the excited chatter. 'Bottoms on the floor, eyes this way, fingers on lips and ears pinned back.' The noise subsided. 'This morning, children, we have a special visitor in our classroom.'

'It's the vicar, miss!' shouted a child.

'It is, Philip,' said Mrs Golightly.

'We saw him in assembly, miss,' said another child.

'Yes, we did, Penelope. Just listen, children. No more shout-ing out. Mr Pendlebury is going to watch our rehearsal for the Nativity play which we will be performing in the church next week. I am sure he will leave us this morning very much impressed. Now, quickly and quietly get into your places.' The children jumped to their feet and scrambled to take up their positions. Mrs Golightly exhaled loudly and frowned. 'I said quietly, children. I don't think Mr Pendlebury will be very much impressed by such noisy children, and he will not be at all impressed with what you are doing, Malcolm Oglethorpe. Donkeys don't roll about on the floor making silly noises, now do they? They stand up straight and pay attention. Justine, don't do that with Baby Jesus, dear, and Philip, please stop fiddling with the frankincense.' She turned to the vicar. 'I'm afraid they are a little excited,' she told him, smiling weakly.

The cleric nodded but had a pained expression on his face. He could predict more unforeseen and unfortunate incidents in the forthcoming play.

'Miss, I've got my finger stuck,' said a small, sharp-faced boy who was holding up the frankincense (a large plastic shampoo bottle). The child had a scattering of freckles, wavy black hair and a tight little mouth.

'How do you mean you've got your finger stuck?' asked the teacher.

'There's a hole in the lid, miss,' explained the child.

'Well, how did you manage to get your finger stuck?' asked the teacher.

'I don't know, miss. I just pushed it in and it's stuck.'

'My goodness, that was a silly thing to do, wasn't it? Well, if it went in, it must come out. Wiggle it about a bit. No, I don't mean your bottom, wiggle your finger about. He doesn't need your assistance thank you very much, Harry.'

'I was trying to be helpful, miss,' the boy told her glumly. 'Mr Pendlebury said in assembly that we should be helpful to others.'

Mrs Golightly shot the vicar a sharp look, 'Yes, I know what Mr Pendlebury said and that you are only trying to be helpful, but just leave the lid alone.'

'My finger's come out now, miss,' announced the child, holding up the shampoo bottle with a beaming smile on his face.

'Good,' said the teacher. 'Alex, put your crown on straight. It's right over your eyes. We don't want you tripping up.' She thought of the boy in the poncho who played Joseph the year before. 'Justine, I have asked you not to do that with Baby Jesus. Gavin, will you stop that immediately. Crooks are for holding sensibly and not for swinging about. You will have someone's eye out. Megan dear, I really don't think the Angel of the Lord would wipe her nose on her sleeve, now would she? Use a tissue.'

'I've not got one, miss,' said the child, sniffing theatrically.

'Well, go and get one from Mrs Leadbeater. Tyrone, palm trees stand still, they do not wander about the stage. Go back and stand on your spot and don't wave your leaves about. Justine, I shall not tell you again not to do that with Baby Jesus. My goodness, we will never get started at this rate. Jonathan Jones, why are you pulling that silly face?'

'I don't know, miss,' answered the boy.

'Well, stop it at once. One day the wind will change and it will stay like that.'

'Miss, I don't want to be the grumpy innkeeper,' said the boy, sticking out his bottom lip.

'Yes, I know you don't,' said the teacher.

'I wanted to be one of the kings.'

'Yes, well, there are some things in life many of us don't want to do, Jonathan, and we just have to grin and bear it and not pull silly faces. What is it, Justine? Well, I did tell you not to do that with Baby Jesus. Put him back in the crib and leave him alone. We will fix his head back on before the performance. Right, I think we are just about ready to begin.'

The following week the village church was packed for the infant Nativity play. St Mary's was looking especially festive that afternoon. The altar was bedecked with blood-red berries, variegated and green hollies, winterberry, evergreen boughs and ivies. On either side of the nave were two wrought-iron pedestals with elaborate displays of white roses. At the front of the church, the great golden lectern in the shape of an eagle with outstretched wings glistened in the candlelight and the brightly coloured saints in the stained glass windows looked down benignly on mums and dads, grannies and grandpas who sat chattering in the pews, waiting for the Nativity play to begin. The wooden crib in the Lady Chapel, displaying large plaster figures representing the Holy Family and the kings and shepherds, was surrounded by the ox, the ass and several rather strange-looking sheep reclining on the straw, one of them had a blue face, the other a pink. When the children had arrived before the congregation, Mrs Golightly had gathered her class in the Lady Chapel to give out the various costumes and props and remind the little actors to be on their best behaviour. She had enlisted the help of some older children from Tom's class to supervise the little ones and these included Carol and George, who had stared at the figures in the crib, fascinated by the model animals.

'I reckon one of them sheep's a Bleu de Main an' t'other one's a Rouge de l'Ouest,' George had pronounced.

'Gerron with you,' his small companion had replied, resting her hands on her hips and scrutinising the creatures. 'Them's French breeds. They wouldn't have had French sheep at the time of Jesus.'

'All reight, know-it-all,' answered George, 'tha tell me then what breed o' sheep 'as a blue face an' what breed 'as a pink face. They're not Wensleydale, are they, an' they're not Leicesters?'

'I shall ask my granddad,' replied Carol. 'He'll know.' She then turned her attention to the breed of ox.

Later when the audience had assembled, the young actors, out of sight, dressed and ready to perform their play, whispered excitedly. Following a rather long-winded welcome and introduction by the vicar, which made the children restless and their teacher irritated, the Nativity commenced. Everything ran smoothly until the final scene when the feared mishap took place.

Mary (looking angelic in blue silk) and Joseph (in brown dressing gown, cotton-wool beard and tea towel on his head) sat at the centre of a colourful tableau of kings, shepherds and animals (the last being children in cardboard sheep and donkey masks). A group of little angels in white crêpe paper and cardboard headbands with silver stars on the front stood on a raised platform at the back. As the church organist at the piano struck up with the introduction to 'Away in a Manger', Mary rocked Baby Jesus – the large pink doll with tightly curled blonde hair and eyes which opened and closed. When the chorus of heavenly angels began to sing, the doll spoke.

'Hi, my name is Tammy. What's your name? Will you be my friend?'

Mary stared in disbelief at the doll and then shook it in an attempt to stop it talking. Rather than shutting it up, this had the effect of making the doll talk even more, louder and faster.

'Hi, my name is Tammy. Will you change my diapers? I need my diapers changing.'

The audience laughed, Mrs Golightly buried her head in her hands and the vicar, hovering at the side, wondered if he should intervene.

'Hi, my name is Tammy,' began the doll again. 'What's your name? Will you be my friend?'

Mary shook the doll forcefully to shut it up which only resulted in the doll repeatedly crying and demanding to be changed. The little girl in desperation thrust Baby Jesus roughly into the arms of Joseph. 'You have him,' she said. 'He won't shurrup!' The small boy looked at a loss what to do as the doll continued to cry and demand to be changed. He shook the doll so violently that the head became detached from the body and bounced down the front of the stage like a football just as the angels got to the line in the carol, 'The Little Lord Jesus lay down his sweet head.' The children watched fascinated as the head rolled towards the front pew. One of the three kings quickly retrieved the head and passed it to Mary who reunited it with its body. To the sound of more laughter from the audience and the crying of the doll, the angels continued to sing lustily. 'The stars in the bright sky looked down as he lay, the little Lord Jesus asleep on the hay.'

The following Monday morning Mrs Golightly entered the staffroom with a face set in stone. Before any of her three colleagues could open their mouths, she raised a hand, fixed them with a steely look and told them in a cross voice, 'Don't anybody say anything.'

Tom regretted taking on the role of the prince in the pantomime. For a start he felt like a fish out of water surrounded by this strange lot of overconfident, rather vain and garrulous amateur thespians. Then there were the lines he had to say. The script was unbelievably banal and badly written. When he had tactfully suggested to Joyce that a few alterations might improve it, she had reminded him, quite sharply, that she had written it and that she was the producer. Tom could see from the firmness on her face that she brooked no argument. Then, of course, there was Janette Fairborn. She had not been unfriendly or offhand with him but she had remained rather strait-laced and serious.

It was the dress rehearsal before the first performance. This took place at the Civic Theatre in Clayton where the pantomime was to be performed the following week. Tom's heart sank when, having changed into his costume, he looked in the mirror. He was not overly enamoured with the ostentatiously frilly shirt or the boots with gold tassels, but worse was the bulky cream surcoat with puffed sleeves and embroidered with colourful flowers which reached to just above his waist. Below he wore a pair of pale-green tights that left nothing to the imagination. There was no way he was going to enter the stage in this outfit on the first night, he told himself.

'You look wonderful,' enthused Joyce when he emerged charily out of the dressing room. 'Every inch the prince.' She turned to Janette who was dressed in a tight-fitting silk gown. 'Don't you think Tom looks wonderful, Jan?'

Miss Fairborn's face broke into a smile. 'Oh yes, wonderful,' she agreed.

She looked stunning in the simple white silk gown, studded with imitation pearls. She wore a small mock diamond tiara in her flaming red hair.

'I really don't think this costume is right,' Tom complained. 'I just don't feel comfortable in it.'

'Nonsense,' said Joyce. 'The costume is perfect.'

'It's the tights, Joyce,' Tom told her, lowering his voice. 'I'm not happy about the tights.'

'Is it the colour?'

'Well, yes, it's the colour but—'

'They show off your legs perfectly. Don't you think so, Jan?'

'Oh yes,' agreed Miss Fairborn still with the smile all over her face.

'It's not just my legs that they show off,' said Tom, feeling his cheeks becoming hot.

'We'll talk about it later,' said Joyce, turning away. 'I need to start the rehearsal.'

'And you can take the smile off your face, Janette Fairborn,' said Tom, looking at Jan. He spoke good-humouredly and he couldn't resist a small smile himself. 'I look a complete buffoon.'

'I don't think you look a buffoon at all,' she said. 'In fact I think you look rather er . . .'

'Rather what?' asked Tom.

The word 'dishy' came into her head. 'You look rather prince-like – although I'm not all that keen on the colour of the tights.'

Later on stage, things went without a hitch until it came to the entrance of young George, the prince's page. In a loud voice resonant with thick Yorkshire vowels, the boy declaimed his lines:

> 'Prince Florimund's dead un'appy,
> Sittin' on t'throne,
> 'E's lookin' for t'princess
> What 'e can call 'is own.'

'Could we try that again?' said Joyce. 'Listen to how the lines should be said:

> 'Prince Florimund's so unhappy,
> As he sits upon his throne.
> He hopes one day he'll find true love,
> A princess of his own.'

After several unsuccessful attempts to get the boy to speak his lines clearly and correctly, Joyce gave up. 'Oh, it will have to do,' she said.

Then it was Tom's turn to enter the stage. He did so with

his hands strategically placed in front of him and recited the doggerel. It was clear his heart was not in it.

> 'Although I'm young and handsome,
> And rich as rich can be,
> I feel so sad and lonely
> Ah me, ah me, ah me.'

'Could we have a bit more feeling when you deliver the lines, please, Tom,' Joyce shouted from her seat at the back of the theatre. 'Try and sound depressed and look dejected. Perhaps you might brush your forehead in a sort of forlorn way with the back of your hand.'

Tom bit his lip. No seasoned Shakespearean actor could possibly endow such gibberish with any sort of feeling. And as for his hands, there was no way he was going to do anything other than keep them firmly where they were, namely in the same shielding position as on the occasions when, as a footballer, he had stood with his teammates defending the goal mouth from a penalty shot. Then came the climax of the drama. He sighed inwardly at what he had to say next. Prince Florimund reappeared on stage, still with his hands before him and feeling ridiculous. What have I let myself in for? Tom asked himself. He delivered the doggerel as fast as he could.

> 'In this castle dark and damp,
> I see a chamber here.
> It looks as if it's been locked up
> For many and many a year.
>
> Who is this on the golden bed,
> This sleeping maiden fair,
> With skin as white as driven snow,
> And lovely golden hair?

Be still, be still, my beating heart,
Oh this is heavenly bliss,
Why I shall wake this maiden up
By giving her a kiss.'

Tom bent over the makeshift bed. Janette looked as stiff and lifeless as a cadaver with a grave expression on her face and her eyes squeezed tightly shut. He bent and pecked her quickly with a dry little kiss on the cheek.

'Oh no, no, Tom!' Joyce shouted out. 'You will have to do better than that on the opening night. You look as if you are kissing a maiden aunt. Make more use of your hands and put feeling into the words.' Tom was about to respond but she moved on quickly. 'Anyway, we haven't time to go through it again, so let us have King Pelinor, the Queen and all the fairies on stage please.'

That evening after the rehearsal Tom called in to see his aunt, who agreed to lengthen the surcoat a good few inches and buy him a pair of extra-large black tights.

It was the first night of the pantomime performance, something Tom was not looking forward to at all. He had discovered that most of the village would be making the journey to Clayton to watch the show: Mrs Gosling, Mrs Moody, several of the local farmers and their families, Mrs Mossup, the vicar and a goodly number of his congregation, Mr Gaunt and the teachers at the school and, of course, a handful of the children in his class and their parents. He would be a laughing stock and cringed at the thought of having to deliver the dreadful rhyming couplets. At least he would not have the indignity of wearing the garish green tights and the undersized surcoat.

Despite the fact that all the cast had arrived on time, the stage sets looked wonderful and the Civic Theatre was beginning to fill up, Joyce was in an uncharacteristically nervous state of mind, rushing around backstage, checking and fussing and nagging, and transmitting her twitchy nerves to the members of the cast.

When she caught sight of Tom in his revised costume, she hurried over.

'Oh, Tom,' she exclaimed, 'whatever have you done to your lovely tunic and why aren't you wearing the green hose?'

'They were both rather tight, I'm afraid,' he fibbed. 'I've just made a couple of minor alterations. They feel much more comfortable now.' Before she could respond he dashed off shouting over his shoulder, 'I need to put my stage make-up on.'

The Clayton and Ruston Amateur Players put on the performance of their lives. The audience applauded loudly when the little fairies danced, it laughed when George tripped over a stage set and delivered his lines in true Yorkshire fashion, thinking he was one of the pantomime's comic characters, and it hissed and booed raucously each time Maleficent, the Wicked Fairy, appeared on stage. But it was Tom who stole the show. When he made his entrance, he was greeted with rowdy cheers and clapping and not a few wolf whistles. Having heard offstage the enthusiastic response of the audience, their cheering and booing, he realised that the awful doggerel the actors had to deliver was as much a part and parcel of the tradition of the pantomime as the good and evil characters. No one took the bizarre medley of fairy tale, dances, rhyming verse and jokes seriously, they just entered into the fun and frivolity of a scant story where hope and goodness triumph over adversity. So, he entered into the spirit of the evening and hammed up his lines to the delight of the audience.

When it came to the denouement of the drama, the awakening of Princess Aurora, Tom bent to awake the Sleeping Beauty. Janette had her eyes open and she looked straight into his. He had never seen her look more lovely. He stared at her for a moment, taken aback by her beauty: the large almond-shaped green eyes, the pale, flawless complexion that seemed to glow like polished marble and the mass of auburn hair. She looked like a fairy-tale princess.

'Kiss her!' someone shouted from the audience.

Tom leaned close and put his arm around her, his hand in the small of her back. He raised her slightly and kissed her gently on the lips. This was accompanied by wild cheering and clapping. As he began to rise, Janette pulled Tom back and gave him a rather more lingering kiss. This was accompanied by even louder applause.

When the curtain fell and the cast had taken several curtain calls, Joyce danced onto the stage. 'Superlative!' she cried.

At the start of the pantomime, the weather had turned suddenly cold and now there were flurries of snow in the air. By the time the theatre began to clear and the actors had changed out of their costumes, great flakes, like goose feathers shaken from a blanket, started to fall thick and fast.

Everyone was in a hurry to get home before the snow settled in earnest.

In the car park Tom found Mrs Golightly and Mr Cadwallader climbing into Mr Gaunt's antiquated pickup truck. He was revving the engine madly.

'Great show,' said the headmaster. 'We can't stop to talk, otherwise I'll have the devil's own job getting up the hill in this weather. You need to make tracks yourself. It's going to get worse. Probably no school next week. Listen for the alpenhorn.'

'Goodnight,' said Tom, and watched the truck drive off, tyres crunching through the snow.

He smiled as he caught sight of Joyce as she clambered into the passenger seat of a large black Mercedes, the driver of which was a suave, middle-aged man with the patrician face of a Roman senator. A large four-by-four vehicle passed him with Mr Fairborn at the wheel. In the back sat his daughter. She wiped the steam from the window and waved.

Tom waved back. 'Goodnight, Jan,' he muttered. He breathed in deeply. What a night, he thought.

He drove slowly through Clayton. The flakes were settling fast and forming a thick carpet along the pavements. Walls, trees, road signs, letter boxes, rooftops were shrouded in translucent white. Cars growled along the road through the soft snow, throwing cascades of slush in their wake. The steep road to Risingdale twisted and turned and was now becoming treacherous. Several times Tom felt the car veer dangerously one way and then the other. He thought of the words of Mr Gaunt when he had first started at the school. 'You'll find the winters up here at the top of the Dale can be especially severe,' Tom recalled, 'and you will never get up the hill to the school in that fancy little car of yours. You'd be skidding off the road and ending up in a ditch again. By December we start to get thick snow and driving winds, then come the blizzards and treacherous black ice. You need a four-wheel drive.' Thank goodness he had heeded the headmaster's advice. He drove on, past snow-laced hedgerows and skeletal trees draped in white. A pale moon lit up the landscape, luminous and still. The scene was magical.

Finally, with a great sigh of relief, Tom pulled up outside his cottage. He crunched through the snow and was soon settled before a blazing log fire with a generous glass of whiskey in his hand.

The telephone rang several times that evening. First it was Mr Gaunt, then Joyce, then Mrs Golightly and Mr Cadwallader all making sure that he had arrived home safely. The final call was from Janette Fairborn.

'I just wanted to check that you got home all right,' she said. 'The snow came down so suddenly and I knew you had to tackle the hill.'

'I drove extra carefully,' replied Tom. 'It was good of you to call.'

'Well, I was worried about you. I thought you might be stuck in the snow.'

'How did you get my number?' he asked.

'Joyce gave it me. I rang her to see if she had got back safely.'

'Jan,' said Tom quickly before she could replace the receiver. 'I . . . er . . . really enjoyed tonight. It was . . . special.'

'Yes, it was,' she said. 'Goodnight, Tom.' The phone went dead.

Before he went to bed, he looked out of the bedroom window. All around the cottage stretched a strange white world stroked in silence. The wind, which had earlier blown the snow into drifts, had now abated. All was still. No birds called, no animal moved and, save for the sporadic soft thud of snow falling from the branches of the towering dark trees which bordered the drive, all was silent. There was a stillness, as if life itself had been suspended.

Tom thought of the farmers. He had been told how the icy wind could rage, how the snow could pack up in great mounds and pile into drifts which froze until the whole landscape was transformed into one vast ocean of crusted billows. He had heard how the sheep, their coats crusted with ice, sheltered against the drystone walls and how some were buried deep under the snow. Tom saw, in his mind's eye, Mr Olmeroyde and Toby Croft trudging through the wilderness of white, their collie dogs struggling though the drifts, in search of their foundered sheep. They would have grim, determined expressions on their faces. Theirs was a hard life.

As he lay in bed that night, Tom thought of his own life. He reflected on his blessings, of which he had many. He had enjoyed a very happy childhood with parents who had been caring and supportive. At school, sport had been his passion and he had thrived, playing for the county youth team and then, having been spotted as a boy with some talent, becoming a professional footballer. His dream had come true. Eventually, he was made captain of Clayton United. Until his accident, he had enjoyed his time on the pitch, the camaraderie of the other players and some of the notoriety which came with the position. Then he had studied hard, trained as a teacher and realised that he had at last found his true vocation. He had fallen on his feet when he had been appointed to Risingdale School. He really liked the company of the other teachers. None could have been more kind and friendly and no head teacher more understanding and encouraging. Tom loved the company of young people and found a genuine pleasure in sharing his knowledge with them. At college the lecturer had said that teachers take on the most important role in society, for good teachers change children's lives. Tom felt some satisfaction that he had made some positive difference in the lives of his pupils. He thought of Charlie, bright and affable and always with a ready smile, of Carol, the champion shepherdess, and Vicky, who always had a lot to say for herself; he thought of David, small and gangly, whose writing had improved by leaps and bounds, and Marjorie, the mathematics whiz, and Simon, the ferret expert and rat-catcher. Perhaps, more than any of his pupils, he felt he had made a difference in Colin's life. The rude and difficult child had become better behaved and more sociable and someone Tom had come to like.

However, as he drifted off to sleep, there was one person foremost on his mind – Janette Fairborn – and he determined to see a whole lot more of her in future.